Bondwitch

by

Chelsey M. Ortega

Bondwitch

Cover Art by *Jennifer Greeff*

The Wild Rose Press, Inc.
PO Box 708
Adams Basin, NY 14410-0708
Visit us at www.thewildrosepress.com

Publishing History
First Edition, 2023
Trade Paperback ISBN 978-1-5092-5194-0
Digital ISBN 978-1-5092-5195-7

Published in the United States of America

"Annamaria… Prom queen… Congratulations."

"Uh…thanks." Anna grunted as she tried to shove away from him.

"My senior prom was pretty amazing too." His eyes darkened. "But my senior year didn't end so well. Hopefully, yours is better."

Anna stopped trying to push him away and looked up at him. He was older, which must be why Anna didn't recognize him. Their eyes met, and Anna froze as his pupils expanded until they almost covered his brown irises. The surrounding volume lowered, and the music became fuzzy. Anna swayed, and her fear disappeared. Her surroundings were a blur save this handsome man. This man who held her desire in his hand. He was the only thing that mattered. Obeying him was the only thing she wanted.

"Let's leave," he whispered. Goosebumps erupted along Anna's cheek and neck. "Come with me." They stopped dancing, and he gripped Anna's hand and led her toward the exit.

Dedication

To anyone who has ever wanted to wake up to magic powers. To anyone who has laid in bed and tried to magically turn on the light. To anyone who believes magic belongs in the modern world. This is for you.

Chapter 1 Promposals

Anna's eyes flew open as her phone alarm blared through the silence of the morning. She glanced at her window, the rising sun peeking through her blinds. She sighed and closed her eyes while blindly reaching for her phone. *Just a few more minutes.* The next time awareness reached her senses, she was being shaken awake.

"Anna! It's seven. You've got to get up."

Anna gasped and jumped out of bed. She ran to her bathroom, her aunt trailing behind her. "This is the third time this week. What is going on?"

"I'm just tired from everything I have to do for school."

In reality, Anna spent several hours every night on the phone with her boyfriend, but she wasn't about to tell Trinity that and risk losing her cell phone.

"Senior year is very taxing." Trinity patted Anna's shoulder. "Take a quick shower. Breakfast is almost ready."

Anna twisted her long red hair up into a messy bun, covered it with a shower cap, and stepped into the shower. Next week was prom. She was running out of time. She needed to convince Trinity to let her go to prom today. She had to make an exception to Anna's curfew this one time. It had been sixteen years since Chicago. Nothing was going to happen. They were safe here.

After her shower, Anna dressed in skinny jeans and a loose yellow blouse. She styled her hair into a half ponytail and applied her makeup. She hurtled downstairs to share a quick breakfast of eggs, toast, and fruit with Trinity.

Trinity swallowed her last ounce of coffee. "Cody's late."

"He's not picking me up today. Could you take me to school on your way to work?"

Trinity beamed. "I'd love to."

Anna grinned back. Phase one of getting herself to prom complete. They got ready to leave, with Trinity chatting about her current project at the library. Anna "hmmm'd" and "ah'd" at appropriate times. As they drove through the small mountain town of Harrison, Anna bounced her knees while her mind turned with the best way to mention prom.

"Speaking of dancing…" Anna's gaze focused on the dress shop they were passing.

Trinity sighed. "No, Anna, I'm sorry, but school dances always begin after curfew."

"Please. It's senior prom." Trinity shook her head, but Anna persisted. "You know Cody is a good guy. We'll be perfectly safe." Trinity opened her mouth, but Anna kept going. "If you're really worried, Cody's ranch is right next to the school. I could sleep over."

Trinity put her hand up, and Anna fell silent, her heart sinking. "No. No sleeping over. Cody is your boyfriend."

Anna folded her arms and pouted. "You used to let me sleep over there."

Trinity laughed. "That was when the sleepovers

were with Alyssa and Courtney, and you weren't dating Cody yet."

"Please?" Anna rested her chin on top of clasped hands.

"No."

Anna threw her seatbelt off as they pulled up to the school, got out of the car, slammed the door, and stomped away. Trinity called out a goodbye, which Anna did not return. When she reached her locker, she had to try her combination three times due to her shaking fingers.

"So...are you going to prom?"

Anna took her time rearranging her locker so she could blink back tears before shaking her head. She closed her locker softer than she had opened it and faced Stephanie and Jamie.

"That's so unfair." Jamie shook her head in sympathy.

Stephanie rolled her eyes. "What's wrong with Trinity? Doesn't she know how embarrassing this is? And what about Cody? It's his senior prom too."

Anna groaned. "It's not like I haven't tried all of those angles already."

"We'll keep trying." Jamie's eyes held a twinkle. "*And* we need to get Stephanie a date, too. I could get one of Isaac's friends to ask you."

Stephanie shook her head. "I'm good."

"But like you said, it's our senior prom." Jamie waved her arms around.

Stephanie rolled her eyes and smiled. "Yes, but I don't have my eyes on any of Isaac's friends."

Anna's eyes widened. "Who do you have your eyes on? You've been keeping secrets!" She playfully hit

Stephanie's arm.

Stephanie just smiled and shook her head. Anna didn't push her. She would focus on Stephanie's mystery man after she got herself to prom. They kept up an easy flow of chatter into their first period English class, where they separated to their assigned seats.

Anna sat down and plopped her classroom copy of *Little Women* on the desk, glaring at the cover. Jo wouldn't care about prom. She'd view it as an opportunity to write without interruption. But Anna wasn't Jo. How could Trinity do this to her? Stephanie was right. This was so embarrassing. Every homecoming, Valentine's dance, and prom, several girls asked Cody if he would be their date. Every time he said no and spent the evening at Anna's house. But like Stephanie said, this was Cody's senior prom too. What if this time, Cody accepted an invitation from another girl? That would crush her.

A large, gentle hand covered hers and squeezed. "I didn't hear from you this morning. Do I finally get to take you to prom?"

Anna looked up and met Cody's blue eyes. So hopeful. His thumb rubbed circles on the top of her hand. Anna's shoulders slumped, and she leaned back in her chair. She broke eye contact, pulled her hand away, and shook her head. Peeking up through her lashes, Cody's face fell as he sat on Anna's desk, and he ran one hand through his curly, blond hair.

Cody took Anna's hand again. "Don't worry—"

"Please have a seat in an actual chair, Mr. Mills," their math teacher said.

Cody hopped down from Anna's desk and snuck a peck on her temple before taking his own seat.

Anna spent the period with her head down. A few tears broke through her defenses and rolled down her cheeks, staining her assignment. When the bell rang, Anna rushed out the door, but Cody was waiting and engulfed her in a hug.

"Anna, we'll figure this out."

Anna stepped out of the hug and paced down the hall. "How? The fact it's our senior year and you have an impeccable reputation isn't swaying her. I don't see how I could say anything else to convince her."

"What about my dad?" Cody suggested. "He could probably convince her."

Anna stopped in her tracks. How had she not thought of that? She had long suspected Mr. Mills and Trinity liked each other.

Anna hugged Cody and kissed him. "You're a genius, Cody! If anyone could change Trinity's mind, it's your dad." Cody threw his arm around Anna as he walked her to the dance room.

"Mr. Mills, Miss Lyons, no PDA at school, please," called out a passing teacher as they walked down the hall.

They both chuckled, and Cody took his arm off of Anna, then grabbed her hand, which was hidden by their backpacks. When they got to the dance room, Cody leaned her against the wall and kissed her. Catcalls reached their ears from passing students. Cody drew away, a faint blush on his cheeks, mirroring the heat creeping up on Anna's face.

"Jake is asking Stephanie to prom today during lunch," Cody said. "Will she say yes?"

Anna pursed her lips. Stephanie flirted with Jake all the time... Was he her crush? "I think she will. It's prom after all. Who doesn't want to go to prom?"

"Perfect." Cody gave her one last peck on the lips. "Don't let her leave the lunchroom early."

Anna skipped into the dance room, still beaming. She changed into her dance clothes and started warming up and stretching. When the warm-up song was over, Coach Holt gathered the girls to the front mirror.

"Ladies, we have less than two weeks until our end-of-year concert, and we still have one more number to choreograph. I'm concerned we can't get it done. Do I need to scrap it from the lineup?"

"No," the girls chorused.

"All right, let's run through each number once, and if all dances look good, we can start our final number."

The girls all nodded and got ready for the opener. Anna leaped, twirled, and kicked in perfect tandem with her teammates. For the two numbers she choreographed, Anna stood in the coach's position, calling out reminders and encouragement, clapping at the end of each one. The last number before the finale was the senior routine. This year there were four seniors—Anna, Stephanie, Jamie, and a girl named Tally. Based on the mirror's reflection, they looked good, shimmying, leaping, and flirting.

At the end of the run-through, Coach Holt clapped her hands, the corners of her mouth upturned. "Well done, girls! All right, you've earned it. Let's tackle this final number."

****

Anna, Jamie, and Stephanie sat down at their lunch table. Jake and Cody better hurry with whatever they are planning. Spring was finally here, and Anna wanted to enjoy the fresh air and vitamin D before lunch was over. Luckily, they didn't have to wait too long. A cappella singing filled the lunchroom. The entire men's section of the school choir walked toward the girls' table, Jake in the lead. Stephanie looked up and fought back a smile. They were singing "As Long as You Love Me" by the Backstreet Boys, but with altered lyrics to ask Stephanie to prom in the chorus.

As the song ended, Jake produced a bouquet from behind his back. He walked up to Stephanie and held the flowers out to her, the tips of his ears pink, his hand shaking. "So what do you say?"

She met Jake's eyes, shifted her gaze to the crowd behind him, then looked down at her hands. Anna resisted rolling her eyes, her foot tapped impatiently under the table. *Just say yes already!* Stephanie looked up and, with a genuine smile on her face, said, "I would love to."

The lunchroom erupted into applause while the choir boys hooted and hollered. Anna and Jamie clapped and cheered as well. Anna's day was certain to keep getting better.

They met Isaac outside at their usual bench. He stopped dribbling a soccer ball between his feet when he saw them. Walking up to them, he nodded at Cody and Jake. He sat down on the bench and pulled Jamie onto his lap.

Jamie wrapped her arms around Isaac's neck. "Jake finally asked Stephanie to prom, and she said yes."

"Awesome." Isaac gave a polite smile. "Congrats." Stephanie beamed, and Jake shrugged like it was nothing, but still had a huge smile on his face. "And what about you, Anna?"

"I'll be there," Anna said. Both Jamie and

Stephanie raised their eyebrows. "Cody and I have a plan." Anna winked. "I'll let you know how it goes tonight."

****

"What do you think we should do to prepare Trinity for my dad's phone call?" Cody asked as he followed Anna into her house.

Anna counted on her fingers. "Clean the house, fold the laundry, and cook dinner."

Cody put his hand to his forehead and saluted. "Yes, ma'am."

Anna rolled her eyes and shook her head. Cody chuckled and threaded his fingers in hers, pulling her closer and pecking her lips. Anna started on the laundry, and Cody vacuumed. Anna swept, and Cody mopped behind her, sneaking taps on her behind, making her scream and slap his hand away. They made chicken Alfredo for dinner. Anna made the sauce, and Cody stirred the pasta while the chicken boiled and the broccoli steamed. Anna repeated slapping his hand away when he tried to sample dinner.

"What? I'm starving." He pouted.

"You're not the one I'm trying to impress. You can eat at home."

Five minutes before Trinity was due home, Anna walked Cody out to his truck. Cody opened the driver's side door and swooped Anna into the driver's seat to level their faces with each other. He wrapped his arms around her waist, she wrapped her legs around his, and their lips moved as one. She sighed as they separated and pressed their foreheads together.

"This is going to work," Cody said.

Anna groaned. "I hope so."

"It will."

They switched places, kissed goodbye one more time, and Cody drove off. Anna reentered the house, dished up dinner, and set the table. The garage door opened just as Anna finished up.

"Bon appétit!"

Trinity's eyes widened, and her mouth dropped. "Wow, Anna. This looks delicious." She sniffed. "Did you clean as well?" Anna grinned, and Trinity's eyes narrowed. "What do you want?"

"Nothing. Dance just put me in a good mood, that's all."

"I'll pretend to believe you. Let's enjoy dinner." They sat down and dug in. "How was school?"

Trinity chuckled as Anna recounted her day. "You kids sure go all out these days. When I was in high school, we just asked."

Anna's jaw clenched. So Trinity got to attend her prom. "We finished *Little Women* in English."

"Oh, I love that book." Trinity's eyes held a dreamy shine. "I always fancied myself like Jo."

"I relate more with Amy."

Trinity giggled. "And Cody is your Laurie?"

Anna scoffed. "No! He hasn't loved anyone else."

"Anna, be careful with the 'L' word. You're still very young."

Anna ground her teeth. This was not going in the direction she wanted.

Trinity patted her hand. "I'm just looking out for you. I'll do the dishes since you cooked."

The phone rang. Anna jumped up to grab it.

"Hello?"

"Hi, Anna. Can I talk to Trinity?"

Anna accidentally squealed. She ran the phone to Trinity. "It's Mr. Mills. I'll finish the dishes."

Trinity narrowed her eyes at Anna before taking the phone. After a moment of listening, she shooed Anna out of the kitchen. This was it. Anna dropped the plate in her hand and closed the kitchen door on her way out. She turned on the TV in the living room and ran back, putting her ear to the door.

"Hal, I just don't think it's a good idea. Something could happen, neither of us will be there… The teachers really aren't the same as one of us… I know we did, but those were different times… All right, but I'm going to be a nervous wreck the whole night." Trinity giggled. "I'm going to hold you to that."

The faint beep of Trinity hanging up hit Anna's ears. She zoomed back to the living room and jumped onto the couch. She stared at the screen, unable to take in what was going on in front of her. Trinity entered the room and turned off the TV.

"All right, Anna, your plan worked. You can go to prom next week."

Anna screamed as she jumped up and down and hugged Trinity. "Thank you. Thank you. Thank you."

Trinity put her hands on Anna's shoulders. "There are some stipulations." Anna nodded, keeping eye contact with Trinity. "First, you will stay at the school the whole time. No running off early to do other things. Second, as soon as the dance is over, you come straight home."

"I accept." Anna hugged Trinity one more time, then ran upstairs to call Cody, Stephanie, and Jamie.

Chapter 2 Libby's Gift

The next day during lunch, Cody blindfolded Anna, took her up a flight of stairs, and then what felt like a ladder. When he tugged the blindfold off, they were on the roof of the school overlooking the football field. Anna blinked the spots away before the entire football team materialized below, spelling "PROM?" with their bodies.

"Anna," Jake said through a megaphone as he made up the dot of the question mark. "If your answer is no, push Cody off the roof. If your answer is yes, kiss hiiiimmmmm!" Anna giggled as the final words rang in her ears and threw her arms around Cody's neck and kissed him with fervor.

The football coach spoke next over the megaphone. "Mills. Lyons. No PDA at school." Anna and Cody pulled apart, laughing and blushing. "And get down from the roof."

"Yes, sir," they called, and climbed back down into the attic.

Cody threw his arm around Anna. "It's going to be a night to remember. We've got to make up for all the dances before this."

****

When Anna walked into her house with Cody after school, Trinity was already home. Anna rushed to tell her all about Cody's promposal. Trinity grinned. "Well, it looks like you're going to have a prom-themed day because I'm taking you dress shopping."

Anna squealed and clapped. "Right now?"

Trinity nodded. "Right now. I'm sorry, Cody. I know you like to spend Friday nights with Anna."

"Not a problem, Miss Lyons." He pecked Anna on the cheek. "Have fun. I can't wait to see you in your dress."

Anna ran upstairs and dropped her backpack off in her room. When she returned downstairs, she bounced on the balls of her feet.

"Let's go," Trinity said, her eyes twinkling.

Anna ran ahead of Trinity, putting her seatbelt on before Trinity could sit down. Trinity held a knowing smile during the drive out of the neighborhood. As they neared the local dress shop, Trinity drove right past it. Anna's breath caught in her throat and her blood pounded in her ears.

"I thought you were taking me dress shopping?"

"I am. We are going shopping in Casper."

A deafening, high-pitched sound enveloped the inside of the car. "We are going on a trip? Are we staying in a hotel?" Trinity nodded. Anna's next squeal was cut off by a gasp. "But you didn't tell me to pack."

Trinity flashed a sly smile. "I packed while you were at school."

****

In Casper, they had dinner at a local pizzeria. The place had a great atmosphere, and true Italian pizza inspired the recipes. They looked over the menu while they waited for a table. Once seated, Trinity ordered a beer and Anna a soft drink. Spinach and Artichoke dip was their starter and a Margherita pizza followed.

Trinity scooped a tortilla chip through the hot dip. "I imagine you aren't too pleased with my lack of support for you going to USC in the fall?"

Anna looked up from her soda. "Is it because Cody is also going?"

Trinity shook her head. "This summer I want to take you on a trip to meet Grandma."

Anna blinked. She had not been expecting that. Grandma Libby never visited Anna and Trinity, and they never visited her. Libby communicated with Anna through birthday cards and Christmas presents.

"I would love to meet Grandma, but what does visiting her in the summer have to do with going to USC in the fall?"

Before Trinity could answer, their pizza arrived. They thanked the server and handed off the empty chip basket and dip bowl. Trinity waited until the server was out of earshot.

"Grandma lives in a special community, and she has a lot of knowledge about our family history to teach you."

"And what she has to teach me will...what? Keep me from going to college?"

Trinity shifted. "It might."

Anna rolled her eyes. "That's not very convincing."

Trinity squeezed Anna's free hand. "That's all I can tell you for now. I need you to trust me. Will you let me take you to Grandma's during the summer? At the end of the summer, you can decide, and I'll support you in your decision."

Anna nodded. "Okay."

The sun had set by the time they left the restaurant.

Anna stopped and breathed in the night air. She was outside past curfew. And she was outside of Harrison.

When they got into the car, Trinity groaned. "I left my card in there. Come on."

"Can I just wait in the car?" Anna asked. Trinity opened her mouth, her eyes already saying no. "I'll lock the doors."

"Okay… I'll be fast."

Trinity got out of the car and hustled into the restaurant. Anna scoffed. Trinity's paranoia could be so annoying. She studied the surroundings of the pizza place. Casper was beautiful. She couldn't wait to shop around and explore more tomorrow. As Anna's eyes raked over the area, she zeroed in on a figure sneaking in between parked cars, ducking down, and reappearing after a few seconds.

Anna's gaze followed the figure. What a strange thing to do. Were they hiding from someone? Sneaking away? Her heart rate sped up and her breathing stopped when the figure headed toward Trinity's car. All the streetlights went out, along with the neon sign over the pizza place. Anna double-checked the locks and looked back out the window, squinting her eyes. She couldn't see a thing. What if they were right there, staring at her?

The lights came back on. The figure was gone.

Anna jumped at the sound of the door opening. Trinity slid in without a word, turned the ignition, and gunned the car out of the parking lot. Anna wanted to ask Trinity about the lights, but Trinity stayed focused on the road, her gaze never wavering from the windshield.

****

During breakfast, Anna texted her friends about how the night had gone. She told them about the pizza place, promised to send Stephanie and Jamie pictures of each dress, and told Cody she would let him know what color the chosen dress was. As Anna and Trinity ate bagels, fruit, and yogurt in the hotel dining area, they looked up bridal shops in Casper. With only two shops that looked promising, Anna could spend a significant amount of time in each one.

At the first shop, Trinity convinced Anna to focus on the princess styles. She tried on pink, blue, and yellow dresses, each bodice covered in intricate beading patterns, coupled with layers and layers of tulle for a skirt. Trinity gasped with each reveal, and even teared up while Anna was in the pink one. These dresses were too young. Anna was a senior and wanted to look mature, like a Hollywood starlet. After convincing Trinity that tulle dresses were out, Anna tried on mermaid skirt styles. They looked gorgeous but pinned her legs too tightly together before fanning out. She tried on the evening gowns, but nothing screamed "the one." Anna sent pictures to Stephanie and Jamie, but they were unhelpful as they approved of every single dress.

In the second store, Anna skipped the princess and mermaid dresses and walked straight to the evening gowns. She tried on a gold one with a plunging neckline, which Trinity vetoed immediately. Anna didn't even try to fight it. She would have been uncomfortable showing so much skin, anyway. Next, she tried on a blue chiffon dress with a solid silk layer underneath. The chiffon embodied a whimsical element that worked better as a dance costume. The third dress left Anna speechless.

The bodice was a dark purple halter top, the thick beaded strap twinkled like stars in the night sky. How the bodice hugged Anna's curves was exquisite. She straightened her back and gave it a slight arch as she studied herself in the mirror. She looked like a woman. The waist fanned out as a full circle skirt, laying light around the legs, and a faux belt made of beads trailed around her waist. Anna spun, the skirt rippled outward, the fabric snapping against itself as a full ball gown.

"This is the one." A warm feeling spread from Anna's chest outward. She could not stop smiling while looking at herself in the mirror.

Trinity wiped her eyes and called over the sales associate to begin the purchase. A seamstress measured Anna in the dress and determined only the hem of the skirt needed to be shortened. She told Anna they could pick up the dress in a week.

"We live two hours away. Since it's just the hem, could you get it done today? You can charge us more," said Trinity.

The seamstress looked Anna up and down, playing with her lip. "Yes, I can do it today. I will need to charge double, though."

Trinity waved her hand as if it were nothing. "Deal."

The seamstress left the dressing room so Anna could change.

"Trinity, are you sure?"

Trinity's eyes twinkled. "Yes. Grandma sent money to pay for your dress. She said cost is not an issue."

"Wow. I don't know what to say."

"Be sure to thank her when we visit this summer."

Anna smiled and intertwined her fingers in the smooth fabric of the skirt. "Oh, I definitely will."

She couldn't believe it. The perfect dress for the perfect night. Cody was going to die when he saw her in it! She for sure needed to meet her grandma now so she could thank her in person.

They spent the rest of the afternoon running errands unavailable in Harrison, which included shoes and jewelry to match the dress. When the dress was ready at seven thirty, Anna tried it on one last time to make sure the hem was perfect.

Anna looked longingly back at Casper as they drove out of the busy city to head back home. Anna couldn't wait for the day she could travel again. Though, this time she hoped it would be with her friends or Cody and definitely longer than one night.

Chapter 3 The Need to be Perfect

Other than finding out that Anna and Cody had been nominated for prom king and queen, the week leading up to prom dragged. She struggled to focus during class and often could not respond correctly when her teachers called on her. She also took almost twice as long to complete her homework at night. She might not have finished at all if Trinity didn't remind her to stop daydreaming and focus. Finally, the day had arrived.

Anna woke much earlier than normal for a Saturday. She was just too excited, so she exerted her energy into helping Trinity weed the garden and the flower beds to prepare the soil for planting. Their garden was a source of pride each summer. They grew yellow squash, green zucchini, beets, onions, tomatoes, peas, carrots, and green beans every year. They also had permanent strawberry and raspberry plants. The garden grew more than the two of them could eat, so they sold the extra to the neighbors. While they were working in the garden, a black crow flew into the backyard and landed on Trinity's shoulder.

"Gwen, it's been a while." Trinity stroked the bird's beak.

She fed the bird some seeds. Gwen was Trinity's transient pet. She didn't live in a cage and was inconsistent with her nights spent in the house. But she visited Trinity often, and they communicated with each other. Anna didn't quite see the appeal, but she made her aunt happy.

Anna didn't have much of an appetite for lunch, but she forced a sandwich down into her squirming stomach. She could finally get ready. She texted Cody's sisters, who had asked if they could help her get ready earlier in the week. Anna sat on a stool in her bathroom while Alyssa curled Anna's hair.

"Are you excited?" asked Alyssa.

"Yes. And nervous. This night has to be perfect. I have to be perfect."

"I seem to remember you saying something similar before your first kiss," said Courtney, laying on the bed.

Anna blushed. "Hey, I was only fourteen. That was scary for me. And you two didn't help hiding around the corner giggling." The two sisters laughed. "Plus, we're up for prom royalty. What if Cody wins and I don't?"

Alyssa paused curling and turned Anna to look in her eyes. "You're going to win."

Anna sighed with a smile. When Alyssa finished curling, she pulled half of Anna's hair up and clipped it together with a gold hair piece they gave as a gift. Then Courtney started on Anna's makeup by first smoothing Anna's face with foundation. She gave Anna a smoky eye, light pink blush, and soft pink lip gloss. Both sisters helped Anna into her dress.

Anna put her shoes and jewelry on. Her heels a sparkly silver, thick enough to comfortably wear for several hours. She adorned her wrist with a dozen silver bangle bracelets. She straightened up to look in her full-length mirror.

Her hair and makeup enhanced the dress beyond the first impression. She was beauty personified. Anna rolled her shoulders back, straightened her spine, and turned her head. She was ten years older, posing for pictures on the red carpet. Cody's arm draped around her waist, and Anna leaned into him. Cody's arm was replaced by his sisters as they hugged Anna and squealed.

"You look beautiful," said Alyssa.

"Absolutely stunning," Courtney said.

Alyssa's phone dinged. "Dad and Cody are on their way! We've got to prepare the stairs. We'll tell you when to come out." The two girls ran out of the room.

Anna paced her room, fanning herself and trying to slow her breathing when Trinity poked her head in. She smiled wide as she studied Anna. "Oh, sweetie, you look beautiful. Cody is here, by the way."

Anna clutched her stomach and groaned.

Trinity ran to her. "Are you okay?"

"Yes. Just nervous. Give me a minute." Anna gasped.

"Take your time." Trinity hugged her tight, kissed her forehead, and left the room.

Anna took a few more deep breaths, then walked out into the hall. Her mouth dropped. A long train of red fabric covered the hallway floor and trailed down the stairs. White string lights were wrapped around both railings. Cody stood at the bottom of the stairs, dressed in a tux, with a purple vest and tie to match Anna's dress. He held a plastic box with a wrist corsage inside. She met those familiar green eyes and her stomach relaxed. Cody couldn't take his eyes off of her as she walked down the stairs. The satiny fabric grazed her legs, her heels peeking out with each step. The twinkle in his eyes increased if it were possible, and his jaw dropped an inch. Mr. Mills was sandwiched between his daughters and Trinity as he filmed the scene with a handheld video camera. His shoulders brushed with Trinity's as she brought her hands up to her smiling lips.

When she stopped in front of Cody, they held their gaze before breaking into giggles. They hugged, and Cody whispered, "You look beautiful."

Anna blushed. "And you look handsome."

They exchanged the corsage and boutonniere, and Trinity called for pictures.

"Okay, bye now!" Anna said after the tenth picture. She grabbed Cody's hand and darted to his truck. "Thanks for everything," she threw over her shoulder to Alyssa and Courtney.

"Wait!" said Trinity. "What are the rules?"

Anna skidded to a halt and sighed. "No leaving the school and come straight home when the dance is over."

"Very good." Trinity gave Anna a hug. Cody helped Anna into the passenger side of his truck before getting in the driver's side. They both waved as he drove away from the house.

Cody laced their fingers and kissed the back of her hand. "We're going to prom."

"I know." Anna smiled and sighed. "What are we doing for dinner?" She had an idea. There was only one fancy restaurant in town.

"We're meeting Jake and Stephanie at Romeo's."

Romeo's was a mixture of Italian, French, and Hispanic food, with a small American menu. The owner's goal was to provide favorites from those three popular styles of food.

Anna squeezed his hand and leaned over to kiss his cheek. She was finally experiencing prom night like everyone else, dinner at the best place in town in a fancy dress with the perfect date.

Chapter 4 Prom

After an enjoyable dinner, Cody parked next to Jake's car, and the four friends walked into the school together. Anna's mouth dropped. The prom committee had transformed the gym into a world of balloons, streamers, and lights. "I Wanna Dance with Somebody" by Whitney Houston started playing. Anna's head bobbed, her shoulders rolled, and she just couldn't stand there looking at the decorations. She dragged Cody onto the floor, and they started dancing.

A couple of songs later, they spotted Jamie and waved her over. She grabbed Isaac's hand and dragged him over to them. The three friends hugged, and Anna pulled out her phone so they could take a picture. They called their dates over for the next picture, and Jake, who was the tallest, held Anna's phone up high to fit all six of them. When the first slow song of the night started, they broke apart into couples. Anna threw her arms around Cody's neck, and Cody wrapped his hands around Anna's waist.

Cody rubbed his thumbs over her lower back and lowered his head. Anna met his lips, opening her own for his tongue to sneak in for a few seconds. Anna blushed and giggled as their lips separated.

"No PDA at school." She attempted to mimic their teachers.

Cody laughed and rolled his eyes. "It's dark. No

one will see." He kissed her again.

"I love being here with you," Anna said.

Cody squeezed her waist. "Same. Sometimes, I can't believe you're mine."

Anna smiled. "Why? It's always been you. Ever since elementary school I've lov...liked you."

Cody's eyes darkened at Anna's slip of the tongue. He brushed his lips against her ear. "I *like* you too."

Anna blushed, then met his gaze. "But why can't you believe it?"

Cody shrugged and distracted her with another kiss. They spent the song hugging, pressing their foreheads together to talk, and Cody periodically lifted his hand to spin Anna under it. Cody and Anna continued to dance in a small group with Jake and Stephanie on the fast songs, and Jamie and Isaac rotated between them and Isaac's soccer friends. At the start of the next slow song, Stephanie stepped between Cody and Anna.

"Let's switch, just for fun."

Anna glanced at Cody, hoping he'd say no. Cody smiled. "Sure."

Stephanie threw her hands around Cody's neck, and he placed his hands on either side of her waist. At least he wasn't hugging her. Anna placed one hand in Jake's, and the other on his shoulder. She wasn't going to hug him like she did when she danced with Cody.

"So how are things going?" Anna asked him.

"Really well, I think. Stephanie is so beautiful. I want to ask her to be my girlfriend. Do you think she would let me kiss her tonight?" Jake looked nervous.

Anna smiled. "I can't say for sure. She hasn't been willing to tell me her feelings for you, but if you're feeling the vibe, go for it."

"You sure?"

"Yes. She said yes to prom, didn't she?"

Anna spent the rest of the song giving Jake a pep talk. A few songs later, the student body president, Kelsey Rimmel, got everyone's attention to announce prom royalty. Anna played with her fingers as Kelsey read off the names, starting with second runner-up. The only name that stuck out to her was Tally, her teammate, who got first runner-up. Anna clapped as Tally walked forward in a light purple dress. King and Queen were next. Her heart beat in anticipation.

"All right, Harrison, your prom king is Cody Mills!" Anna cheered, jumped, and clapped. Cody sauntered to the front beaming and accepted a sash and crown. Everyone in the room held their breath.

"And the moment you have all been waiting for. Your prom queen is Annamaria Lyons!"

Their friends' cheers were louder than everyone else. Anna rolled her shoulders back and held her head high as she walked forward. Anna bent for the sash and crown next to the other prom court members, then took her rightful place next to Cody and smiled wide for the yearbook photo.

After the dance for prom royalty was over, Cody left Anna to go to the bathroom. Anna walked over to the refreshments and served herself some punch. She took a sip and coughed as the punch burned her throat.

"Not interested in drinking?" asked an alluring voice behind her.

Anna spun around and found herself much too close to a pair of brown eyes and a smirk that sent her heart thumping. She coughed again. "No."

The handsome stranger held out a pale hand. "The water is still pure."

She accepted it and took a long sip as a means to study him. He was tall, with light brown hair. His pale skin stood out against the black of his tux. Unusual for a youth in a mountain town where outdoor activities were all there was to do. Even with his pale complexion, he was quite attractive, and every girl who walked past did a double take, looking him up and down, trying to catch his eye.

Anna set the cup down. "Thanks. Who are you? Do you go here?"

The young man didn't answer. "Do you want to dance? I love this song."

"No thank you. I'm waiting for my boyfriend to get back from the bathroom." Anna took a step toward one of the perimeter tables but was stopped by a strong hand grabbing hers.

The boy dragged her onto the floor. Anna wriggled and jerked against his hold, but he was too strong. She looked around, hoping to send a silent message that she needed help. Jamie was in a dark corner making out with Isaac, and Jake and Stephanie were nowhere in sight. He pulled her into a formal dance position, even though the song was upbeat and fast. His grip was strong, and Anna struggled to follow his lead.

"Annamaria… Prom queen… Congratulations."

"Uh…thanks." Anna grunted as she tried to shove away from him.

"My senior prom was pretty amazing too." His eyes darkened. "But my senior year didn't end so well. Hopefully, yours is better."

Anna stopped trying to push him away and looked

up at him. He was older, which must be why Anna didn't recognize him. Their eyes met, and Anna froze as his pupils expanded until they almost covered his brown irises. The surrounding volume lowered, and the music became fuzzy. Anna swayed, and her fear disappeared. Her surroundings were a blur save this handsome man. This man who held her desire in his hand. He was the only thing that mattered. Obeying him was the only thing she wanted.

"Let's leave," he whispered. Goosebumps erupted along Anna's cheek and neck. "Come with me." They stopped dancing, and he gripped Anna's hand and led her toward the exit. She followed him without a fight. They were halfway across the gym when Cody interrupted them.

"Is everything all right?" His eyes traveled back and forth between Anna and her captor.

The young man looked into Cody's eyes with a smirk. "Everything is fine. Annamaria is coming with me. You have fun with your other friends."

Cody narrowed his eyes. "I don't think so."

Her captor finally relented. "All right, you win. You can have her back, for now." He nudged Anna into Cody's arms, winking. The room returned to full volume. Anna turned away from the stranger and hid her face in Cody's chest. Cody hugged her.

"He's gone. What happened?" Anna recounted the incident at the refreshment table. "I don't recognize him either. He can't be that much older than us, so we should know him. Oh look—" Anna looked up to where Cody pointed. "—his date is also wearing a purple dress. He must be too drunk to tell you two apart." The boy was walking out of the gym with his arm around a girl who was, in fact, wearing a dress similar to Anna's, but Anna couldn't see the girl's face and couldn't tell who it was from behind.

"Did you see who his date was?" she asked Cody.

"No." Cody tugged on Anna's hand, trying to lead her back onto the dance floor.

"But he knew my name," said Anna. "He congratulated me on being Queen."

"Drunk people don't always make sense." Cody shrugged.

Anna's shoulders slumped, and her hands shook. She didn't want to ruin the rest of the night, so she shook her head, put a smile on her face, and followed Cody's lead back to dancing. None of their friends joined them the rest of the night, so Anna and Cody danced to the last songs of prom happy and alone.

Dancing in Cody's arms while wearing their King and Queen sashes and crowns was heaven. The tighter she held on to him, the longer she gazed into his eyes, the farther she was able to push her strange encounter into the back of her mind. Tonight was about her and Cody. Anna could not have created a more perfect night.

When the last notes of the final song finished and the lights came on, Cody and Anna looked around for their friends again and, still unable to find them, headed to Cody's truck. As Cody opened the passenger door for Anna, they both turned at the sound of Stephanie calling them. She was dragging Jake toward them, who put up a terrific struggle with clumsiness.

"Jake is drunk," she said, panting, as she caught up to them. "Can you help me get him home?" Her jaw was clenched, her eyes glaring.

"Of course," said Anna and Cody together.

"I'll drive Jake's car." Cody grabbed Jake's arm and fished his friend's keys out of his jacket pocket. "He can ride with me. That way if he throws up, he'll ruin his car, not mine. Anna, Stephanie, do you two want to follow in my truck?"

"Yeah," Anna said.

Stephanie grinned at Cody, her eyes twinkling. Cody tossed his keys to Anna along with his crown and helped Jake get into his car. Jake's car trailed forward, and Anna began following.

"I'm so sorry," Anna said.

Stephanie folded her arms and looked out the window. After a minute of silence, she asked, "Did you tell Jake to kiss me?"

"What?" Anna shook her head. "No, I didn't *tell* him to. He asked if I thought you would accept a kiss, and I said I didn't know for sure, but if he was feeling the vibes to try it."

Stephanie turned her angry gaze on Anna. "Apparently those vibes told him to drink for liquid courage."

Anna clenched the wheel. "I'm really sorry. I swear I didn't know that would happen."

"Whatever." Stephanie looked away again.

They spent the rest of the drive in uncomfortable silence. When they got to Jake's house, Anna got out of the truck and helped Cody remove Jake from the car and walked him to his front door. Stephanie stayed in the truck, glowering.

"Wait!" Jake slurred. "I have to kiss her goodnight."

"Not going to happen, bro." Cody wrapped one

arm around Jake's torso and knocked on the door with his free hand.

Jake's mom opened it, looked her son up and down, yanked him inside, and thanked Anna and Cody. When they got to the truck, Stephanie had moved to the middle seat. Anna chose not to say anything and jumped into the passenger seat while Cody took the wheel. During the silent drive to Stephanie's house, Anna peeked over. Stephanie spent the ride leaning against Cody's shoulder. Anna bit her tongue and looked out the window. All of them were on edge over Jake's actions. That's all this was.

Anna pulled out her phone and texted Trinity.

—*Jake got drunk, so we have to help him and Stephanie get home.*—

Anna's heart hammered as she watched the three dancing dots.

—*Okay. Get home as soon as you can. Be safe.*—

When they arrived at Stephanie's house, Cody walked her to the door and gave her a brief hug, rubbing her back. Anna slumped in her seat on the drive to her house. What a way to end the night.

Cody grabbed Anna's hand and kissed it. "Don't be upset. We got Jake and Stephanie home safely. Everything was great beforehand. Let's end it great."

She straightened up and smiled. "You're right. Let's end this right."

When they got to Anna's house, Cody walked Anna to the porch. Anna turned around at the door and threw her arms around Cody's neck. He drew her in and kissed her with fervor, pushing her up against the door, hands caressing her waist and arms. Anna got lost in Cody's kiss, but after a while, the surrounding silence unnerved her. Anna leaned away.

"What's wrong?" Cody asked.

"Trinity isn't interrupting us."

"I'm not complaining. I enjoy having more time to kiss you."

Anna giggled and let Cody keep kissing her. After another minute, Anna sighed and pulled away again. She did not want the night to be over. "Do you want to come in? Maybe Trinity will let you stay longer."

"Yeah." Cody grinned.

Anna took out her house key, stuck it in the lock, and found the door unlocked. Odd. Trinity always locked the door at sundown. "Trinity," Anna called out as she and Cody walked into the house. All the lights were on. "I'm home. Can Cody stay and watch a movie or something?" No answer. The silence created an eerie vibe.

Anna checked the first floor while Cody remained in the entryway. Nothing. She ran upstairs and checked Trinity's room. It was empty too. Anna treaded back downstairs and checked the garage. Trinity's car was still there. "I can't find her."

"Maybe she's with my dad." Cody shrugged and walked farther into the house. "We have the house all to ourselves. Let's take advantage of that." Cody tugged Anna by the waist while lowering his head, his eyes hazy.

Anna squeezed his shoulders. "Cody, I have a really weird feeling."

Cody pursed his lips. "Look—" He gestured around him and led Anna through the living room. "—if something happened to her, we'd see a sign of a struggle. The house looks the same as when I picked you up." Anna sighed. Cody was right. Trinity would not have let anything happen to her without a fight, but still, something was off. "We are rarely alone like this. Let's enjoy it until Trinity comes back and makes me leave."

"All right." Anna's shoulders slumped in defeat, though she blushed and couldn't fight the smile appearing on her lips.

Cody backed her up against the couch and lay her down. "Is this okay?" Anna nodded. He kissed her lips, her jawline, her neck, and back up. After a few minutes, Cody pulled her back up to a sitting position. "Let's go to your room," he whispered, as he gave a soft tug on the zipper of Anna's dress. Anna froze. "Is everything okay?"

"Yeah," Anna said, avoiding his gaze. "Um, I need to clean up real quick. My room is a mess from Lyssa and Courtney helping me get ready."

"I don't care about that." Cody grinned, his eyes mischievous.

"Well, I do."

Anna got up, leaving Cody on the couch, and ran upstairs. When she entered her room, she put her hands on her stomach and doubled over. She had pictured this moment before. Cody was the only guy she could imagine herself with, but too many bad things had happened tonight, and the time wasn't right.

Anna changed out of her dress and put on regular clothes. This should send a subtle message without the need to have an awkward conversation. When Anna returned downstairs, Cody was back in the entryway talking to Trinity.

"Trinity!" Anna threw herself into her aunt's arms.

Trinity hugged Anna back and giggled. "I was worried. You weren't in the house."

"I'm sorry." Trinity cupped Anna's cheek with her hand. "Something strange happened. But I'm home now."

"Can Cody stay for a movie? Please?" Anna squeezed Trinity's hand. "It's prom night."

Trinity shook her head. "I'm sorry, it's after midnight."

Anna opened her mouth to argue some more, but Cody spoke over her. "It's okay."

Trinity smiled. "You'll see each other again tomorrow. Your dad invited us to dinner after you two drove off."

Cody nodded, his eyes a little pained. "Bye, Miss Lyons. Goodnight, Anna."

Chapter 5 Family History

Anna turned toward the stairs, refusing to look at Trinity. She should be grateful Trinity let her go to prom at all, but the end of the dance had been a disaster, and ending the night on good terms was paramount.

"Anna, wait. There is something we need to talk about."

"Can it wait for tomorrow?" Anna forced a yawn.

Trinity shook her head. "I'm afraid not. There is someone in the kitchen you need to meet."

Anna stopped trying to go up the stairs. Someone was here after midnight? She followed Trinity across the living room to the kitchen. Before they opened the door, Trinity stopped again. "Anna, all of that stuff you were going to learn at Grandma's this summer, you are actually going to learn it tonight."

Anna's eyes widened, and her mouth opened in a toothy grin. "Is Grandma here?" She bumped past Trinity and opened the kitchen door. The woman sitting at the kitchen table was much too young to be a grandmother. Her hair was red like Anna's, pale skin, and a familiar face. In fact, the more Anna looked at her face, the more she was sure she recognized it. The woman sitting in Trinity's kitchen looked just like Anna's... "Mom?" Anna's heart pounded.

The woman gave a half smile. "No, I'm sorry, Annamaria. I've heard I look like her, though."

"Yeah, you do. Who are you?"

"I'm um…" the woman started and looked down at her hands.

Trinity stepped forward and took a hold of Anna's hand, gave it a squeeze, and took a deep breath. "Anna, this is your sister, Marianna."

"What?" Anna looked back and forth between the two of them. "No, I'm an only child." Trinity shook her head, sat down at the table next to Marianna, and gestured for Anna to sit as well. Anna kept standing and folded her arms.

"Anna, I haven't been honest with you about Marianna because, until tonight, I didn't even know she was alive. Will you sit down and let me start from the beginning?" Anna sat down on the opposite side of the table. She glanced at the woman named Marianna.

"Most of what I'm about to tell you is going to sound unbelievable, so I ask that you not interrupt," Trinity prefaced. Anna nodded. "Grandma Libby, myself, your parents, and the both of you come from a long line of powerful witches." Anna's eyebrows shot up into her hairline, and she pursed her lips to keep from snorting.

"It's true," Marianna said, looking at Anna. She lifted one of her hands from the table, her palm facing the ceiling, and all the lights went out. Anna jumped.

"You could have put the lights on a timer," she said after a brief silence.

"Go try a light switch," said Marianna.

Anna got up and felt her way to the light switch by the garage door and flipped it. Nothing happened. "So someone turned off the power." Anna shrugged. "Do I have any other long-lost family members hiding around?"

"Go look out the window." Marianna sounded amused.

Using the counter as a guide, Anna shuffled over to the window above the sink. She couldn't see the outlines of the trees, or moon, or the stars. Only darkness pressed on her vision. She couldn't think of an explanation. The lights came back on, and Anna's stubborn determination returned. "That means nothing."

Trinity sighed and lifted her own hand, pointing at the refrigerator. The door swung open of its own accord, and a bottle of wine floated out of the fridge and onto the table. Trinity pointed at the table and two wine glasses and a bottled water appeared out of thin air. She poured the wine into each glass and offered one to Marianna, gave Anna the water bottle, and drained the glass she kept for herself.

"I'm sure there is an explanation for that," Anna stuttered.

Marianna let out a soft giggle. "Maybe you should unlock her powers. I don't think she'll fully believe until she can feel her magic and do something. Teach her a simple spell."

"You're right." Trinity nodded. "Anna, sweetie, will you come here?"

Anna walked from the sink to stand by Trinity. Her heartbeat increased with her breathing. "What are you going to do?"

"I'm going to unlock your powers. I locked them when you were two. This won't hurt."

Trinity placed her pointer finger over Anna's heart and began muttering in an unfamiliar language. While she chanted, she traced the perimeter of Anna's body.

As Trinity did so, a warmth traveled through Anna's bloodstream and finished in her heart, as if a swallow of hot chocolate advanced beyond the esophagus and traveled through her entire body. When the warmth reached her fingertips, they grew hot. Anna gasped and looked at them, her eyes widened. A golden light briefly shown out of her fingers. As the light disappeared, so did the warmth.

Anna took a shuddering breath. "What was that?"

"Your powers." Trinity raised her hand, and her fingers glowed the same golden color Anna's had.

Anna raised an eyebrow and pursed her lips, her brow lowered as she contemplated what just happened. She could not think of a logical explanation for the warmth that had just traveled through her body, nor the golden light she and Trinity had emitted.

Trinity placed a spoon on the table in front of Anna. "I'm going to teach you levitation. Levitation requires calling on the element of air. Air is the easiest element to call on because it is everywhere."

"How do I call on it?" Anna asked.

"From within. Your head, your heart. There is no specific incantation. You connect with your magic, and you can connect with the elements."

"And how do I do *that*?" This didn't make any sense. What was she supposed to do?

"You call on your magic from your heart with your mind," said Marianna. "Your heart is the center of your magic, and your mind tells your magic what to do. Connect with your magic in your heart, call on the air, and raise the spoon."

Anna pointed at the spoon on the table. She tried to think about the warm feeling she had felt when Trinity dragged her finger across Anna's body. Inside her mind, she pictured the spoon floating. *How do I call on the air?* It's not like it was alive. Was it? Was it supposed to be like a prayer? Anna had never prayed before. She wouldn't know how to begin. They weren't religious, and she hadn't been interested in attending any church services her friends invited her to. After a while, Anna dropped her hand and turned around to leave the kitchen before Marianna and Trinity could start laughing. They must be pranking her, and she fell for it. She was about to place her hand on the door when Marianna appeared between Anna and the door, blocking it.

"How did you—"

"Don't be upset, please don't leave. No one gets it on their first try. We probably started too big. Let's try just getting some magic out of you. Connect with your heart, feel the magic, and guide it out through your hand. Don't try anything specific, just try to drive the magic out."

Anna looked at Trinity, who nodded with a small smile. Anna once again envisioned the warm feeling that had flowed through her body. She closed her eyes and focused on her heart. A warm pulse developed in her chest. After a minute, the warmth grew, expanding beyond her heart. When the warmth arrived at her shoulders, it snapped like a rubber band back to nonexistence. Anna sighed.

"How far did you get it? I could tell by your face you felt something." Trinity's eyes twinkled.

Heat flooded Anna's face. "My shoulders."

Marianna smiled. "Try again. You'll get farther each time."

Anna tried again. This time, the warmth appeared in her heart instantly. As it grew, Anna gained control of the warmth and guided it down her right arm toward her hand. Right at the tips of her fingers, the warmth had nowhere else to go, and snapped back again.

"I got it to my fingertips!"

"Excellent!" chorused Trinity and Marianna.

"Try again. Third time's the charm." Marianna winked.

Anna grasped control right away. The warmth spread through her arm and shot out of the tips of her fingers. The magic looked like gold particles, the way dust looked when caught in the sunlight. Anna squealed, a smile taking over her face. Marianna and Trinity cheered, and Anna and Trinity hugged.

"Okay, now try to levitate the spoon," said Marianna. "Just picture the spoon rising, and your magic will do the rest."

"That's it?" Anna asked.

"That's it," Marianna said.

Anna took a deep breath, pointed her finger at the spoon, and imagined the spoon floating. The magic left her hand, and the spoon rose into the air. Anna's eyes widened, and her lips parted into an enormous smile. Trinity and Marianna were both smiling as well. Anna dropped the spoon back to the table.

"Is that how magic works?" Anna asked. "I just picture what I want, and it happens?"

"Only for simple magic, like levitation and summoning." Trinity sat back down at the table. "More advanced magic will require an incantation."

"So why did you keep this from me my entire life?"

"That's what I was trying to explain when we went on this tangent. Care to sit down and let me explain?"

Anna bobbed her head and sat back down. Marianna joined her.

"Like I said earlier, our family, the Lyons, is a powerful magical family. Your ancestors made the rules in the magical world. Those rules affected witches, vampires, and werewolves. Most witches and werewolves have been compliant, but vampires, not so much. Over the centuries, the number of witches who sympathize with vampires has grown. They call themselves Black Market witches. Sixteen years ago, one witch named Valentina advocated for our family to step down and let the magical community live how they want. Of course your great-grandmother, Celeste, refused, and Valentina attacked with her followers. Almost everyone in our family died. You two, Grandma Libby, my sister Dawn, and I survived. We barely escaped."

Trinity dabbed her eyes with a tissue. "We were pretty sure we were being followed, so we split up and planned to meet up after a week of traveling in order to get them off our trail. Dawn took Marianna, who at the time was four years old, and I took you, you were two years old. Dawn and Marianna never showed up. We waited for a week. We reached out to everyone. No one had seen or heard from them. We couldn't find them. I figured something horrible must have happened, so I hid you here and locked your powers to protect you. Until tonight, I didn't know what happened to Marianna."

"So when you told me my parents died in a home invasion, you didn't mean the burglary kind?"

Trinity looked embarrassed. "No."

"Did this even happen in Chicago?"

"No, we used to live in an all-magical community known as Outer Salem, very near present-day Salem, but I believe everyone has since migrated out."

"Where is Grandma now?"

"In a new all-magical community on the border of Canada and the US."

"Why aren't we living there?"

"Because back then I didn't know if Valentina wanted to finish the job she started, and I wanted to protect you. And as the years have gone by, I thought letting you grow up human would remove the stress and expectations I believe my mother would have placed on you. My plan was to let you meet her after graduation and make your own decision."

"My decision on what? Whether to be a part of Libby's community?" Anna asked.

"Yes," said Trinity.

Anna sighed. She always wondered why her grandma never called or visited. She had assumed Libby wasn't the grandmother type. Now, however, she wondered if Trinity kept her away on purpose.

"No offense, Trinity, but it sounds like our family were the bad guys," Anna mumbled. Marianna's eyebrows rose, and the corners of her mouth twitched.

Trinity sucked her cheeks in. "I wouldn't say we were the bad guys, but we definitely have made very grave mistakes over the generations. Grandma Celeste should have been willing to talk with Valentina, maybe even make some compromises. Her pride led to her death and the death of most of the family."

At the word family, Anna remembered Marianna.

"She really is my sister?" Anna nodded at Marianna.

"She really is," said Trinity.

"Why didn't you ever tell me about her?"

Trinity raked her fingers through her hair. "It's not a good excuse. You were so young, and little kids just ask so many questions. I didn't have the answers to those questions. I had hoped we would find her a long time ago, and I would introduce you then, but obviously I waited much too long. I'm so sorry, honey."

Anna nodded her forgiveness. She could have argued against Trinity's reasons. She could have told Trinity what she should have done all those years ago. But rehashing now wouldn't do anything. They couldn't go back in time and change it.

Anna looked at Marianna and gave her a small smile. Marianna grinned back. "So what happened to you?" Anna asked.

Marianna looked down at her hands and played with her fingers, pursing her lips. "I don't remember too much from the beginning. From what I have been told, Dawn thought we were close to getting caught, so she dropped me off with a friend she could trust, Caroline. Dawn told Caroline to keep me safe until she returned, but she never did. Caroline raised me and trained me in magic. When I turned eighteen, I left to look for you, but it took me two years to find you."

"Why didn't Caroline ever contact us?" Anna asked.

"You and I have been hiding," Trinity said. "There aren't very many people who know where we are or if we are even alive."

"Is this why I've had such strict rules all my life?"

"Yes, I'm sorry. I know it was hard for you, but

even here I can't be one-hundred-percent sure that we are safe. The fact that Marianna found us proves my point." Trinity turned her attention to Anna's sister. "Not that I'm upset you found us. I am so happy you are alive. But if you found us, then others can, too."

"I'm not offended," said Marianna. "I understand."

"What do we do now?" Anna asked.

"You are going to bed." Trinity placed her hands on the table and stood up. "It's been a long night. We need to rest and can pick back up in the morning."

"You just dumped a ton of information on me, and you expect me to go to sleep?" Anna asked.

"Anna, it's almost two in the morning."

"But—"

"I'll still be here tomorrow. I'm not going anywhere," Marianna said.

Defeated, Anna got up from the table. "Goodnight."

"Goodnight, Annamaria," Marianna said.

Anna paused. "Goodnight, Marianna."

Ten minutes later, Anna lay in bed, unable to fall asleep. She was a witch, she had an older sister, and she came from an infamous powerful family. Crazy is what this was, and yet, she knew it was real. Something warmed her body—her magic, perhaps—when she thought about it.

As Anna reviewed all the information, the silence and darkness of her room focused her thoughts on two bombshells Trinity had glossed over—vampires and werewolves. Anna shivered. She was sure the books and movies didn't have everything right, but stereotypes come from some sort of truth. Anna's eyes became heavy, and she made a mental note to ask

Trinity and Marianna for more information about vampires and werewolves later.

Chapter 6 Magic 101

Anna had such a strange and cool dream. Trinity introduced her to a woman who turned out to be Anna's long-lost sister, Marianna. Anna and her family were witches, and a vengeful witch named Valentina had murdered most of Anna's family. Trinity unlocked Anna's powers, and Marianna helped her gain control over them, which led to Anna levitating a spoon.

Anna checked her phone once her eyes were fully functioning. Half a dozen text messages from Cody flashed on her screen.

—*What happened last night?*—

—*Are you ok?*—

—*Did I do something wrong?*—

And on it went. Anna sent him a brief text stating everything was all right. He responded with a kiss and heart emoji.

Anna headed downstairs and stopped dead in her tracks when she entered the living room. Sitting on the couch, reading a book, was Marianna. Anna stood there, her mouth agape. Marianna looked up from her book and beamed.

"Good afternoon, Annamaria," Marianna said. Anna continued to stare. As if she could read her mind, Marianna raised her eyebrows. "No, last night was not a dream." No, it certainly was not. Anna got a much better look at Marianna. Her pale skin and beautiful red hair stood out against a black blouse, dark jeans, and black boots.

Anna exhaled. "I'm sorry. I didn't mean to be rude. This is just so surreal."

"I know what you mean," Marianna said, not taking her gaze off Anna.

Anna was speechless again. Her cheeks flushed, and she giggled to cover her embarrassment. "I'm sorry, I'm just feeling shy, and awkward, and I have a million questions." When she finished talking, her stomach growled. Both Anna and Marianna laughed. "And apparently hungry."

"Let's go in the kitchen," said Marianna. "You can eat, and we can talk."

In the kitchen, Anna made herself a sandwich. "Do you want one?"

"Oh, no thanks. I already ate," Marianna said. Anna poured herself a glass of grape juice, and she and Marianna sat down at the table. "So fire away."

"You've always known you were a witch?" Anna asked.

"Yes. Caroline used her powers daily and taught me how to use mine."

"How old were you when you started learning magic?"

"I was five. Most witches start learning between four and six years old. When they can push their powers out, like what you did last night, is the sign one is ready."

"Have you always known about me and our family?"

"Yes, I remembered your name and have a fuzzy memory of what you looked like at two years old.

Caroline taught me about our family, so I yearned to be with you one day."

"Why did it take you two years to find us?"

"Like Trinity said, you two have been hiding."

"How did you find us? Did you use magic?"

"Yes, though it's complicated to explain." Marianna pursed her lips and shifted her gaze.

"Something I'll understand better when I know more?"

Marianna nodded and smiled. "Yeah."

"Do you remember Mom and Dad?" Anna looked down.

Marianna took a while before answering. "Yes, a little. I remember what they look like, and I have a few happy memories. But I don't remember the night they died."

Both girls sat in silence as they contemplated their lives, their family's tragedy, and the "what-ifs" had their parents survived. Anna sniffed and wiped her eyes. Marianna wasn't crying, but her face looked just as sad. Trinity walked into the kitchen with Gwen on her shoulder.

"What's wrong?" she asked.

"I was asking Marianna about herself, and my questions turned to Mom and Dad, so things got a little emotional," Anna said.

Trinity hugged Anna and patted Marianna's shoulder. "Well, you two are going to need to have those moments now that Marianna has found you."

Gwen cawed and flew toward Marianna. She put her hands up to shield her face, and Gwen pecked her hands, drawing blood. Anna yelled at Gwen, and Trinity grabbed her tail feathers and yanked her away from her niece. Trinity put the bird's face up to hers. "You leave her alone. She is perfectly safe." Gwen cawed again and flew up to the second floor toward Trinity's bedroom, her caws ringing in their ears.

"What the heck?" asked Anna.

"Gwen doesn't like strangers, but don't worry, she'll get used to Marianna," Trinity said.

"Gwen isn't an ordinary bird, is she?" Anna cocked her head.

"She is my familiar," Trinity answered.

"Like your animal partner?"

Trinity laughed. "In layperson's terms. Gwen and I can communicate on a deeper level. She can go places and sense things I can't. She looks out for me."

Anna perked up. "Does every witch get a familiar?"

Trinity nodded. "Yes. When a witch is full grown. You technically are since you're eighteen, but you haven't been practicing magic, so yours may take a while to find you."

"Are only crows familiars?"

"No, any animal can be."

Anna turned to Marianna. "What kind of animal is your familiar?"

"A wolf." Marianna smiled. "Her name is Luna."

Anna's eyes lit up. "Cool. Is she here with you?"

"No, but you will meet her eventually," Marianna said.

"Anna," said Trinity. "Would you like to have another magic lesson today?"

Anna jumped up and clapped her hands. "Yes!"

Trinity beamed. "Clean up your lunch and meet me in the living room."

Anna washed her dishes at top speed and ran into the living room. There were three objects on the coffee table ranging in size from small to big—a spoon, a coffee mug, and a bowling ball.

Rubbing her hands together, Anna looked at Trinity. "Ready."

Trinity chuckled. "We are going to continue levitation today. You can't just levitate anything right off the bat. It requires building your physical strength and a connection with your magic. So I would like you to levitate each item one at a time, starting with the smallest and lightest and going to the biggest and heaviest. Also, an important part I didn't teach you last night is to control the descent. Just dropping the object shows a lack of control. Controlling the descent will help build up your skill."

Anna looked at the spoon. She lifted it into the air without a problem. However, the spoon fell with a loud clang when she let go of it. Trinity nodded. "Try again with the spoon, but work on controlling the descent." Anna's second attempt was more successful, and she lowered the spoon with perfect control.

Trinity smiled. "Good. Now the mug."

Anna pointed at the mug. Her magic flowed and left her fingers, but the mug remained still. She furrowed her brow and tried with all her might, but it still wouldn't budge. Anna dropped her hand and sighed.

"Pick up the mug with your hand, without magic," said Marianna. Anna picked it up. "Memorize its weight and the effort your arm and hand muscles have to put in to raise and hold it."

Anna raised and lowered the mug, noted how her

forearm and hand tensed and flexed. When she was ready, she placed it back on the table. Anna pointed at the mug again, imagining its weight, imagining her hand holding it. The mug wiggled but didn't rise.

"Use your entire hand instead of your finger," Marianna said.

Anna unclenched her other fingers and spread them out. The mug rose. Anna exhaled. Marianna was so good at talking her through this. As Anna lowered the mug, it wiggled and crashed to the coffee table, shattering. "Trinity, I'm so sorry."

"It's easily fixable." Trinity waved her hand over the mug, and the pieces sprang back together, good as new.

"Whoa," said Anna. "Is it like levitation, where you think it and it happens?"

Trinity shook her head with a smile. "No. That one needs an incantation. You'll learn it, eventually."

Anna spent the rest of the afternoon levitating and lowering objects. She broke the mug several more times, and Trinity repaired it over and over. When Anna succeeded, she progressed to the bowling ball. She ended the night drenched in sweat and panting.

"Let's call it a day," said Trinity

"No. I just need a drink of water and a few minutes of rest."

Trinity grabbed Anna's hand. "Anna, be patient. I know this is exciting, but we'll work some more tomorrow. You'll get better each day."

"But I'm at least ten years behind other witches my age," Anna said.

"I wouldn't worry," said Marianna. "You may be new to magic, but you aren't a child. I think you'll catch up quickly."

"All right." Anna sighed but still smiled.

"I'm sure you're starving," Trinity said. "I know I am. What do you want for dinner? I'll show you how to cook with magic."

"Aren't we supposed to have dinner at Cody's house?" Anna asked. She needed to shower and do her hair and makeup. She had been so invested in practicing magic, she spent the day in her pajamas.

"Sorry, Anna, but I called Hal this morning and canceled," Trinity said.

"What? Why?"

"Because we can't take Marianna with us, and it would be rude to leave her here alone."

"Why can't she come with us?"

"Because we can't tell anyone about her, or us."

"Well, I figured the witch part, but I don't see why we have to keep Marianna a secret."

"You two can go to dinner without me," Marianna said. "I don't mind."

"No, Marianna, it's okay," said Trinity. "Family comes first."

Marianna didn't respond, but her eyes shone, a small smile on her lips. Anna conceded as well. Trinity was right. They had known Marianna for less than twenty-four hours. Of course they needed to focus on her. Besides, what were they going to talk about at dinner, anyway? Anna would end up acting weird since she would try so hard to not let something slip. But she still didn't understand why no one could know about Marianna. Why couldn't they come up with something believable to tell the town?

During dinner preparations, Trinity showed Anna

how she used levitation and some other spells to flatten the chicken, fold the ham and cheese slices into it, and chop up the vegetables. Anna didn't get to try any of it herself. This was an observational lesson. However, for the actual cooking, Trinity recommended the human way. She said magical speed cooking tasted very similar to leftovers in the microwave.

When the chicken was ready, the three women sat down with their plates. While they ate, they talked about Anna's lesson that afternoon, and Trinity and Marianna reminisced about their own training years. Marianna ate less than half of her food, and when Anna pointed it out, Marianna said she had a small appetite.

While Anna was brushing her teeth, her phone vibrated with a text from Cody.

—Why didn't you guys come to dinner?—

Anna ignored it and moved on to washing her face. Her phone vibrated again.

—Are you mad from last night?—

Anna changed into clean pajamas and climbed into bed. Her phone vibrated with an incoming call. It was Cody. Anna rejected the call and turned her phone off. What was she supposed to say? She couldn't tell Cody the truth, and she didn't want to lie to him. Why couldn't anyone know about Marianna?

Chapter 7 Secrets

Trinity handed Anna her car keys during breakfast. Anna raised her eyebrows.

"You can take my car to school this week."

Anna's eyes lit up. "Awesome! Why?"

"Because your rehearsals will go late. You can just drive my car home instead of calling me or asking for a ride."

"What rehearsals?" Marianna asked.

"Dance," said Anna. "The concert is this Saturday, so we have extra practice after school."

This was the first year Trinity had done something like this. Anna had a feeling it was more to do with keeping her from being in a position which could accidentally reveal Marianna. Regardless, driving Trinity's car for a week would be fun.

At school, Jamie was waiting for Anna at their lockers, but Stephanie was nowhere to be seen. "Hey," said Jamie, the normal pep in her voice faltering.

"I will not force small talk," said Anna, her good mood from driving Trinity's car dissipating. "Just tell me what Stephanie said."

Jamie's forced smile disappeared. "She's still really mad at you."

"Obviously." Anna gestured around the Stephanie-less hallway.

Jamie avoided Anna's eyes. "Well, that was a

pretty crappy thing to do. Why would you do it? Jake and Stephanie aren't even a couple."

Anna gritted her teeth. "I told Stephanie this, and I'll repeat it to you. I didn't *tell* him to kiss her. He asked me if I thought she would let him kiss her if he tried, and I told him if he was feeling the vibes to give it a shot. It's not my fault he got drunk." Jamie opened her mouth, but Anna kept going. "And that conversation wouldn't have even taken place if Stephanie hadn't demanded we all switch dates for one dance."

Jamie nodded her head toward their English class and started walking. Anna refused to follow. She could not believe Jamie took Stephanie's side. Jamie was usually a great mediator. The tardy bell rang. She stomped toward class when Cody called out her name.

"Hey." She forced the same smile Jamie had given her just minutes before. She stopped walking and let him catch up. He didn't throw his arms around her, kiss her, take her hand, or touch her.

"Let's get out of here," he said. "Do you want to go up into the mountains?"

"I can't."

"Anna, come on! You've been ignoring my texts and calls."

"It's hell week! If I ditch and Coach Holt finds out, she'll take away my solos, maybe even take me out of the entire show."

"Oh, right," mumbled Cody.

"Mr. Mills, Miss Lyons, class started five minutes ago," said the vice principal as she walked down the hall.

"Sorry," they both said, then scattered.

Anna didn't receive any grief from Mrs. Caldwell. She always offered leniency to students when things were stressful, and this week was the dance team's turn. Stephanie shot Anna the stink eye, and Jamie kept her head down. Anna sighed and spent the class period with her head in her arms.

Pre-Cal was just as frustrating. Cody kept looking back, his face a mixture of hurt and confusion. Anna could not deal with this today. When class was over, Cody was at Anna's desk before she could stand up.

"At least let's eat lunch at my house?"

Why was he so desperate to get her away from school? Anna's heart sped up. Was he planning on breaking up with her? Their breakup would be the talk of the school. Maybe Cody was being kind enough to spare her from an audience. The reason he had been bugging her about if she was upset was because *he* was upset. Anna caught her breath. He was upset she got cold feet on Saturday night, and her refusal to talk yesterday just fueled the fire. She needed to avoid this conversation. She had to stall him.

"I can't," she said. "I have to go home for lunch."

"Why?"

"Um… Trinity needs her car."

"So I'll follow and drive you back."

"No. I'm sorry, but I can't tell you." Anna scooted around him and ran to dance class. She heard Cody kick her desk.

In team, they spent class time getting all the costumes ready. Anna worked in silence while Stephanie refused to look at her, and Jamie's eyes shifted between the two of them. When the lunch bell rang, Anna raced to Trinity's car before the tears started flowing. She cried the entire drive home. When she got home, Anna threw herself onto a kitchen chair and cried into her arms.

"Annamaria? What's wrong?" asked Marianna. Anna jumped. "Oh, sorry."

"It's okay," Anna said. "I just didn't hear you come in."

"What's wrong?" Marianna repeated.

Anna shook her head and waved her hand. "My friends and I are in a fight. You know how high school is."

Marianna looked away. "Actually, I don't."

"Really? You didn't go to high school?"

Marianna shook her head. "I was homeschooled."

"Oh, that must have been lonely."

"It was."

Anna closed her eyes and put her head in her hand. "I'm sorry, that was tactless."

Marianna shrugged. "It's okay. It's the truth. Do you want to tell me what happened?"

Anna told Marianna everything. She expressed her fears of losing her two best friends and the possibility of Cody breaking up with her. Marianna pushed a tense hand across the table as if to put her hand on top of Anna's, her face pained. Right as her cold fingertips touched Anna's knuckles, Marianna pulled her hand back. "I'm so sorry. I wish I knew what to say to help you feel better."

Anna shrugged. "It's okay. It's not your fault."

"Well, I think the stuff with Cody is. If I weren't here, you would have been able to spend yesterday evening with him. I'm sorry."

"Don't be." Anna placed her hand on Marianna's

shoulder. "Things would have been weird, anyway. Because of prom night, Cody and I now have to have *the talk*, which is the real reason I'm avoiding him. You just made the perfect excuse."

Marianna chuckled. "I'm happy to be of service."

Both girls giggled. Anna spent her lunch break talking instead of eating, so she rushed through making herself a sandwich and scarfed it down as she drove back to school. Back at school, Anna struggled to pay attention. Would her exams even matter in the magical world? Now that she knew who she was, she didn't know if USC was even in the cards anymore.

Practice was miserable. Nothing went right, and Coach Holt spent the afternoon yelling at everyone. Anna wasn't concerned with the actual dance routines. The start of hell week was always like this. Everything would come together by Saturday. When practice ended for the night, Coach Holt called Anna up to the control booth. Her stomach dropped at the sight of Jamie and Stephanie standing there as well.

Coach Holt looked at each girl. "I don't know what's going on, but whatever it is, it has got to stop. Do not ruin your last show at this school just because you're mad at each other. Fix it and come tomorrow prepared to do better. Understood?"

The three of them dipped their heads and mumbled. Coach Holt stomped away to clean up her things, and the three girls walked out to the parking lot together. Jamie and Stephanie walked shoulder to shoulder. Anna walked a foot away but kept their pace.

"So…" began Jamie.

Anna looked at Stephanie. She didn't need to explain herself a third time. This was Stephanie's problem.

"I'm sorry I let this affect rehearsal," Stephanie said. She didn't sound sorry at all.

"I'm sorry too," Anna said, just as stiff. She sighed and dropped her shoulders. "Stephanie, I'm really sorry about prom and Jake. I honestly did not know I said anything wrong. Can you please forgive me?"

Stephanie shrugged and walked away. "That's it?" Anna asked. Stephanie continued to walk as if she had not heard Anna. Jamie looked just as shocked as Anna. "This has got to be bigger than prom. What is it?"

"I don't know," Jamie whispered, then hurried after Stephanie. Anna didn't believe Jamie either.

Anna's vision blurred, and she rubbed her eyes. She unlocked Trinity's car and threw her bag onto the passenger seat. Before she could fall into the driver's seat, a hand grabbed her shoulder. Anna screamed and swung her fist around but stopped when she realized it was Cody. He didn't even apologize for scaring her.

"Can we please talk now?"

She pointed to her tearstained face. "Seriously?"

"Look, I'm sorry you aren't getting along with them, but I really—"

"*I'm* not getting along with them? They are the ones who are freaking out about something stupid."

"I know. But can we please focus on us for a minute?"

Anna groaned. "Cody, please. I'm hungry, I'm tired. I just want—"

"Damn it, Anna. Can you please give me a few minutes?" Cody hit the side of Trinity's car, planting his hands on either side of Anna, trapping her between him and the car. Anna stopped breathing. Her body froze.

Cody studied Anna's face, and he dropped his head down into her neck. "I'm so sorry. We haven't talked in two days. I've missed you." Anna sat down in the driver's seat with her legs hanging out toward the ground. Cody sat on the ground next to Anna's feet and took one of her hands, kissing it.

"Can you please tell me how you feel about Saturday night? I feel like you put up a wall between us, and I don't know how to break through it."

Anna's eyes widened. He wasn't mad at her. He thought she was mad at him. Anna exhaled. "I thought you were going to break up with me."

Cody chuckled. "Why would I do something like that?"

Anna's face flushed. "Because I didn't want to, you know... Isn't that why couples our age break up?"

"Only if they're immature." Cody threw his head back and laughed. "So you're telling me we just spent the past two days not talking because we were afraid of the same thing?"

It was Anna's turn to laugh. "I guess."

Cody groaned and put his head in his hands. "I'm so sorry I boxed you in like that. I don't know what came over me."

Anna's eyes softened. "It's okay. We've all been on edge."

"So we're all good?" Cody looked up from his hands, his eyes hopeful.

"Yes," said Anna, letting Cody kiss her. "But I really have to go. I have Trinity's car, and I need to eat."

"All right. Call me later?"

"Sure."

Back at home, Trinity saved a plate of food for Anna in the microwave. Anna ate in silence.

"Marianna told me about your morning. Did the afternoon get better?" Trinity asked. Anna recounted what had transpired at dance practice and in the parking lot. "I'm sorry about Stephanie and Jamie, but I'm glad you and Cody could work things out."

"Yeah."

"Are you too tired to practice magic?"

"No." Anna jumped up, energy miraculously flowing through her body, or was it magic? Her fingertips glowed. "See?"

Anna warmed up by levitating the spoon, mug, and bowling ball first. Trinity then instructed Anna to fluctuate weight and sizes. She levitated the kitchen chairs, plates, decorations, even Trinity. Anything Anna could have lifted with her hands or arms, she was able to levitate. Trinity told her to practice levitation every day until it became second nature. Only then would she be able to levitate objects she couldn't physically lift.

"Where's Marianna?" Anna asked at the end of practicing.

"She's out. You'll see her in the morning," said Trinity.

Anna looked confused. "But nothing is open this late."

"She's not doing human stuff," said Trinity.

"Oh."

Up in her room, Anna had three missed calls from Cody. She called him back via video call. His face appeared with his elbow behind his head and his pillow as his background. "Hey babe." He wiggled his eyebrows.

Anna blew him a kiss and fluttered her eyelashes. "Hey."

"What have you been doing all night?"

"Bonding with Trinity."

Cody squinted. "You live with her. What kind of bonding could you possibly do?"

"The grown-up kind." Anna tried to keep a straight face.

Cody rolled his eyes. "You're such a goof. Really? What did you do?"

"She taught me some stuff about my family."

"Oh, cool. That seems to have put you in a better mood."

Anna smiled. "Getting out of that school and eating dinner also helped."

Cody chuckled. "I hear ya." He gazed through the screen.

Anna blushed. "What?"

"I just like looking at you. I've missed you."

"I've missed you too."

"Have lunch with me tomorrow? Just us."

Anna nodded. "Yeah, that sounds nice." She yawned.

Cody sighed. "I'll let ya go. I like you."

Anna giggled. "I like you, too."

****

Anna woke up an hour earlier to practice. She couldn't believe she had only been practicing magic for three days, and she was already good at levitating. Marianna must be right about Anna being older, making the simpler stuff easy and fast to learn. At Trinity's usual breakfast time, she still had not come downstairs, but Marianna did.

"Good morning, Annamaria."

"Good morning." Anna smiled. "Do you know if Trinity is awake?"

"She left early. She said you can still drive her car, and she should be home by dinner," Marianna answered.

"Huh." What did Trinity need to do at the library that required her to leave so early? "What are you doing today?"

"Hanging around the house. Do you want to come by for lunch again?"

Anna hesitated. She had already agreed to eat with Cody, but Marianna was her sister. They were still getting to know each other.

"It's okay if you have other plans."

Anna shook her head. "It's not a problem. I'll come."

Marianna's face lit up. "I'd love that. I'll have lunch ready."

Anna shook her head. "Don't stress yourself. I can have a sandwich again."

Marianna waved Anna off. "I want to."

Anna smiled. "All right, I'll see you in a few hours."

At lunchtime Anna snuck out to her car. Before driving away, she sent Cody a quick text canceling lunch. Even if she had stayed at the school with him, it would have been miserable. The entire school knew Anna and her friends weren't talking. Though, from what she could gather through eavesdropping, no one knew the details. However, lack of knowledge didn't stop her classmates from choosing sides, and they didn't choose hers.

When Anna walked into the house, she licked her lips at the restaurant-worthy sandwich waiting on the kitchen table. Marianna toasted the bread, turkey, and cheese and added avocado, bacon, and tomatoes.

Anna sat down and took her first bite. "Wow. Marianna, this is delicious. Are you going to eat with me?" Anna looked around for a second sandwich.

"I already ate," Marianna said. "How are things at school today?"

Anna rolled her eyes and told Marianna the same things she had told Trinity the night before, plus her discoveries from the morning.

Marianna's brow furrowed. "Those girls don't sound like good friends to me."

Anna leaned onto her elbow. "I thought they were my best friends. We've known each other since kindergarten. Did you have friends like this?"

Marianna shook her head, then stopped. "Well, I had one friend, but she really wasn't the same as your friends."

"Was she a witch like us?" Anna's eyes lit up.

"She is a part of the magical community," Marianna said.

"Any boyfriends?"

Marianna grimaced. "There was one who liked me growing up, I guess. But I didn't like him back, and our friendship didn't really end on good terms."

Anna looked down. "I'm sorry."

Marianna shrugged. "It's not a big deal. I have a much better boyfriend now."

"You do? What's his name? Did he come here with you? Will I get to meet him?"

Marianna grinned. "His name is Will. Yes, he's here, but he has his own thing to do right now. And yes, I hope you get to meet him soon."

Anna's lunch break ended much too soon, and she headed back to school with slumped shoulders. "If I didn't have my spot in the dance concert to protect, I would just stay here with you."

"Keep your head up and be strong." Marianna leaned toward Anna like she wanted to hug her but stopped herself. Anna grabbed Marianna and hugged her. They said goodbye, and Anna drove off.

****

After an improved dance practice, Anna found Cody leaning against Trinity's car. Anna rubbed his biceps and kissed him. "I'm sorry about lunch today."

Cody grimaced, then closed his eyes and took a deep breath. When he opened his eyes, he flashed the smile that made Anna's knees go weak. "Make it up to me by coming to dinner?"

Anna bit her lip and bounced her leg. She could miss seeing Marianna for a couple more hours. "Let me ask Trinity." Cody nodded as she pulled out her phone. She leaned against him while Trinity's phone rang, and he massaged her shoulders.

"Yes?"

"Hi. Can I eat dinner at Cody's?"

"No, sorry. You need to come home if practice is over."

"But—"

"We are having dinner as a family."

"Ugh. Fine."

"I love you."

"Love you too." Anna hung up. She turned in

Cody's arms. "I'm sorry, I can't. I have to go home and have dinner with Trinity."

Cody groaned. "What's going on?"

Anna stilled in his arms. "What do you mean?"

Cody squeezed Anna's waist. "I mean, ever since prom, you and Trinity have been acting weird."

Anna avoided his eyes. "How so?"

Cody folded his arms, causing Anna to readjust and step back. "Trinity was all mysterious on prom night, then canceled dinner. And you keep going home for lunch, and now you have to go home again."

Anna sighed. "I'm sorry, I'm just busy with dance, and Trinity wants to make sure I don't fall behind in school."

"Why do I get the feeling you aren't being honest?"

"Please trust me." Anna cupped his cheek and rubbed it with her thumb.

Cody nodded and kissed her palm before walking toward his house.

Anna groaned as she settled into the car. She hit the steering wheel. She wasn't doing this on purpose. She should just tell him. Her stomach squirmed. What if Cody told other people? Or he didn't take the news well? Until Anna better understood how things worked in her new world, she couldn't even consider telling Cody. But there had to be something she could tell him now to appease him. Maybe Trinity would have some advice.

When Anna got home, Trinity wasn't. *Are you kidding me? After she told me to come home.* "Where's Trinity?"

"She must still be working. I haven't seen her all

day," Marianna said from the couch.

Anna called Trinity's cell, but she didn't answer this time. Anna threw her phone on the couch and warmed up some leftover chicken cordon bleu. "Are you going to eat?" She gestured to the empty spot in front of her.

Marianna looked out the window. "I already ate."

"Hm."

"Are you okay?" Marianna studied Anna with concern.

Anna deflated and nodded. "Yes. Sorry. It's been a long day."

Marianna nodded, and Anna ate in silence. The only time she witnessed Marianna eat was on Sunday night, and she had only eaten a few bites. Was Marianna anorexic? She was very skinny, but she didn't look unhealthy. Quite the opposite. Her shape was beautiful, and she was toned. Maybe she had some weird issue with eating in front of an audience?

Trinity arrived home just as Anna finished her dinner.

"Where have you been?" Anna asked.

"I had a lot of work to do." Trinity waved Anna's question away. "Good, you've eaten. Let's start on your next lesson." Anna swallowed her questions at the chance to practice magic.

This time, the living room didn't have any objects set up to be levitated. "Tonight we are going to start on summoning. Summoning is when you make an object appear out of thin air. Like levitating, you connect with your magic and tell it what to do. However, you aren't actually creating something out of nothing. You take the object from somewhere else. So when you are first learning, it's best to summon an object you already know exactly where it is."

Trinity held her hand out, palm up, and an apple appeared. Anna grinned and shifted in her seat. "I summoned this apple from the fridge," said Trinity. "But you'll start by summoning objects you can see." Trinity set the apple down on the coffee table. "Now, hold your hand out, and tell your magic to put the apple into your hand."

Anna held out her hand and concentrated. After a minute, the apple soared into her hand. Darn, she meant to summon it, not levitate it. Anna tried several more times, but every time the apple levitated into her hand. Anna groaned. "What am I doing wrong?"

"It takes time," said Trinity. "Keep trying."

Several minutes later, Anna still could only levitate the apple to her hand. "May I make a suggestion?" Marianna asked.

"Please." Anna groaned.

"I think you are imagining the apple traveling to your hand. Especially if you are looking at the apple. Imagine it simply appearing in your hand. Look at your hand."

Anna held out her hand again and stared at it, picturing the apple without looking at it. After several seconds, the apple appeared in Anna's hand. She jumped and looked at the empty coffee table. "I did it!"

Trinity clapped. "Yes. Well done. Marianna, you are such a skilled teacher. I'm so glad you are here." Marianna smiled and looked down.

Anna summoned several more objects from around the room. When there was a small pile on the couch, Trinity called it a night.

Anna's magic coursed through her veins as she got ready for bed. Warm tingles flowed with the magic. She was whole. She hadn't been miserable before. But with her powers unlocked, she recognized there had been a void before. She no longer needed to go to USC. She was content to see where her magic might take her—whether it was college or somewhere else. With these thoughts, Anna drifted off to sleep.

****

She woke up to the sound of a loud banging on the door. When her brain focused, she discovered someone knocking on the front door, not her bedroom door. She looked at her digital clock. 12:38 a.m. Who was visiting at this time of night? She got out of bed, opened her bedroom door, and walked out into the hall. She was about to descend the stairs, but two voices made her stop.

"Just tell me what's going on," Mr. Mills said.

His voice dropped, and Anna couldn't decipher what he was saying. Trinity responded, and it sounded like they were arguing. Was that her name and Cody's? Anna scooted down the stairs on her behind so she could hear better. When the arguing stopped, Anna froze. Kissing sounds reached her ears. Anna clapped her hands over her mouth to prevent giggles escaping down to their ears. Mr. Mills began to lead Trinity up the stairs, and Anna ran back to her room. At the top of the stairs, Trinity pulled Mr. Mills' hand.

"Wait. No," she whispered. "Anna is in the house."

"Is she a heavy sleeper?" Mr. Mills asked.

Anna's jaw dropped, and she gagged. It was cute when they were kissing, but there was no way she wanted them to do *it* just down the hall from her. What was going on with the Mills men this week?

"Hal, you're going to have to be patient."

Hal sighed and pecked Trinity's lips. "All right. Don't make me wait much longer."

Trinity hummed. "Graduation."

"It's a date."

They headed back down the stairs, and Anna stayed in her room. What were they arguing about in the middle of the night? Was it possible the Mills were also connected to the magical world? If so, Anna should be able to tell Cody, and everything would be all right. Plus, they were going to hook up on graduation!

****

Anna once again woke up an hour earlier to practice magic. She worked on levitating for thirty minutes, then summoning. She did great at levitating, and summoning was easier than the previous night. At breakfast, Anna ventured to ask Trinity about her late-night rendezvous with Mr. Mills.

"Trinity? Are we the only witches in Harrison?"

"Yes. That's one reason I picked this place to raise you."

"And the other reasons?"

"It's a small town, surrounded by mountains. No one would expect us to be here," Trinity said.

Anna wanted to ask if Mr. Mills knew about magic, but something in Trinity's tone stopped her, and she dropped the subject. As Anna got ready to head out the door, Marianna ran downstairs.

"Hey, Annamaria, can I have your cell number? Maybe we could message each other throughout the day?"

Anna's eyes lit up, and she whipped her phone out

of her pocket. "Yeah." Her fingers flew as she unlocked her phone and typed in Marianna's number. She sent her sister a heart emoji to give Marianna her number. "I could use the distraction. Text me every class period, K?"

Marianna smiled and nodded. "Are you coming home for lunch?"

"Most definitely," said Anna.

Marianna grinned. "I'll see you then."

English was unbearable with Jamie and Stephanie, but Anna survived with kind messages from Marianna. Pre-Cal ended up being really fun. They were working in small groups to prepare for the end-of-year exam. Anna and Cody were in the same group, which they used to their advantage to split off as a duo, which resulted in no studying.

"Did you know your dad visited last night?" Anna whispered.

Cody looked up from his paper. "What? What was he doing there? When?"

"He came in the middle of the night, at twelve thirty in the morning. He and Trinity were talking downstairs, then they started kissing."

Cody's jaw dropped. "No way!"

"It's true."

"Did you hear what they were talking about?"

Anna shook her head.

"Hm…my dad said he needed to talk to me about something important after school today. Maybe they are going to come clean to all of us?"

"Maybe."

The bell rang. Anna and Cody stuffed their incomplete papers in their backpacks and walked down the hall holding hands.

"Are you staying here for lunch?" Cody asked before Anna entered the dance room.

"No," said Anna.

"We don't have to eat in the lunchroom." Cody played with her fingers. "We can eat in the courtyard, or the field, or my house."

Anna shook her head. "I'm sorry. I need to run home."

"You *need* to?"

"Fine, I want to."

Cody dropped Anna's hand. "What for?"

"I just need to be alone right now," Anna said. Cody sighed and stomped away without saying goodbye. Anna threw her head back. She didn't know what else to say. She needed to talk to Trinity soon.

Lunch was ready for Anna again when she arrived home. Anna ate in silence at first, her mind wandering to the night Trinity shared their family history. Trinity had said vampires did not like the rules their family enforced.

"Are vampires real?" Anna asked Marianna.

Marianna stilled. "Yes."

Anna put her lunch down. "Have you ever met any?"

Marianna bit her lip and looked away. "I know a few."

"What are they like?" Anna leaned onto her elbow.

"Well, some are jerks, and I don't talk to them anymore. Some are really great, and we are good friends."

"Whoa," Anna whispered. "And werewolves?"

"I've never met one, but I know people who have."

"What have you heard?"

"They have terrible tempers and can be quite aggressive."

Interesting. Trinity had said the werewolves got along with their family, and the vampires didn't. What would Anna think when she got to meet some?

"Can I ask you a question?" Marianna asked.

"You just did," Anna said. Marianna's lips parted in surprise. "I'm sorry." Anna giggled. "That was a lame joke. Yes, you can ask me a question."

"Do you want me to call you Anna?"

Anna looked up and pursed her lips, then made eye contact with Marianna. "No, I enjoy hearing you say Annamaria."

Marianna grinned. "I like it too."

"What about you?" Anna asked.

"I have always been Marianna."

"Do you know why our parents gave us such similar names?"

Marianna shook her head. "Does it bother you?"

"No," Anna said. "I was just curious. I like it."

"Me too." Marianna smiled.

****

The next three days went by in a flash. Anna had finals, dance rehearsals, and magic lessons. Each day she could levitate heavier objects and summon objects from further away. Cody also stopped talking to her, so whatever his dad told him, he didn't share with Anna. When Anna would sneak peeks in Pre-Cal, he didn't look angry, he looked hurt. Anna didn't know how to fix it. She focused on dancing and planned to make things up to Cody after the concert.

Anna continued to go home for lunch and spend

time with Marianna. After lessons, Trinity also joined their girl time. Anna continued to observe Marianna's eating habits—which were nonexistent.

When Saturday morning finally rolled around, Anna could not keep Marianna a secret any longer. She wanted Marianna to see her dance, and she wanted to be able to tell Cody something. "Trinity, can Marianna come to my concert?"

Trinity sighed. "You know I want to let her, but it's not a good idea."

"Why not? We can still keep our magic a secret. Humans find lost family members all the time."

Trinity rubbed her forehead.

"What if we told people I'm her cousin?" Marianna asked.

Trinity pursed her lips and studied the two girls. "All right. We can try it and see how tonight goes."

Trinity dropped Anna off at the school several hours before the show. Anna used this as an opportunity to discuss Mr. Mills' late-night visit.

"Does Mr. Mills know about us being witches?" Trinity cocked her head and twisted her mouth but didn't respond. Anna twisted her hands in the silence and took a breath. "I'm really sorry, but I kind of overheard you and Mr. Mills on Tuesday night."

Trinity looked out the windshield. "I dated him a long time ago, before he met Cody's mother. I introduced him to my world, and I eventually realized a permanent relationship with him would not work, so I ended things. When we went into hiding, I remembered him, and we moved here."

"Well, if he's kept our secret for this long, why can't he know about Marianna?" Anna asked.

"Because Marianna showing up after sixteen years raises a lot of questions we need answers to before we let anyone else know what's going on. I haven't even told Grandma," Trinity explained.

"Why?"

"Because I want to find answers without her interfering. It's better we wait until we have more information before telling her."

"What answers are you looking for?"

"I want to meet Caroline and hear for myself what she knows. And I want to figure out what happened to Dawn."

"And Grandma can't help?"

"No, because I'm going to have to contact people who don't like or trust her."

"But they'll trust you?"

"I'm hoping to gain their trust, which will have to be without my mother."

"Who are these people?"

"Vampires and Black Market witches."

Anna's eyes widened. "Won't that be dangerous?"

Trinity nodded. "Yes, but necessary."

In front of the makeup mirrors, Coach Holt dictated what the team's hair and makeup were to be. Unlike previous years, Anna did her hair and makeup alone. She combed her hair half up and sprayed until it was unyielding. She curled the loose strands into tight curls. After an eternity, it was showtime. Anna's gaze scanned her teammates, who all avoided her. She set herself up on the dark stage and waited for the lights and music to come on.

The show was perfect. They were on fire, and the crowd loved it. When the senior number was over,

Coach Holt stepped out on stage to introduce them one by one and announce their plans for after high school. Anna still let the human audience believe she would attend USC in the fall.

When the show was over, Anna called to Stephanie and Jamie. She hoped the success of their final dance concert could rekindle their friendship. However, both glanced at Anna, then ran off to their families. She dragged her feet over to Trinity and Marianna. They both held a bouquet for Anna and gave her a big hug.

"Good job, sweetie," said Trinity.

Marianna rubbed Anna's shoulder. "Yeah, you were amazing."

Anna forced a smile. "Thanks."

"Romeo's is staying open late tonight for this. Do you want to go for dessert?" asked Trinity.

"No. Let's eat at home."

"Okay. We'll be in the car while you get your stuff."

Chapter 8 The Whole Truth

When Anna walked out of the main doors, she found Cody sitting on a bench in front of the school. She sat down next to him. "Hey." She tried to smile but was unable to meet his eyes.

"Hey," said Cody, just as awkward. "You danced really well tonight."

Anna smiled and bumped his shoulder. "Just really well?"

Cody stroked her cheek. "I mean amazing. You were amazing."

Anna's smile widened. "Thanks."

"Who was the redhead sitting with Trinity?"

Anna blinked and paused. "She's my cousin."

"I didn't know you had any cousins." Cody frowned.

"Oh, she's a distant cousin. I just met her this week."

"Is she why you kept going home for lunch?"

"Yes."

"Why couldn't you just tell me that? And why couldn't I meet her?"

Anna rubbed her hand down her face. "I don't know how to explain it."

Cody raked his hands through his hair. "Listen, I know this is crappy timing, but to be honest, there is no good timing." Anna's heartbeat sped up, and her breath got caught in her throat. "I… I don't think things are going to work out between us."

Anna couldn't breathe. Her blood roared in her ears, and she stared at Cody. "Why do you think that?"

"Because you haven't been honest with me. You have been hiding your cousin from me all week, and running away at lunch, and ignoring my texts and calls. I've tried to be patient with you, but you won't let me in."

Anna looked down. "I'm sorry. It's this family stuff. Let me talk to Trinity firs—"

Cody growled. "No, Anna. Look me in the eyes right now and tell me the truth, or I'm done."

Anna sat in shocked silence for a minute. When she failed to speak, Cody glared, stood up, and stomped through the parking lot toward his house. The tears Anna had been holding in all night spilled over. She walked to Trinity's car with her shoulders drooping, carrying the weight of her failed friendships and failed relationship.

Both Trinity and Marianna's faces were full of compassion and pity. Trinity put her hand on Anna's shoulder and gave it a gentle squeeze, and Marianna gave her a side hug. As they drove away, they passed Cody's house, and Anna's heart broke into a million pieces. Cody, Stephanie, Jamie, and Isaac were walking up the long driveway together. Fresh tears fell down Anna's cheeks. Marianna hugged her, and Anna cried on her sister's shoulder for the rest of the drive.

After parking the car, Trinity turned around, sympathy swimming in her eyes. "I know it hurts, sweetie. Your first heartbreak is the worst. You don't have to get over it right away, you can cry all night long, and we'll sit with you and offer our shoulders." Anna listened for the "but." "*But* there will come a time where you don't hurt as much. You will get through this."

Anna sniffed. "Now I'm really out of here after graduation."

"And I'm coming with." Trinity patted Anna's shoulder.

The three of them got out of the car. Trinity led them up the garage steps. "I'll make us something special. Anna, you can choose. What would you like?"

Anna became distracted from answering when her feet couldn't advance from their current position. Anna bent her right knee and put pressure on the ball of her foot, but it wouldn't lift. She tried the same thing with her left leg, same result. No matter how hard she tried, she couldn't walk. "What the… What's going on?"

Trinity turned around. "What?"

Marianna reached Anna's side and pulled on her arm. Anna remained glued to the floor. She pulled harder, nearly yanking Anna's arm out of its socket. "Ow!"

Marianna let go and grimaced. "Sorry."

Trinity reached Anna's side, knelt down, and felt around Anna's feet. She looked up, her eyes wide. "Someone's here. Marianna, get in the house. I'll help Anna."

Marianna shook her head. "No. I want to help. I can sm—"

Anna's arms became pinned to her sides, as if invisible ropes wrapped around her torso. "Trinity, what's going on?" Marianna and Trinity stopped arguing to look at Anna. The invisible force holding

Anna yanked her out of the garage. Both Trinity and Marianna ran after her. At the line where the garage and driveway met, they crashed into an invisible barrier. "Trinity! Marianna!" Trinity's and Marianna's mouths moved like they were yelling back, but Anna couldn't hear them. Trinity looked like a mime as she started feeling out the invisible barrier. Meanwhile, Marianna clawed at it like an animal.

The sound of footsteps accompanied Anna regaining control of her body. She spun around. Two women she didn't know stood a foot away. One was blonde, with curly hair, the other straight black hair. Both were smirking.

"Annamaria Lyons," the blonde spoke. "We have been looking for you for sixteen years."

"Who are you?" Anna gestured to her family trapped in the garage. "Let them go."

"I'm afraid they have to stay," the blonde said. "Now, come."

"I'm not going anywhere with you."

The woman with the black hair cackled. "You don't have a choice, sweetheart." She grabbed Anna's arm and a current traveled through her body. The slightest movement from the woman commanded Anna from her shoulders down, like she was a puppet. She turned Anna around and walked her away from the house.

The blonde turned to Marianna and Trinity. "Marianna, when the barrier comes down, you're free to go. Valentina doesn't consider you a problem. Trinity, you get to be the messenger. Please inform your mother the Lyons line is about to end."

Sweat beaded along Anna's hairline. She tried to

turn around, but her captor dug sharp nails into Anna's skin and dragged her away. She turned her head to look behind her. Marianna still thrashed at the invisible barrier like a cat. Trinity's palms rammed against it, her eyes were closed, and her mouth moved. The blonde messenger caught up to Anna and her puppeteer. "Valentina is excited to meet you, Annamaria. I've been told she has quite the proposition prepared for you." Fear turned to full-blown panic. Anna wriggled against the control of the other witch's magic, but she might as well have been pushing against a boulder for all the good her struggling did.

Past the driveway, a black car was parked against the sidewalk. The blonde opened the back door, and the talons digging into Anna's skin receded as she was pushed inside. The black-haired witch muttered under her breath, and once again, invisible ropes wrapped themselves around her torso. A flash zoomed by the car, taking the black-haired woman with it. Then Marianna was on top of the black-haired woman, pinning her to the ground.

"Run, Annamaria!"

Anna got out of the car with difficulty. The invisible ropes were still holding her arms down. She didn't go very far when she was yanked backward and landed on her back. She looked into the face of the blonde. "Oh no you don't." The blonde was thrown off of Anna. Anna sat up. Trinity now pursued the blonde with her hands out in front of her. The two women engaged in the strangest combat Anna had ever seen. They both shot spells at each other without moving their mouths or uttering a sound. Trinity leaped out of the way of the blonde's spell and threw back her own curse as soon as her feet hit the ground. The blonde ducked and spun, responding with another spell. They continued ducking, spinning, and leaping out of the way, neither gaining the upper hand. They were evenly matched.

Meanwhile, the black-haired woman had gotten away from Marianna and shot spells out of her talons, but Marianna wasn't firing any spells back. She was, however, dodging them so fast she was a blur, popping into existence from one spot to the next. The black-haired woman circled around Marianna, positioning her close to Anna again. She used one hand to hold off Marianna and the other to levitate Anna back into the car. Then she dove into the driver's seat, turned on the ignition, and floored the gas pedal.

Before the car could leave the street, the driver's side door flew off the car with a deafening screech. Anna screamed, while the witch behind the wheel cursed. Marianna appeared in the doorway. She reached in and yanked the keys out, making the car come to an abrupt stop, throwing all three of them forward. Marianna grabbed the black-haired woman by the neck and dragged her out of the car. She growled, opened her mouth wide, and bit into the woman's neck. The woman let out a gurgled scream. Blood flowed from the woman's neck, Marianna's jaw stayed clamped to the wound, and her neck convulsed. The woman struggled against Marianna, but her movements slowed down and became feeble until her body became limp. The force of the invisible ropes disappeared. Anna's jaw dropped, and she scooted away from the driver's side of the car.

Marianna dropped the lifeless body to the ground. Remnants of the woman's blood were on Marianna's lips. Their eyes met. Marianna's eyes held a spark of anger which changed to fear. Anna remained frozen against the back door.

"What are you?" Anna whispered.

"Annamaria, this is not how I wanted you to find out," Marianna said.

"What are you?" Anna screamed.

"A little help here," said Trinity.

"I'll explain everything, I promise," Marianna said, then ran toward Trinity and the blonde. The blonde was not a better fighter, but Trinity was tiring. The blonde focused one hand on Trinity and one on Marianna. Marianna tackled her and shifted her to hold her as a target. Trinity shot some power out of her hand, hitting the blonde in the face. Her eyes closed, and her weight slumped in Marianna's arms.

"Go tie her up." Trinity gestured at the house. Marianna flung the blonde over her shoulder without a grunt or change of breath. She walked normally, her muscles still relaxed. Trinity ran over to Anna and hugged her tight. "Are you okay?"

"I don't know." Anna's voice shook.

Trinity looked her over. "Are you hurt?"

"No."

Her eyes wandered over to the dead, bloodless woman in the road. Trinity sighed, walked over to the body, and hovered her palm over it. Wind blew, concentrating into a funnel over the body. The body spun, and dust spun around as well, growing until Anna couldn't see the body anymore. The funnel exploded, the dust fell, and the body was gone.

"What did you do to her?" Anna asked.

"I returned her to the earth," Trinity said. "Let's go

inside and talk."

In the kitchen, the blonde sat propped in a chair, with ropes wrapped around her torso and legs. Her eyes were closed, her chin drooped into her chest. Trinity threw some more power at her, but Anna couldn't see a change in her. "The ropes are now locked, so she can't free herself when she wakes up," Trinity said.

Marianna looked at Anna with mournful eyes. Anna kept her gaze down. Her stomach churned at what she had just witnessed. Why was Trinity so calm? Trinity walked into the living room and called for the other two to join her. Trinity sat down on the big couch, and Marianna joined her. Anna sat alone on the love seat, facing her aunt and sister…if that's who she really was.

Trinity leaned forward. "Annamaria—"

"What are you?" she asked Marianna for the third time.

Marianna lowered her gaze, her body concave. "I think you know."

Marianna never left the house during the day, never ate, and never performed magic, except for the light trick on the first night. She ran faster than any human Anna had seen, was stronger than a female of her size, and Anna had watched her drink the now dead woman's blood. After a minute of uncomfortable silence, Anna forced herself to speak.

"A… v… vampire?" Marianna put her head in her hands and nodded. Anna's heart pricked at how uncomfortable and sad Marianna looked, but she was still so shocked and a little angry. "Are you even my sister?"

"Yes!" said Marianna and Trinity at the same time.

Marianna's voice pleaded, while Trinity's was stern.

"Marianna, you have my permission to tell her everything. Annamaria, please listen to your sister," Trinity said.

Anna folded her arms. Big reveals on Saturday nights better not become a habit in this family.

"Caroline lived with a coven of vampires," Marianna said. Anna's eyes widened, but she remained silent. "She served them with magical protection and helped them gain power with her abilities. They allowed Caroline to hide and protect me at Dawn's request, so I grew up in their home and in their coven. Most of them were nice to me, and I didn't know a different life, other than my fading memories of you, and Mom and Dad.

"During my teenage years, I grew restless living there. I loved Caroline, and I was so grateful for all she did for me, but I wanted to be among more witches. I wanted to find you and Trinity and Grandma. When I turned eighteen, I packed up and said goodbye to Caroline. She was sad, but she understood. Diego, the coven leader, had other plans for me. Several others were waiting for his orders, and they ambushed me. They held me down, and Diego turned me."

Both Anna and Trinity had tears in their eyes. Marianna continued, "I was so angry. I left once the transition was complete. I haven't spoken to or seen any of them since. A few weeks after I turned, I met Will. He took me into his coven, and I have lived with him ever since. For the past two years, I have been searching for witches who might know where you are. I followed several false leads. The clue which sent me here was an anonymous message. I tried to track who I think was the messenger, but I lost her. I followed the message on blind faith and was ecstatic to discover you and Trinity."

Anna leaned forward. "Why didn't you tell me all of this last Saturday?"

"I'm afraid that's my fault," said Trinity. "I told her not to overload you with too much information on night one."

"I also wanted you to get to know me before you knew what I was," Marianna said. "I'm sorry for hiding it, but I was worried you would fear me."

Heat rose to Anna's face, and she looked down. Based on her reaction from moments ago, their worries were not unfounded. Marianna turned her head toward the kitchen door. "She's awake."

Trinity jumped up from the couch and headed into the kitchen with Anna and Marianna close behind. The blonde woman tested against the ropes. "You're wasting your energy, Lica," said Trinity with a smirk.

Lica stopped wiggling and smirked as well. "I thought I'd test your abilities since you've been living as a human for the past sixteen years."

Trinity raised her eyebrows. "What? You think I've done no magic this whole time?" She waved her hand over the ropes, and they fell to the floor. Trinity helped Lica stand up, and the two women embraced. Both Anna's and Marianna's jaws dropped. Trinity kept her arm around Lica's shoulders. "This is my good friend Angelica Byrne."

"You can call me Lica," she said, extending her hand to Marianna, then Anna.

"Okay, I'm sorry, but I'm getting whiplash. What is going on?" Anna asked.

"Let's head back into the living room and talk," said Trinity.

Once the four women were seated, Trinity began the new story.

"Shortly after Valentina killed our family, Lica went underground to live among the Black Market witches and vampires. She's kind of a spy, but I'm the only one who knows, and now you two. The rest of the magical community thinks she converted over. Even Grandma thinks she's a traitor."

"Oh my gosh, Trinity. I almost killed her out there." Marianna had her hand on her heart.

"I wouldn't have let you," Trinity said.

Anna, however, was not ready to jump on the sympathy train. "Then what the heck was tonight all about? If you are supposedly on our side?"

"I'm sorry for scaring you," Lica said. "I had to be convincing outside in front of Priya and any others who were watching us. Now, whoever was watching will report Priya is dead, and I am being held captive."

"It sounds like we are lucky you got the job of finding us," Trinity said.

"You have no idea." Lica rolled her eyes. "I originally didn't get the job. But when Marianna took out Scott in Casper, Priya needed a new partner."

Trinity cocked her head, confused, but a memory sparked in Anna's mind. "Wait, was that you in the parking lot of the pizza place?" she asked Marianna.

"I wasn't the one stalking you between the cars," Marianna answered. "It was a man. I could tell he was a witch, and he was up to no good. So I turned out the lights and took care of him."

"Good thing, too." Lica smiled at Marianna. "If

you hadn't, Annamaria would have never made it back to Harrison."

"How does Valentina know about me?" Marianna asked.

Lica shrugged. "She has connections with all the powerful covens. Diego probably told her at one point, or she might have even visited. I wouldn't be surprised if he turned you on her orders." Marianna's lips parted, her eyes wide.

"If you've been following us since we were in Casper two weeks ago, why did you wait so long to attack?" Anna asked.

"Before Marianna took out Scott, we didn't know what her end goal was in searching for you. Because she's still a new vampire, we didn't know where her emotions were and whether her plans were nefarious. When we realized she was here to strike up a familial bond, we took a step back and created a plan B."

"What does Valentina want with me?" Anna asked.

"I actually don't know. I only said what I was told to say," Lica said.

"Let's back up a minute," said Trinity. "How does anyone know we are here?"

"I honestly don't know." Lica sighed. "I didn't know others were going after you until they commanded me to take Scott's place."

"You don't know a lot for someone who has spent sixteen years as a spy," Anna said.

Trinity glared. "Annamaria."

Lica put a hand up. "It's okay. She's been through a lot in one week. There isn't a single soul who follows Valentina who knows everything. She gives some pieces to one person, and other pieces to another." Lica looked to all three Lyons women. "The one thing I know for certain is because Priya and I failed, others will come. You can't stay here anymore."

No one spoke as Trinity, Marianna, and Anna took in those words.

"How much time do we have?" Trinity asked.

Lica shrugged. "Not much, I imagine. You should leave tonight, if you can."

"We can," Trinity said.

Anna gasped. "But what about the senior campout? And graduation? I can't miss those."

Trinity rubbed Anna's shoulder. "I know it will be hard to miss those milestones, but this is your life we are talking about. I have been preparing ever since Marianna showed up. I knew if she found us, others could, too." Trinity waved her hand, and two black suitcases appeared on the floor in between the TV and the table.

"Where are we going to go?" Anna asked.

"That's the hard part," Trinity said, getting choked up. "The stuff I told you this afternoon, the people I need to visit, the answers I need… I have to go alone."

"What? Why? Where am I going to go? You can't leave me."

"I'm sorry, sweetie, but I have to spend some time in the Black Market, and it's too dangerous for you. Your powers aren't strong enough, which I know is my fault. But now that we have been compromised, I can't put this off anymore. I need to go underground. Marianna, will you take her with you, protect her, and teach her?"

Marianna put her hands to her heart. "Yes, of course I'll look after her."

"Is your coven safe for Anna?"

"Yes. No one knows where I live."

"Is that true?" Trinity asked Lica, who nodded.

"To my knowledge, no one was watching Marianna until she started traveling across the country."

"Good." Trinity stood up.

This was all happening too fast. Just a few hours ago, she danced in a high school concert and expected to start introducing Marianna to the town. Marianna left the room to grab her stuff. Trinity strode over to Anna and drew her into a hug. At first, Anna remained stiff, but then she fell into Trinity's arms and sobbed. Trinity sniffled as well. They held each other for several minutes, crying.

"I love you so much, Annamaria," Trinity whispered.

"Please take me with you," Anna said.

"I wish I could. I promise I will come and get both of you when it is safe to do so."

Anna sniffed. "Okay."

Marianna reentered the room with her own black suitcase. "I called Will while I was upstairs. He's a few minutes away." Anna's stomach knotted itself tighter. Her sister's boyfriend was a *vampire*.

"Good, thank you." Trinity sounded like she struggled to get the words out. Her aunt cleared her throat, and when she spoke again, she had a little more control over her voice. "Annamaria, I have new cell phones for us with new numbers." Trinity handed Anna a cell phone box. "Leave your old one here. Do not contact any of your friends on your new phone. Do you understand?"

"No," Anna said. She didn't plan on contacting

Stephanie or Jamie, but she wasn't ready to give up on Cody.

Trinity looked up at the ceiling. "Annamaria, you are entering a world your friends do not belong in. If you contact them, you could put them in danger."

"But you told Mr. Mills. Why can't I tell Cody? He'll take me back if I tell him."

Trinity shook her head before Anna finished talking. "Hal and I were together long before Valentina attacked our family. She knows where we are. If you stay in contact with anyone here, you will put the entire town in danger. She could use Cody or Lyssa or Courtney to draw you out. Do you want that to happen?" Anna dropped her head and shook it. "Good, neither do I. When we leave this place tonight, we cannot look back."

Anna stayed silent. Trinity handed Anna a thick, white envelope. "Here is some cash for emergencies." Anna peeked inside. Every single bill was a one hundred-dollar bill.

"Will's here," said Marianna.

Trinity hugged Anna one last time. They both started crying again. "I love you, Annamaria."

"I love you too, Trinity."

"I'll come for you when it's the right time."

"When will that be?"

"When it's safe or when you are powerful enough. Whichever comes first, so train hard, okay?"

"I will, I promise."

While they hugged, Marianna took her and Anna's suitcases outside. When she returned, Trinity hugged Marianna. "It's been so nice to get to know you, Marianna. I can't wait to see you again."

"You too." Marianna smiled.

Lica stepped forward. "It was a pleasure to meet you both," she said, shaking their hands again. "And may the next time be under better circumstances."

"Are you going with Trinity?" Anna asked.

"No, Trinity is going to tie me up again when you leave. She'll get out of here, and I'll be rescued in no time. In fact, we are about an hour past when Priya was scheduled to contact Valentina to confirm we were successful, so all of you better get going."

Trinity, Marianna, and Anna all thanked Lica for her help and headed outside. Another black car was outside with the engine running. The outline of a male figure sat in the driver's seat. Trinity walked over to the window and talked to him in a low voice. Anna's heartbeat increased again, and she stopped walking. She breathed fast and shallow. She could not take one more step forward.

Marianna put a comforting arm around Anna's shoulders and gave her a squeeze. "I'll be with you the whole time. I won't let anything happen to you. Would you like me to sit in the back with you?" Anna nodded. Marianna took Anna's hand and led her to the car, where she opened the back door. Marianna climbed in, still hanging on to Anna's hand. Trinity ran over to Anna, and they hugged one more time. Marianna gave Anna's hand a gentle tug, and Anna plopped down into the back seat. Trinity shut the door and waved, tears falling down her cheeks. Anna barely clicked her seatbelt into place when the car took off. She didn't have time to look back at the house she had grown up in and wave one last time at the woman who had raised her.

Chapter 9 The Daylight

Will drove so fast, they left the city limits and were on the highway in less than five minutes. Anna and Marianna were still holding hands, and Anna started squeezing Marianna's. Anna loosened her grip and let go. "Sorry."

"It didn't hurt," Marianna said. "I'm sorry. Vampires don't like to drive slower than they can run, but I assure you, Will is in complete control."

Anna's lips twitched, and she would have laughed in much different circumstances. She turned away and looked out the window. She spent the next hour watching the landscape change as they descended out of the mountains. They were heading east, and Anna wondered where they were going. Lica had mentioned following Marianna across the country, so they were for sure leaving Wyoming.

Silent tears leaked out of Anna's eyes. She wanted this to be a bad dream, and she wanted to stop crying for heaven's sake. Anna closed her eyes and leaned her head against the window. Maybe if she fell asleep, she would wake up in her bed, and it would still be Saturday morning. Several minutes later, Anna was still wide awake, and her forehead was cold from the window. She opened her eyes and glanced at her sister's boyfriend. She was unable to distinguish any of Will's features in the dark. He stared straight ahead, focusing on the road, so all she could see was the back of his head and his hands.

Anna thought back to earlier in the evening when Marianna divulged her actual history. She had so many questions. But in the car's darkness, the thought of voicing those questions made the blood pound in Anna's ears. She wiggled her legs and drummed her fingers against the door handle.

"Is something the matter?" Marianna asked.

Anna took a deep breath in and out, wiggled some more, and looked out the window. "What was it like, growing up with vampires?"

Marianna's body relaxed. "When I was a little girl, I feared all of them. I used to hide under the kitchen sink whenever any of them would come talk to Caroline. I think Diego felt bad, so he always offered me candy. I would refuse it at first, and he would coax me until I gave in. When I stopped hiding, his partner, Jade, gave me piano lessons in their ballroom. Those lessons are my favorite memories from my years there."

Marianna was smiling. "Was it just Diego and Jade?" Anna asked.

Marianna shook her head. "There were eight others. Though I wasn't as close to any of them as Diego and Jade. Most of them stayed away from me, on Diego's orders, I presume."

"And they just expected you to be a happy family at the snap of their fingers?" Anna asked.

Marianna rolled her eyes. "More like the snap of my neck." Anna gasped. "I'm sorry, that was too graphic."

Anna shuddered at the image. How did one become a vampire? She shook her head. Hopefully it wasn't like the movies. "So are you still a witch? Can you still do magic?"

"Kind of. I'm what the vampire community calls a hybrid. I can control light, brew potions, and I still have a connection with my familiar."

"Are there a lot of hybrids?"

"Not that I'm aware of. I only know of one other, Alistair. He lived in Diego's coven when I was a girl. I'm the only one in Will's coven."

"Can Alistair do the same stuff as you?"

"Brewing potions and having a familiar are standard for hybrids. But instead of light, he kept the ability to control water. Mighty handy for putting out fires, which could kill him and the rest of the coven."

"What are the standard abilities of a vampire? From what I saw tonight, you have super speed, super strength, and super hearing."

Marianna giggled. "Those are the basics, yes. We can also see well in the dark. Our fangs have a venom which temporarily paralyzes when we bite, and we can hypnotize."

Anna's mouth fell open. "Good grief, do you have any weaknesses?"

Marianna rolled her eyes with a smile. "Yes. We can't enter a house without being invited in, and wooden stakes, fire, and the sun will kill us."

"Really? Wooden stakes?" Anna had been so sure that one was all Hollywood.

Marianna giggled, then called up into the front seat. "Sunrise is less than an hour away."

"Yeah, I'm paying attention," Will answered without turning his head. His voice was, to be frank, sexy.

Ten minutes later, they exited the freeway. Will drove the car down the empty streets of the town they were in until he pulled into the parking lot of a hotel. In big, bright red letters, Anna read "The Daylight." Will parked the car and cut the engine. Taking the keys out of the ignition, he turned around, smiling. "Hello, Annamaria, I'm Will."

In the light of the parking lot, Anna could finally see Will's face. She recognized those eyes, the sweeping brown hair, the pale skin, framing a confident smirk. Her own eyes widened in horror. She was looking at the mysterious boy from prom. She remembered looking into his eyes and feeling light and unable to talk. Vampires could hypnotize. Anna pressed herself into the cushion of the back seat, hyperventilating.

"What's wrong?" Marianna looked between her boyfriend and sister.

"He... I..." Did Marianna know what Will had done a week ago? Was she the girl in the purple dress?

Marianna's brows furrowed. "Have you seen Will before?"

Anna's breath shuddered. "Yes. He was at my prom."

Marianna growled low in her throat, and she glared at Will. "What. Did. You. Do?"

"Nothing!" Will blinked, taking on an innocent look.

Marianna rolled her eyes. "I told you to behave yourself while we were there. You could have ruined everything."

Will put his hands up. "I behaved. No one died, no one even got hurt. I simply enjoyed a snack from a pretty little girl. She won't remember a thing, and I didn't leave any lasting damage."

"Then why is my sister scared out of her mind?"

"We danced together for one song," Will said.

Anna straightened up and glared. "You hypnotized me!"

Marianna leaned into the front seat and slapped Will across the face.

Will's eyes flashed for a split second before returning to doe eyes. "Okay, I deserved that. But can we please go inside? Let's get a room and duke it out in there, where we aren't in danger of being burned to a crisp."

Marianna looked at the lightening sky and ground her teeth. "Fine. Get the luggage." She grabbed Anna's hand. "I am so sorry about this. I promise we will get this resolved inside."

Anna bobbed her head and got out of the car with Marianna. As they headed toward the hotel, Anna leaned into her sister and focused on the hotel doors. Will followed behind with their suitcases.

Anna's eyes widened when they entered the lobby. This was not a normal hotel, and she could barely see a foot in front of her. The carpet, tile, walls, and ceiling were all black. The furniture and light fixtures were dark silver, and the lights themselves were red. Not a bright, Christmas red, but a dull, dark red. Marianna led her to a large silver counter.

The man at the counter wore a black long-sleeved button-up shirt with a silver vest the same shade as the counter. His name tag read Bryce. As they approached, he picked up a black tablet. "Welcome to The Daylight. Do you have a reservation?"

"No." Marianna shook her head.

Bryce smiled. "Not a problem." His pointer finger punched on the tablet screen. "How many days?"

"Just today."

"How many guests?"

"Three."

"What species?"

"Two vampires, one witch."

"How many beds? What size?"

"Two queens, please."

"And the décor?"

"Normal."

"Would you like your room to be public or private?"

"Definitely private."

"All right, give us a few minutes to make up your room. Have a seat, and we'll let you know when it's ready."

Marianna thanked him and led Anna over to a silver couch. They shared the couch while Will sat in a cushioned chair nearby with the luggage between them. Anna looked around. From what she was able to see, the other guests dressed like Marianna—all black or dark colors. The only bright color was red. Will also wore dark jeans with a dark gray button up in what looked like silky polyester. Anna grimaced at her pastel purple blouse, light blue jeans, and white pumps. She stuck out like a sore thumb.

Marianna put her mouth to Anna's ear and whispered, "I think you should borrow my clothes until we get to Will's house." Anna dipped her faced toward her chest, hiding it. Were any of these people walking around looking for her or at least willing to turn her in if they recognized her?

Anna jumped. Bryce materialized out of the darkness to inform them their room was ready. He handed the keys to Marianna, along with two pamphlets, and explained one was a list of the amenities for vampires, the other for witches. A new employee materialized out of the darkness to escort them to their room. His name tag read Adam. He gave Marianna and Will a professional smile, but his gaze landed on Anna, and his eyes darkened. He looked her up and down, the tip of his tongue licking his lips. Marianna put a protective arm around Anna's shoulders and cleared her throat. Adam returned to his professional demeanor and led them down the hall. Marianna kept her arm tight around Anna's shoulders. Anna leaned into her, shaking, and kept her gaze locked on the floor.

When they stopped walking, Anna looked up at a black door with a silver handle. Marianna thanked Adam and slid the key card into the door. "I'll provide your room service for any of your needs," Adam said, his gaze only on Anna. Marianna finished unlocking the door, guided Anna inside, and stormed in after her. Will squeezed in before Marianna slammed the door.

The room sported bland wallpaper, stereotypical bedding, and wooden furniture. It passed for a regular hotel room. The simplicity and normalcy calmed Anna's heart.

Marianna threw her hands in the air. "I do not know why they let vampires work with the guests. All it takes is a pretty face for them to forget their manners. I'm calling the front desk and making a complaint."

"Oh come on, give the guy a break." Will grabbed Marianna's arm. "Annamaria screams innocence, she's much too tempting."

Marianna ripped her arm out of Will's grip. "Like on prom night?"

Will swallowed and glanced around the room. "You know, that guy was inappropriate. File a complaint."

"Don't change the subject. I would like to know exactly what happened at prom." Marianna cornered Will up against the wall, her face an inch from his. Anna sat down on one bed and tucked her knees into her chest.

Will wrapped his hands around Marianna's waist. "Look, your aunt wouldn't invite me in, so I had to go somewhere. I wanted to meet Annamaria. I offered her water when she discovered the punch was spiked. We danced for one song, her date showed up, and I left. I snagged a little snack, who is still alive, and she won't even remember me."

"What about the part where you hypnotized her? Never mind, I don't have time to force five different versions out of you before I get the truth." She turned to Anna. "Annamaria, what did he do to you?"

Anna looked past her sister. Will's eyebrows crinkled, his eyes begging, but she just shrugged at him. Anna told Marianna everything.

Marianna's eyes blazed. She poked Will in the chest. "What were you planning on doing with her once you got her out of the school?"

"I wasn't going to feed on her. I just wanted an invitation into the house. I thought I could get her to do it since Trinity wouldn't."

Marianna relaxed as she cupped Will's face with her hand. "I know that wasn't fun for you. I'm sorry. I appreciate you being supportive. Still, do not hypnotize Annamaria ever again."

Will took Marianna's face in his hands. "Cross my heart."

Marianna leaned into Will. He lowered his lips to Marianna's, and she kissed him back. Anna looked away and swallowed the lump in her throat. Marianna then said something to Will in a voice so low Anna couldn't hear it. Will responded in the same low voice, and Marianna hissed. After some back and forth where Anna could not catch a single word, Will sighed and pecked Marianna one more time.

Will walked over to the bed Anna sat on. He took her hands in his and stood her on her feet. "Annamaria, I am deeply sorry for hypnotizing and scaring you." He brushed some stray hairs from her face. "I promise as long as you are under my protection, no more unruly vampires will get close enough to smell you."

Anna looked at Marianna, her eyes wide. Why was her sister's boyfriend touching her like this? In front of his girlfriend, no less. Marianna rolled her eyes and pulled Will backward. "Sorry, he's a little too friendly sometimes. Anyway, this is a genuine apology for him."

"Okay," Anna said. She glanced at Will. His lips were puckered and downturned, his doe eyes returned. "I forgive you." She looked away. She didn't forgive him, but if she was going to survive this, things needed to calm down. She fought an enormous yawn.

"You need sleep," Marianna said.

Anna shook her head. There was no way she could sleep in this place, but she yawned again. Marianna rolled back the covers from the bed behind Anna. Anna kicked off her shoes, climbed into bed, and didn't even feel childish about letting Marianna tuck her in. She mumbled a thanks and fell asleep the minute her head hit the pillow.

****

Anna woke up in darkness. She squinted at the digital clock on the bedside table. 5:02 p.m. Marianna was on the other bed, asleep. Will did not appear to be in the room. Anna pushed the covers back and tiptoed to the bathroom. After relieving herself and washing her hands and face, she studied herself in the mirror. Her makeup was gone, but her eyelids were sticky and droopy. The curls in her hair were frizzy, and the top of her head was crunchy. She needed a shower. Anna opened and closed the bathroom door, keeping the handle turned to prevent any noise.

"Hey," Marianna said from her bed.

Anna jumped. "Oh, I'm sorry, did I wake you up?"

Marianna waved her hand. "No. I can't really sleep anymore, just rest. Did you sleep all right?"

Anna nodded. "Yeah." Her stomach growled. They both giggled.

"I have got to remember you need to eat more often than me. Here." Marianna handed Anna the pamphlet from Bryce. "You can order whatever you want."

The Daylight had quite the extensive menu. Anna chose the soup and salad combo. Her stomach was too squirmy to handle anything too heavy. Marianna showed her how to call from the room's phone and place her order.

"Do you want anything?" Anna asked Marianna, gesturing to the pamphlet for vampires.

"No." Marianna shook her head. "I already got something while you were sleeping. I figured it would be easier for you."

Anna looked away. "Thanks."

While she waited for her food, Anna picked up the vampire pamphlet, which advertised all blood types and different sizes of containers. Anna let out a breath. Thank heavens the hotel didn't offer actual humans. She shuddered. Still, the blood was taken from someone. She dropped the pamphlet.

A knock rang out on the door. "Room service."

Anna opened the door to Adam. He beamed. "Oh, hi," he said, as if surprised. Yeah right. Anna "screamed innocence." There was no way he forgot this was her room. Her heart pounded at the hungry look in his eyes. "May I?" He gestured with his head while holding the tray with Anna's food.

"No thank you. We can take it ourselves," Marianna said behind Anna. She took the tray out of Adam's hands. Adam's smile faded to a hard line as he surveyed Marianna. Marianna ignored him and headed back into their room.

"Thanks." Anna started to shut the door, but Adam grabbed her hand. He brought her hand just below his lips, turned her hand so the inside of her wrist almost touched his mouth, and breathed in. When he breathed out, his lips brushed her skin, which resulted in a tingle on the surface of Anna's wrist. Anna jumped back and let the door shut. He chuckled as the lock clicked.

Anna sat down at the small table in the corner where Marianna laid her food. Marianna glared at the door.

"So what exactly is this place?" Anna asked after a

couple of bites.

"It's a refuge for vampires during the daytime when the sun is out," said Marianna. "From what I've heard from older vampires, it used to be strictly for hiding out. But now it's turned into a cross between a fancy hotel and a club. Will is at a gathering in someone else's room right now."

Anna's stomach twisted. "Is that what the front desk meant when they asked if our room was private or public?"

Marianna nodded. "If your room is public, then your name goes on a list, which usually means you have snacks to share."

Anna shuddered. "People die here?"

"No, thank heavens. Killing is not allowed. It's the number one rule for staying here. The police would become suspicious if too many humans entered but never left, and witches would tear the place down. Vampires who kill on the premises get thrown out immediately, even if it's in the middle of the day."

"Well, I appreciate you not sharing me." Anna let out an awkward giggle.

Marianna smirked, then her gaze bore into Anna's. "I will never let a single vampire bite you, Annamaria."

After dinner, Anna opened up her suitcase. She squinted at the contents and scooted them around. The new clothes Trinity had purchased were not anything Anna would have chosen. Anna wore bright or pastel colors. Inside the suitcase were the type of clothes Marianna wore and the same colors which adorned the other clients in the lobby—black, dark gray, green, purple, blue, and red.

Marianna looked over Anna's shoulder. "You

know, the mall is open for another hour after sunset. We could get you some new clothes before we head out."

Anna sighed. "No, it's okay. Trinity knows what she is doing." Anna's new phone started ringing, and Trinity's name flashed across the screen. Anna accepted the call. "Trinity."

"Annamaria! How are you?" Trinity's voice asked.

"I'm as good as can be, considering," Anna said. She closed her eyes and tilted her head, swallowing a lump. Anna switched to speakerphone. "You're on speakerphone now, Trinity. Marianna is here with me."

"Hello, Marianna, did everything go all right last night?" Trinity asked.

"Yes," said Marianna. "But Trinity, I'm really sorry. I didn't know what to do during the day, so we are at—"

"Don't say it out loud. I understand. I know where you are. You should be fine, as long as you used the proper precautions while checking in?"

"Yes, we did," said Marianna.

"Good," said Trinity. "Anyway, I have to go soon. I just wanted to hear your voices. Text me updates as you can, but don't call. I will call you when it is safe, okay?"

"Okay," both girls said.

"I love you, girls," Trinity said.

New tears brimmed in Anna's eyes. "Love you, too." When they hung up, Marianna gave Anna a big hug.

Sunset was less than an hour away, so Anna took a fast shower, dressed in dark jeans, a dark blue blouse, and black boots similar to Marianna's. She brushed the hair spray out of her hair, which loosened the curls to a nice wave. She applied her makeup in her traditional style of neutral colors. Anna packed the clothes she had been wearing. At least she had one reminder of who she used to be.

The click of a key card prefaced Will strolling into the room. "The sun has set."

"Excellent, let's get out of here," said Marianna. "Carry the suitcases?"

"Sure thing." Will grinned and winked. Anna looked away. "Annamaria, you clean up nicely. You look ravishing in those colors." Anna took a step backward as he bent closer to pick up her suitcase. Will pouted. "Oh, don't tell me you're still scared of me?"

"Well, what do you expect when you keep saying things like that?" Marianna said.

Will flashed Anna a charming smile. "Sorry." He gestured to the door. "Ladies first." Anna scurried around him and caught up with Marianna.

In the car, Marianna sat with Anna in the back again. Anna took deep breaths as they drove away. Images of Adam and what could be going on in the other rooms invaded her mind. Before getting on the freeway, they stopped at a gas station to fill up and allow Anna to stock up on snacks for the night.

"What exactly is the Black Market?" Anna asked after a few minutes on the freeway.

"It's essentially anything vampire related, but it stems from witches who ally with vampires, sell products to vampires, befriend vampires, hence the term Black Market witches. So it's not one particular place. The Daylight is a part of the Black Market since it's made for vampires," said Marianna.

They passed most of the drive in silence. Anna's heart steadier than when they first left the hotel. She still had a million questions, but she paced herself. After a while, Anna had a question for Will, and she took almost an hour to pluck up the courage to address him. Their eyes kept meeting in the rearview mirror, and he would stifle a chuckle every time Anna looked away, blood rushing to her cheeks. He could hear her heart pounding.

"Um, Will?" Anna said.

"Yes, Annamaria?" He smirked through the rearview mirror.

"My classmate from prom you...um...drank from, who was it? I saw you leave with someone, but I didn't see her face."

Will rubbed his chin. "I think her name was Tally."

Anna exhaled. Tally was at school all the following week, and she danced just fine at the concert on Saturday night.

"You're sure she won't remember anything?"

"Positive."

"But I remember being hypnotized."

"That's the magic in your witchy blood."

Anna looked at Marianna and cocked her head.

Marianna smiled. "Witches have some natural defenses against vampires. You can remember everything that happens if you get hypnotized. In fact, the stronger you get in your powers, the harder it is for a vampire to hypnotize you, and if you train really hard, you'll eventually get to where you can't be hypnotized."

Anna exhaled. "That's a relief."

"I think it's a shame." Will sighed. "Because

witches taste divine compared to humans, or so I've heard."

Marianna hit the back of his seat, and he stopped talking. "Your blood will also heal your body faster should you ever get bitten. Vampire venom can't paralyze you for as long as it can a human." Anna's face paled. "But you won't experience it if I can help it."

They got off the freeway an hour before sunrise and found another Daylight hotel. Since Anna slept well the day before, she wasn't as tired and couldn't fall asleep right away. She tossed and turned until she drifted off while Marianna and Will cuddled up and rested their eyes.

When Anna woke up, Will was gone again. "Is Will in another public room?"

Marianna nodded and rolled her eyes. "His friend, Jordan, is here."

"You don't like Jordan."

Marianna sighed. "He's all right. Will just gets rowdy when he hangs out with him. Anyway, Will really wants us to join him when you wake up. But I told him it would be up to you."

Anna shrugged. "Didn't Trinity tell us to be careful and stay hidden?"

"She did." Marianna nodded. "However, Jordan is mostly trustworthy. I can't see him blabbing he met you. It's still up to you, though."

Anna looked around the room. "Well, I really need to wash my hair and eat. So I guess if there's time after."

"Take your time." Marianna winked.

Anna took a full shower and blow-dried her hair

straight. She put on a long black blouse, which she coupled with dark silver leggings and black boots. She scrunched her face at her reflection. This was so far off from her normal style, but it would help her fit in with the new crowd she would live with. Early in the morning, they would arrive at Will's house where the other vampires were. Anna didn't want to "scream innocence" when Will's house wasn't going to be a temporary twelve-hour stay.

"Wow, straight hair suits you, Annamaria," Will said, after he strolled into the room.

"Thank you." Anna gave a small smile.

As they headed down the hall, a young man materialized out of the darkness, blocking their way. "Marianna, I missed you at my party this afternoon." Anna looked down at her feet, her hair covering her face.

"I'm sorry, Jordan," Marianna said. "I was busy with other things."

"Clearly," said Jordan. "Who is this mysterious witch I'm not allowed to know about?"

"That's really none of your business," Marianna said.

A hand cupped Anna's chin and turned her head up. She met his eyes. He smirked, his eyes glinting.

"Ah." He breathed. "It appears the long-lost Annamaria has been found." Anna trembled. She shuffled her feet backward, but his grip was too strong to free her face.

Marianna dug her nails into his forearm. "And if you value your life, she will remain lost."

Jordan let go of Anna's face, shaking Marianna off him, and clasped one of her hands in both of his. "No need to worry, Marianna. I was just curious." He traced shapes in Anna's palm. Their eyes met again. "I'm not going to hurt you, child. I just wanted to meet you." He kissed Anna's hand, sending a stronger tingle than Adam. Anna bit down on a yelp. Jordan and Will gave each other a hearty goodbye. He gave a slight bow to Marianna, then disappeared into the darkness of the hallway where he originated from.

Marianna collapsed into the car a few minutes later. "I'm so glad we are almost done traveling. Between Adam and Jordan, we are lucky to get Annamaria home in one piece."

"I'm sorry," Anna said.

Marianna waved her off. "It's not your fault. It's theirs for not exercising any control."

Will scoffed. "They didn't bite or try to hypnotize her. I call that control. Not all of us have the patience of a hybrid." Marianna rolled her eyes.

"What do you mean?" Anna asked.

"It means the witch blood in your sister prevented her from going through the years of bloodlust and lack of control like most new vampires. Which is why at only two years old she can sit in the back seat with you without sucking you dry."

"Oh." Anna looked out of the window, watching the landscape. "Where are we?"

"Ohio," Marianna said.

"Where are we going?"

"The Appalachian Mountains in Pennsylvania. Which reminds me, I need to let the others know when we'll arrive." Marianna took out her phone and started texting. Anna's heart rate sped up.

"Um, how many… Who are they?" Anna struggled

to breathe.

Marianna counted on her fingers. "There's Anthony. He's the oldest, over three hundred. Then there is Tyler and Kylie. They're fifteen years. They are dancers, so they travel a lot. And there's me and Will. Will is in his seventies, and he's the coven leader."

Anna surveyed Will. He didn't look a day over eighteen, and he acted like a teenager. Marianna had also been eighteen when she was turned, technically making her and Anna the same age. Marianna acted much older than eighteen. Were the others like Marianna or Will? She hoped they were like Marianna because if they were like Will, Adam, or Jordan, Anna didn't think she would survive.

When they passed the "Welcome to Pennsylvania!" sign, Anna's breath caught in her throat. About an hour later, they headed into the mountains in front of them, and the road inclined, weaving up the mountain, zigzagging with the road's switchbacks. They passed through a sleeping town. The only lights on were what looked like the local police station. Once out of the town, the incline steepened, the switchbacks were more frequent, and the trees thickened. Anna's heart beat out of her chest.

At the top, the trees cleared. A tall wall of iron bars with a gate in the middle surrounded the biggest mansion Anna had ever seen. They rolled up to the gate, and Will pushed some buttons on a little box. The gate opened, and Will drove the car up the drive, around the house, and into a large, multi-car garage. Once parked and the car turned off, Will pressed the button to close the garage door. Anna froze as the door descended. The sound of the garage door sealing against the cement echoed throughout Anna's entire body.

Chapter 10 Holland Manor

"Welcome to your new home," Will said.

Anna's body shook, and she breathed in quick gasps. How was she going to survive this separation from Trinity? How was she going to learn magic surrounded by vampires? Her new reality crushed her like a boulder to the chest. She could not go into that house, not when they outnumbered her five to one, not when she was so inexperienced compared to everyone here, and not when this world was still brand new.

Marianna patted Anna's back. "Are you okay?"

Anna wrapped her arms around her legs and hid her face in her knees. She shook her head. Marianna rubbed Anna's back, but Anna continued to shake and gasp.

"Go inside and tell Anthony, Kylie, and Tyler to stay out of the hallway. I'm going to take Annamaria straight to her room. They can meet her after she has rested," Marianna said. Anna didn't hear Will answer, but the car door shut, and a distant door opened and shut.

"Can I take you to your room? You don't have to see anyone else this morning."

Anna lifted her face out of her knees and wiped her eyes. "Yes. Sorry. It's just…a lot…you know."

Marianna's face was sympathetic. "I know."

Anna got out of the car and wobbled a bit. "Would

you like help?" Marianna asked. Anna shook her head. Anna followed Marianna to the garage door leading into the house. Marianna opened the door, and they stepped into a small entryway. At the sound of the door swinging shut, Anna's knees buckled. Marianna caught her and cradled her like a child. "I'll just carry you."

Even though Will had gone to tell the others to stay out of their way, Anna hid her face in Marianna's shoulder. Marianna walked down the hallway, her breathing never changing. When they turned a corner, new voices reached Anna's ears. She tightened her grip on Marianna's neck, and her shaking returned.

"Oh look at her, she's shaking. Poor thing," a woman's voice said.

"Wow, her hair is the exact shade of red as Marianna's. It's exquisite," a male's voice said.

"Guys, Will told you to scram. She's not a spectacle," Marianna said.

"Sorry, Marianna," said another male voice.

Anna heard a quick breeze, followed by silence. Her body rose one step at a time. Anna opened her eyes and peeked around when Marianna's footsteps flattened again. They were at the start of another long hallway.

"Your room is at the end," Marianna said.

"I think I can walk."

Marianna put her down but kept a protective arm around Anna. Anna glanced at the other doors as she passed them. There were three on one side, and three on the other. They stopped at the third door on the right-hand side of the hallway.

Marianna opened the door, and Anna walked into the biggest bedroom she had ever seen. The room was at least twice the size of her bedroom back home. There was a king-size bed against the center of the wall on the right. There was also a nice dresser, bedside table, vanity, and bookshelf. To Anna's left, a door opened into an enormous bathroom.

"Wow." Anna breathed out.

"I'll send for Will to deliver your suitcase." Marianna took out her phone. "You know you haven't slept in pajamas this whole trip?"

"I'm afraid to." Anna looked down.

"Why?"

"They make me feel vulnerable." Anna looked up.

Marianna's eyes were soft. "Would you like to try a sleeping potion?"

"A what?"

"A sleeping potion. You will fall asleep and stay asleep until your body and mind are ready. No noises, hunger, nothing will wake you until you are ready. Your body will be able to set itself back on track."

If nothing could wake her up, how will she protect herself? Yet she couldn't see how she could fall asleep on her own otherwise.

"I promise you'll be safe."

"Okay."

"Are you okay if I run to my room and grab it? It's just next door."

Anna bobbed her head and sank onto the bed.

While Marianna was gone, Will entered the room with Anna's suitcase. Anna looked away from him, her cheeks flushed. Will walked over to Anna and sat down on the bed next to her. All of his swagger and charm was gone, instead he looked penitent.

"I know I've been a jerk for the last three nights, but I want you to know you are perfectly safe here. Not very many people know where my place is. Plus, Anthony, Kylie, and Tyler are so much better behaved than me. They won't do anything to you. I'm honestly the worst one here, so if you can survive three nights on the road with me, you'll be just fine here at the house."

Anna smiled and let out a quiet giggle. "Thanks, Will."

Marianna reentered the room, holding a small bottle in her hand. Will patted Anna's leg, walked over to Marianna, and gave her a quick kiss on the lips before leaving.

"Here." Marianna held out the bottle to Anna. The liquid inside was midnight blue.

Anna took it. "Do I drink the whole thing?"

"Yes. Do you want me to stay with you?"

Anna shook her head. "No, it's okay. I'm just going to get in my pajamas and take this."

"Okay," said Marianna. "When you wake up, you can come out and go anywhere in the house. We'll give you a tour when you're ready. This isn't like the hotel. You aren't confined to this room."

"Thanks."

Marianna hugged her and left. Anna found a pair of black pajama pants and a black tank top and changed into those. She looked at the bottle for a minute. Would the potion really work? She had seen and experienced some incredible things over the past week and a half, but potions were brand new. She picked up the bottle, counted to three, and gulped the warm liquid down. The warmth flooded her body as the potion traveled down her trachea. Anna pulled back the dark blue covers of the bed, tucked herself in, and drifted off as the potion worked its magic.

****

Annamaria opened her eyes. She didn't have to rub the sleep out, blink several times, or lie around waiting for her body to stir. Where had this potion been her whole life? Not in Trinity's medicine cabinet. Or had it? There was no way Trinity completely gave up magic during the past sixteen years.

Annamaria frowned. She had missed out on so much. And yet, even though Annamaria was mad at Trinity, she still understood. Annamaria couldn't imagine being in charge of a young child's safety and future. She couldn't say if she would do any better than Trinity.

Annamaria sat up and grabbed her new phone from the bedside table. She widened her eyes at the date and time. She reviewed the calendar in her head with their traveling schedule. She was sure they arrived at Will's house early Tuesday morning. Her phone showed it was now Wednesday at 8:02 a.m. She had slept for twenty-four hours.

Annamaria got out of bed and headed into the connecting bathroom. This bathroom was larger than hers back home, with a jetted tub, a separate shower, a long counter connected to the sink, and a walk-in closet. How did Will own this house? Annamaria was certain she didn't want to know. She looked at herself in the mirror. Her eyes were no longer puffy from crying, and they no longer looked tired and fearful. The potion really did its job.

"Annamaria," she said out loud to her reflection. Hearing Marianna and Will say her full name felt right. There had been a change when Trinity started using it, and this was the first time she had said her full name out loud in years. She was a new person now, her real self. She was a witch who was living with her vampire sister and vampire roommates. She wasn't Anna anymore. She was Annamaria.

Annamaria figured Marianna was eager to know how she was, but she didn't want to head out into the vast house alone, in her pajamas, and not showered. She grabbed a pair of jeans, a dark green blouse, and bodywash from her suitcase and headed back into the bathroom.

After getting ready, Annamaria put her hand on the door handle and stood there. Her heart pounded. She let go and backed away. What else could she do? Her gaze landed on the unmade bed. When that was done, Annamaria's breath quickened looking at the door handle. She unpacked her suitcase and organized her new wardrobe in the walk-in closet. But after she finished, she still couldn't turn the door handle.

Annamaria looked around the spotless room. She was out of things to do. The bookshelf. She looked over the titles but didn't recognize any of them. They looked old, and she wondered if they might be magic books. She opened one and read a page. The text was in a language Annamaria didn't know, though some words looked familiar. Latin based, perhaps? Shoot. She hadn't practiced magic at all since leaving Harrison.

Practicing magic should help. She levitated everything around the room she could lift. Then she summoned everything from the bathroom. She didn't know what else was in the house, but maybe that was the next step. Annamaria pictured an apple, opened up her hand, and concentrated. A plump, red apple appeared in her hands. She grinned and took a bite. The apple was real and juicy. She summoned a banana and ate it as well. She summoned a bowl, a spoon, a box of cereal, and a jug of milk and ate breakfast in her room.

When she was done, Annamaria's heart and breathing had slowed. She needed to return the milk, bowl, spoon, and cereal box to the kitchen. She didn't know how to send those items back by magic, so she had no choice but to leave the bedroom.

With her breakfast in hand, Annamaria opened her bedroom door and poked her head out. She breathed out and relaxed at the empty hallway. She tiptoed out into the hall. Annamaria walked down the hall on the balls of her feet. She imagined the kitchen was downstairs. At the end of the hallway, the door on the opposite side from Annamaria's opened, and a young man stepped out. She squeaked, jumped, and dropped all the breakfast stuff. The young man caught everything before it hit the floor, moving so fast it almost gave her whiplash.

Annamaria blushed. "Thanks."

His lips turned upward. His skin was pale like Marianna's and Will's, and his black hair stopped just above his eyes and fanned out below his ears. He also dressed in dark colors that suited his outdated hairstyle.

"You must be Annamaria. I'm Anthony." He held out his free hand. Annamaria accepted his hand and shook it. Their eyes met. Anthony's eyes were dark like Will's, but where Will's eyes were wicked, Anthony's were charming. He held Annamaria's gaze until she looked away.

"Nice to meet you. Um, thanks again." Annamaria reached for her breakfast things, but Anthony held on to them.

"I can take them. Can I show you where the kitchen is?"

"Sure." She followed Anthony down the stairs.

"How are you feeling?" Anthony asked over his shoulder.

"I'm better now. I'm sorry about yesterday morning. Everything is still so new to me."

"You don't have to be sorry. Marianna told us about the past week. I imagine everything has been pretty overwhelming."

At the bottom of the stairs, a large entryway ending in a tall door loomed in front of them. There was a hallway going left and a hallway going right. Anthony gestured to the hallway on the left. They passed the first door and entered the second door.

As Anthony was putting stuff away, Marianna walked in. Annamaria's face lit up and so did Marianna's. "Good morning." Marianna walked over and gave Annamaria a big hug. Annamaria hugged her back, squeezing her torso.

"Morning."

"Did you enjoy your breakfast? I'm assuming you summoned it since I didn't hear you come downstairs until just now?" Marianna's eyes twinkled.

Annamaria smiled. "I just needed to warm myself up before venturing out."

Marianna clapped. "Good job. I wish I could have seen that. I used to do the same thing. When I didn't want to see anyone, I would summon food from the kitchen to my room. Mostly Caroline didn't mind, but every once in a while, I would accidentally summon something she was holding, and that would drive her crazy."

The two sisters giggled, and Anthony observed from the other side of the kitchen, smiling.

"I guess I don't have to worry about that here," Annamaria said.

"Well, I actually forgot to tell you, one human lives here," Marianna said. Annamaria blinked. "She's our housekeeper. Her name is Sandy."

"When you say human, do you mean—"

"She's not a witch."

"And she knows what you all are?"

"Yes. She gets paid. No one touches her," Anthony said.

"What does she do exactly?"

"She cleans the house and takes care of the grounds," Marianna said. "In fact, she is really excited to meet you. She's hoping you'll join her for dinner tonight?"

"Oh, yeah, sure." Annamaria glanced down at her feet, then over at Anthony. His gaze was still on her. She shifted her gaze to Marianna.

"So what do you want to do today?" Marianna smiled.

"Um, I don't know," Annamaria said. Without magic lessons and travel, she didn't know what to suggest.

"How about a tour?" Anthony asked.

Marianna beamed. "Are you up for that?"

Annamaria glanced around. "Yeah, sure."

Marianna gestured in an arc around the room. "Well, you know where your room is, and now the kitchen. Let's head back upstairs so you can know where everyone else lives."

She left the kitchen, and Annamaria followed her.

Anthony caught up to them and offered Annamaria his arm. Annamaria stared at his arm, then looked at Marianna, her brows raised. Her sister giggled and inclined her head toward him. "Anthony is old-fashioned. It's one of his more endearing qualities." Annamaria put her arm through Anthony's and let him guide her down the hall and up the stairs.

At the top of the stairs, Marianna started with the first door on the right. "This is Will's room." She knocked. "Will, honey, coming in." She opened the door and walked in. Annamaria peeked in but didn't enter. Will was sprawled out on a black bedspread covering a king-size bed.

"Annamaria, come on in, I won't bite."

Anthony groaned. Annamaria stepped in, her eyes scanning the perimeter. Will's room was decorated in black. Black bed, black furniture, black curtains, and the walls were painted dark gray. His room reminded Annamaria of The Daylight.

"Why do you need a bed if you don't really sleep?" Annamaria asked. She blushed and clapped her hands to her mouth.

"Well, at the moment, I'm waiting for your sister to finish showing you around so we can get back to what we were doing before." Will gave a cheeky grin. Marianna grimaced. Annamaria's blush deepened.

"Oh come on, man," said Anthony. He turned to Annamaria. "What Will meant to say is it's nice to have our own private space."

"My room next," Marianna said, zooming out of Will's room.

The colors of Marianna's room were silver and gold. Her bedspread was a pattern of gold and silver swirled together. The furniture was light gold, and the walls were painted silver. On the other side of the hall, the room across from Annamaria's was Kylie's. Tyler's was next to Kylie's and across from Marianna's, though they didn't go inside either since Kylie and Tyler weren't home. They had gone on a trip while Annamaria slept.

"They can't wait to meet you when they return in a few weeks." Marianna smiled.

The last door was Anthony's. He opened the door and invited her in. Anthony's theme was gold like Marianna's, but brighter and without the silver. The bedspread was all gold, as was the furniture. The walls were sky blue, with big, bright suns. There was an easel near the gold curtains and a tall table with paints and paintbrushes on it.

"Did you paint everyone's walls?" This old-fashioned vampire was a modern artist.

Anthony nodded. "I can paint yours when you know what you want?"

"That's very kind of you, thanks." Annamaria cast her gaze to the floor, heat rising to her cheeks.

Back downstairs, they turned right. There were only two doors down this hallway, one on either side. The one on the left opened up into a vast ballroom. Annamaria's mouth fell open. In the far corner was a grand piano.

"Is that yours?" Annamaria asked Marianna.

"Yes." Marianna smiled with pride.

"Will you play something?"

"Right now?"

"Yes, right now."

"I don't think so."

"Come on, please?"

"Just one song?" Anthony said. "We all love listening to you play."

Marianna sighed. "All right." A small smile creeped up her lips as she walked to the piano.

She sat down and played a piece Annamaria didn't recognize. The style sounded classical. Marianna's hands traveled with ease over the keys. The sounds and vibrations conjured a dancer on a stage as Annamaria choreographed in her mind. When Marianna finished, both Annamaria and Anthony clapped.

"Kylie and Tyler also use this room for dance rehearsals. Will throws parties in here, and you and I are going to hold your magic lessons in here." Marianna stood up from the piano bench.

Annamaria straightened. "Really? When do those start?"

"I was thinking tomorrow."

Annamaria squealed.

"There is also a built-in stereo and speaker system," Anthony said, guiding Annamaria over to the wall near the piano. He opened up a cupboard Annamaria hadn't noticed because it blended in with the wall itself. A CD and record player were built into the wall, along with shelves and shelves of CDs and records. The ballroom was the best room in the house so far.

The door across the hall was a library as grand as the ballroom. Books lined the walls, and the middle of the room held several comfortable-looking couches and chairs, with a couple of large desks. Anthony showed her how he organized the books by topic, then author's last name. He also showed her a few empty shelves for anyone in the house to use as a to-read pile.

The living room was in the same hallway as the kitchen. A large entertainment center, a couch and love seat, and two cushioned chairs—all black—adorned the room. Across from the kitchen were two doors. Sandy's bedroom, and a guest bedroom. At the end of the hallway was the entryway connected to the garage and a staircase leading to the basement.

Down in the basement were the laundry room and several locked doors. Both Anthony and Marianna ignored the locked doors and tried to guide Annamaria back up the stairs.

"What are they?" Annamaria refused to move.

Anthony hesitated and glanced at Marianna. "The dungeons, where Will and Anthony used to lock up captives and prisoners," she said.

"What?" Anna's eyes widened, and her jaw dropped.

Anthony looked at his feet. "Vampires aren't really a peaceful breed. It's not uncommon to feud with another coven or a werewolf pack." He looked up. "But we haven't fought with anyone in a long time. We've been living under the radar for a couple of decades now. I'm pretty certain you don't need to worry about these rooms being used while you are here."

"And that's Holland Manor for you." Marianna threw her arm around Annamaria.

"Holland Manor?"

"Holland is Will's last name. It's his house, his coven, his name," Marianna said.

They left the basement and headed back upstairs. Was Annamaria truly safe here?

Chapter 11 The Housekeeper

Back upstairs, Marianna asked, "Are you okay if I leave you for the afternoon? Will felt left out the week I was with you and Trinity, and traveling here, I focused all on you. Not that I don't want to spend time with you, but I feel like I should give him my attention right now." She grimaced.

Annamaria forced a smile. "It's okay. I'll be fine." Marianna hugged her and zoomed toward her boyfriend's room, leaving Annamaria alone with Anthony in the hallway. She met Anthony's eyes, then looked away again.

"You know, you can do anything you want," he said. "You aren't a guest here. This is your home."

"Right." Annamaria nodded. She walked toward the hallway where the ballroom was located. Anthony remained a few steps behind, looking around. "You can come with me," Annamaria said. Anthony grinned and caught up. Why did she just do that?

In the ballroom, Annamaria looked through the CDs, pulling out specific artists and searching the back for a song title. There were a couple of empty shelves, and she asked Anthony if they were similar to those in the library, where anyone could create a playlist.

"Yeah. Kylie and Tyler mainly use the music, but they won't mind sharing with you. What do you want to do in here?"

Annamaria shrugged. "I danced in high school."

"Will you show me something?"

"Um, I don't think so, not today." She blushed.

"Marianna played the piano for us."

"Well, you've known Marianna for a couple of years, and she's my sister. I just barely met you this morning."

"Fair enough." Anthony winked.

Annamaria returned to the CDs, looking for the songs from her dance concert and stacking the CDs on the empty shelf when she found them. When she was done, she turned to Anthony. "So what's your story? How did you become… I mean, how did you end up here?"

"You mean, how did I become a vampire?" Anthony asked. Annamaria dipped her chin down, looking up through her eyelashes. "It's a long story. Do you want to sit down in the library?"

"Okay."

In the library, Annamaria sat on a love seat and tucked her feet under her while Anthony sat in a cushioned chair next to her.

"I was born and raised in Salem, Massachusetts, in the late seventeenth century." Annamaria's eyebrows rose. That's right. Anthony was over three hundred. "I was nineteen during the witch trials. Most of the poor souls who lost their lives were innocent humans. I fancied one of the young women accused, so I helped her run off. After we left Salem, I learned Elizabeth was an actual witch. We stayed away and began a new life together. We lived together for about a year before a coven of vampires captured us. They turned me within days of taking us. I was twenty years old. They wanted

Elizabeth to remain a witch. A witch's magic can be very useful to a vampire, and those who can convince one to live with them become pretty powerful. Elizabeth didn't want to be confined, and the ensuing conflict killed her. I lived with them for a couple of decades while I learned control, then I moved on. I have traveled from coven to coven, spending a decade or two on my own in between, until I met Will about seventy years ago. This is the longest time I've ever stayed in one place and with one group."

Annamaria had her hand over her heart by the end. "Wow, I'm sorry."

Anthony shrugged, but his eyes were pained. "It's okay. It was a long time ago."

"The part about the vampires wanting Elizabeth's magic. Is that why you guys let Marianna bring me here?" Annamaria asked.

Anthony shook his head. "Marianna said you two needed a place to hide while you train."

"Well, yes, but why did the rest of you agree? I mean, the little I've gathered over the past week and a half, vampires don't really like my family."

Anthony leaned forward. "Like I said earlier, we've been living under the radar for a while, and Marianna is family, which extends to you. We know you aren't responsible for your ancestors' actions."

Annamaria leaned forward as well. "What were those actions? Trinity told me about Valentina, my great-grandma Celeste, and my grandma Libby, but I don't actually understand what these rules were everyone was fighting about." Anthony looked away from Annamaria. "Anthony, please tell me. Trinity kept everything from me all my life, and she finally told me some, and we separated a week later. You've lived a long time. You probably know more than Trinity."

Anthony leaned back and stabbed his chest with his hand. "Ouch." He smirked. "I am not that old." His hand framed his face.

Annamaria rolled her eyes with a smile. "You know what I mean." She discretely scooted back as well, her heart pounding at how close she had gotten to him.

Anthony sighed. "When I was turned, vampires were constantly in danger of being hunted down and killed by witches and werewolves. That's why taking witches like Elizabeth to protect a coven was so popular. Your family sanctioned the executions. Over time, they made some compromises. The new law allowed vampires to feed if they didn't kill their food. But if they killed, they were executed in return."

"How did they keep track of that?"

"They couldn't exactly. So they amped up the hunting. Werewolves and witches were constantly on the lookout for "suspicious" activity. Vampires reacted by preemptively hunting witches and werewolves. We were at risk of a full-on war. Then Valentina showed up with her ideas of compromise and freedom. Your family didn't take to her at all, and Valentina wasn't one to take no for an answer, and well, you know the rest."

Anthony's story sounded worse than Trinity's. Annamaria didn't know how much to believe. As a vampire, Anthony would side with Valentina, but even Trinity admitted Celeste could have handled things better.

"What have things been like since?" Annamaria

played with her hands.

"Vampires have slowly started living more openly. Not to humans. They are still unaware of the magical world. I'll admit, it's nice to go hunt without looking over my shoulder, though I am sorry it cost you your family."

Annamaria shuddered at Anthony's casual use of the word hunt, but she still wanted to get information out of him, so she hid her shudder with a cough. "And is Valentina the new leader or something?"

"No, she kind of disappeared after everything. I guess she really meant it when she said to let the masses govern themselves. She could have easily turned the tables and set herself up as the new dictator, but she didn't."

I wonder what she wants with me then.

****

Annamaria ate a small lunch in the privacy of her room. Her room had blue wall-length curtains. Neither Marianna nor Anthony shared what was behind the curtains during her tour of their rooms. Annamaria guessed a window, which would be why they would keep them closed.

She slid the curtains to the side and was greeted by beautiful double glass doors with a balcony behind them. Annamaria opened the doors and stepped out onto the balcony. Fresh air enveloped her. The sun warmed her. The green grounds were well taken care of and looked a little out of place surrounded by the wildlife of the Appalachian Mountains. Annamaria dragged the chair from her desk out onto the balcony and ate her lunch. The mountain air brought her back to Harrison, the sun relaxing.

Annamaria spent the rest of the afternoon on the balcony. She texted Trinity. —*Made it to Will's. I start up lessons again tomorrow.*—

Trinity responded several minutes later. —*Glad to hear it! Stay safe. Love you.*—

Annamaria furrowed her brows. Where was the Trinity who needed to know every single detail?

—*Love you too. You also stay safe. Keep me updated?*—

Ten minutes passed, and Trinity still hadn't responded. With her phone in her hand from checking every minute, Annamaria opened up the app store and typed in one of the social media platforms she frequented. Her thumb hovered over the install button. If she looked, she would be tempted to comment. Trinity's warning that she could endanger her friends if she contacted them echoed in her head. Were they even her friends anymore? Certainly not after the way they treated her. Annamaria exited out of the store and locked her screen. She summoned a book from her to-read list in the library and began *Pride and Prejudice* until the sun hovered over the opposite mountains.

A knock on Annamaria's door interrupted her stroll through nineteenth century courtship. She opened the door to a middle-aged woman with dirty-blonde hair dressed in work clothes. Her skin had a fleshy hue.

"Hello, Annamaria. My name is Sandy. I'm the housekeeper." She held out her hand.

Annamaria shook it. "Nice to meet you."

"I wanted to invite you to eat dinner with me." Sandy smiled, her eyes hopeful.

"Marianna mentioned that. I'd love to."

"Wonderful! I'm going to go work on it. You are

welcome to join me in the kitchen when you are ready. I trust you know where the kitchen is?"

"Yes, I'll come with you right now." Annamaria stepped out of her bedroom and walked down the hall with Sandy.

"Are you settled nicely?" Sandy asked as they walked.

"Yeah, I think so."

"Good. I can help you with anything human related…food, laundry, going into town during the day," Sandy said.

Annamaria smiled. "Thanks. But I can prepare my food and do my laundry. I don't want to add to your workload."

Sandy waved her hand. "I'm already doing everyone else's laundry, and I already prepare my food. Really, it's nothing. It will be like my son is back here."

While passing Will's room, the door opened. Marianna poked her head out. "How are you doing?"

"Good," said Annamaria.

"Glad to hear it. I'll see you after dinner?" asked Marianna.

"Yeah."

"Perfect. See you then." Marianna closed Will's door.

Annamaria and Sandy headed down the stairs. "You have a son?"

Sandy's eyes twinkled. "My pride and joy. He's twenty-two and is finishing up college."

The kitchen smelled of tomatoes, meat, and cheese baking. Sandy took out lettuce, carrots, cucumbers, tomatoes, and avocado from the fridge. "Can I help?" Annamaria asked. "I used to cook a lot at home. I would get home from school before my aunt got home from work."

"Of course," Sandy said. "I haven't had a helper in the kitchen in four years. Why don't you pick a vegetable and start chopping?"

Annamaria grabbed the cucumber as Sandy handed her a knife. Annamaria cut the cucumber into circles, and Sandy washed the head of lettuce before ripping the leaves into little pieces and dropping them into a large bowl. Annamaria stacked the circles and quartered them. She was about to pick them up by the handful and toss them on top of the lettuce when an idea entered her mind. She pointed her hand at the slices of cucumber, levitated them into the air, and guided them to the bowl, where she placed them on top of the lettuce.

Sandy clapped, Annamaria did a mock bow, both giggling. Sandy shredded the carrots while Annamaria chopped the tomato, then the avocado. Like with the cucumber, Annamaria levitated them and put them in the salad bowl. Sandy opened the cupboards and placed two plates and two glasses on the counter.

"Can I set the table?" Annamaria asked.

"Be my guest." Sandy stepped back, her eyes twinkling.

Annamaria focused on the plates and levitated them off the counter to hover over the island. Annamaria willed them to separate, something she hadn't tried yet. She beamed with pride when they did. She transferred one plate to be under the direction of her free hand and lowered them with perfect control. She floated the glasses over with both hands as well. Next, Annamaria focused on her open hand and imagined silverware. Two forks and two knives appeared in her hand. Annamaria placed them on either side of each plate and stood back to admire her work.

The timer dinged, and Sandy took lasagna out of the oven. She cut into it and placed a slice on each plate, gesturing for Annamaria to sit down. Before she did, Annamaria summoned a pair of tongs and placed them in the salad. Annamaria served Sandy and herself some salad.

"What dressing would you like?" Sandy asked. "I have ranch, Italian, and poppy seed."

"I can grab the dressings for you two," said Anthony as he walked into the kitchen. He strolled over to the fridge, grabbed all three dressings, and placed them on the table.

"Thank you, Anthony," Sandy said, a slight blush forming on her cheeks.

"Not a problem. Can I join you two?" he asked, sitting down on an empty barstool.

"Absolutely." Sandy smiled.

Was Sandy as comfortable with everyone else, specifically Will? Annamaria was itching to know why Sandy worked in a house full of vampires. They started eating, and after a couple of bites, Annamaria couldn't stand the anticipation anymore. "I'm sorry, Sandy, but I have to know. Why are you here?"

Sandy let out a loud laugh. "Yes, I suppose I'm the true elephant in the room, being one-hundred-percent human, and old." Annamaria made to apologize, but Sandy cut her off. "Not to worry, dear. About twenty-two years ago, I had just given birth to my son, Daniel. I was a single mom. Daniel's father didn't even know I was pregnant. Anyway, I hadn't spoken to my family in years, and I didn't think I could turn to them. I didn't have a car, or a job, or money for rent. A women's shelter took us in, and after a couple of weeks of living there, I found a notice on the jobs board that was perfect for my situation. Some rich bloke named Anthony Chambers needed a live-in housekeeper, and the flyer said room and board would be taken care of. I called the number, and Anthony answered."

Sandy paused and simpered at Anthony. Annamaria ate while she listened, and Sandy took a few bites during her pause. "I explained my situation, and he said it wouldn't be a problem. Daniel could come too. Anthony hired me over the phone and told me he would pick me up from the shelter that night."

Annamaria's eyes widened. "So you just got in his car without knowing where you were going?"

Sandy smiled. "Anthony has a very trusting persona about him. I will admit, when I climbed in, I almost jumped right back out. I was not expecting to open the car door to a young man my age. But I really needed this job. He drove us back here, and I got nervous when I saw the house. How could someone so young afford a place like this? With an honest living? I was sure I had just been picked up by a drug lord or something."

Anthony chuckled.

"Anthony introduced me to Will and three gals who don't live here anymore. He gave me a tour and told me what my duties would be—cleaning the house, taking care of the grounds, and doing laundry. 'What about cooking?' I asked him. 'Oh, you can cook for yourself and your baby,' he said. Then Anthony told me they were all vampires, and if that was too much, he would take me back to the shelter and I would never hear from any of them again."

"Did you believe him?" Annamaria asked.

Sandy shrugged. "I didn't want to, but he showed me his fangs. I was so desperate to get out of the shelter, and I could build a savings if I could live rent and grocery free, so I accepted them for who they were. I raised my son here, and I had saved enough by the time he was five to buy a car with cash, and I could drive him to school in the nearest town. It's been a good life."

"Did any of them ever…you know?" Annamaria asked, avoiding a look in Anthony's direction.

"Anthony forbade it," Sandy said. "On my first night there, I overheard him telling the others, 'She's an employee, not a snack.' "

Sandy laughed again, and Annamaria gave a small smile. Annamaria looked back and forth between them. Even though Marianna proved herself to be trustworthy, and Anthony seemed nice, she couldn't forget Will hypnotizing her or the other vampires at The Daylight. Sandy seemed enamored with Anthony, so was her judgment reliable?

After dinner, Annamaria headed up the stairs and stopped in front of Will's door. She paused, and her heart rate increased. "Marianna's in her room right now." Annamaria jumped and turned around. Anthony smiled apologetically. "Sorry."

Annamaria shook her head. "I didn't hear you come up the stairs. Is that another vampire power?"

Anthony chuckled. "Yeah."

Annamaria walked to Marianna's door and knocked. Marianna swung the door open. "You done with dinner?" Annamaria nodded as Marianna gestured her inside, and Marianna shut the door on Anthony. Marianna plopped onto her bed, and Annamaria joined her. "How was your day?"

"Full," Annamaria said.

"Did you discover your balcony?"

"Yes, I spent the afternoon there."

"And what do you think of Sandy?"

"She's really nice. She has quite the story."

"Yeah, she does. She's been here longer than me, Kylie, and Tyler. Anyway, now that the sun is down, do you want to go outside with me?"

Annamaria smiled. "Yeah."

"Great." Marianna jumped off the bed and grabbed Annamaria's hand. "Do you mind if the boys come too? All of us are always itching to get out as soon as the sun goes down."

"Sure."

When Marianna opened her door, both Anthony and Will were standing there as if they had been listening. Will wrapped his arms around Marianna's waist and drew her close. Annamaria looked away. When she looked back at them, Anthony was looking at her again. Their eyes met, and once again, Annamaria looked away first.

Will led the way. "So Annamaria, how do you like my house?"

"It's really beautiful."

"Why thank you."

At the bottom of the stairs, he started toward the garage, but Marianna tugged on his arm toward the front door. "Let's show Annamaria the grounds first," she said.

"All right," Will grumbled. Anthony shot him a

look and said something so low Annamaria couldn't understand it. He sounded angry. Will replied in the same low, unintelligible volume. They argued back and forth, hissing and growling at each other. Marianna told them to knock it off at a normal volume.

"What's going on?" Annamaria looked from Marianna to the boys.

"Anthony and Will were having a private conversation in front of you," Marianna said.

"More superpowers?" Annamaria asked.

Marianna's mouth twitched. "Yes. It was quite rude, wasn't it?"

"Sorry," both Will and Anthony said to Annamaria.

"Will wanted to take you hunting with us, and Anthony thinks that's a bad idea," Marianna said.

"Oh, um, no offense, but I'm okay staying here," Annamaria said.

"That's what I thought." Anthony glared at Will again.

Will put his hands up. "Well, excuse me for trying to include her in our evening activities."

"That was very thoughtful of you, honey." Marianna patted him on the arm while rolling her eyes. "But we can go hunt when she's asleep."

Annamaria's stomach clenched, yet she still wanted to spend time with Marianna. Will seemed to always say uncomfortable things. Annamaria would just have to get used to him for the time being.

The lawn surrounding Will's house was smooth and perfect. The opposite side from the garage was a garden similar to the one Trinity and Annamaria tended back home. Annamaria's eyes shone, looking at the garden.

"I'm sure Sandy wouldn't mind if you helped in the garden during the day, in the sun," Marianna said.

"That would be great," said Annamaria.

Marianna had her own herb garden for potions. Behind the house was a large patio decorated with small tables, benches, and bushes. At the conclusion of the grounds tour, Annamaria was tired and ready to go to bed.

Marianna hugged her goodnight. "We go out most nights, so if you wake up in the middle of the night, don't be alarmed. You're welcome to anything in the house, and Sandy says you can wake her up if you need to. If it's really important, call me."

"You can also call me or Will," Anthony said. "Just in case." Marianna gave him a look. Annamaria handed Anthony her phone so he could punch in his and Will's numbers.

"Have fu… I mean, goodnight."

As Annamaria walked to her room, she looked at her phone. Anthony had texted himself from Annamaria's phone, giving him her number as well, but he hadn't done the same with Will's number.

Chapter 12 Elemental Magic

Annamaria met Marianna in the ballroom after breakfast. Marianna stood next to a table holding four bowls lined up in the center. Shortly after Annamaria walked in, Will and Anthony followed. "What are you two doing here?" Marianna asked them.

"We want to watch Annamaria perform magic," answered Will.

"We're just curious," said Anthony.

Marianna pursed her lips and tapped her foot. She looked at Annamaria. "It's up to you. These are your lessons."

Annamaria glanced at the two boys, then back to her sister. "I'm sorry, but I'd like lessons to be just us two for now."

"Of course," Marianna said. "You heard her. Scram."

Will pouted, but Anthony smiled and bowed his head. He grabbed Will by the arm and marched him out of the ballroom.

Annamaria raised her eyebrows. "Is this normal behavior for those two?"

Marianna rolled her eyes. "No. A witch has never lived here before. So this is as new to them as it is to you. Are you ready?"

"Yes."

Marianna cleared her throat, straightened up, and

placed her hands behind her back. "Magic comes from the earth, the sun, and the moon. Our powers are a gift which must be cherished and respected. In order to connect with the givers of this gift, we start with elemental magic." She gestured toward the table with the four bowls. Annamaria stepped closer. One bowl held sand, one held water, one held matches and small twigs, and one was empty.

"You have already practiced your command of the air with levitation. Air is the easiest because it is always around us. The other three will be learned in two stages. Stage one will be about controlling and expanding the existing element. Stage two will be about summoning them."

Marianna scooted the bowl of sand forward. "Now, this first part should be easy. I want you to levitate the earth and then the water. Practice controlling them in small sizes, then we'll expand them."

Annamaria stretched out her hand and raised the sand out of the bowl. She guided the sand around the room and even separated the individual grains like the dinner plates the night before. Marianna gave a thumbs-up and a "good job." She pulled the bowl back to the line and pushed the water forward. Annamaria did the same thing with the water.

"Fire is the trickiest element," Marianna said. "Because it doesn't simply exist like water, earth, and air do. Fire must be created. It's also the hardest to control, which makes it the most dangerous. So I'm going to light these twigs on fire, and then I want you to raise the fire so you can memorize how controlling the flames feel, then carefully lower them back down."

"Okay." Annamaria flexed her fingers. "I'm

ready."

Marianna picked up the matches.

"Can I light those for you?" Annamaria reached for the matches. "I don't want you to get hurt."

"I know how to light a match." Marianna smiled. "But thank you for your concern." Marianna struck the match, lit the twigs, and blew on them lightly. When the flames were above the rim of the bowl, she stepped back. "Go."

Annamaria took a deep breath and focused solely on her magic and the flame. The tips of her fingers grew hot, the feeling of flames licked them, but no pain followed. The flickering flames rose away from the sticks and crackled in midair. Annamaria kept them floating for several minutes to see if the flames would die down. They didn't. Smiling, she lowered the flames back onto the sticks. Marianna doused them with the bowl of water.

Marianna grinned widely. "That was perfect. Questions before we continue?"

"Yes," Annamaria said. "You said something about the givers of the gift of magic. Who are they?"

Marianna pursed her lips. "I actually don't know. Those were the words Caroline used when she taught me. She said those who gave us magic are our creators, and we show respect and gratitude by using our magic appropriately."

"What is the appropriate use of magic?"

Marianna shrugged. "It's different for each witch. I guess we'll figure it out together?" Annamaria nodded. "So the next thing you need to do is multiply the amount or increase the size in front of you. Unlike levitation, multiplying requires an incantation. The incantation to multiply the amount is *pullulate*."

"Pu…llu…late?"

"Yes. *Pullulate*. Try saying it more fluid."

"*Pullulate*."

"Good. Now, *pullulate* doubles the amount, so you need to say the incantation each time until you have the amount you want. For water, you'll be doubling the amount of water molecules, and for earth, you'll be doubling the amount of grains of soil. Try with water first."

"*Pullulate. Pullulate. Pullulate*," Annamaria said under her breath. "Okay, I'm ready."

Marianna gestured to the water with an encouraging smile. Annamaria raised the water out of the bowl. "*Pullulate*." The water bubble grew.

"Again," said Marianna.

"*Pullulate*." The water doubled again. Marianna talked Annamaria through doubling the size several more times until the bubble resembled a backyard pool.

"Can you hold it?" Marianna asked, with a glint in her eye.

"I think so." Annamaria steadied both of her hands.

Marianna took a step toward the giant floating water bubble and jumped up into it. She swam around in it, diving, somersaulting, and twirling, like a graceful mermaid. When she jumped out, some water splashed with her, wetting the floor. She had a youthful smile that matched her laughter.

"Oh, I forgot to tell you how to shrink it down. You can either shrink it, or you can undo the spell. The shrinking incantation is *subtraxerum utilium* and to undo is *reditus*."

"Does shrinking work the same as growing?"

Annamaria asked.

Marianna nodded.

"*Reditus*," Annamaria said. The water returned to its original size, and Annamaria dropped it back into the bowl.

"Do you mind drying me?" Marianna asked.

"Not at all." Annamaria called upon the air, commanding it like an invisible hair dryer, drying up the floor and Marianna in less than a minute.

"Thanks, now do the same thing with the earth."

Annamaria raised the earth out of the bowl and repeated the incantation until there were several large sand dunes in the ballroom. Marianna's frolic in the water gave Annamaria an idea. "Have you ever been sandboarding or snowboarding?" she asked her sister.

"I have been snowboarding, but I don't know what sandboarding is."

"It's very similar." Annamaria focused both of her hands on the floor in front of her, summoning two sandboards. She handed one to Marianna and took the other one for herself. "I'll race you to the top!" Peeking over her shoulder, Marianna looked dumbfounded for a minute, then zoomed ahead of Annamaria in a blur. Annamaria was panting when she got to the top.

"What is this?" Marianna asked.

"A sandboard."

"And what do I do with it?"

"You ride down the sand, just like snowboarding."

"Have you done this before?"

"No, but I have also gone snowboarding, and I imagine they are pretty similar."

Both Annamaria and Marianna strapped their feet into their sandboards. Anna counted them down, and they both took off. Annamaria's hair waved and rippled behind her as she gained speed. Almost immediately Marianna bypassed her sister, sliding across the hardwood in a graceful stop. Annamaria wobbled when her sandboard transferred from the sand to hardwood. When the board stopped completely, Annamaria kept going, crashing onto the floor. She caught herself with her elbow, banging her funny bone.

Marianna laughed. "Oh, if I were still mortal, I would have been way too scared to try that!"

Annamaria winced. "Well, I am still mortal, and I think I got a wood burn from my fall." Annamaria showed Marianna her arm, and sure enough, there was an angry red welt across the skin.

"I'll tell you how to heal when we are done. I have a feeling you'll be getting a few more," Marianna called over her shoulder as she ran to the top of the hill.

They continued to board down the sand dunes for almost an hour until Annamaria was exhausted and out of breath. Marianna, however, hadn't broken a sweat. Annamaria reduced the sand, returned the particles to their bowl, and summoned a glass of water. After gulping the water down, she held out her injured arm to Marianna.

Marianna studied it. "Since it's a surface wound, *salutem* will be good enough. More serious injuries require potions, but we'll get to those later." Annamaria repeated the incantation with her hand over the burn and gasped when she removed her hand and the welt was gone.

"Good. Now on to fire. Fire uses a different incantation because you are increasing the size. The incantation is *incrementum*. Repeat."

"*Incrementum. Incrementum. Incrementum.*"

"Excellent. So because fire can be disastrous, I need Will and Anthony in here to be on standby just in case. Can they come in?"

"I understand. Yes, they can come in." Annamaria rubbed her arms. The door opened and Will and Anthony walked in with several large buckets, one of them sloshing with water. "Were you guys standing outside listening this whole time?"

"No, we could hear you two from our rooms," said Anthony.

"And I'm deeply hurt you didn't invite us to go sandboarding with you. The past hour has been very long and boring." Will pouted.

Marianna simpered. "Sorry, girls only. Okay." She clapped her hands. "Annamaria, can you multiply the water and fill the remaining buckets so we can douse the fire if need be?"

"Sure thing." Annamaria scooped some into another bucket and multiplied the water until the bucket was full. She did the same thing until each bucket was filled. Marianna lit a few sticks on fire and backed away.

Annamaria raised the flames up into the air. "*Incrementum*," she whispered. Nothing happened.

"It's okay," Marianna said. "I trust you."

Annamaria cleared her throat. "*Incrementum.*" The fire glowed and doubled. Annamaria repeated the incantation a few more times until there was a large ball in between her and Marianna. The heat touched Annamaria's body. The warmth reminded her of summer nights back in Harrison. Annamaria tilted her head up and closed her eyes, basking in the glow and memories.

"Okay, that's good enough." Marianna's voice shook.

"*Reditus,*" Annamaria said. The fire zoomed back to its original size, and Annamaria flung the flames into a bucket of water. The room was silent. Annamaria glanced around. The other three had wide eyes and were exchanging looks with each other.

"Did I... Was that all right?" Annamaria asked.

"Oh. Yes." Marianna smiled. "It's just a little unsettling to be so close to something that can kill you."

"Yeah, I don't know what that feels like at all." Annamaria rolled her eyes and smirked. The others giggled.

"Well, anyway, you are doing really well, and I had full confidence you were in control," Marianna said. "So *pullulate* and *incrementum* are not for elements only. They are for anything you wish to multiply or expand. I think that's good enough for today."

"Okay." As Annamaria's focus broke away from magic, she became light-headed, and her stomach growled. "I'm going to eat lunch now."

Marianna nodded in approval. "Get yourself back on a normal eating schedule. Do you want to watch a movie or something after?"

"Yeah, that'd be great."

Annamaria headed toward the kitchen while Marianna stayed in the ballroom and started playing the piano. Anthony caught up to Annamaria. "Can I join you?"

"Sure," Annamaria said. Anthony followed her into the kitchen while she prepared her lunch. He sat down at the counter with her. "So how far can your super hearing go?" Annamaria asked Anthony as she ate.

"Not too far." Anthony shrugged. "It's kind of like a circular perimeter. Since the ballroom was right below us, we could hear."

"Can you hear every part of the house?"

"It depends on the level of noise," Anthony said. "Normal to loud, yes, we can hear everything. We can hear quiet noises, but it's harder to decipher exactly what is going on. You'd like some privacy, I imagine?"

"Yes."

"Well, most of the time, we tune each other out. So unless anyone is deliberately listening, it's just white noise."

"So you were deliberately listening to my lesson?"

Anthony held up his hands and grinned. "Sorry, I couldn't help it."

Annamaria's breath caught in her throat. She sucked in her lips before the smile trying to form completed itself. *Stop it! So what if he's charming. I just barely met him. But he is really cute.*

****

The next day was Friday, and Marianna decided it would be the last day of lessons before the weekend. The sisters agreed to hold a normal school schedule for lessons. Friday's lesson comprised of Annamaria learning to summon earth, water, and fire into her palm. Unlike summoning other objects, summoning those three elements required an incantation—*aqua*, *ignis*, and *terra*. Once she recited the incantation, the element appeared in her hand as a palm-sized sphere, and from there, Annamaria could guide and multiply it. According to Marianna, control of the elements took young witches months, sometimes years, further proof that Annamaria was learning at a fast pace since she was full grown.

On Saturday afternoon, Sandy took Annamaria into town and showed her around. Most of the shops catered to tourists by selling wildlife souvenirs and T-shirts. There were a few shops meant for the locals which provided groceries, medicine, books, electronics, and clothing. The town reminded Annamaria so much of Harrison. Though every once in a while, someone they passed would do a double take upon meeting eyes with Annamaria.

At the end of dinner the next night, Will strode into the kitchen. "Annamaria, come with me to the living room." Annamaria furrowed her brows and remained sitting. "Now." Will's face and voice were serious. An expression Annamaria had yet to see on him. She jumped up and followed him. Marianna and Anthony were already in the living room. Both looked confused.

"What's going on?" Annamaria's body tensed.

"Jordan just called." Will folded his arms. "He said you were on the news."

"What?" Both Annamaria and Marianna wore matching expressions.

Will turned on the TV, and a news broadcast blared out of the speakers. Annamaria sat down next to Marianna. Will sat on Marianna's other side, throwing his arm around her. Anthony sat next to Annamaria, keeping several inches between them. They all turned their attention to a middle-aged, fake blonde anchor with a face-lift.

"Today marks almost a week since Wyoming residents Trinity and Annamaria Lyons have gone missing from their home. Last Monday, Trinity did not show up to work. And her niece, Annamaria, did not show up for school. Concerned neighbors and police investigated the home and found décor had been smashed and furniture upturned. The garage door was opened, and Trinity's car was gone. By Tuesday morning, the police declared the two women as missing persons, though police believe they may have been missing since Saturday night, as that is the last time anyone saw either of them. Wyoming officials are asking for the Nation's help as police believe the two are no longer in Wyoming." Side-by-side pictures of Trinity and Annamaria popped up on the screen. "If you see either of these two, or know anything, call the number on your screen. Annamaria also answers to Anna."

Will muted the TV. Marianna and Annamaria looked at each other, eyes wide, lips parted. "Do you think something happened to Trinity?" Annamaria asked.

"I don't know." Marianna raked her fingers through her hair. "We both talked to her on the phone, and I've been texting her."

"Me too," said Annamaria. "Do you think something happened to Lica after Trinity left?"

"Could be." Marianna frowned.

Annamaria took out her phone and typed out a text to Trinity. *—Have you seen the news?—*

—We are missing persons!—

—What do we do?—

Annamaria's phone vibrated in her hand. "Trinity, what happened?"

"I don't know. Everything was in order when I

left," Trinity answered.

"Could something have happened to Lica?"

"That was my first thought too, but I called her first, and she's just fine."

"Then what happened?"

"I don't know. I told my junior assistant I had to go out of town for a family emergency, and she was in charge indefinitely. I even left Hal a message, telling him he could regain control of the house. So this doesn't make any sense."

"So are you saying the destruction of the house is fake?" Annamaria met Marianna's eyes. Marianna's gaze rotated between Annamaria and her phone.

"Oh, I'm sure the destruction is real to get the police's attention and get a search party going. But I don't think whoever orchestrated the destruction actually thinks something happened to us. I think this is a ruse to lure us out of hiding," Trinity said.

"Who would do this?"

"I have a few ideas, but we can't fall for it. Stay hidden and keep training. You understand me?"

"Yes, but shouldn't we at least tell the Mills so they know we are okay?" Annamaria crossed her fingers.

"They know we are okay. I left Hal a note. Annamaria, remember what I said? You can endanger yourself and them if you contact them. Don't do it."

Annamaria sighed. "Fine."

"Good, I love you."

"Love you, too."

Trinity hung up. Both Marianna and Will were looking at Annamaria. Both furrowed their brows and pursed their lips. Anthony, however, surveyed Will.

"How does Jordan know she is here?"

"We ran into him while we were traveling." Will shrugged.

"I thought you guys were going to be careful," Anthony said.

Marianna put her hand on Will's knee. "It's not his fault. We didn't know Jordan would be there ahead of time. He ambushed us on the way to check out and got his claws on Annamaria before I could stop him."

Annamaria wrinkled her nose. Had she really been that weak? "Marianna threatened Jordan just for looking at me. She didn't think he would tell anyone." Anthony met Annamaria's eyes and gave a slow nod.

"Anyway, until the humans are no longer looking for her, I don't think Annamaria should go into town anymore," Will said.

Annamaria straightened up. "What? Why?"

"Honey, I think that's a little extreme."

Will waved both of them off and stood up and started pacing. "Annamaria, your face is all over the news. What are you going to say if the police question you? How are you going to explain why you are here? They don't even know this place exists."

Annamaria stood up and pointed out the window. "Those people down there probably aren't even looking for me. I grew up in a similar town. The only news they care about is what's going on next door."

Will narrowed his eyes. "All the same, we should be cautious. Besides, the entire magical community is looking for you, even if those humans are not."

"Do any other vampires live near here? Any witches or werewolves?"

"No."

"Then me going out shouldn't be a problem." Annamaria kept eye contact with Will.

Will pointed his finger in Annamaria's face. Marianna stood up and placed her hands on his shoulders. He shrugged her off. "Look, I shouldn't have to explain myself to you. This is my coven. I'm in charge."

Annamaria shoved Will's finger away. "I'm not a member of your coven."

"But you are my guest."

Marianna stepped between them. "Will said only until the humans stop looking for you. You'll be forgotten in the next big news story, which won't be long."

Annamaria looked at the three vampires. Will glared. Marianna held a small smile, her eyebrows high, and Anthony's gaze traveled from person to person. He had not taken part, but his silence said everything. Annamaria huffed and stormed out of the living room.

Annamaria spent the next hour in her room with three spheres of water, fire, and earth, levitated and circling above her head. The balcony doors were open, letting the cool mountain night air in. Annamaria glared at the circling globes. She did not leave Harrison to be placed under new and stricter rules. Especially when the one enforcing the rules was her age and a stranger. Sure, Will had been eighteen for seventy years, but it's not like his mind was that of a ninety-year-old man. He still acted like a teenager. And how could Marianna have sided with him? On the road she had been one-hundred-percent the boss. What happened? They couldn't expect Annamaria to live under Will's authority when she wasn't a vampire. And Anthony, he had been so kind and attentive. Why didn't he say something? Annamaria clenched her fists. His charm must be an act. He was like Will.

Annamaria dropped the three spheres when a knock on her door startled her. She caught the fire as the earth and water fell on her bed. Annamaria summoned the water back and doused the fire. Annamaria got off her bed and opened the door. Anthony stood in the doorframe with his hands in his pockets.

"Oh, hi," she said.

"Hi," said Anthony. "I'm really sorry about what happened downstairs. Can I come in? I'd like to explain."

"I dunno." Annamaria looked down. Think of the devil, and the devil shall appear.

Anthony put his palm on his forehead. "I'm sorry. That was forward of me. Would you be willing to go someplace else and talk?"

"Where is Will?"

"Marianna took him out for the night to cool down."

Great. Will would take his anger out on innocent humans. "We can go to the library," she said.

Annamaria sat on the same couch as before, and Anthony sat in the same chair, facing her. "I know you are upset neither Marianna nor I stood up for you when you were arguing with Will. The thing is, we couldn't. As the coven leader, Will has an authority that is very difficult for a vampire under him to oppose. It's almost impossible to disobey an order by the coven leader unless a vampire is leaving the coven for good."

Annamaria blinked and kept her face passive.

"Why would you want to live like that?"

Anthony chuckled. "Will doesn't exercise his authority often. He must be serious about keeping you safe to have done so tonight."

Annamaria scoffed. "Are you trying to make me feel guilty for arguing with him?"

"No, not at all. I just wanted to let you know how things are on my end."

Annamaria slouched. "Does Will expect me to act like the rest of you?"

Anthony shifted in his chair. "Will is used to being in charge. I don't think he consciously planned to force you to obey him, but when you challenged him, he retaliated."

"I won't be a prisoner here." Annamaria stared at Anthony.

Anthony leaned forward. "Trust me, none of us want that either. Like Marianna said, when things die down on the news, things can go back to normal."

Annamaria sighed. She didn't want to concede, but she couldn't get anyone on her side. "What's Will's story?" Maybe she could understand him better if she knew his background.

"Will turned the summer after his senior year in high school. His change was abnormal because the vampire who changed him didn't stick around. There are no accidental changes. The way the change works, it has to be deliberate. So when a vampire changes someone, they have a purpose. I met him a few weeks after he turned and was the first vampire he met. I had left my previous coven, and I took Will under my tutelage. This house belonged to his family, and he took it from them. We created a coven together, though we are smaller than most. He found your sister as quickly after her change as I had found him. He brought her right here, and they have been inseparable ever since."

Wow. No wonder he expected Annamaria to obey. He was used to being the boss. Annamaria looked at her hands. "Thank you for telling me that. I'm still mad at all of you, but I understand better now." She stood up. "I'm going to bed now."

"May I walk you to your room?" Anthony asked.

Ugh. "Sure."

They walked in silence to Annamaria's room. She opened the door and turned around. Anthony took her right hand in both of his. "Goodnight, Annamaria," he whispered.

"Goodnight." She tugged her hand, but Anthony kept a gentle but firm hold.

Anthony raised her hand to his lips and Annamaria's hand jerked more forcefully. His lips brushed the back of her hand. The same tingles erupted on her skin, but this time the feeling was pleasant. She exhaled. Anthony gave a small smile and zoomed down the hall so fast he was a blur.

Chapter 13 Messages

Annamaria's magic lessons continued to go very well over the next few weeks. Once she mastered the elements, she progressed to a reverse summoning called casting.

"Casting is where you send an object from your hand to a different location. Instead of appearing in your hand, it disappears from your hand and appears elsewhere. There is one difference between summoning and casting—you always have to know where you are sending the object." Marianna placed an apple in Annamaria's hand. "Cast it into my hand."

Annamaria willed the apple into Marianna's hand. *Yes!* Instant success. Annamaria then cast it across the room, into each individual room in the house, and various places outside.

The next level of casting was sending it to a location farther away. The next time Sandy traveled down the mountain, she picked a spot in town, called Annamaria, and described it to her.

"I'm behind the movie theater. It's the employee parking lot with the dumpsters."

Annamaria closed her eyes. She had only seen the front of the theater during the one time Sandy had taken her into town. In her mind, she drove through the main street, past the police station, and stopped in front of the theater. From here, it would have to be imagination.

She pictured walking around the side of the building and to the back. She pictured Sandy standing there with her phone to her ear, her light blue purse resting in the crease of her elbow. Annamaria opened her eyes, and the apple disappeared.

"Did it work?"

"I don't know," Sandy said. "I can't see anything."

"Go look around front," said Marianna.

The sound of Sandy breathing and walking came out of the speaker. "I see it! It ended up on the corner of the front and the side."

Annamaria grimaced, but Marianna beamed. "That's a good first try. Sandy, you up for hanging around town a bit longer?"

"Absolutely."

It took Annamaria an hour to cast the apple exactly where Sandy chose. Sandy cheered through the phone, and the two sisters hugged and jumped. "Thank you so much, Sandy. Are you willing to do this each time you go into town?"

"Of course."

After Annamaria mastered casting, she learned how to summon, control, and extinguish light, which was what Marianna could do. Like summoning the elements, summoning light required the incantation *lux*. *Luxmea* connected the light fully to her magic so that her thoughts could control it. *Nonlux* extinguished it. Annamaria discovered she, as the spell caster, could still see their surroundings after reciting *nonlux*.

"Why don't you use *nonlux* to go out during the day?" asked Annamaria.

Marianna gave a sad smile. "It's only an illusion. I can't actually turn off the sun, so its rays would still kill me if I stepped outside and magically darkened the sky. Electric lights, yes, but not the sun."

Since magic lessons were only in the morning, Annamaria was free to do whatever she wanted the rest of the day. After lunch, Annamaria rotated through reading in the library, learning to paint from Anthony, listening to Marianna play the piano—where Annamaria would sometimes dance to the music—and spending time outside in the sun. Sandy was happy to let Annamaria help in the garden, and after working in the garden, Annamaria also read outside.

Spending afternoons outside meant spending less time with Marianna and Anthony. However, they both encouraged Annamaria to go outside when she could. She made it up to them in the evenings after dinner. They would watch a movie or play outside. Some evenings were a girls' night for the two sisters. Sometimes the four of them would hang out. When Marianna gave Will attention, Annamaria ended the night with Anthony. He was always kind and charming. But Annamaria could not get over how he let Will bully her into staying stuck on the property. So she kept him at arm's length. Besides, Cody still lingered in the back of her mind.

One night while the four of them were playing volleyball on the lawn, a loud howl interrupted them. Good timing. Annamaria and Marianna were losing by an incredible amount because of Annamaria's lack of speed. Though her magical connection to the air did help, it wasn't quite enough. Everyone's attention turned to the front gate.

A large, beautiful black wolf stood outside the gate, poking its nose through the bars. Marianna squealed and ran over in a blur to the gate, letting the wolf in. The wolf tackled Marianna, and she giggled and wrestled with it. She led the wolf over to Annamaria. "This is Luna, my familiar."

Annamaria held her hand out. "Hi, Luna. I'm Annamaria, your mommy's sister."

Luna's tail wagged. She licked Annamaria's hand and let out a bark. Will and Anthony stayed far back. They seemed tense watching the exchange. "They don't care for Luna?"

"Luna doesn't care for them." Marianna stroked Luna's neck. Luna huffed. Marianna giggled.

Every night Anthony escorted Annamaria to her bedroom, and before parting, he would kiss the back of her hand. His kisses continued to leave the warm, tingle feeling from the first time. Annamaria's stomach erupted in butterflies every time, then would clench in guilt for liking it. She also wanted an explanation for the tingle feeling. However, every time she tried, she lost her nerve. So each night she accepted the kiss with a strained smile.

Annamaria ate every dinner with Sandy. They became fast friends. Every once in a while, Sandy would come back from a trip into town with a little gift for Annamaria, who was still confined to the house. Although the original news story died like Marianna predicted, Cody and his father aired on the news without the police to send a message to Annamaria or "whoever might have her" to "do the right thing" and return Annamaria to Harrison. Will took no time in extending Annamaria's prison sentence, which resulted in another argument between the two.

Annamaria hated being near him now, but he and

Marianna were inseparable. So if Annamaria wanted to spend time with her sister, she had to endure Will. Will and Marianna were pretty comfortable with intimacy, and Annamaria had to deal with the embarrassment of walking in on them all over the house. Marianna always sent an apologetic smile, while Will would flash a wicked grin. Annamaria would clench her teeth, roll her eyes, and slam whatever door she had just entered.

"You'll eventually get used to it," Anthony said.

I hope I never do.

On the occasion Annamaria ran into Will alone, he had a nasty habit of trying to intimidate Annamaria. He would get too close, caressing her face, neck, and arms and pretending to bite her. Annamaria would fend him off by threatening him with a fireball. She never burned him because Marianna would get upset, and she also feared Will's retaliation. Annamaria kept these altercations to herself because neither Marianna nor Anthony could do anything about it, and she didn't want to increase the tension. So she dealt with the situation on her own.

At night, Annamaria also suffered from a recurring nightmare. In her nightmare, Annamaria was back at her house on the night Priya attacked. When Priya drove off in her car with Annamaria, Marianna failed to catch them. Once they were out of town, Priya changed into Will. Will would feed on Annamaria, and while she kicked and screamed, Anthony would show up and heave Will off of her. However, he wasn't there to save her. He kept Annamaria in Will's car.

"Don't struggle." His voice was gentle. He'd caress the side of her face. "We'll be happy. I promise."

Whenever Annamaria woke up from this

nightmare, she couldn't go back to sleep. To pass the time and get the nightmare out of her mind, Annamaria would go to the ballroom and dance until she was so exhausted, she would sleep without dreaming. At first, she danced through her old concert routines, but terrible memories accompanied them. She then turned to choreographing new routines, getting lost in the music, movement, and creativity calmed her.

Cody's birthday passed during the month of May, as well as what would have been Annamaria's high school graduation. Annamaria spent the afternoon and evening alone. Even though Annamaria enjoyed her magic and living with her sister, she still missed her old life, and most of all, she missed Trinity.

One afternoon, Annamaria was outside with Sandy, soaking up the sun and working in the garden. Sandy stood up to take her bucket of vegetables inside to prepare them for dinner when her cell phone slid out of her pocket and onto the grass. Annamaria leaned forward and opened her mouth but stopped herself. After Sandy shut the back door, Annamaria grabbed the phone and ran behind a tree. *Sorry, Trinity, but I have to.*

"*Recludo*," Annamaria whispered, and Sandy's screen unlocked. She clicked the message icon, opened up a new conversation, and typed in Cody's number.

—Cody, this is Anna. I want you to know I'm okay.—

—I had a family emergency.—

—Please stop asking the news and police to look for me.—

Annamaria pressed send, her heart racing. The three dancing dots appeared on the screen.

—Who is this? Prove it.—

Annamaria took a quick selfie, a small smile with her lips closed, and sent the picture.

—Is this good enough?—

The phone started ringing, Cody's number flashed on the screen. Annamaria rejected the call and typed a new message.

—I can't talk, text only. I can't be overheard.—

Cody responded right away.

—Whose phone is this? Where are you?—

Annamaria pursed her lips. How much should she tell him? Would he take her back if he knew everything? Even if he did believe her, and by some miracle wasn't scared, she couldn't lead him here. She shook her head. Her goal was to regain access to the town down the mountain.

—I can't tell you who or where. It's too dangerous, I'm sorry.—

—I just wanted you to know I'm okay and ask you to stop putting my face on the news.—

Annamaria's eyes filled with tears after she sent the texts. Sandy's phone dinged.

—Seriously?! I haven't heard from you in over a month and that's what you say to me?—

—Consider it done. We'll stop looking.—

Annamaria's mouth fell open as she stared at the phone. Even though she had forced it, his response still hurt. Sandy's phone started ringing again, only this time Anthony's name flashed across the screen. Annamaria swiped with shaking hands. "Hello?"

"Oh, Annamaria," said Sandy's voice. "Where are you?"

"Outside. Your phone was in the grass. I didn't

notice it until it started ringing." Annamaria's heart pounded as she kept her voice level.

"Oh phew! Will you bring it in for me?" Sandy asked.

"Sure thing." Annamaria hung up and typed one last message.

—I'm really sorry. I have to go.—

—Don't text back.—

Annamaria hit send and deleted the conversation.

Throughout the evening, Annamaria kept shaking her leg and playing with her hands and would jump at unexpected noises. Anthony asked her several times if everything was all right, and she told him she was fine. What would the consequences be if anyone read those messages? Sure, she deleted the conversation, but she couldn't delete the record of the phone call. What if Sandy called Cody back? Or the unrecognizable number led her to find the deleted conversation? What if Cody didn't listen and contacted Sandy? Sandy liked her life here. Would she tell Will?

Annamaria retired early and failed to notice Anthony's kiss on her hand. She tossed and turned for a long time. She eventually got out of bed, put on her dance clothes, and headed downstairs.

In the ballroom, Annamaria put the CD in the stereo with the song she was currently working on. When Annamaria had started her choreography, she had been thinking about Anthony. Tonight, however, her mind was on Cody. What if he were here? Would he accept this world? Would he accept her? His dad had accepted Trinity once upon a time. She finished the choreography and danced through it three times in a row. When she looked up from her last run-through, two figures were watching her from the other end of the ballroom.

Annamaria stayed still. She didn't recognize them. One was a tall, skinny yet built, light tan man with sleek black hair. The other was a darker tan woman with wavy black hair. They must be Kylie and Tyler. Annamaria's blood rushed through her veins. They approached Annamaria with careful steps. Oh gosh. They could hear her heart. How embarrassing.

"Hi, you must be Annamaria." The woman extended her hand. "I'm Kylie, and this is Tyler."

Annamaria accepted Kylie's handshake, and her mouth fell open as she got a closer look at their faces. They weren't just any Kylie and Tyler. They were Kylie Johnson and Tyler Vasquez, stars of the online video channel "Dancing in the Moonlight." Kylie and Tyler were professional ballroom dancers. Their channel had hundreds of thousands of followers, and each video had millions of views. Annamaria, Stephanie, and Jamie watched every single video together.

Annamaria closed her mouth. "I'm sorry. I'm just kind of starstruck right now. I watch your channel, and I didn't know you were vampires. Oh jeez, I'm so sorry." Annamaria blushed deep red and looked down at her feet.

Kylie and Tyler both chuckled. "No need to apologize," Tyler said. "Vampire isn't a dirty word." Annamaria couldn't respond other than to keep blushing. This was the best surprise so far.

"When we were told a witch was moving in, we didn't realize we'd be sharing the dance floor." Kylie gestured to the floor space behind Annamaria.

"Oh, I can get out of your way." Annamaria only danced for fun. This was their career.

Kylie waved her hand. "No, stay. You're great. Would you like to dance with us?"

Kylie thought Annamaria was good. Annamaria pinched her palm. Yep. This is real. "I'd love to!"

Tyler set up the music while Kylie zoomed upstairs to grab an extra pair of Latin heels. The three of them spent the next few hours following each other in their different styles.

While Annamaria's school didn't offer ballroom classes, her coach had incorporated some steps into different routines over the years, so she already knew the basics. Dancing with an actual partner was a new experience, however. Annamaria picked up on the steps and choreography pretty quickly. When Annamaria taught them her old routines, they looked so much better than she did, but she wasn't the least bit jealous. Just being in the same room as them was an honor.

Toward the early hours of the morning, Annamaria's feet were on fire, and she was breathing hard. Like Marianna with the sandboarding, neither Kylie nor Tyler were sweating or showing signs of tiredness. They called it a night so Annamaria could get some sleep.

"So Annamaria, how has your time here been so far?" Kylie asked while Annamaria stretched.

Annamaria looked up from hugging her ankles. "It's been all right. I'm adjusting, I guess."

"Yeah, I imagine. Sorry we weren't here when you woke up. We had to go do some shows," said Kylie.

Annamaria smiled and shook her head. "Don't worry about it. It was really awkward, anyway."

"I bet." Tyler laughed. "No one in the house, apart from Anthony and Marianna, has ever met a witch before."

"I'm sorry I wasn't willing to meet you guys when I first arrived. I'm still new to this world and coming here was not planned. I was just so nervous." Annamaria looked at her hands, her face turning redder with each phrase.

Kylie waved her off. "Not a problem. We completely understand. We were ignorant humans before we turned, so we experienced a similar shock."

Annamaria fell asleep as soon as her head hit the pillow. No nightmares plagued her. Instead, swirling movement and color kept her sleep calm as she dreamed about her new friends.

****

Two books were on the table when Annamaria entered the ballroom. An elegant inscription of *Marianna* was printed on the cover of one, the other was blank.

"Each witch writes their own magic book throughout their life," Marianna began. "This is the one I started." Marianna gestured to the one with her name on it. "I'm going to let you study it, though there's not much since I only made it to eighteen. But you should write everything you have learned so far and continue to write as you learn more." Marianna gestured to the book with the blank cover. Her shoulders were slumped, her mouth downturned.

"Wow, thank you." Annamaria's heart hurt a little watching Marianna's emotions.

"It is important you begin your own book because we are nearing the end of consistent incantations.

Magic is a part of each individual soul and therefore is as different as each person. You will need to learn how to communicate with your magic as we study deeper abilities because how you call forth your incantations will look and sound different from another witch, though you will get the same results. Which is why it's important to write down what you learn and pass the information on to future generations."

"Thanks again. I understand how hard this is for you. I will appreciate your writings." She gave Marianna a tight hug.

Marianna hugged Annamaria back. "I want you to know I'm not abandoning you because handing over my book hurts. This point of magic is deeply personal. You need to further connect and communicate with your magic and learn from each other. Of course you can always come to me with questions. And I would absolutely love if you showed me the spells you discover."

Annamaria stepped back to look into her sister's eyes. "Of course I will keep you engaged in my magic. You are an amazing teacher and an even more amazing sister."

Marianna patted Annamaria's shoulders. "Use my book to get started on yours. And I would suggest some caffeine and sunshine since you didn't get a lot of sleep last night." Marianna winked.

Annamaria reddened. "Did you hear us? I didn't know you were home."

"We came home while you were dancing, but we didn't interrupt because it sounded like you were having fun with them." Marianna smiled. "I'm glad you met Tyler and Kylie in your element."

Annamaria grinned. "Me too."

Annamaria took both books outside and sat down at one of the round tables on the back patio. Luna appeared and curled up next to her, nuzzling Annamaria's feet with her head. Annamaria traced Marianna's name. Marianna's life had been so unfair.

Annamaria opened up Marianna's book and looked through it. The beginning was all the basic spells Annamaria already learned. She opened up her book and copied them down, adding her own notes for specific positions to hold her hands and fingers for each incantation. Comparing Marianna's notes to her own helped Annamaria understand what Marianna meant about each witch figuring out their own style. When Annamaria practiced on her own, she found a tiny change of one finger or angle could make her incantation come out faster, stronger, or obey her direction easier. While she wrote, she took breaks to scratch Luna's head, receiving licks and nuzzles in return.

After an hour, Annamaria put down her pen and stretched. She was so tired from the night before. She flipped through the pages of Marianna's book, skimming the spells Marianna had recorded. How did one discover new spells? The spells she already learned were Latin for what they did. She could start there and see if her magic would respond to other Latin words. She would need a Latin dictionary. The library was sure to have one. Annamaria would check after lunch.

After lunch, Annamaria was on her way to the library when someone grabbed her arm. She turned around, her fist flying, but instead of Will's face, Tyler's hand caught her knuckles. "Hey," he whispered, with a smirk. "Can you come talk to me and Kylie upstairs?"

"Um, okay." Annamaria dropped her hand and shook it. "Sorry."

"Yay!" Tyler flung Annamaria over his shoulder and zoomed upstairs, making their surroundings a temporary blur. When he put Annamaria down in the back of the upstairs hallway, she swayed and grabbed his arm. Tyler chuckled. "Sorry, I'm just so excited."

He led Annamaria into Kylie's room, the room across from hers. The walls were lined with costume racks full of all the costumes from their videos.

"Annamaria, darling." Kylie ran over and hugged her. "So Tyler and I have been talking all night since we met you."

"And all morning, and while you were eating your lunch," said Tyler.

"Last night was so fun dancing with you. You have an incredible talent for both technique and choreography. And you caught on quickly to the Latin and ballroom steps we taught you, so..." Kylie grabbed Tyler's hand, they looked at each other, turned to Annamaria and said in unison, "We want you to join our channel!"

Annamaria clasped her hands to her mouth, a giant grin forming on her face, and she squealed like she was back in high school. "Oh. My. Gosh. Oh my gosh. Oh my gosh! YES!" She jumped up and down. Kylie and Tyler cheered and jumped up and down with her. The three ended in a big group hug.

"Thank you so much. This means so much to me." Tears formed in Annamaria's eyes.

"No, thank *you*," said Tyler. "We were running out

of ideas for how to shake things up. Adding a third dancer is perfect. Plus, your fiery red hair is going to look sexy flipping around in front of the camera. And maybe you could even conjure up some actual fire?"

Annamaria scrunched her brows. "So you want my magic?"

"Both," said Kylie. "We think you and your magic are just what we need to take our routines to the next level."

"You still down?" Tyler asked.

Annamaria grinned. "Of course."

"Excellent. Can you practice with us Monday through Friday in the afternoons?" Kylie asked.

"Absolutely."

"Can you start right now?" Kylie asked.

"Give me a few minutes to change?"

"Meet us in the ballroom," said Tyler.

Annamaria ran across the hall to her room and changed as fast as she could. As she walked out of her room in her dance clothes, Will cut her off.

"So little Annamaria is going to become an internet star?"

"That's right." Annamaria cocked her head, her magic humming.

Will grabbed her collarbone and forced her against the wall. Annamaria curled her fingers, her palm warmed. "You better hope no one recognizes you. The longer your pretty little face stays on the news, the longer you'll be stuck here."

"It won't happen anymore. I took care of it." Annamaria held his gaze.

Will's eyes narrowed, and he applied more pressure to Annamaria's shoulder. "What did you do?"

Annamaria gasped at the pain. "The details don't matter, but I can assure you, you won't see me on the news again."

"You better be sure," he growled.

Annamaria called fire into her hand and burned Will's hand on her shoulder. Will swore and let go. "I am sure, and stop touching me." Annamaria kept the fireball alive and raised her hand to eye level. Will growled but remained where he was. Annamaria ran down the hall and downstairs, keeping the fire burning in case Will followed her.

If Kylie and Tyler overheard the confrontation, their faces remained unaware when Annamaria entered the ballroom. Tyler was dressed in black dance pants, a satin stripe on the side of each leg, black Latin shoes, and a tight black T-shirt. Kylie was in spandex leggings, a practice Latin skirt, and a light pink tank top. She wore Latin sandals and had an extra pair on the floor. Annamaria put the shoes on and was ready to go.

"So what we want to do is tell a story through several routines. We'll film and publish them consecutively," said Tyler. "We want to tell your and Marianna's story from your separation to being reunited. But we are going to tweak a few details to make the retelling more artistic. We have already talked to Marianna, and she has given us permission to do so. Are you comfortable with this?"

Annamaria nodded. "That sounds really cool."

Annamaria's chest swelled. Dancing her way through her complicated history could help her process everything and heal. Perhaps the same could happen for Marianna.

"We also haven't started any choreography at all.

So today is going to be kind of slow as we start from scratch, but we want you to be a part of the entire process," Kylie said.

"Thank you." Annamaria beamed.

"The first number we are going to work on will be your parents' love story. Obviously, we don't know it, so we are going to make something up. We would like you to dance the part of your mom, and Tyler will be your dad," Kylie said.

"And what are you going to do?" Annamaria asked Kylie.

"I'll man the camera and the music." Kylie shrugged. "Don't worry, I'll be in the next one."

Tyler put the CD in the stereo and pressed play. They listened to the song all the way through once while sitting. They played the song all the way through two more times while each dancer did some individual improvisation. Once all of them had some ideas flowing, they started on choreography.

By the time dance practice and dinner with Sandy were over, the sun had set. Annamaria hadn't seen Marianna since morning and proceeded to look for her. When Annamaria stepped into the upstairs hallway, Marianna exited her room.

"I was about to come find you. I want to start potions soon. Do you want to come learn about my herb garden?"

"Ooh, yes."

Marianna guided her down the stairs. "Herbs and several other plants are used in potions and some spells. They are all harmless on their own, and humans use them to flavor their food as you've experienced. But when mixed properly by someone with magical blood, they can heal, harm, and control."

They arrived at the herb garden, and Annamaria took in the vast strip of earth covered in straight rows of herbs.

"I don't expect you to memorize them all immediately, but I have an herb book I'll give you to help you learn how to identify them and what they can be used for." Marianna handed Annamaria a book titled *The Modern Herb for the Modern Witch.*

"Thanks." Annamaria took the book and hugged it to her chest while she watched Marianna.

"I will not stand here and lecture you on each herb since you can read about them on your own. So what I want to do is invite you to tend the garden with me. Would you like to?"

"Yes, I would love that," Annamaria said.

"Let's get started. I just like to check for weeds, make sure everything looks good, and water them."

The two worked in silence while they weeded. Annamaria peeked over at Marianna, who was smiling and singing under her breath as she tended to her babies. Annamaria smiled at her sister's readiness to share this with her. When they finished weeding, water was the last thing needed.

"Isn't there a sprinkler system?"

"Yes, but I put some Magi-Grow in the water. It's kind of like what plant food does for regular plants, but Magi-Grow amplifies the magical properties in plants with magical potential." Marianna poured the magically induced water on the herbs.

"Where do you get it?"

"A witch's apothecary."

"Really? How do you find those?"

"They are quite common. Over time, you'll learn how to see the magic hidden in the normal."

"Like The Daylight?"

"Exactly."

As they headed back toward the house, Annamaria yawned. They met Will and Anthony as they entered the house. Will drew Marianna into his chest.

"Are you ready, babe?"

"Yes." She turned to Annamaria. "We are going out. I'll see you in the morning?" Annamaria clamped her mouth shut and hugged Marianna goodnight. Will and Marianna zoomed out the front door.

"It sounds like you enjoyed an enriching time out there with Marianna?" Anthony said.

"Yeah." Annamaria narrowed her eyes and looked away. Of course he had been listening. Again.

"Do you want to watch a movie or something?" Anthony asked.

"Not tonight. I'm exhausted."

"Okay." Anthony's face fell.

Annamaria's stomach twisted. "Don't take it personally. I didn't get a lot of sleep last night, and today was really busy." She swayed and stumbled backward. Anthony grabbed her.

"Whoa. Okay, I believe you're tired. Can I carry you so you don't fall down the stairs?" Anthony asked.

"Oka—"

Anthony swooped her up. Upstairs, Anthony set Annamaria on her bed. He bent to kiss her hand as usual, but Annamaria stood up and embraced him around his middle, her head in his chest. Why did she just do that? She was supposed to be keeping her distance. He hugged her back, wrapping his arms around her, and traced the curve of her back with his fingers. His lips brushed the top of her head, and he buried his nose in her hair, inhaling deeply. Annamaria stepped away, but Anthony kept his hands around her waist, so she placed her hands on his forearms and looked into his dark brown eyes.

"Thank you so much for being kind to me from the beginning."

"You're welcome." Anthony smiled.

He lowered his face toward Annamaria, and she bowed her head, causing him to kiss her forehead. She looked up at him with a sheepish expression but relaxed when neither anger nor pain graced his features.

"Goodnight, Annamaria."

"Goodnight, Anthony."

He left Annamaria's room, and she collapsed onto her bed, her heart beating a mile a minute. What was she doing? She was drawn toward Anthony, no doubt about it, but there was a forbidden air surrounding him that she couldn't explain. And what about Cody? Annamaria shook her head. He broke up with her before she left. Time she spent with Anthony wasn't unfaithful, right? Then why did she feel guilty?

Chapter 14 Black Hole of Sound

Annamaria got her hands on a Latin dictionary and, for the next week, spent the mornings studying from Marianna's books, experimenting, and writing in her own book. Annamaria had a specific goal in mind as she used the Latin dictionary to help her figure out how Marianna's spells translated. She wanted to find or create a spell which would allow her to protect her room from the vampires' super hearing.

Annamaria succeeded with *sonusopstructio*. When she said it, a bright blue square the size of her face appeared in front of her, then disappeared.

"Anthony!"

Annamaria waited. In the time it would have taken for Anthony to have arrived via vampire speed, he did not appear. Annamaria walked to the other side of her room and called Anthony again. This time, he showed up in less than a minute.

"Yes?"

"Oh sorry, I'm experimenting." Annamaria tapped her lips.

"Experimenting with calling my name?" Anthony winked.

Annamaria blushed and rolled her eyes. "No, I'll let you know when I have it figured out. Can you go back to where you were?" Anthony pouted, but his eyes sparkled as he left Annamaria's doorway.

"*Sonusopstructio.*"

This time Annamaria held the blue square in her magic hold and, using her arms, guided it to expand and surround the perimeter of her room. All four walls of her room glowed blue, then faded back to normal. Annamaria called Anthony's name and waited. Nothing. Good, she was making progress. She looked down at the floor and called Anthony's name again. This time, Anthony showed up.

"Still experimenting? Can I help in any way?"

Annamaria beamed. "You are helping. And I just figured out the last detail. Thank you."

"Does that mean I have to leave again?"

"Yes."

Annamaria undid the first spell, her walls flashed bright blue again. She repeated the incantation one more time, grabbed the blue square and guided it around her walls, up over her ceiling, and onto the floor. She did the same thing in her bathroom. Annamaria called Anthony's name one more time. He didn't come. "Yes! Yes! Yes!" Annamaria danced, cheered, and clapped.

She threw open her door and started running down the hall. Before she got halfway, Anthony appeared and hugged her tight. "Annamaria, are you okay?"

She giggled. "Yes. Why do you look so scared?"

"Suddenly I heard nothing. I thought whatever you were doing had gone wrong, and you were hurt, or worse…"

"No, everything went right."

She grabbed his hand and towed him toward her room. She stopped at the door. "Wait here." Annamaria returned to her room and shut the door. She sang and yelled and knocked on the walls. She opened the door to Anthony's stunned face.

"Why can't I hear anything?"

"I cast a sound barrier spell." Annamaria bounced on the balls of her feet.

Anthony didn't respond right away. "Wow, that's great." His smile didn't convince Annamaria.

Annamaria didn't miss the tone of his voice. "Wait. Do you like to listen—"

"Annamaria." Marianna appeared, Will right behind her. "What did you do? Your room has no sound." Her eyes were shining.

"I cast a sound barrier spell." Annamaria beamed. Marianna would understand.

Marianna gasped. "Really? Go inside your room and say something."

Annamaria skipped inside, shut her door, and made noise again. No response. Annamaria opened her door again, and Marianna's smile reached her ears. "This is brilliant. It's like your room is a black hole for sound. I wish I could have figured this out when I was the witch surrounded by vampires."

"Caroline didn't have her own version?"

"Well, she wouldn't have chosen to if she did." Marianna looked away briefly.

Will frowned with his arms folded across his chest. "Is this a good idea? Us not being able to hear her?"

"Will, this is Annamaria's first spell she created on her own, and it's amazing," said Marianna.

"Obviously." Will rolled his eyes. "I'm not talking about how amazing the magic is. I'm talking about the implications. Is it wise for us to not hear her? What if she plans something, and we aren't prepared?"

Annamaria snorted. "What am I going to do? I'm outnumbered by five to one. I just want some privacy. You guys have your quiet talking thing. Now I have this."

Will opened his mouth, but Anthony cut him off. "It's not really about distrust. I worry about your safety. What if something happens to you while you're in here? No one would know."

Marianna snickered. "Anthony, don't make me laugh. Her safety? Yeah right." She gave him a look and rolled her eyes, then turned to Annamaria. "Let's talk in my room while these two work out their nonsensical issues."

Once inside Marianna's room, she gestured to the gold and silver walls. "Can you show me how you did the spell? Step by step?"

"Sure." Annamaria's magic hummed.

She showed Marianna the blue square and talked her through how the barrier worked, going through each level of the barrier she had done with Anthony. Marianna's gaze followed the blue like a kid in a candy factory.

Together, they experimented with whether the inhabitant of the room could hear anything from outside. The spell worked both ways. This posed a problem. Annamaria would like to know when someone approached her room. With a slight change in the incantation, *caveasonus*, Annamaria could prevent sound from leaving Marianna's room but could hear normal sounds from just outside the room—knocking, someone yelling, or running. She then changed her own room before rejoining Marianna.

"This is amazing," Marianna said. "Just imagine

what kind of witch you'd be right now if you were raised as one."

Annamaria sighed. "Yeah, I've been thinking about a lot of different 'what-ifs' since coming here. But I have no room to complain. You had it worse. Being raised by someone who wasn't family, and getting screwed over by a pack of vampires to boot."

"Coven," Marianna corrected her, smiling. "Werewolves live in packs, vampires live in covens, just like witches. Oh, this is so exciting. Let's write it down."

Annamaria summoned both books. As Marianna wrote, her eyes darted with the sweep of her pen, taking deep breaths and letting out soft squeals.

"Marianna, why don't you keep your book? I'll show you everything I discover, and we both can record the spells. You can continue your book and continue to be a part of the magic."

"I would love that. Thank you." Marianna's eyes shined.

When she finished writing, she sat down on her bed, patting the spot next to her. Annamaria sat down, and they spent the next hour talking and laughing in their sound bubble.

"What do you like about Will?" Annamaria asked toward the end of the conversation.

"Well, he was the first vampire I ran into after leaving Diego's coven. He brought me here and showed me how his house lived. He accepted me and my past without judgment and helped me find you and Trinity," Marianna said.

Annamaria wondered if Marianna was aware of the private run-ins between herself and Will over the past several weeks. There was no way she didn't. What did Marianna think of those? Did she have enough romantic power over him to make him stop?

"He just doesn't seem like an amiable person." Annamaria played with her hands.

Marianna pursed her lips. "He's a tough shell to crack, but you can't help the one you love."

"You love him?"

"Yes, I do."

"Does he love you?"

"Yes, I believe so."

"Enough to leave me alone if you asked him to?"

Marianna pulled her hair over her shoulder and twisted it.

Annamaria placed her hand on her sister's knee. "I haven't wanted to involve you. I know it's not fair to ask you to get in the middle of this, but I just—"

"I have been asking him to stop." Marianna let go of her hair. "I'm so sorry. It's caused a lot of drama between us, but I've been hiding it. I don't know what else to do. This is his kingdom, and he is not used to being challenged."

Annamaria took in a deep breath, her heart hurting for Marianna. "Oh Marianna, I'm so sorry. You don't have to fend for me anymore. I'll figure something out, okay? I don't want you to feel you have to choose between me and him." Annamaria hugged Marianna, and Marianna hugged her back.

"Thanks," Marianna said. "I guess I'm not a great sister."

Annamaria rubbed her arm. "We are both learning."

Marianna squeezed her hand. "Yes. Do you mind

undoing the spell on my room? I don't mind being heard anymore."

During dinner, Annamaria told Sandy all about her sound barrier spell.

Sandy's eyes grew wide, and her lips parted. "Can you do that to my room?"

After dinner, Annamaria put the spell on Sandy's room. Sandy's face lit up watching the blue light. She tried it out by standing outside the door and pressing her ear to it while Annamaria made noise inside. Sandy reentered her room laughing and clapping.

Afterward, both Marianna and Annamaria spent time in the herb garden to gather some herbs to begin potion lessons. Marianna kept expressing her excitement since she could brew potions herself—she would be a participant, not just a verbal instructor. When they returned to the house, Will and Anthony were waiting by the door. Marianna narrowed her eyes at Will, put her hands on her hips, and stared at him.

Will dropped to both of his knees and took Marianna's hands in his. "Baby, I'm so sorry for questioning you today. I know next to nothing about magic and witches. Forgive me?"

Annamaria scrunched her face. She just could not understand the conflicting power dynamic between the two. Marianna's lips curved upward, and she ran her fingers through Will's hair. She raised him up and kissed him so long, Annamaria shifted and looked down.

"I forgive you, my love."

Will growled, scooped Marianna up, and zoomed upstairs.

Annamaria groaned, shaking her head. "They have

no shame." She headed toward the stairs as well, her arms full of herbs.

"Can I accompany you?" Anthony asked. His hands were clasped behind his back, his head bowed.

Annamaria sighed. "Yeah, I suppose."

She walked to her room, not checking to see if Anthony followed her. She allowed him into her room and shut the door. At least the rest of the house wouldn't hear their conversation now.

"Annamaria, I'm so sorry for earlier today. I was wrong to expect you to be okay with having your privacy imposed upon."

"What's the real reason you like to listen to me when I'm in here?" Annamaria had her hands on her hips.

Anthony looked into Annamaria's eyes. "I know you're physically safe, but I hear you cry and sometimes scream at night. I worry about you."

Annamaria looked away and shook her head. Of course he heard her nightmares. She should just deny them. There was no way she could tell him what they were about, but Anthony had been honest just now. Annamaria owed him some honesty, too.

"I have a recurring nightmare about traveling here."

"Oh Annamaria, I'm so sorry. Do you want to talk about it?" Anthony stepped toward her. Annamaria sat down on her bed, and Anthony sat next to her.

"I don't know." Annamaria played with the ends of her hair. "They are just dreams. They started after Will and I fought for the first time. I just don't understand why he's connected to the attack back home, or why you are there, too. I mean, you weren't in Wyoming."

Annamaria peeked at Anthony.

"I'm in this nightmare?" Anthony grabbed her hands. "Annamaria, I never want you to be afraid of me. I will never hurt you."

Annamaria shifted but did not pull her hands away. "That's what's so confusing. During the day, you're so kind, and I think I feel safe. But at night in my dreams, you're with him, and there's blood everywhere. I just feel so conflicted. I'm becoming friends with all of you, but I can't forget what you are and what you do."

Annamaria pulled her hands out of Anthony's and hugged herself, hiding her face in her chest. Her cheeks were burning. Anthony's gentle fingers pulled her chin up. Annamaria squeezed her eyes shut but forced herself to open them. Once again, Anthony's face held no hint of anger or hurt. How was he so good at controlling his emotions?

"I don't kill," he said.

"You don't?"

Anthony shook his head. "I don't. At least, not anymore. The early years are hard as a vampire figures things out. I don't have a clean record, but it's been over a hundred years since I have last killed a human."

"How do you manage?"

Will had said Marianna had amazing self-control because of her witch background. He made it sound like traditional vampires struggled with control. So while she never pictured her sister as a killer, she wasn't sure about the others.

Anthony looked away. "It's not a perfect solution. I don't know exactly what you may have witnessed or learned from Will and Marianna already, but we can control how much venom we secrete into our prey. So I just do enough to make them loopy, and I don't drink too much. Then I leave them in a safe place."

Annamaria tried very hard to keep a poker face. "Won't they remember and tell people?"

"Well, when they wake up, they think they were high or drunk, and they were hallucinating." Anthony shrugged.

Annamaria sighed. "You're right. It isn't perfect, but I will admit it's better than killing."

Anthony's body relaxed, but he still looked hesitant. They were saved from the awkward silence creeping in by a knock on Annamaria's door. A beaming Kylie was on the other side of the door.

"Your debut video just got published! Do you want to watch it with us?"

Annamaria gasped and smiled. "Oh my gosh, yes. Come on." She beckoned to Anthony. He grinned and followed her to the living room.

The first routine was a Viennese waltz. They told the story of a man and woman meeting and falling in love. Tyler and Annamaria portrayed a couple starting off as shy, then blossoming into comfortable and loving. The entire process had been so fun, like swaying through clouds.

Will and Marianna were also in the living room for the showing. Marianna sat on Will's lap. Both of them relaxed into each other, faint smiles on their faces. Tyler plugged his laptop into the large flat screen.

"Everyone take your seats," he said as Kylie, Annamaria, and Anthony walked in.

Annamaria sat on the love seat, and Anthony joined her. Kylie sat on the floor in front of them. The TV showed the preview screenshot of Annamaria with her right arm around Tyler's neck, the left trailing behind her with her left foot popped. Tyler's right arm was around her waist, his left trailing behind him. Both leaned away from each other in a frozen twirl. Tyler clicked play and ran to the couch by Will and Marianna.

Kylie and Tyler were in the ballroom wearing practice clothes. "Hello, moonlight dancers," Tyler said. "We have a special announcement for you. This video is the first of a new series called Reunited."

"Reunited is a special story we are excited to tell," Kylie said. "But we don't want to give everything away just now. So put on your critical thinking hats and let us know in the comments what you notice in the story."

"We will also use this series to introduce a new dancer to our family, Selene. This is her debut performance, and we hope you will give her the same love and support you have given us," Tyler said.

The screen faded to an empty ballroom. Annamaria tucked her knees to her chest and bit down on the tops of her knees. Selene was her mom's name, and their hope was no one would recognize her in heavy makeup and studio lights. Marianna's gaze twinkled at her from across the room.

The music started, and Annamaria danced into view. Tyler danced in from the opposite direction, and the duet began. They spun and swayed, Annamaria's light blue dress swirling around her, the rhinestones catching the light. For the last verse of the song, Annamaria completed a seamless onstage costume change by using magic to replace her blue dress to a flowing white gown. Their human audience would think it was just superb editing.

When the video ended, Annamaria had tears in her eyes. Representing her mom in such a beautiful way was an honor. She looked around at her new friends.

"Annamaria, Tyler, that was beautiful." Marianna's hand pressed to her heart.

"Now, will you be willing to play the piano for us?" Tyler nudged Marianna's leg with his elbow.

"I don't know." Marianna looked down, a small smile forming.

Annamaria straightened up. "Do it! Don't you think it would be so wonderful for both of us to work on this?"

"Maybe for the final number," Marianna said.

"Yay!" Annamaria, Kylie, and Tyler cheered.

"That was beautiful to watch," Anthony whispered in Annamaria's ear. "You were beautiful to watch."

****

Selene became an internet sensation overnight. The likes and comments came rolling in. Kylie and Tyler were ecstatic, and Annamaria's head spun. She never in her wildest dreams imagined she would dance with the likes of Kylie and Tyler *and* receive such worldwide popularity. She had taken her first small step back into the human world. Annamaria could live in both worlds.

Trinity's reaction was the only thing that worried Annamaria. She feared Trinity would tell her to stop because she risked exposing herself.

"You danced so beautifully! And using your mom's name, I loved it. You should be fine to keep dancing. Unfortunately, I actually have to hide this phone for the time being. So don't try to contact me anymore until I contact you."

Annamaria looked at her phone. "Why?"

"Because I'm in disguise, and I can't risk connecting myself to you and accidentally sending someone after you."

"Okay." Annamaria pouted.

"I love you. Keep working hard. Be safe."

"You too."

The next episode in the series detailed the murder of Annamaria and Marianna's parents. Kylie danced the part of Valentina, while Tyler and Annamaria returned for their original roles as her parents. They danced a paso doble. Annamaria and Tyler rotated, fighting with Kylie and trying to protect one another. Kylie whirled fast and ferocious around the floor, striking with quick and efficient movements. Annamaria used her magic to produce fire, flashes of lightning, and raise Kylie up into the air for dramatic effect. In the end, Kylie overpowered the other two, and Annamaria and Tyler lay dead on the floor as Kylie stood over them in her final pose of triumph.

During the editing, Annamaria contemplated Kylie's and Tyler's own experiences as victims of violence. She still did not know exactly how one became a vampire but was certain a mortal death was part of the process. What had Kylie's and Tyler's deaths been like?

"Can I ask you two a personal question?"

"Sure," Kylie said, as Tyler worked on his laptop.

"How did you two become vampires?"

"Will changed us," said Kylie. Annamaria's mouth popped open. "As you can tell by this house, his family is filthy rich. His younger brother is the last living sibling, and he currently funds Will's lifestyle. Anyway, he used to throw these parties where half the guests were vampires and half were human. The whole point was to provide a wild ruckus for the vampires to snack and play. We scored an invitation without knowing what we were getting ourselves into. When we figured out what was going on, we begged Will to change us."

"You wanted to change?"

"It was change or get eaten." Tyler shrugged. "What would you have picked?" Annamaria didn't answer, but grimaced and nodded.

"Will agreed, and he separated us from the rest of the party to avoid accidents. He changed us the next day." Kylie's voice and face were nonchalant.

Annamaria lowered her gaze. She couldn't imagine what it would feel like to choose between death and vampirism. "Are you happy with your choice?"

"We could see the silver lining." Kylie smiled. "In that moment, we wanted to save our lives. And afterward, we recognized this would be wonderful for our dancing career. Our bodies will never change. No weight gain, no pregnancies, we don't sweat or get tired, the chances of injury are pretty much nonexistent."

"But we had to sacrifice attending competitions and performances in person." Tyler raised a finger. "It would have been unfair and eventually noticeable for us to perform with perfect ease, not to mention the not aging thing. So we started our channel. Humans ignore the passage of time online, so we can get away with looking fifteen years younger than we actually are."

"I'm so sorry." Annamaria loved dancing on stage to a live audience.

"It's not a big deal." Tyler clicked "save" on his

edits. "We still accept performance invitations every once in a while, provided we don't have to arrive until after sundown. We just don't compete anymore. And this online thing has been great."

"How do you become a vampire?" Annamaria played with her hands.

Kylie looked at Tyler. He nodded. "The vampire who changes you drinks as much of your blood as they can without killing you. Then you drink their blood. Then they kill you. Or they kill your body, anyway. Their blood in your system keeps you from truly dying and changes you. And it has to be the same vampire throughout the process, or the change won't work because drinking each other's blood connects you."

Annamaria shuddered. Tyler grabbed Annamaria's hand and rubbed her knuckles. "You don't have to worry, dear. Your magic is much too valuable for us to give up."

Kylie glared at him. "We also like you for who you are, not just your magic."

Annamaria scoffed, then pursed her lips, smiling a little. Whatever selfish reasons each vampire had for keeping her mortal, she was glad she wasn't in danger of being turned.

****

Annamaria spent so much time choreographing, practicing, and recording with Kylie and Tyler, she had decreased her time with everyone else. She wanted to keep dancing, but she had abandoned her original people. What should she do? She should at least be more conscientious of her time. Annamaria apologized to Sandy at dinner one night.

"Not to worry, dear." Sandy waved her hand. "You

need to bond with the others. I'm thrilled for you. Just continue to eat dinner with me. I've grown accustomed to it and don't want to go back to my solo dinners." Sandy winked.

Annamaria smiled and nodded. Over her many dinners and gardening with Sandy, she had learned that Sandy's son, Daniel, had not returned home since going to college. Instead, Sandy visited him for a couple of weeks each summer and for a week each Christmas vacation. This summer, she planned to visit for the first two weeks of July, which was a week away.

Annamaria continued to involve Marianna in her magical study. She worked on her own at first, but once she perfected a spell, she would go through everything with Marianna, and the two would write in their books together. Sometimes, Annamaria would get stumped and tell Marianna what she was trying to accomplish, and Marianna would make suggestions based on her previous knowledge, which led to success.

Marianna also started teaching Annamaria potions. "Unlike spells, potions are exact and do not vary from witch to witch." Marianna owned several potion books they used to practice brewing from.

"It's just like following a recipe." Annamaria skimmed the instructions with her finger.

Marianna giggled. "Yes."

"So could humans make a potion?"

Marianna looked thoughtful. "Technically, yes. Anyone can, as long as they have the ingredient that truly makes a potion work."

"Which is what?" Annamaria looked up from the book.

"Witch's blood."

Annamaria looked back down at the sleeping potion instructions. "I don't see that in here."

"It's not printed on purpose." Marianna placed their pot of ingredients on the stove's burner. "No witch, Black Market or otherwise, wants to be hunted for their blood."

Annamaria let out a nervous giggle. "That makes sense."

Marianna suggested Annamaria have a constant storage of healing potions, sleeping potions, and memory potions, as those were a witch's staple.

Annamaria hadn't been on the news in weeks, yet Will refused to lift his prison sentence. Anthony tried to calm her temper by accessing the latest movies and television shows, taking long walks outside in the moonlight, reading in the library, and painting in his room. He hadn't attempted to kiss her again or touch her at all. Annamaria didn't believe he had given up on her because she caught him staring at her constantly. Annamaria made sure not to send any more mixed signals because she still wasn't sure if she wanted to move on from Cody. Kylie and Tyler took things out of her hands when they brought the subject up during the third routine of the Reunited series.

This routine was to be a contemporary duet between Annamaria and Kylie. Kylie danced the role of Marianna, while Annamaria danced as herself. Annamaria summoned a wall right down the middle of the dance floor. At the beginning of the choreography, Annamaria and Kylie danced right next to the wall, mirroring each other. Annamaria then constructed two magical costume changes. Their first costumes were overall shorts, with Kylie in a rhinestoned pink T-shirt and Annamaria in purple. Their second costumes were floral dresses ending above the knee. For their third set, Annamaria transformed Kylie's costume into a black bodysuit while she changed into a flowy pastel yellow dress that ended halfway down her shin. With each magical costume change, Annamaria's choreography led her farther away from the wall, no longer mirroring Kylie. Kylie's choreography kept her clinging to the wall, trying to reach out to Annamaria.

Annamaria's heart ached watching Kylie's run-through. However, she believed the process was important to her and Marianna's healing, regardless of how uncomfortable parts of it made her.

Tyler watched the end of the routine with a thoughtful expression. "I'm trying to decide if this would be a good time to bring in myself as your ex, Cody. How serious were you two?"

Annamaria surrounded the three of them in a sound barrier spell.

"This must be juicy since you're blocking the rest of the house from listening." Tyler chuckled as the bright blue box surrounded them before disappearing.

Annamaria rolled her eyes. "I wouldn't say juicy. I just want to tell Ant...the others on my own terms." Tyler and Kylie exchanged looks. Annamaria relayed her history about Cody, his sisters, his dad, and her aunt. "I thought I loved him on prom night." Annamaria put her face in her hands. "He wanted to have sex, and I wasn't ready, so I ran up to my room. Then Trinity appeared and sent him away. She introduced me to Marianna and unlocked my powers. I couldn't tell him what was going on, so he broke up with me. And then Trinity, Marianna, and I got attacked, and I had to come here. But then he shows up on the news like he still cares? I'm just so confused."

Kylie put her hand on Annamaria's back and rubbed it. "Oh sweetie, I know it's hard. Relationships are hard." She pulled Annamaria into her arms and hugged her.

Tyler patted Annamaria's shoulder. "So I'm going to keep this number just the two of you. The next part of the story we will have Cody and a Diego-Will hybrid character."

Tyler opened the routine by speaking to the camera to explain the couple from their previous recording had two daughters who were separated after their parents' death. They finished up the final bits of choreography, ran through the routine a few times, and called it a day. While they were packing up, Kylie pulled Annamaria aside.

"Come have a girls' chat in my room?"

"Sure."

Once up there, Annamaria cast the sound barrier spell around them.

"What's up?"

"It's obvious you still have feelings for Cody, but have you thought about your feelings for Anthony?" Annamaria was about to claim they were just friends, but Kylie put a hand up. "Don't even try to lie to me, girl."

"I just don't know." Annamaria sighed. "He makes me feel safe and happy, and he treats me really well, but I don't even know if I'm still Cody's girlfriend or not. Yes, he broke up with me, but on more of a condition. He said if I was honest with him, things could work. So when I can tell him, he'll take me back.

I guess I'm still hoping I'll get to see Cody again and figure things out."

Kylie gave her a half smile. "Sweetie, you and Cody don't belong in the same world anymore."

"I'm still mortal." Annamaria folded her arms.

"Yes, but you are going to outlive him by about nine hundred years." Kylie's eyes were sympathetic.

"What? Marianna didn't tell me—"

"I imagine she has been too focused on getting your magic up to par, and she forgot to mention it. Witches can live for around a thousand years. You won't even look older than thirty when Cody is a grandpa."

Annamaria's heart deflated. Yes, it was exciting she would live for several centuries and stay young for most of them. But now she and Cody were incompatible because of it?

"Well, Anthony is going to outlive me by forever." Annamaria flipped her hair behind her shoulder.

"Spending a thousand years with someone is better than only ninety. Look, I'm not telling you what to do. I care about you, and I care about Anthony, so I just wanted to give you some information to think about."

Annamaria spent the next few days thinking about what Kylie had said. She wasn't quite ready to give up on Cody, but she also didn't know when or if she would see him again. Anthony was right here, and the lure Annamaria experienced around him threatened to yank her the rest of the way. Over the next several days, Annamaria sat closer to Anthony, laughed with more energy, placing her hand on his shoulder as she did so, and made eye contact with him when they talked.

One night during a walk outside, Anthony snuck

his fingers through hers. Annamaria tightened her grip and smiled at him. They held hands the rest of the night, Anthony rubbing circles over Annamaria's knuckles. Her pulse raised from his touch. And Anthony returned to kissing her hand each night before bed. She welcomed the tingles back when his lips touched her skin.

The next time they watched TV together, Anthony progressed to putting his arm over her shoulder. Annamaria leaned into his chest, hugging her stomach. She couldn't remember what they watched because she was so concentrated on her breathing.

****

Kylie kicked Annamaria out of her own bedroom for the remainder of June. She had a surprise planned, which for some reason required Annamaria to bunk with her sister. Kylie refused to say anything, and Marianna only giggled and winked. Over the next several days, Annamaria looked for clues among the other members of the house and the house itself but found nothing.

Sandy, Marianna, and Will were tasked with distracting Annamaria while Kylie, Tyler, and Anthony worked on the surprise. Will even temporarily lifted Annamaria's prison sentence and allowed Sandy to take her into town. No incidences happened. Just as she predicted.

On the first day of July, Sandy left to visit her son. She gave Annamaria a long, tight hug goodbye. "I wish I could take you with me. I just know you and Daniel would get along." After Sandy drove away, Annamaria found herself surrounded by Kylie, Tyler, Anthony, and Marianna.

"We have a surprise for you," Kylie said.

"Really? I had no idea."

Everyone laughed.

"But you need to put this on." Tyler held out a blindfold.

Annamaria took a step back.

"You'll get your room back," Marianna said.

"Okay." Annamaria sighed and closed her eyes. Tyler tied the blindfold around her head. Tyler and Anthony each took one of her hands and led her down the hall, Marianna's and Kylie's footsteps sounding behind. Tyler stopped everyone at the stairs.

"Let's just zoom her up the stairs. I'm too excited."

"No! We need to do this nice and slow to build the suspense," said Kylie.

"Okay, you guys are really making me nervous." Annamaria tried to wiggle out of Anthony's and Tyler's hands.

"Will you trust me?" Anthony asked.

Annamaria blushed and continued following Anthony's and Tyler's lead. When they got to the top of the stairs, they continued to walk the full length of the hall. Annamaria heard a door open. Tyler let go of her hand, and only Anthony guided her in. The blindfold was removed. Annamaria looked at her room and took a deep intake of breath. The walls, once plain cream, were now a midnight blue background with larger-than-life dancing figures. One of them even had Annamaria's red hair. A new comforter covered her bed, midnight blue covered in small silver sparkles. The bathroom was a light purple and decorated in lavender.

"Oh my gosh, is this for me?" Annamaria's eyes brimmed with tears.

"It is." Anthony's eyes sparkled.

"We want you to be officially part of the family." Tyler hugged her from behind. "And everyone else's rooms are just as extravagant. We couldn't let you keep the plain room you used to have."

Annamaria's tears spilled over. Her three friends and sister surrounded her and gave her a big group hug.

"I miss being able to cry." Kylie gave an exaggerated sniffle.

"Me too," Tyler said. They both made sobbing noises. Annamaria's cries turned into giggles.

"Thank you so much." Annamaria wiped her eyes with a tissue Anthony handed her. "This means so much. I love you all." Kylie and Tyler both kissed her on the cheek, leaving the same tingle Anthony's kisses caused. Annamaria touched her cheeks and grinned. "I don't need to ask who painted the walls." He smiled at his feet, and Kylie, Tyler, and Marianna snuck out of the room.

"You've been inspiring me for the past month."

Annamaria walked around the room to study each figure. The figures were in positions from the different routines Annamaria danced with Kylie and Tyler, but Anthony had made each figure unique in their features.

"You have incredible talent." She smiled at him, playing with his fingers.

"You do too." Anthony tucked some hair behind her ear, tracing her jawline.

Annamaria blushed and looked away. Why did she have to get so nervous whenever he touched her? She walked into the bathroom with the intent to ignore the pounding in her chest and the squirming in her stomach. She grabbed her hairbrush and brushed her hair up into a ponytail. Her heart pounded as Anthony followed her into the bathroom.

"Back in high school, we were reading *Little Women* in my English class. Have you read it?"

"Mmm hmmm"

"It used to bug me. I was jealous of Jo and all of her sisters because I didn't have a proper family. But I guess, now, I realize I don't need to be biologically connected to have a family."

What the heck was that? What a lame thing to say.

"Yeah, biology would get in the way." Anthony's voice was right in her ear. Goosebumps erupted along her neck and arms.

Annamaria turned around. He was right there. Of course he was. She had seen him in the mirror and heard him in her ear. Anthony placed his hands on her waist and lifted her up onto the bathroom counter, leveling their eyes with each other. Annamaria stopped breathing. She was dangerously close to the point of no return. This time she kept her head up as Anthony placed his lips on hers. Annamaria closed her eyes and kissed him back, her lips exploding in tingles. Anthony wrapped his arms around the small of Annamaria's back and tugged her closer. She wrapped her arms around his neck and trailed her fingers through his hair.

Annamaria didn't think she could kiss anyone other than Cody. She feared she could not adapt to Anthony's style. But as her lips moved with Anthony's, she was able to follow him. Her blood rushed, her magic hummed, and she beamed through the best kiss she ever had.

When they leaned away, Annamaria couldn't breathe, or look at Anthony, or do anything other than listen to her heart pound in her eardrums. Anthony hauled her off the counter and took her hands in his. "I'll give you some time to enjoy your room on your own." He kissed both of her hands, then zoomed out of her room. When he was gone, Annamaria fell onto her new bedspread and stared up at the ceiling, smiling, squealing, hyperventilating, and heart beating in frantic bursts.

Chapter 15 Daniel

No one said anything after Annamaria and Anthony kissed, but everyone threw them knowing looks, winks, and thumbs-ups. Annamaria and Anthony didn't discuss what they were right away. They simply followed their desires, which was lots of kissing.

The next video in the Reunited series was published as a duet between Kylie and Tyler, telling the story of Marianna's upbringing. They combined Diego and Will into one character danced by Tyler. In a contemporary piece, Tyler took Kylie away from her solitude, with her fighting him every chance she got. They also left out the vampire element in their story. Kylie would keep her powers but become captive to Tyler. Annamaria used her magic to create the illusion of Kylie doing magic for the routine. By the end of the routine, Kylie submitted to Tyler.

On the morning of the Fourth of July, Kylie and Tyler called everyone into the living room. "We want the whole family to go out tonight," said Tyler. "We want to go into town at sunset and party with the humans."

"That sounds like fun, but what if someone recognizes Annamaria? Perhaps she should stay behind for her safety," Will said.

Annamaria gritted her teeth and clenched her hands.

"I'm pretty sure most people will be too drunk to recognize her. And besides, all of us are going to be there," Kylie said.

Will and Marianna looked at each other, and Marianna's eyes were pleading. "Sounds like a plan." Will licked his lips. "I haven't partied in a while." He winked at Annamaria. Annamaria looked away. Will hadn't accosted her since she threatened him with a fireball, but he still liked to make faces at her and sneak in snide comments whenever he could.

"Excellent." Kylie rubbed her hands. "Us girls have matching tops to put on."

"Oh, I don't think that's necessary." Marianna shifted her weight.

She and Kylie did not dress remotely similar. Kylie wore bright colors at every opportunity.

"Oh come on," said Annamaria. "It will be fun."

"Just try it on." Kylie batted her eyelashes.

Marianna sighed. "Fine."

The three girls bounded upstairs to Kylie's room. "Tada!" she sang, producing three white tank tops. Across each bodice was a rhinestone US flag pointing horizontally down the front. At the bra line, the rhinestones changed to red and white fringe.

Annamaria put hers on and twisted her torso, making the fringe dance. Kylie twirled, and the fringe flared out. Marianna cracked a smile, looking at the three of them in Kylie's mirror. "Okay, I'll wear it."

Annamaria and Kylie jumped up and down, squealed, and hugged Marianna. The girls spent the day together in Kylie's room. They curled each other's hair, applied their makeup, and helped each other pick out the perfect shoes. When they headed down the stairs, the boys were speechless.

"Fabulous," said Tyler, spinning Kylie under his arm.

Will looked from one sister to another. "Damn, if Annamaria's blood didn't smell so irresistible, I wouldn't be able to tell you two apart." Marianna rolled her eyes. Anthony hit Will in the stomach.

"What is wrong with you? Why are you so disgusting?"

Will chuckled. "No need to get territorial. I won't do anything."

He threw his arm over Marianna's shoulders and led her toward the garage. Tyler and Kylie jumped into Tyler's car and zoomed off. Marianna and Will followed in Will's car. There were two cars left in the garage, Kylie's and Anthony's. Anthony opened the passenger door for Annamaria, and she climbed in.

"Why are we taking so many cars?"

"Because the others are probably going to return with guests." Anthony avoided Annamaria's eyes. Her stomach churned. She sighed. There was nothing she could do about it.

"I'll make sure we stay away from them." Anthony took Annamaria's hand as they drove out of the gate. Cody used to take her hand like this when he drove his truck. Annamaria pulled her hand out of Anthony's.

"Sorry," she said.

Anthony seemed to get used to the trial-and-error experiences with Annamaria in their physical relationship. He wrapped his arm around her shoulders and played with her hair while he focused on the road.

They entered town to a celebration like what Annamaria experienced in Harrison. Once out of the car, they followed the crowd to the high school football field to watch the fireworks. Both Kylie and Tyler already had human dates they were cuddling with. Marianna was snuggled up against Will. Annamaria and Anthony sat down with the group, and Anthony put his arm around her waist, scooting her so their sides were pressed into each other. With the first explosion of red, white, and blue, Annamaria laid her head on Anthony's shoulder. Anthony rubbed her back throughout the whole show.

At the conclusion of the fireworks, their little group clapped along with the rest of the town. "We are going to the bar!" Tyler called out to the rest of them. "It's the only place open after this." Both Tyler's and Kylie's dates were dragging them toward a lit up building with the sign "Al's Place."

"Do you want to go?" Anthony asked Annamaria.

"Sure. I don't drink though. Do vampires drink?"

Anthony chuckled. "Only if it's mixed with blood. But there is a dance floor and soda."

Annamaria brightened. "Okay."

When they entered the building, Annamaria looked around for a bouncer or a security guard to check her ID, which she didn't have. However, no one stopped her. Perhaps the busyness of the holiday made checking IDs too difficult for the employees. After looking around, Annamaria grabbed Anthony's hand and led him to the dance floor. He was no Tyler, but she had a lot of fun following his casual lead. Kylie and Tyler were making out with their dates, and Marianna and Will were off in a corner, talking to a police officer.

"Do you guys know the people in town?" Annamaria spun under Anthony's arm.

Anthony shook his head. "No, not really."

"Then what's going on with the police?"

Anthony glanced at Marianna and Will. "He's just checking them out since they aren't locals." Will gestured to the dance floor. "Looks like they're covering for us, too."

A couple of songs later, Kylie broke free from her date and grabbed Annamaria and Marianna, leading them to the center of the floor. The other women joined, which lead to appreciative cheers from the men. Annamaria and Marianna spent the song hip-bumping, spinning each other, and shimmying. When the song faded out and a new one began, a stranger broke through the crowd and asked Annamaria to dance. She hesitated. The last time she danced with a stranger, she was almost hypnotized out of the building. "Don't worry, he's human," Marianna's voice whispered in her ear. Annamaria accepted his invitation.

Annamaria had no trouble following his lead. She relaxed, interacting with another human. "You look familiar," the guy said. "Do you live here?"

Annamaria shook her head. "No, just visiting."

"Hm… I know I've seen you someplace."

"Maybe the fireworks?" Annamaria's heart sped up.

"Yeah, maybe." He shrugged. They finished the dance with the guy dipping Annamaria. "I know!" The guy pulled Annamaria back up. "You look like that girl on the news."

"Oh, I'm not her." Annamaria ran into the crowd.

An hour later, Annamaria fell asleep at a table in the back. "Are you ready to head back?" Anthony gently shook her shoulder.

"What? Oh, yes please." Annamaria yawned.

"Can I carry you?"

"Mmm hmm."

Anthony cradled her to his chest and walked to his car. As he placed Annamaria in the passenger seat, two beams of light hit them. "Sir, is she okay?" asked an authoritative voice. Annamaria opened her eyes and could make out two police officers.

"Oh, yes," said Anthony. "She's just tired. We are going home now."

"Mind if we check for ourselves?" asked the officer, though his tone made it clear he wasn't asking.

"Okay." Anthony's hand stayed on Annamaria's knee. The beams of light dropped to the ground, and the two officers walked closer. One of them lowered himself into a squat.

"Miss, are you oka... Wait a minute, hang on. What's your name?"

Before Annamaria could answer, a third officer joined them. "Captain, the Hunter boys are trashing the bar again. I need help."

The officer whose light shone on Annamaria's face swore. "I'll join you in a minute. I need to make sure she's all right."

"Sir, it's urgent," said the other cop in the dark.

"I will join you in a minute. Damn, Stevens! Let me do my job. What's your name, sweetie?"

"Selene," Annamaria said.

"And do you know this man?"

"Yes, he's my boyfriend."

"Okay, drive safe, you two."

"Thank you," said Anthony.

The first part of the drive up the mountain was

silent.

"Why did you lie to the police?" Anthony asked.

"Because they think I was kidnapped, and I wasn't. How am I supposed to explain any of this to the police?" Annamaria groaned. "Please don't tell Will, or he won't let me out of the house again."

"I won't, I promise." Anthony squeezed her knee and slid his hand up her thigh. "So am I your boyfriend?"

Annamaria huffed. "I don't know. It just seemed the easiest thing to say at the time." Anthony chuckled and stopped talking. Annamaria leaned against the window and struggled to keep her eyes open. Anthony traced circles on her leg with his free hand.

When they got to the house, Annamaria wandered to the kitchen and downed an entire bottle of water. By the time she finished, the rest of the house arrived. Both Kylie and Tyler had their dates with them and were taking them up the stairs. Marianna and Will also held a person balanced between them. Marianna avoided looking in Annamaria's direction.

"Oh, I am not sleeping upstairs if that is going on right next door, and across the hall, and all over."

"I could make a bed on the couch for you? I'll stay in the living room with you." Anthony rubbed her shoulders.

Annamaria slumped into his chest. "Yes, thank you."

She dragged her feet into the living room while Anthony zoomed upstairs and returned with a pillow and a blanket. Annamaria laid down, and Anthony tucked her in. He kissed her on the lips as she fell asleep. Later on, Annamaria woke up to the sound of the door closing.

"Who's there?" She sat up, her heart pounding.

"It's just me."

Annamaria flopped back down and breathed. "Where were you?"

"Just getting some fresh air." Anthony took her hand and kissed her as she drifted back to sleep.

****

A couple of days after their adventure into town, Sandy returned early without a heads-up. She strolled in from the garage door with a young man who Annamaria was sure was Sandy's son. He was taller than his mom, with a wider build than the other males in the house, and had Sandy's dirty blond hair. Kylie, Tyler, and Anthony all greeted him with smiles and hugs, commenting on how much he had grown in four years. He and Will nodded at each other.

"This is my son, Daniel." Sandy wrapped her arm around his waist. "This is Marianna." Marianna and Daniel shook hands, letting go after a split second. Marianna's hand trembled. "And this is Annamaria." Sandy gave Annamaria a tight side hug.

"It's nice to meet you." Annamaria shook Daniel's hand. "Your mom talks about you a lot."

Daniel smiled, but it didn't reach his eyes. "Likewise. I've heard a lot about you as well." His gaze bore into Annamaria until she looked away.

"Oh?"

Still in the side hug, Sandy squeezed Annamaria's shoulders. "It's because Annamaria is my favorite person in the house. Well, second favorite now my son is back."

"What? I thought I was your favorite?" Tyler

winked. "Annamaria is everyone's favorite right now."

Annamaria kept her lips pursed as she forced a smile. "Dinner is almost ready, but I didn't know you were coming. I can quickly make more, though."

"Let me help," said Sandy.

"Not to worry, you've been traveling. A simple spell will do the trick." Annamaria waved off Sandy.

Sandy and Daniel followed her into the kitchen. Annamaria set the island for three and noted there were a few minutes left before dinner was ready. Even though Annamaria could magically cook dinner faster, she discovered Trinity had been telling the truth—magically cooked food didn't taste as good as cooking at a human pace. She used her magic to make prep work go faster.

"Do you want anything special to drink?" she asked the two of them.

"I think tonight is an occasion for some wine." Sandy smiled, her eyes twinkling. "The bottles are stored downstairs. I'll go get them." She left Daniel and Annamaria in the kitchen while she ran downstairs.

"Remind me where you go to school?" Annamaria asked.

"U-Penn."

"The University of Pennsylvania? Cool."

Sandy returned with a bottle, and the timer dinged. Annamaria took her solo dinner out of the oven, waved her hand over it, and the number of chicken breasts, potatoes, and peas on the sheet pan tripled.

"Nice," said Daniel.

"Is this your first time seeing magic?" Annamaria asked as she dished up everyone's plates.

Daniel shook his head. "No, I know a couple of

witches."

"Really?" Annamaria sat down. "I just barely learned about myself a couple of months ago."

"Yeah, I know." Daniel gave her a look that appeared to have some hidden meaning.

Sandy looked between Daniel and Annamaria. "Daniel will start his last year of college this upcoming fall."

Annamaria smiled. "What are you studying?"

"Biology. It's just my undergrad. I'm going to apply to veterinary school next."

"Wow." Annamaria leaned back in her chair. "I was going to start at USC this year, but now I'm not sure what I'm going to do."

"Would you like some wine?" Sandy asked Annamaria, pouring herself and Daniel a second glass.

"I'm not old enough," Annamaria stuttered. Sandy knew that, right?

"Sh, no one will tell." Sandy winked.

"How old are you?" Daniel asked.

"Eighteen. I'll be nineteen in September."

"See. You're an adult." Sandy waved her hand. "I drank at your age."

"And that's how you ended up pregnant with me," Daniel mumbled.

"Hey." Sandy wagged her finger at her son. "You respect your old mom, young man."

Daniel chuckled. "Yes, Mom."

Annamaria declined the wine again, and Sandy stopped asking. When dinner was over, Sandy yawned and slouched. "Wine makes her sleepy," Daniel whispered. "Sorry, she can't help with the dishes. I'll help once I've tucked her in."

"Not to worry." Annamaria smiled. "I can clean them in a few seconds." She turned toward the sink, and another hand snuck into hers, leaving a folded piece of paper in it. Annamaria turned around, and Daniel led his mom out of the kitchen. Annamaria unfolded the paper.

We need to talk privately.

Come to my mom's room when you can.

Annamaria had a strange feeling to keep this visit with Daniel to herself. Not telling Will made sense. But the others? Annamaria was good friends with them, and they embraced Daniel when he arrived. Annamaria followed her gut and hoped she could get across the hall to Sandy's room without the others noticing. When Annamaria finished the dishes, she crept across the hall and knocked on Sandy's door. Daniel opened the door and yanked Annamaria inside by her wrist. Sandy was snoozing in her bed.

"What the—"

"My mom said you put some sort of sound spell in this room?" he asked in a whisper.

"Yes." Annamaria nodded.

"No vampires can hear us?"

"Nope."

Daniel's body relaxed. "Can you also lock the door against their strength?"

"Yes." Annamaria waved her hand and chanted the spell. "Daniel, what's going on?"

"I know who you are," he said.

Annamaria swallowed a smirk. "Yeah, I think the entire country does."

"I'm not talking about that." Daniel waved his hand. "I mean, I know who you *are*. Your grandma is looking for you."

Annamaria blinked. "How do you know? Do you know my grandma?"

"I've never met her, but I'm in contact with someone who knows her." He sat down in one of Sandy's chairs, and Annamaria sat in the other.

"How are you in contact with magic?" Annamaria glanced at Sandy.

"I'm a werewolf," Daniel said.

"You are?" Annamaria's eyes widened. The tension in the house suddenly made sense. She narrowed her eyes. "Prove it."

Daniel sighed and held his hand up between Annamaria and himself. Annamaria's lips parted in a smile as the nails on his fingers grew into claws. She shifted her gaze from his hand to his face to see his irises were now yellow, and canines one would see on a wolf were poking out from his lips. In the blink of an eye, his canines receded, his irises returned to a soft brown, and normal fingernails replaced the claws.

He smirked. "Believe me now?"

Annamaria cocked her head. "Why didn't you shift all the way? I was kind of hoping the full moon thing was a myth."

Daniel chuckled. "It is, but I still need the moonlight to fully shift."

Annamaria's eyes lit up, and her smile widened. "Can we go outside and you show me?"

Daniel shook his head. "It wouldn't be safe in such proximity to vampires."

Annamaria inclined her head in understanding. "Does your mom know? Does the rest of the house know?"

"Yes," said Daniel. "That's why I haven't been around in four years. I shifted for the first time when I was eighteen, surprising us all. Will almost murdered me, but Anthony stopped him. My mom is human, and I never knew my dad, so he must have been a werewolf."

"You weren't bitten?"

Daniel chuckled. "No, that's a myth. Werewolves are biological, like witches. Vampires are the only ones who breed through violence. Anyway, your grandma is supposedly going crazy looking for you and your aunt."

"Does she know about Marianna?"

"Not that I'm aware of." Daniel shook his head. "She knows vampires took you, and you are dancing online. She just doesn't know where you are."

"Except I wasn't taken," Annamaria said. Daniel squinted his eyes and cocked his head. "I came here willingly." Annamaria gave Daniel a summary of Marianna showing up in Harrison. However, she left out the details that would compromise Trinity and instead made it sound like she was here to get to know her sister and train under her tutelage.

"So what happened to your aunt? Where is she?"

"I don't know." Annamaria sighed. "Are you going to tell your friend I'm here?"

"I would prefer not to. I don't want my mom to get caught in the cross fire when Libby's forces show up. My mom refuses to leave this place." Daniel glared over at his mom's sleeping figure. "So I'm begging you to get out of here on your own. Convince your sister to come with you if you can. I'll help if you need it." He handed Annamaria another piece of paper. "This is my phone number. I'd be happy to drive you once you got a safe enough distance away."

Annamaria took the paper and looked down. She couldn't tell him why she couldn't leave without compromising Trinity. So she settled on a half-truth. "I need to get my magic up to par. I'm still brand new."

Daniel sighed. "Well, at least keep my number. When Will drives you over the edge, and trust me, he will, call me? I'll come help you."

Annamaria nodded. "Okay, thank you."

After leaving Sandy's room, Annamaria ambled up the stairs. Anthony poked his head out of his room before she could walk by. "Did you fall in the dishwasher?" Translation—he heard her disappear, which meant she was in Sandy's room.

"I got invited into a conversation in Sandy's room, is all." She smiled.

"What do you think of Daniel?" Anthony stepped out into the hall.

"He seemed more comfortable in Sandy's room than he was in the kitchen. I think he enjoyed knowing he couldn't be overheard."

Anthony nodded. "Oh yeah, he and Will had a rough relationship by the time he was ready to go to college."

"He told me."

"All of it?"

"Yes, he told me he's a werewolf. What's up with vampires and werewolves, anyway?"

Anthony shrugged. "We just don't like each other. It's innate, a part of our DNA."

Marianna and Will came out of their rooms with a small suitcase each. "We are going to go on a couple's vacation for the week." Marianna beamed, her eyes twinkling.

One week was how long Daniel planned to visit.

"Have fun." Anthony clapped Will's back. Will smirked.

"Bye. Be safe." Annamaria hugged her sister.

Will and Marianna headed downstairs, and Anthony took Annamaria's hand, pulling her into his room. Annamaria threw open the curtains and the door to the balcony, walked outside, and leaned on the railing, looking over the forest and Will's car zooming down the road.

Daniel was right. Will would eventually do something to force Annamaria to flee. If that happened before Trinity contacted her, she would have no choice but to find her grandma. Will made sure she didn't know the code to open the gate, but Annamaria could levitate herself over it. The challenge would be convincing Marianna to go with her.

Anthony materialized behind Annamaria, put his hands on top of hers, and kissed her neck. "What are you thinking about?"

"I want to get out of the house again. The Fourth of July gave me a taste of what a semi-normal life here could be like, and I want more." She turned around and looked into Anthony's eyes. "You all said I was part of the family when you painted my room, and I haven't been on the news in over a month. I should be able to come and go just like the rest of you."

Anthony smiled and pecked her lips. "You are right. I'll take you somewhere tomorrow night."

"Really?" Annamaria searched Anthony's face.

"Really. But tonight I just want to kiss you."

Anthony picked up Annamaria and sat her on the

railing. Annamaria giggled, wrapped her legs around Anthony's waist, and kissed him. Their lips moved in tandem, like they were made for each other.

They still hadn't talked about what they were, other than the awkward moment when Annamaria told the police they were dating to get them off her back. Annamaria didn't want to just yet. She enjoyed holding hands, cuddling, and kissing for the time being. This was a new feeling, the excitement of a new relationship without planning where they would go. She found she enjoyed physical attraction without a label.

Anthony picked Annamaria up off the railing and carried her inside, never taking his lips from hers, sucking on her bottom lip as he walked. He lowered her onto her feet and leaned her against the wall, tracing his finger from her face down the side of her body to her hips. Moving his hand around the small of her back, he drew her closer. While his hands explored the outside of her body, his tongue explored the inside of her mouth. Annamaria combed her fingers through his hair and tickled his neck. Anthony circled her around, walked her backward to his bed, and sat her down on it. He tipped her backward, but Annamaria pulled her lips away, breaking the spell.

Anthony sighed, and Annamaria gave him a tight-lipped smile. "Goodnight," she said, kissing him again, and left his room. She was aware he wanted more, but she wasn't ready. They had time. Hopefully, he would be patient.

*****

Annamaria spent a lot of time with Sandy and Daniel during his visit. They spent the mornings outside on the lawn, hiking, or in town. While in town,

Annamaria used some of the money Trinity had given her to buy summer clothes. The Black Market fashion had rubbed off on her over the past two months, and she mixed her new style with her previous style in her purchases.

In the afternoons, Annamaria continued to dance with Kylie and Tyler, which allowed Sandy and Daniel mother-son time. During the week, they finished Tyler and Annamaria's duet, which portrayed her relationship with Cody up to prom.

The dance was a foxtrot-tango medley. During the foxtrot, Annamaria's character focused on Tyler, and they danced like a loving couple. During the tango, a dark shadow conjured by Annamaria followed them. Only Annamaria could see it, and Tyler kept trying to get her attention. At the very end, when Annamaria said goodnight to Tyler, the shadow enveloped her.

True to his word, Anthony took Annamaria into town every night after sunset while Marianna and Will were gone. One night, they laid on the football field of the local high school, and Annamaria recounted her own memories from high school. Another night, they returned to the bar from the Fourth of July and danced again. They also took night hikes around the mountains and walked through the neighborhoods.

Annamaria hadn't told Sandy about her and Anthony, and one morning, right before breakfast, Sandy and Daniel walked in on them. Annamaria was preparing her breakfast when Anthony grabbed her waist and spun her around, making her squeal, and kissed her up against the counter. They hadn't been kissing long when a soft "Oh!" broke them apart.

Sandy's hands were over her mouth, a twinkle in

her eyes. Daniel, however, glared with his hands balled into fists. Annamaria blushed and looked away. Anthony excused himself.

"Oh Annamaria, you've made quite the change since I left." Sandy giggled.

She started helping Annamaria with breakfast. "I must admit, I had actually hoped you and Daniel might hit it off, but Anthony is great too."

Annamaria blushed and mumbled something inaudible. Daniel looked at his mom in complete surprise. For the rest of the day, Daniel observed Annamaria and Anthony, and his eyes narrowed every time Anthony touched Annamaria.

On Daniel's last night there, he made steaks for the three of them. Sandy and Annamaria made homemade ice cream for dessert. When Annamaria prepared to turn in for the night, Anthony told her he would go out, but he would be back before dawn. "Going out" meant hunting. Sometimes Kylie, Tyler, Will, and Marianna would be gone for a day or two when they went hunting. But Anthony never was gone longer than a night because he liked to be back to spend the day with Annamaria. When Annamaria had first moved in, Marianna also would return before dawn. However, when Annamaria started her independent study, Marianna was more willing to be gone longer, which pacified Will when she wasn't rushing back to her sister.

Annamaria forced a smile and kissed him goodbye, but inside her blood boiled. This was the one thing about Anthony and the others that bothered her. She hated that they hunted humans for sustenance. One time, Annamaria asked Anthony if he could drink animal blood. He had laughed and said drinking animal blood was a myth. Vampires had once been human, so only human blood would sustain them. Anthony's breath always smelled terrible afterward, like blood and death. Even before their first kiss, Annamaria could smell his breath when they would just talk. It helped that Anthony hunted only when necessary, and he only drank what was necessary to keep him strong and coherent. Annamaria convinced herself everything was okay because Anthony didn't kill, but she still struggled when she pictured him hunting.

After saying goodbye, Annamaria strolled into the kitchen for a glass of water. Daniel was in there alone, sipping a can of beer. Daniel invited her to sit across from him as they both drank their beverages. "Annamaria, I know we just met, and I'm probably out of line, and I certainly hope I'm reading the situation wrong, but I think you should be careful with Anthony."

"And what is it you think you are reading?" Annamaria narrowed her eyes.

"You are romantically involved with him." Daniel set his drink down and stared at Annamaria.

"Well, we haven't exactly put a label on it." Annamaria glanced away.

"But he's touching you, and kissing you, and you're kissing him back. Have you spent the night with him?" Annamaria's eyes flashed. "I'm sorry. What I'm trying to say is, even though Anthony is kind, he is still a vampire. Yes, he has mastered control compared to others, but those innate urges are still there. Just please be careful, and don't let him distract you from getting to your grandma."

Annamaria cocked her head. "Why are you talking about this in the kitchen?"

Daniel tapped his nose. "No one is here."

"You can smell them?"

"Yep."

"Do you have super hearing as well?"

"Only in my wolf form. Back to the topic at hand. Promise me you'll be careful?"

Annamaria sighed and rolled her eyes. "All right, I promise." She inched her way toward the door.

Daniel grabbed her hand before she could leave. "I'm serious, Annamaria. You don't know how important you are."

"If you are referring to my 'royalty' status, I don't want it. Not if it's going to create the drama that killed my parents." Annamaria yanked her hand out of Daniel's.

Daniel looked at his drink for a few seconds. "Look, I don't know all the intricacies of witch's politics. I just know you getting to your grandma's community is important to them."

Annamaria frowned. She wished Daniel goodnight and left the kitchen. Annamaria fell asleep with her vision of Daniel's reaction to her kissing Anthony mixing with her vision of Anthony out there somewhere hunting.

Annamaria and Cody were dancing to a slow song, holding each other and kissing. When the song ended, the lights came on, and they were the only ones in the empty school gym. No student body, no DJ, no decorations. Daniel appeared and yelled at them to run.

"Get inside *the house."*

Cody grabbed Annamaria's hand and led her

toward the exit. But Annamaria resisted and pulled her hand out of Cody's.

"How do you know us?" Annamaria asked Daniel. "You're not supposed to know me yet."

Daniel shook his head and continued to lead them to the exit.

"Come on!" Cody tugged on Annamaria, but she wouldn't budge.

A new pair of hands yanked Annamaria from around her waist, separating her from Cody. Cody and Annamaria both screamed, reaching for each other. Annamaria was shoved against the wall of the gym, the rough brick scraping her shoulder blades. Expecting to see Will, her mouth dropped when she recognized Anthony's face. He kissed her lips with a fierce intensity. He kissed down her jawline, stopping at her neck, where he bit her and sucked her blood.

Cody roared and ran toward them, but Daniel blocked his path.

"It's too late," Daniel said. "She made her choice. We have to get inside your house NOW!" Daniel and Cody ran out of the gym. Cody looked back, fury shining in his eyes.

Annamaria woke up screaming, "I haven't!"

She opened her eyes. She was in her bed at Will's house, over a thousand miles away from Wyoming. Sweating and shaking, she got out of bed and paced her bedroom floor. *It was just a dream. A dream that means nothing. It's just my thoughts getting jumbled from my conversation with Daniel.* She wiped her face down with cold water in her bathroom. She lay back down, but she spent the rest of the night tossing and turning.

Chapter 16 Defense

Annamaria and Anthony went on one of their late-night hikes. Sitting on a large boulder overlooking the forest below them, Annamaria failed to register Anthony rubbing her back. She had been quiet all day, thinking about her conversation with Daniel the previous evening and the horrible dream which had followed.

"Do I get to know what's been on your mind?" Anthony asked.

Annamaria sighed and continued to stare down the mountain for a minute. "Last night, after you left, Daniel warned me about you."

Anthony looked confused. "But I've never hurt you."

Annamaria met Anthony's eyes. "I know. And so does Daniel. He thinks that you being a vampire is enough to make you dangerous." She flushed and looked back down the mountain. "My mind couldn't let go of what he said, and I had this dream. I was back at prom with Cody, and Daniel showed up and was trying to get us to run. Then you showed up and…and…drank my blood." Annamaria hid her face in her hands and peeked through her fingers.

Anthony rubbed his face. "I've known Daniel his whole life. I'm pretty sure there was a point when he used to love and trust me. But I guess there is no fighting the natural animosity between vampires and werewolves. I don't fault Daniel for saying what he said, and I imagine he has found his own kind to be with these past four years, which would only further fuel the terror he experienced when Will almost killed him."

Annamaria shook her head. Will was at the center of everyone's terror.

Anthony turned Annamaria to face him. "Annamaria, I'm so sorry we have placed any amount of fear in your heart. I know I'm not perfect, but I believe I am doing the best I can with the cards I have been dealt. I promise with all of my heart I will never hurt you. I care about you too much."

Annamaria couldn't fight the smile that crept up her face. "I care about you too." Anthony drew her into his torso, she rested her head in his chest. He inhaled the scent of her hair. "Is it hard for you to be with me like this?"

"No. I love spending time with you." He played with her hair.

"No, I mean like physically hard? Do you have to fight off any impulses?" Annamaria blushed some more. Great. Just what she needed during this topic.

Anthony chuckled and nuzzled his nose into Annamaria's neck. "No. I'm old, so I have lots of practice. You smell incredible, though."

He licked her neck. Annamaria squealed and jumped away from him. Anthony tackled her in the grass behind the boulder. Anthony lowered his lips to hers. She opened her mouth for him and wrapped her arms around his neck. Anthony briefly pressed into her as he finished the kiss, then rearranged themselves to look up at the stars.

"Can I ask you a personal question now?" Anthony asked.

"Yeah."

"Do you still have feelings for your ex?"

Ex? Was Cody her ex? Yes, he was. Annamaria needed to accept that. He broke up with her. His conditions didn't matter because she didn't deliver. Even if she did, would he have accepted her true self? Annamaria put her hands over the bridge of her nose and closed her eyes. She was not ready to have this conversation, but Anthony had been patient, and she owed him the truth.

"I don't know." She removed her hands. "He's the only person I have ever dated. He was my first kiss, my high school sweetheart. I loved him, and I thought he loved me too, but…" She still didn't know if she should tell Anthony about the text messages.

"But?"

"He broke up with me the night everything happened, and I had to leave with Marianna and Will. But it wasn't a permanent breakup. He could tell something was going on, and after a week of me refusing to tell him, he said we were over until I could be honest. I didn't get the chance to be honest, and Trinity wouldn't let me, even though she told his dad about her when they dated a long time ago."

"I'm sorry," whispered Anthony.

"It's just high school." Annamaria shrugged. "Even if I never came here, and we never met, I still couldn't be with him. I would have gone to my grandma's during the summer, learned I was a witch, and I probably would have assimilated into her community.

Cody and I don't belong in the same world."

Annamaria met Anthony's gaze. "I'm sorry. This is probably not what you wanted to hear at all. But it's why I've been so hesitant about us."

Anthony twisted strands of her hair in his hand. "It's okay, I understand. You didn't get closure."

When Annamaria and Anthony returned to the house, Marianna and Will were back from their trip. Will neither commented on nor questioned where Annamaria had been. In fact, he gave a genuine smile when their gazes met. Hopefully, this was a sign she would not be denied leave of the house anymore.

****

Marianna spent the next several days playing the piano every day, and by the sounds of it, composing something original. She wouldn't let anyone in the ballroom while she practiced. When she finished it, she called everyone into the ballroom to listen to the final product. The composition started out soft, then built in power. After the climax, the melody changed to an upbeat staccato and finished full circle to how the song started, soft and pleasant. When she took her hands off the keys, everyone clapped and cheered.

After her bow, she looked at Tyler and Kylie. "Will that work for your finale?"

The two squealed and ran and hugged her.

"Will you play it live for the video?" asked Kylie.

"I'll play live, but I don't want the camera on me," Marianna said

With Marianna's song, Kylie, Tyler, and Annamaria finished their final number in the Reunited series. The choreography showed Tyler bringing Annamaria to the same place as Kylie. They discovered each other and did similar mirror choreography to their earlier number. They turned against Tyler and fought him. He gained the upper hand at first, but they worked together and became victorious. When Tyler was defeated, they celebrated and finished running off into the distance, holding hands.

Will glared at the TV by the end of the number. "Are you calling me the bad guy?" He shifted his glare to Tyler.

Tyler rolled his eyes. "It's called creative licensing, Will. Inspired by true events, not this-is-exactly-what-happened."

"I think the entire series was very artistic." Marianna patted Will's leg.

****

Annamaria became a very adept spell caster and potion brewer by the end of July. She could now cast spells without verbalizing the incantation. Magic was a part of her, and she wielded it for everything. However, she was close to the point where the books Marianna gave her could no longer challenge her. She wanted new books or to meet with other witches and learn from them. She needed to broach the subject with Marianna. However, her sister was a staunch rule follower, and Trinity had instructed they be careful. One morning, before Annamaria made it downstairs for breakfast, there was a knock on her door.

"Marianna, come in."

Marianna entered and sat down on Annamaria's desk chair. "We have gone beyond everything in these books." She gestured to the bookshelf. Annamaria nodded with a small smile. "And I'm guessing you are wondering what the next step in your magical study should be?"

"Of course. Do you know how to connect with other witches?"

"Yes." Marianna bit her lip. "But I would like to train you in defensive magic first, before we venture out into the magical community."

Annamaria blinked. Of course that made sense. "Oh, gosh, yeah. I don't want to be vulnerable the next time Valentina's followers attack."

Marianna nodded. "I think we should practice outside so we don't destroy the ballroom. Will you do lessons out on the lawn when the sun goes down each night?"

"Yes." Annamaria smiled, getting excited. She couldn't wait to fight like Trinity.

When Annamaria met Marianna out on the lawn, her face fell at the sight of Will standing next to Marianna.

Marianna gave an apologetic smile. "I know you like lessons to be just us two. However, if you are going to be successful, you need someone attacking as close to a genuine attack as possible."

"And you can't be that person? Or Anthony? Or Kylie or Tyler?" Annamaria threw her hands in the air.

Marianna giggled. "No, your reaction is exactly why it needs to be Will. But the others will join us once you get a single attack down and need to practice against multiple attackers."

Annamaria gulped. "Okay."

Will smirked. Marianna raised her brows at him, then turned back to Annamaria. "So the first branch of defensive magic is just like our first lessons—using the elements. Will is going to charge you, and I want you to throw him backward by calling on the air."

Will started before Marianna finished speaking. Before Annamaria could raise her hands, let alone cast a spell, Luna lunged from the side, tackling Will to the ground. Both Marianna and Annamaria collapsed to the ground howling with laughter. Will struggled with getting Luna off of him.

"Will you two shut up and get this thing off of me?"

Marianna stood back up, but Annamaria had a harder time doing so. "Luna! Luna girl! Get off him." Luna obeyed and ran over to Marianna, her tongue lolling, her eyes shining. Marianna patted Luna's head. "I know you love your aunt, but we are just practicing. She's not in real danger right now."

Luna cocked her head and rose a brow but trotted back to the side. Marianna commanded both Will and Annamaria to set up again. However, the same thing happened. Marianna scolded Luna again. They tried again, and Luna continued to interfere. So Marianna put her in the garage, where she howled for several minutes before going quiet. "Let's try this again."

Just like before, Will charged before Marianna finished talking. Annamaria found herself on her back with Will on top of her. "Will one, Annamaria zero."

Annamaria growled, called on the wind, and threw Will from her. He landed about twenty feet away. Annamaria got up, and Will charged her again. She blasted him again, but he dug his feet into the ground. The air slowed him down, giving Annamaria time to back up and run to a different location. She kept the wind on him with one hand, called on water with the other. Encasing him in water, she raised him up in the air and threw him to the ground.

"Stop!" Marianna held a hand up as Will got back up. She clapped and cheered, ran over and picked Annamaria up, and spun her around. "You were amazing. I knew Will could drive it out of you."

Annamaria giggled along with Marianna. "Yeah, I've been dying to do something like that to him."

Loud laughter came from the house. Anthony, Kylie, and Tyler ran outside to join them. Kylie screamed, just like Marianna. "We were watching from the window. I have never seen something like that before."

Anthony grinned. "I have, but you were still great."

"You showed him." Tyler gave Annamaria a high five.

Will humphed, but even he couldn't contain a smile either. Annamaria defended herself against each vampire one-on-one. Using only three elements, she buried them in earth, whipped them around in water, and threw them backward with the air. The only thing she didn't call upon was fire, which Marianna said would only be for life-and-death situations. They ended the night panting, laughing, and talking amongst each other.

"Tomorrow we'll have two at a time against Annamaria, which will double the pressure," Marianna said.

****

Marianna was right.

The first two to double up against Annamaria were Will and Tyler. Annamaria made the mistake of focusing on Will. She had Will encased in water when Tyler's arms wrapped around her neck, shoving her face-first into the ground.

"Oh my gosh, girl. Are you okay?" Tyler pulled Annamaria up and tried to inspect her, but Anthony ripped Annamaria out of Tyler's grasp.

Annamaria rubbed her nose. "It stings, but I don't think it's broken."

Anthony caressed her face. "No blood." He glared at Tyler. "What the hell, man?"

Tyler put his hands up. "It was an accident. I thought I was going soft enough, clearly not. I'm sorry."

"It's okay. Let's try again." Annamaria returned to her starting position.

With the second try, Annamaria balanced her magic between the two of them, and they both broke through and tackled her at the same time. The third time, Annamaria tried throwing water at Will, then Tyler, and rotated until they slowed down. However, they once again broke through, and for the third time in a row, Annamaria found herself on her back being held down by two vampires.

"Let's mix it up," Marianna called out.

For the next half hour, no matter the combination, Annamaria could not gain the upper hand. Her arms ached from keeping the magic going for so long, her shoulder blades and behind were sore from banging into the ground over and over, and she was out of breath.

"I need a break."

Marianna nodded. "Let's call it a night." She hugged Annamaria. "Don't be too hard on yourself. I honestly didn't expect you to succeed at all tonight. In fact, how long you lasted before you needed a break is pretty impressive. We'll try again tomorrow night."

Back in the house, Annamaria lay on her bed while Anthony massaged her sore body and rubbed a relaxer potion mixed into lotion over her muscles.

"Did I look terrible?"

"No." He rubbed her calves, and she moaned. "You looked like you were fighting for your life. It was hard to see you go down so many times."

"You didn't seem to mind when you were the one going at me." Annamaria tapped his head with her toe. "I could tell you weren't holding back."

"Because this is incredibly important for you to master if you're going to survive living with vampires."

"You promised you guys wouldn't hurt me."

"Not us, but vampires feud with other covens often. Their witches help too."

"*Their* witches?" Annamaria sat up and surveyed Anthony.

"I meant the witches that live with them." Anthony pulled her face to his and kissed her deeply.

Annamaria brought her hands up to his shoulders and groaned, pulling away. "You gotta finish putting that stuff on my body if we're going to do any of that tonight."

Anthony chuckled and got to work on her shoulders.

****

Annamaria gathered everyone around her before starting. "I'm not going to spend energy defending myself tonight. I would like to study your angles and techniques. So can you just stop right before you get to me?"

Marianna smiled and nodded. "Good idea."

Will liked to charge head-on, while the others used

him as a distraction to sneak up on her from the sides or behind. Tyler also ran straight at Annamaria, but came at her from behind. Kylie would zigzag all over the place, seemingly popping in and out of existence. Marianna wouldn't attack, but would make defensive movements until the last minute, then she would materialize in front of or behind Annamaria. Anthony would full-on disappear until he was there, wrapping his arms around Annamaria, nibbling her neck.

"Hey, lover boy! She said no touching." Tyler laughed as he ripped Anthony away from Annamaria.

Annamaria laughed. "Anthony's exempt."

She studied while they ran toward her repeatedly until at the very end of the night she blasted Will backward, then turned around and threw Anthony up into the air.

"Yes!" Annamaria and Marianna yelled at the same time.

Over the next couple of weeks, Annamaria got better and better at holding off more than one vampire. As she improved with two, Marianna threw in three, then four, then all of them. On the first try against all of them, Anthony reminded everyone not to bite or scratch Annamaria.

"That's rich coming from the guy who touches her all the time." Tyler scoffed, then winked. "But in all seriousness, relax, Anthony. No one's going to hurt her."

"Yeah, we want her to be just as intact as you do. She's completely changed our channel," Kylie said.

"Enough." Annamaria smiled. "Get ready."

They attacked from all sides. Annamaria called on the air to raise her up. Will and Tyler crashed into each other, but Marianna, Kylie, and Anthony skidded to a halt just in time. Annamaria levitated herself away from them, landing a safe distance away, and they started again. She threw water and earth at them and blasted individuals as they got too close. After some time, she couldn't keep up, and Tyler and Kylie got behind her. They yanked her hands behind her back, squeezing her wrists. Annamaria called on the wind, ready to blast them off her, but nothing happened. She tried two more times, nothing. Annamaria screamed, and everyone stopped.

"What's wrong?" Anthony zoomed over and pulled Annamaria out of Tyler and Kylie's grip.

"My magic." Annamaria held up her hands. She tried again, and wind flew from her fingers, rustling the nearby trees. "What the? Kylie, Tyler, do that again."

"The whole thing?" Kylie asked.

"No, just squeeze my arms." They did so, but a blood pressure gauge squeezed harder. "No. As hard as you did the first time." They increased their strength until Annamaria winced. Annamaria called on the air. Nothing. "*Aqua.*" Nothing. "*Ignis.*" Nothing. Kylie and Tyler let go, their eyes wide.

"It's like kinking a hose." Annamaria stared at her hands. "Did you know this could happen?" She looked at her sister. Marianna shook her head, looking just as surprised as Annamaria.

"I'm sorry, I did." Anthony palmed his head. "I had forgotten because I've only seen it a few times. You're going to have to strengthen yourself in order to overcome that position." Annamaria's heart beat hard, and she breathed in short gasps. "Are you okay?" Anthony took her hand and rubbed it.

"No."

Annamaria put her fingers through her hair and walked away. This was the most vulnerable she had been since she started lessons. She had gotten used to having magic over the past several months, and to know she could lose it, albeit temporarily, made her blood run cold.

Marianna walked over alone. "Do you want to be done for the night?"

"Yes please."

Marianna and the others trudged inside, throwing glances her way before they crossed the threshold. Annamaria stayed outside to catch her breath. When she entered the house, she could see a bruise on each arm in the shape of Kylie's and Tyler's hands.

****

Annamaria's defensive lessons continued into the middle of August. She advanced beyond elemental magic, and she learned how to summon an invisible shield that attackers bounced off of or crashed into. Annamaria figured out how to spread the shield like the sound barrier, encasing her entire body. She couldn't send magic through the shield, so she used the protective barrier to get herself at a safe distance to start again.

Marianna also taught her a sleeping spell to throw at witches. Since vampires couldn't sleep, the spell didn't fully work on them, but it would knock them down for several seconds. There was one spell Annamaria could not get down. The incantation was *incarcero*. When done right, a witch could summon a flexible golden cage which trapped their opponent. When done right, only the witch who produced the cage could remove it. Every time Annamaria tried, the vampires threw the spell off after a few seconds, sometimes even knocking the cage away before the golden bars could encase their bodies, causing it to dematerialize.

Defense lessons were now down to once a week. They included a warm-up of what Annamaria could do, then she would practice *incarcero* and try to do any kind of magic with her wrists getting the life squeezed out of them. Anthony didn't want her to practice too much because he was worried they would damage her wrists beyond repair. However, both Annamaria and Marianna were of the same mind—she needed to get this down.

One night at the end of a successful practice in which Kylie struggled in the golden cage for five minutes before escaping, Annamaria pulled Marianna away from the group.

"So you said we could connect with other witches when I got defensive magic down?"

"I did."

"Do you think we are there?"

Marianna contemplated, then nodded. "Yeah, I think so."

Annamaria took a deep breath. "Will you go with me to meet Grandma?"

Marianna's eyes widened. "I don't know." She looked away.

Annamaria took her sister's hand. "Look, I know Trinity wants us to stay here, but she abandoned her phone, and she was going to take me to meet Grandma this summer, anyway. Grandma will probably be thrilled to know both of her granddaughters are okay."

"Annamaria, I won't stop you if you want to go find Grandma, but I don't think I can go."

"Why not?"

"Because she has a terrible reputation against vampires, and granddaughter or not, I don't think she'll accept me."

"Will you just try? I'll protect you, and if she's really terrible, I'll come back with you." Annamaria squeezed Marianna's hand.

Marianna pursed her lips and took a breath, but Will stepped between them. "No."

Annamaria scoffed. "Will, this is a private conversation."

"Then you should have taken her into your black hole of a room." He smirked. "Neither you nor Marianna are going anywhere near your vampire-hating grandma." He put his arm around Marianna. "It's for her safety, of course, and you need to obey your aunt. She said you need to hide here."

Annamaria glared at Will. "You don't care about Trinity. You just like controlling me. Why?"

Such was the authority Will had, he didn't even answer. He tugged on Marianna's waist and led her to his car, where they took off to go hunting. Marianna mouthed *Sorry* as she let Will take her away from their unfinished conversation.

Annamaria plopped down on the grass, laid her head on her knees, and wrapped her arms around herself. Luna nudged her, and she wrapped her arms around the warm wolf and cried into her beautiful black fur. Why did Will do this? Every time things were improving, he would ruin it. She hated him. And she hated that the others wouldn't do anything about it.

After a while, Luna growled. Annamaria looked up and discovered Anthony standing a few feet behind her. "It's okay," she whispered to Luna, patting her on the back. Luna stopped growling but stayed close.

"Annamaria, I'm so sorry."

Annamaria didn't respond. She looked into the trees on the other side of the wall. Anthony continued to stand, not coming closer. Luna picked up a low growl again, and when Annamaria didn't quiet her, Anthony backed away.

****

Kylie and Tyler surprised Annamaria with an invitation to choreograph a solo routine. She would have total control over the song, choreography, costume, and cinematography.

This would be the best way she could get closure with Cody. The routine would be a goodbye dedicated to him. After careful deliberation, Annamaria chose a song about forbidden love. While Annamaria's love for Cody wasn't forbidden, the lyrics matched their inability to see each other again. She would always love him, even if they weren't compatible. The dress she designed was a replica of her prom dress, but with a skirt that ended just above the knee.

On the day of dress rehearsal, Kylie presented Annamaria with her costume. Annamaria opened the box and unwrapped the tissue paper. She gasped and tears filled her eyes. The purple fabric in her hand was the same as her actual prom dress.

"How did you pull this off?"

"We have connections." Kylie winked.

When the routine was over and Annamaria held her final pose, Tyler yelled, "That's a wrap!" Annamaria collapsed to the floor, sobs wracking her body. Kylie rushed over and threw her arms around Annamaria, but Tyler pulled her back. "Let her cry. She needs to let it all out."

Annamaria had a lot to let out. This goodbye wasn't just for Cody, but everything about her previous life. Being human, Stephanie and Jamie—regardless of how they treated her in the end—Trinity, Alyssa, Courtney, Mr. Mills, and Harrison itself. She missed it. She was so happy to have Marianna, and she wouldn't give up her magic, but this new life had come at a price.

Annamaria cried all of her makeup off, and after several minutes, slowed down to little sniffles. "Sorry. I didn't know I would react like that."

Kylie handed her a tissue. "We all suffered through similar things in the beginning. Of course, Tyler and I couldn't cry."

"Who did you have to say goodbye to?" Annamaria wiped her eyes.

"Our family and friends." Kylie's eyes were sad.

"I'm sorry. But since you're online, don't they know you're all right?"

"Well, yes. But we always come up with excuses for why we can't meet in person. I suppose things will get easier in a few decades when they all die." Tyler played with his hands.

Annamaria's closure helped heal her anger from the night Will had once again denied her access out of here. She still wasn't happy with Will, but she was no longer mad at the others. In a better place, Annamaria and Anthony watched a movie in the living room, but neither of them were paying attention.

"So the video Tyler posted of you today, is that

really your closure?" Anthony asked.

"Yeah."

"It just looks like you are still in love with him."

Annamaria studied him. "Well, yes. I will always feel something for him. Have you completely stopped loving Elizabeth?"

Anthony grimaced. "No, I guess I haven't."

"Which doesn't bother me," said Annamaria. "Neither of them are here, but you and I are. Can you accept me as is?"

Anthony's eyes twinkled, and he tightened his hold on her. "Yes."

Anthony shifted himself on top of Annamaria, sucking her neck and sneaking his hands under her shirt and caressing her waist. Annamaria giggled and squeezed Anthony's biceps. He worked his way up her jawline to her lips while his hands inched her shirt up. Tyler ran into the room. He smirked and didn't even apologize.

"Annamaria, your video has the most views in the first few hours of posting than any of our past videos!"

She gasped and sat up. "Really?"

She took the laptop from Tyler and skimmed through the comments. One account made her heart stop. The user's name was "Wyoming Rancher," and Annamaria was certain the profile picture was of Cody's horse.

The comment read —*Please respond.*—

Annamaria scrolled through the comments of every video she was in and looked for the same account. Cody had commented on every single video.

Things like —*I miss you.*—

—*Beautiful.*—

—Where are you?—

—Be strong.—

Annamaria reread the comments several times. Why was he commenting all over her videos? Annamaria needed to send a private message to Cody.

"I'm in the mood for a dance flick. Can Kylie and I take over the TV?" Tyler asked.

"Of course. We'll join you." Annamaria smiled. Tyler skipped upstairs to get Kylie. "Will you make me some popcorn?" she asked Anthony.

"Sure."

Lucky for Annamaria, Anthony walked at human speed. She signed into her email as soon as she was alone. Skimming dozens of junk emails, she found a recent one from Cody.

Anna,

I don't know if you have access to your email, but if you do and you can reply, please tell me where you are. I can't go into details in case the wrong person reads this, but WE CAN HELP. Please trust me. I miss you.

- Cody

The sent date showed a couple of weeks after the text messages. Annamaria clicked "Reply."

I'm sorry. It's too dangerous. I can't tell you for your safety.

Annamaria bit her lip as tears welled in her eyes. The blurry keyboard and screen making her struggle to type the next part.

I will be okay. Enjoy USC, good luck.

Love, Annamaria

She hit send, exited out, and closed Tyler's laptop as everyone else sauntered back into the room.

Annamaria wiped her eyes but didn't fool anyone. Kylie and Tyler exchanged a glance but said nothing. Tyler let her pick the movie, provided she chose a dance flick. Annamaria picked *Save the Last Dance.*

Kylie sighed during the romantic scenes. Her happy aura rubbing off on Annamaria. Annamaria snuggled deeper into Anthony's arms. She looked at him with twinkling eyes and a soft smile to help him feel better about earlier. He smiled back, hugged her tight, and kissed the top of her head.

Inside, Annamaria couldn't stop thinking about the email she sent. It was the right thing to do, but her gut still twisted. Cody and Annamaria would have had to say goodbye, anyway. Her feelings for Anthony also made the goodbye necessary. She desired to spend every waking moment with him and was anxious when she was away from him. When he left to go hunting, Annamaria didn't sleep well. When she was outside, she counted down the hours to sunset. He consumed her every thought. Annamaria would always care for Cody. No one ever forgets their first love, but like the rest of Harrison, Cody was becoming a memory.

Chapter 17 Bondwitch

Tomorrow would have been Annamaria's first day of college. The late August sunshine and singing birds streaming through her balcony doors did not match her sour mood. She sighed and trudged downstairs to the kitchen in her pajamas.

"Surprise! Happy Graduation!"

Annamaria screamed and jumped. Holding her chest, she looked around at everyone squished in the kitchen. On the kitchen island was a stack of pancakes with strawberries and whipped cream. Hanging from one wall to the other was a banner reading, "CONGRATS GRAD!"

"Wow, thank you, but I don't get it." Annamaria looked between the sign and her friends.

"We should have done this much sooner, back in May," said Marianna. "I wanted to give you a high school graduation since you missed yours. Would you like that?"

Annamaria stared for a minute. The breakfast, the banner, the smiling faces of her new friends. She needed this. "Yes, I would love it."

"Great. Eat up and then get dressed," Kylie said as she handed Annamaria the plate of pancakes. She, Tyler, and Will left the kitchen with a wave and a wink.

"Where are they going?" Annamaria sat down. The warm pancakes and sweet strawberries wafted into her nose, making her mouth water.

"To set up the ballroom." Anthony sat next to her and trailed his fingers up and down her back.

Annamaria dug into her pancakes and moaned. "Sandy, these are so delicious. Marianna, this whole thing is so sweet of you."

Sandy smiled as she cleaned up the pan and empty batter bowl.

"I figured you needed it. And I also hope the day could be a peace offering?" Marianna sat down on her other side.

"A peace offering? For what?" Annamaria asked.

"For me being so weak and letting Will walk all over you and spending less time with you." Marianna looked down.

Annamaria sighed. As the summer had gone on, Marianna had grown distant. She was always involved in Annamaria's magic, but other than that, she and Will kept to themselves most of the time. If the others hadn't been around, Annamaria would have been so lonely. She knew better than to blame her sister. She placed all the blame on who deserved it. Will was jovial enough in the kitchen with everyone else. Which only meant the whiplash Annamaria would receive the next time he challenged her would be more frustrating and painful.

"I accept your peace offering." Annamaria hugged her sister.

When Annamaria finished eating, Marianna gave her two dress bags and sent her up to her room, but not before Anthony insisted on carrying them. He laid them on her bed, then drew her in for a kiss. She sighed at the tingling sensation which always danced around her lips when he kissed her.

"Early graduation present." His eyes gazed into hers.

"I'm guessing you didn't get a graduation ceremony in Salem?" Annamaria kept her hand on the back his neck.

Anthony chuckled. "No, modern-day festivities would definitely be considered a sin."

"What would they think if they could see you now?"

"Oh, they'd definitely burn me with the witches." He smirked.

"I'd save you." Annamaria trailed a finger down his cheek. She stood on her toes and met his lips, hugging him tightly and sucking on his top lip.

"Anthony, quit distracting her and come downstairs."

They stepped apart, laughing, and Anthony zoomed downstairs with Kylie. Annamaria turned to the dress bags on her bed. She opened the first one and found a shiny black dress with a pattern of dark green roses.

The dress was a perfect fit. Tight on the bodice, with a slight flare at her waist. The skirt ended just above her knees, and the shoulder straps were about an inch thick. Black open-toed heels were in the bottom of the bag. Annamaria looked at herself in the mirror. She settled into her left leg, popping her hip. She was a woman, and she was dangerous. Her red hair shone in contrast to the dark colors.

Next, she opened the second bag and gasped. A sky blue Harrison High School graduation gown lay before her. She had watched both Alyssa and Courtney graduate in this gown. How did they get the exact gown? She also found a gold braid representing high honors. Annamaria would have graduated with high honors had she attended her actual graduation. Annamaria put the robe on, covering the alluring witch she had been moments before. The robe swallowed her, and she was a teenager again. A teenage girl who was about to receive her high school diploma.

Annamaria met Marianna at the doors of the ballroom. She wore a sleeveless purple dress with a three-layered ruffle skirt ending mid-thigh.

"Don't come in until you hear the music," Marianna said before she slipped into the ballroom.

The notes of "Pomp and Circumstance" filtered through the wooden doors. The melody that entered Annamaria's ears wasn't coming out of the speakers, but the piano. Butterflies danced in Annamaria's stomach, and she clasped her hands to her mouth. She counted to three, took a deep breath, and opened the door.

Marianna sat at the piano, her fingers drifting over the keys with poise. There were seven chairs set up near the piano. The rest of the house occupied all but two. Everyone else was dressed as nice as Marianna. The chairs were facing a small stage which was underneath a balloon arch of Harrison blue and gray. Annamaria stopped as she took in the scene. The other members of the house beamed at her. She walked over to an empty chair and sat next to Anthony. Marianna played the last note and walked over to the stage.

"Welcome to Annamaria's graduation. And specifically, welcome, Annamaria, and congratulations. You have accomplished what only three others in this room before you have—graduate from high school. I am so proud of you. I know Mom and Dad are looking on you with pride, and I know Trinity would be proud if she were here as well." Marianna took a deep breath with her hand to her heart, and Annamaria found a tissue tucked into her hand from Sandy behind her. She dabbed her eyes. "This isn't just a human ceremony. This is also a celebration of your magical accomplishments. You have gone so far in just four months, and it is apparent you will be an amazing witch. Congratulations!" Everyone clapped, cheered, and gave Annamaria quick hugs. "Before you receive your diploma, Annamaria, the rest of the house would like to say a few words as well."

Sandy spoke next and cried as she declared Annamaria was like a daughter, and she was sure Annamaria would go far in life. Tyler and Kylie both made Annamaria blush and hide her face as they talked about how sexy she was on the dance floor, but she straightened and grinned when they expressed how grateful they were for her friendship. Even Will said something positive when he expressed how impressed he was with what a "badass" Annamaria was for holding her own against him. Anthony spoke last. Like Marianna, he acknowledged both human and magical accomplishments, but then ended in a romantic direction.

"I will forever be grateful you came into my life when you did. I have never known a more beautiful and passionate woman. Today is for you. Tonight is for you. May we have many more reasons to celebrate in the future."

Kylie, Tyler, and Will catcalled and whistled. Annamaria blushed profusely and hid her face in her hands. What was Anthony talking about? Or was he just being eloquent?

When Anthony sat down, Marianna got up to the stage again. "And now I will call the names of the graduates. When you hear your name, come up one at a time, and you may take your diploma." Annamaria giggled along with everyone else. "Annamaria Lyons."

"She skipped half the alphabet," Kylie whispered in a fake rage.

Annamaria walked up on stage beaming. Marianna handed her a thick paper. Annamaria looked down and gasped. It was her real high school diploma.

"How did you get this?" Annamaria whispered.

Marianna jerked her head in Kylie's direction. Kylie mouthed, *connections*. While everyone stood and clapped, Annamaria took her cap off her head and threw it in the air. She hugged and thanked everyone and took pictures with everyone on her cell phone.

"You're an adult now." Tyler rubbed her shoulders. "Your relationship with Anthony is now legal." He winked.

"What? I've been eighteen this whole time."

"Yeah, but you were still a high school student, which is a big no-no for someone as old as Anthony." Tyler wagged his finger.

"Even then, I don't know if I'd call this relationship legal, though." Kylie smirked. "What are you, three hundred years older than her?"

"Shut up." Anthony shook his head. "It's not like I knew her when she was a little kid." The others laughed. Anthony turned to Annamaria. "In honor of your graduation, you get to choose everything today."

Annamaria deliberated, and her face sunk. What

Chelsey M. Ortega

she wanted to do was not possible.

"You want to go into town during the day?"

Annamaria answered with an apologetic look on her face. Anthony chuckled. "I had a feeling you would want that. I gave Sandy the day off. She'll take you."

Annamaria squealed. "Really? Are you sure?" She didn't want to be unfair by abandoning them right after they had just thrown the best solo graduation a girl could ask for.

"Yes, we'll prepare the house for the evening when you get back," Marianna said, smiling.

"Thank you." Annamaria hugged Anthony and kissed him. Tyler whistled. But Annamaria was too excited to blush. Then she hugged everyone else, even Will. On her way to Sandy's car, Will pulled her aside in the hallway. Annamaria tensed, preparing her magic.

"I know Marianna hasn't told you because she wanted today to be about you, but today is her birthday," Will said.

"It is?" Annamaria's eyes widened. She was a terrible sister. Not once had she asked Marianna when her birthday was. "Why did she do all of this for me on her birthday?"

"Because she doesn't enjoy celebrating her birthday since she stopped aging. Anyway, can you acknowledge it in your plans for the day?"

"Absolutely."

"Thanks." Will gave her a genuine hug.

Annamaria and Sandy started the day at a matinee in the small theater. Even though the movie was from last year, Annamaria still enjoyed sitting in the theater, eating popcorn, and watching something on the big screen. After the movie, they ate lunch at a local restaurant. Eating near them were a couple of police officers. One kept looking over at Annamaria and Sandy, squinting his eyes and looking them up and down. What would she do if he approached and questioned her? She'd have to tell a convincing lie like on the Fourth of July.

"Are people still looking for me?" Annamaria's tone was low.

"Hm… I don't know. You haven't been on the news since early June."

"I know nothing has been on TV, but I just wondered if you knew more since you actually get to leave the house?"

"I haven't seen or heard anything. I'm sorry, honey." Sandy patted her hand.

"So no one connected me with the dancer online?" Annamaria glanced at the officers again.

Sandy gave a closed-lip smile, her eyes sad. "Living between the two worlds, I have learned most humans ignore magic at all costs. Were you wanting to be found? I thought you were here by choice?"

"Well, yes, I did technically come here willingly." Annamaria sighed. "I just want to stop hiding. I want to let my friends back home know I'm okay, but I also don't want to lose any of you. But I don't see how both things are possible. If I come out into the open, there will be a police investigation, and I don't know where Trinity is, nor could I answer questions about her. And how do I explain my sister to my human friends? Then there're the complications with my grandma. I've never met her, but Marianna fears her, and Daniel thinks I need to get to her as soon as possible. I'm just feeling pulled in so many directions right now."

Sandy squeezed Annamaria's hand. "I can't tell you what to do, dear. But I will support you, whatever you decide. I love you very much. You've become a daughter to me."

Annamaria wiped a tear away. "Thank you. I feel the same way."

They finished their lunch, and the officer's gaze followed them on their way out. They spent the afternoon shopping. Annamaria chose some books, which Sandy paid for as her graduation present. Annamaria bought Marianna a birthday present—a gold ring with the word *sisters* in cursive at the top part of the band. She also bought a matching one for herself. After purchasing the two rings, she stepped off to the side and placed a spell on both of them. She couldn't wait to tell Marianna about it. While they were walking around, the same flyers stared at them in the windows of every shop.

HAVE YOU SEEN ME?
Tiffany Meyer, 22
Jonathan Reed, 24
David Lewis, 21

Above each name was a picture. Annamaria grabbed Sandy and pointed out the flyers. Sandy nodded in sympathy. "Poor dears. They disappeared over the Fourth of July." Annamaria dragged Sandy in between two shops.

"They were at the house," she whispered. "Kylie, Tyler, Will, and Marianna brought them home the night of the Fourth."

Sandy's color drained from her face. "That's not good."

"What should we do?"

"Tell Anthony. He always puts the others in place when they get out of hand."

Annamaria's heart calmed a bit. Yes, Anthony would know what to do. However, the memory of what Annamaria had witnessed, and the revelation of what happened while she slept, put a knot in her stomach. She was done spending time in town.

The drive up the mountain was quiet. Annamaria wrung her hands as they got closer to the mansion. Will had always been evil and ruthless, but because of the way the others had treated her, she assumed they were like Anthony. Annamaria sighed. What was Anthony's part in this? He promised Annamaria he didn't kill, yet he didn't stop his friends from killing. Where did that put his moral compass? And what about Marianna? She killed Priya right in front of Annamaria, though she had been defending Annamaria. How was Annamaria supposed to party with them tonight knowing this information? Should she draw a line? If so, where?

Annamaria's inner battle disappeared when she walked into the house decorated with balloons and streamers. Annamaria blushed. "You guys did not have to go this far."

"But we wanted to." Anthony threw his arms around her and kissed her temple.

Sandy made sandwiches for dinner at Annamaria's request. They had eaten a lot in town, so she wanted something simple. Afterward, Sandy produced a beautiful cake, which only she and Annamaria ate.

Marianna carried a small pile of presents into the kitchen. The first one she handed Annamaria was from her and Will. Annamaria opened two delicate frames, one with Annamaria's diploma in it, and the other with the group picture from right after the ceremony. Next, Kylie and Tyler gave their present, a new pair of Latin shoes. Annamaria wouldn't have to borrow Kylie's extra pairs anymore. From Anthony, Annamaria unwrapped a small jewelry box. Her hand paused over the lid, and her heart hammered. She forced herself to lift open the top in a calm manner and sighed in relief when it was a necklace. The pendant was a gold heart, hallowed in the middle, where a capital *A* sat and hung from a gold chain. Anthony clasped the chain around her neck, and she touched the charm with her thumb and middle finger.

"So does the *A* stand for Annamaria or Anthony?" Tyler shimmied and chuckled.

"Annamaria, of course." Anthony scowled.

"Wow, thank you, everyone." Annamaria hugged them. "And now…" She twirled her right hand, and the wording on the "CONGRATS GRAD!" banner changed to "HAPPY BIRTHDAY!"

"Happy birthday, Marianna!" Annamaria spread her arms out.

"What? How did you know?" Marianna's brows furrowed, but her lips were smiling.

"Will told me. Now it's your turn to open presents." Annamaria produced a jewelry box like the one Anthony gave her. Marianna gasped at the ring. "It's more than just a piece of jewelry. I have a matching one. They are both charmed. I put a beacon spell on them, and all you have to do is rub yours three times when you need me, but you can't call or speak. My ring will guide me to you, and vice versa."

Marianna put her ring on and wiggled her fingers. "That's some impressive magic. And the ring itself is beautiful, thank you."

"Okay, now from the rest of us." Kylie put her hand over Marianna's eyes.

Will took Marianna's hands and guided her to the front door and outside under the newly darkened sky. Kylie removed her hands, and before Marianna was a brand new black luxury car. She squealed and jumped into Will's arms, hugging and kissing him. Then she hugged Kylie, Tyler, and Anthony.

"Are you okay celebrating your birthday now?" Will asked her.

"Yes!" Marianna gave him more kisses.

"Why don't you pick the activities for the rest of the night?" Annamaria said.

Marianna put her finger to her lips, but she had a smile on her face. "Do you remember the sand dunes you made during your first week of lessons?"

Annamaria smiled. "Yes."

"Could you do that with snow? I want to go snowboarding."

"Oh my gosh, yes!" Annamaria jumped up and down, clapping. "But let's go outside so there is more room, and I can make the hills bigger. In fact, take your car for a spin while I prepare everything." Annamaria hugged her sister and ran to the side of the house where her defense lessons took place.

Annamaria called on water and cooled the surrounding air so the water froze to the consistency of snow. She expanded the snowball and made three large hills. Next, she summoned enough snowboards, sleds, and inner tubes for everyone in the house. Annamaria walked inside and ran into Sandy.

"Are you going to join us?"

Sandy shook her head. "No. My old bones couldn't last for too long. I just wanted to say goodnight." Annamaria shook her head. Sandy was not as old as she acted but maybe taking care of a large mansion day after day wore her body out more than her age. They hugged. "Oh, and I talked to Anthony. He said he'll take care of it." Annamaria relaxed. She could enjoy the rest of the evening, after all.

Marianna and the others returned from their drive as Annamaria finished. The boys zoomed inside to grab snow gear for everyone to wear. While too much heat or cold wouldn't harm a vampire, their bodies were like a reptile, where they took on the temperature of their surroundings. Like mortals, they preferred to be warm.

They raced each other several times on each of the snow vehicles, Annamaria losing by several feet every time. She and Anthony and Marianna and Will shared the bigger sleds and tubes, going down the hills as couples. Luna also ran up and down the hills, chasing the sleds and rolling around in the snow. After about an hour, Annamaria was exhausted and sat on the porch, watching everyone else with a smile. Anthony was the fastest on a snowboard, and after claiming victory over the others several more times, he joined Annamaria on the porch.

"I have something else for you. Come with me?" Anthony held out his hand. Annamaria took his hand and followed him into the house and up into his bedroom. Her heart pounded when he closed the door. She had no reason to be nervous. She had been in his room almost daily. But tonight somehow felt different.

He opened the top drawer of his dresser and took out an old book. "I know it's not a very traditional present, but it's special to me, and I want you to have it."

Annamaria took the book and read the cover, *Elizabeth*. "Is this Elizabeth's magic book?" she asked.

"It is."

"Oh, Anthony, are you sure?" Annamaria's heart was swelling and breaking at the same time.

"Yes, if anyone deserves it, it's you." Anthony rubbed her hand with his thumb.

Annamaria sat down on Anthony's bed, handling the pages with reverence. "How old was she when she died?"

"Nineteen."

She had only one more year of magic written in her book than Marianna. Annamaria's gaze fell on one page, and she stopped turning.

Inside Sun

(Safe for vampires)

Solis-Deceptiomen

The above incantation creates the illusion of the sun indoors.

The brightness and warmth can be seen and felt.

For: Anthony

"Anthony, did she ever show you this spell?" Annamaria asked, pointing at the page.

Anthony looked over her shoulder and read it. He had a pained smile on his face. "No, she must have created it right before she died."

"Lay down." Annamaria pushed on his shoulders.

Anthony obeyed, stretching out on his bed, his hands behind his head, watching Annamaria. Annamaria laid Elizabeth's book open on the table Anthony stored his paints on. She raised her hands to the ceiling. "*Solis-decpetiomen.*" A small, bright light appeared above them and grew to the size of a basketball. Annamaria could feel the warmth, and based on Anthony's reaction, he could too. His eyes were wide, the corners of his mouth turned up as he touched his skin and looked up at the duplicate sun. Annamaria turned off the electric lights in Anthony's room and joined him on the bed. She called on air and water and threw some clouds up by the sun to circle around.

Anthony tugged Annamaria onto her back, nestling her into his arm. "I haven't felt the warmth of the sun in over three hundred years." His voice choked. Annamaria turned and kissed him, then lay her head on his chest. They laid there in comfortable silence while Anthony enjoyed the mini oasis Annamaria had conjured in his room.

"Anthony?"

"Hmmm?"

Annamaria opened her mouth, but no sound escaped for several seconds. "Am I the first person you've been with since Elizabeth?"

"No, I have been in three other relationships in between." Anthony shifted and surveyed her face. "Did I give the wrong answer?"

Annamaria exhaled. "No. I'm actually relieved. I was worried I might have this pressure to fill a three-hundred-year void."

Anthony chuckled and put his other arm around Annamaria's stomach, nestling his face into her neck. "You are the first witch since Elizabeth, though."

"Oh, well, I'm flattered." Annamaria giggled. Anthony pressed his lips to hers, tingles exploded all over her lips. Annamaria pulled away. "What are those tingles?"

Anthony looked away from Annamaria. "They're part of a vampire's, for lack of a better word, charm. It acts like a drug on human skin to make a potential victim more agreeable."

Annamaria furrowed her eyebrows. "So are these feelings not real?"

Anthony sat up. "Of course they are. The charm can't affect your mind or your heart. The magic in your blood protects you from feeling the full effects."

Annamaria scooted away from Anthony. "Do you use that on humans?"

"Not since I've met you." Anthony rubbed his eyes with his thumb and pointer finger. "For me, it's not out of lust or dominance. I need blood to be coherent and strong. I wish it could be different, but it's not. I just want them to not fear or feel pain."

Annamaria pursed her lips. She didn't like it, but she couldn't judge Anthony for it. He had been turned against his will and remained in order to protect his first love. He could not control what his body now required, and she couldn't fault him for trying his best to remain as humane as possible with his dietary needs. Annamaria sighed and allowed Anthony to tuck her back under his arm.

"How long do vampire relationships normally last?"

"You are full of questions tonight."

Annamaria couldn't read Anthony's tone, so she looked at him. His eyes were sparkling.

"Just humor me, it's my graduation party after all." Annamaria smiled and batted her lashes.

"All right, but only because I can't say no to those

pretty eyes. We're just like humans. Some find their forever partner and stay with them for centuries. Others date around from decade to decade."

"So am I just another name for your little black book?"

"What? I thought you were relieved I had dated around?"

"I am, I'm sorry. I'm just trying to figure us out, I guess." Annamaria sighed.

"You're trying to figure out if I'm some player?" Anthony laughed. Annamaria didn't say anything, hiding her face in her hands. Anthony removed her hand from her face so he could look into her eyes. "Every relationship I have been in was meaningful. And how I feel about you is one hundred times stronger than any of the past ones."

"How can you know after only a few months?"

Anthony shrugged. "Time? Experience? I just know."

He sat up, taking Annamaria with him. He took her hands in his, like he had so many times before when he wanted to tell her something important.

"When Marianna called to tell the rest of us her younger sister would accompany her, I didn't think anything of it. To me, you were going to be a witch version of Marianna. I looked forward to having magic in the house, but I wasn't prepared for any emotional connection. That morning, when you were walking down the hall, I opened my door to introduce myself. Our eyes met, something burst open inside me, and I knew I needed to get to know you." Anthony shook his head, his eyes shining. "It was funny to me. I've looked at your sister every day for the past two years and have never felt a thing other than friendship, but with you, the attraction was instant."

"I felt it, too." Annamaria squeezed Anthony's hands. "It took me much longer to accept it, though."

Anthony put one hand on her face, caressing her cheek with his thumb. He pulled her toward him, and she met him in the middle. Their kiss started soft, breathing each other in. Anthony laid her back on the bed, crawled on top of her, still kissing her. Annamaria wrapped her hands around his neck, drawing him down closer. He abandoned her lips and started kissing her forehead, eyelids, and down her neck, sucking just enough to elicit a moan from Annamaria. Everywhere his lips touched, tingles and goosebumps erupted on her skin.

In one swift movement, he flipped them over so he was on his back, and Annamaria straddled him. She bent forward to continue kissing him, and he placed his hands inside the back of her shirt, rubbing the skin of her lower back. Anthony tugged her shirt up to her bra line and caressed her exposed skin. He removed the rest of her shirt with care. He removed his shirt as well, and Annamaria stopped kissing him to enjoy tracing the lines of his inhuman muscles.

Anthony switched their places again, kissing Annamaria's bare stomach while she fought back giggles. He kissed back up to her lips, pressing their skin together. Anthony tugged on Annamaria's shorts, and she called on the air, throwing him off of her. A moment of tense silence followed.

"I'm so sorry."

Annamaria clapped her hands over her mouth, her eyes wide as Anthony lay flat on his back on the floor below the bed. Anthony got up, not meeting Annamaria's eyes, his brows furrowed. He didn't return to the bed.

"Um, what just happened?" he asked.

Annamaria looked down at her knees. "It was a natural reaction. I'm sorry."

"I need a minute."

Anthony walked out onto his balcony and shut the door with a soft click. Annamaria groaned and yanked on her hair. What was wrong with her? Didn't she want him? She was so stupid to send mixed signals like that. Annamaria grabbed her shirt and ran from Anthony's room.

Once in her room, Annamaria changed into pajamas, twisted her hair up, and sat on the floor against the wall. Looking up at the ceiling, she sighed. She was crazy attracted to Anthony. Why did she have to go to pieces every time he tried to go farther?

Several minutes later, there was a knock on Annamaria's door. She remained immobile.

"Annamaria? Can we talk?"

Anthony's voice pulled at her. She opened the door a crack. Anthony's shirt was back on.

"Why do you look so scared? I'm not mad," Anthony said, his hand on the door.

"You're not?" Annamaria opened the door wider.

Anthony took a step into her room and took her hand. "No. My pride was hurt. That's why I needed a minute. Will you come back to my room and talk?" Annamaria nodded at her feet and followed his lead down the hall.

Back in Anthony's room, they sat on his bed. Annamaria looked down and stared at her lap. Anthony raised her face. "Did I do something wrong?"

Annamaria shook her head. "It was me. When you took my shirt off, I thought I was ready, but I guess deep down I..." She looked away.

"You weren't?"

Annamaria bowed her head. "I'm so sorry. I shouldn't have sent mixed signals."

Anthony extended his hand to her, then dropped it. "You don't need to apologize. You can change your mind at any moment. I can wait. You are worth the wait."

Annamaria smiled and leaned into him. Anthony wrapped his arms around her, kissed the top of her head, and buried his nose in her hair.

They spent the next little while lying under the sun in comfortable silence. When Annamaria felt herself drifting off, she got up to leave.

Anthony grabbed her hand. "Will you stay the night here? With me? I promise I won't do anything. I just want to hold you while you sleep."

"Okay." Annamaria smiled and crawled back onto the bed.

Anthony pulled back the covers, and Annamaria laid down on a pillow. Annamaria snuggled against him and closed her eyes. Anthony wrapped his arm around her waist and traced patterns on her lower back. When Annamaria was asleep, the sun and clouds she conjured disappeared, enveloping the couple in darkness.

****

Annamaria spent the first part of September studying Elizabeth's magic book. The beginning pages looked very similar to hers and Marianna's. The later pages held a lot of fun spells, like the indoor sun spell.

Based on her writing, Elizabeth was of the mindset magic was for fun and should be enjoyed. Annamaria recorded everything she learned. The last page read like a journal entry instead of a spell.

BONDWITCH

The Bondwitch spell should not be recorded and needs to be lost and forgotten. It is a horrible ceremony in which a witch is forced against his or her will to become magically bound to a vampire and their coven. Once bound, the witch has no choice but to obey the vampire whom they are bound to. My mother, Sarah, was a bondwitch. She has described the feeling of being stuck inside one's head, screaming for help, yet no help comes. The desires and feelings of the witch are buried deep in their heart, and the desires of their vampire master take precedence. They have no choice, no agency, no liberty. The only way to be free is for the main vampire—who the witch is bound to—to be killed. That is how my mother was freed. The vampires who have captured me want to bind me to them. I will not. I will die first.

Annamaria stared at the page. Her heart raced, and her breathing sped up. Poor Elizabeth. She remembered her first conversation with Anthony. She had asked him if they wanted from her what his old coven had wanted with Elizabeth. He denied it, but something was off. Kylie and Tyler had also been so nonchalant about laying claim to her magic, almost like they were entitled to it. The biggest clue was how possessive Will was about Annamaria's activities and whereabouts. *Oh my gosh, are they going to bind me?* And what about Marianna? Was she a part of this as well? Perhaps this was the real reason she traveled to Harrison.

Annamaria hyperventilated, and she clutched her stomach. She paced her room. What should she do? She needed to confront Anthony and force him to tell the truth. She threw the door open, then closed it. First, she needed an emergency bag. She needed to be ready to escape, just in case. She summoned a backpack, packed her magic book, an outfit, and the leftover money from Trinity, then she shoved it under her bed.

Heart pounding, breathing shallow, Annamaria stomped down the hall to Anthony's room. He opened the door before she even knocked.

"Hey." He went to draw her into his arms, but Annamaria stopped him.

"Come to my room?" She kept her face passive.

"Sure."

As soon as the door was shut, she put the impenetrable lock spell on it. Anthony raised an eyebrow. "How did Elizabeth really die?"

Anthony looked confused. "She didn't want to live with vampires, and the conflict killed her."

Annamaria shook her head. "No. Tell me the truth. What happened?"

Anthony looked around, his gaze falling on Elizabeth's open book. His eyes scanned the open page, and his face fell. "Did you read that?"

Annamaria glared. "So did you forget this was in there, or is this how you planned on telling me?"

"Planned on telling you what?" Anthony held his confused face. What an excellent actor he was.

"Telling me that's what you guys want to do to me." Anthony recoiled at her raised voice. His face softened.

"Annamaria, listen—"

"Has everything been a way to get me to submit to this? The dance lessons with Kylie and Tyler? The relationship with you? Are you guys just manipulating me so I'll give in to the spell?" Tears filled her eyes, but she balled her fists and blinked them away. She must be strong right now.

"No, I swear. Everything has been real." Anthony stepped toward her. She took a step back.

"Then why does it all match? Why does everything make sense?"

Anthony bit his lip. "Can we sit down?"

"No, we can stand." Annamaria folded her arms.

Anthony took a deep breath. "Please listen and let me get to the end." Annamaria stood there with her arms still crossed, staring him down. "Yes, the bondwitch spell inspired Will when you first arrived. But I advised against the actual spell because it can be dangerous. Witches who fight the spell during the process die. That's how Elizabeth died. She fought the spell, and it killed her. The hope at the beginning was to give you a pleasant enough life, you would stay by choice and bless us with your magic. Will didn't make a good start of it, so Kylie, Tyler, and I took over. I had no idea I would fall in love with you, and Kylie and Tyler truly care for you as well. Everything changed and developed as we got to know you. We love you for you. We want you in this family, not just your magic."

Annamaria stood there in silence. Anthony just said he loved her. She shook her head. She couldn't get distracted. "Will doesn't seem to agree with the rest of you. He is still trying to control me."

"He'll come around." Anthony's face said otherwise. Annamaria rolled her eyes. "I won't let him hurt you."

"Was Marianna a part of this entire scheme?"

Anthony shook his head. "She doesn't know anything about it."

Annamaria's body was shaking so much, she was close to collapsing. How could she have been so stupid? At the very beginning of this imprisonment, she put herself on guard. Over time, she let them entangle themselves into her heart.

"Please, believe me." Anthony reached for her, but Annamaria remained still.

"I want to, but now everything Will has ever said and done makes sense." Annamaria blinked and wiped a stray tear.

"I know it looks that way, but he trusts my opinion on this since I have the most experience, and I have been very firm with him not to do the spell."

Annamaria assessed Anthony. She couldn't argue against a conversation she wasn't privy to. Annamaria sighed. She could forgive Anthony on the surface but pay better attention to everyone's words and actions and start planning her exit.

"You fell in love with me?" Her voice and face softened.

Anthony looked relieved. "Yes, I love you. I know you can't say those words back yet. But I want you to know that's how I feel."

He was going to make leaving so hard.

Chapter 18 Familiar

Annamaria showed Marianna the page in Elizabeth's book about the bondwitch spell. Marianna read over it, but her face remained passive.

"You aren't surprised by this." Annamaria studied her sister.

Marianna took a deep breath and closed her eyes. "There's something I need to tell you. Caroline is a bondwitch. She is bound to Diego and his coven. So when Anthony talked about Elizabeth, I put two and two together."

Annamaria gasped. "Why did Dawn leave you in that situation? Why didn't she rescue Caroline?"

"Dawn couldn't take on ten vampires by herself with a four-year-old in tow," said Marianna. "She must have run out of options. I didn't know for a long time. Caroline never told me. She was probably ordered not to. But in my mid-teens, I figured it out. That's why I wanted to leave when I turned eighteen. I was scared they would do the same to me. Ironically enough, they had different plans for me."

"I interrogated Anthony because of things he, Kylie, and Tyler have said, and of course, all of my problems with Will. Anthony admitted Will wants to do this spell on me."

Marianna gasped as her eyes bugged.

"Did you know about this?" Annamaria asked.

Marianna shook her head. "I had no idea. I swear. But I promise, I will not let him."

Annamaria sighed. "Marianna, I can't risk this happening to me. I have an emergency bag packed, and the next time Will tries to control me, I'm gone. I can't wait for Trinity."

Marianna closed her eyes and rubbed her brows. She let out a shuddering breath, her shoulders shaking. "I can't believe him."

Annamaria could, but she didn't say that to her sister. Instead, she grabbed her hand. "Will you come with me?"

Marianna opened her eyes and directed her gaze at Elizabeth's book. "I... I'll help you get out."

Annamaria squeezed Marianna's hand. "Please consider it."

Marianna pursed her lips and nodded, avoiding Annamaria's pleading eyes.

"I'm so sorry." Annamaria shook her head. "I feel terrible asking you to choose between me and Will."

Marianna glared at the wall. "You aren't responsible for this. Will is."

****

Annamaria spent the next couple of weeks on the lookout for signs the others were about to force the spell on her, which proved difficult since neither she nor Marianna knew how the spell was performed. Anthony must have known, but Annamaria was struggling to trust him. Still, she slept next to him each night. However, like in the past, when Annamaria rejected other advances, Anthony never did more than kiss and hold her. Annamaria slept by his side for two reasons. One, she wanted to. She still was so drawn to him, and she wanted to spend as much time with him as possible before she left. Two, she wanted to prevent him from noticing her changes and preparations.

Annamaria, Kylie, and Tyler were working on several fun and upbeat routines—cha-chas, sambas, jives, freestyle, and hip-hop. The energy these routines created allowed Annamaria to hide her suspicions.

One evening, while Annamaria and Anthony were on the couch in the living room reading a book together, Tyler and Kylie burst into the room.

"We have amazing news," said Tyler.

"Everyone, come listen," said Kylie. A few seconds later, Marianna and Will arrived.

"We are going to do a short, live tour of our most popular routines!" Tyler beamed with his arms spread out.

"The tour includes the Reunited series, so Annamaria gets to come with us." Kylie jumped up and down, clapping.

Annamaria jumped off the couch and cheered.

"No." Will, glared at Kylie.

"Well, Marianna will also be with me. She plays the piano for the final number." Annamaria's body tensed, and her magic hummed.

Will shook his head. "No. You and Marianna need to stay here to practice magic."

"I can practice magic while on the road, plus there's tons of magic in the actual show." Annamaria rolled her eyes. "Why do you care about my magic so much?"

Will faltered, then flashed a smile that didn't reach his eyes. "I don't. But your aunt does, so you need to stay here."

Annamaria opened up her mouth, but Kylie spoke first. "Now wait just a minute! You said all of us had equal access to her magic. This is how Tyler and I want to use it."

Anthony put his forehead in his hands. Tyler covered his mouth. Annamaria locked eyes with her sister. They couldn't pretend ignorance anymore. Marianna nodded. Will caught the silent communication and growled at Kylie.

Kylie closed her eyes and let out a breath. She turned to Annamaria. "That came out wrong."

"No, I think it came out right." Annamaria glared at Kylie. She surveyed the room. Anthony now mirrored Tyler, and his leg shook, refusing to look at Annamaria. Marianna had a hand on Will's shoulder, whose hands were balled into fists. "Listen, none of you get to control me or my magic. If I cannot truly be a part of the family, then I don't need to be here anymore."

Silence met Annamaria's declaration. After a few seconds, Kylie, Tyler, and Anthony rushed to her.

"No, that's not what this is."

"It's just a miscommunication."

"We don't want to control you."

Annamaria put her fingers to her temples, trying to block them out. She threw her hands out, enough air flying outward to catch everyone's attention. "I know about everything." She met Will's angry eyes. It was a mistake to wait for him to push her because that still allowed him control. If she wanted to control her life, she needed to control when she left Will's coven.

Will looked at Marianna and gave her a raised eyebrow. Pain and anger swirled in her eyes. Will shrugged. His confident smirk erased, the flirtatious twinkle in his eye gone. Cold, dangerous eyes met Annamaria's. "Fine. I only allowed you to live here to use your magic. So you have two choices, live under my direction, or I'm putting the bond spell on you."

Everyone froze, looking between Will and Annamaria. Annamaria clenched her jaw. Of course no one jumped to defend her from Will. They never had before. She shifted her gaze in Marianna's direction, who gave her a tiny encouraging nod. She called on the air, threw all the vampires backward, and raced from the room. Halfway up the stairs, powerful arms wrapped around her waist, upsetting her momentum and banging her jaw onto the above step. Fingers dug into her waist and turned her, slamming her onto her back. She met Will's predatory gaze.

Two pairs of hands ripped him off Annamaria. Anthony and Tyler held onto Will as he thrashed, his eyes blazing. Marianna appeared in front of him, cupping his face with her hands. "Honey, please, don't hurt her. Let her go."

Kylie moved toward Annamaria. Annamaria summoned a fireball, and Kylie froze, putting her hands up.

"Don't come near me."

Kylie took a step back, her eyes widening. *Sorry,* she mouthed.

Annamaria kept the fire going as she fled up the stairs while Will argued with the others, and Marianna tried to placate him. She slammed her bedroom door and put the shield spell around her entire room before taking another breath.

What should she do? She thought when she left,

Marianna would come with her. She also didn't expect to be *literally* running for her life. She couldn't run when Will could follow her. She would have to wait until the sun rose, which meant Marianna couldn't come with her.

Annamaria rubbed her ring. Her ring grew warm and guided her toward the door. This had to be Marianna's way of saying she received Annamaria's call, and she was on her side. As Annamaria sat on the floor, a knock sounded on her door.

"Annamaria!" Anthony, Kylie, and Tyler said in unison.

"Annamaria, I'm so sorry," said Kylie. "What I said was so stupid. I didn't mean for it to come out that way."

"We don't want you bound," said Tyler.

"Please open the door." Anthony's voice choked.

Annamaria's body shook at hearing his voice. A body slid down the door. Guessing Anthony was on the other side, she put her hand against the door, wishing she could touch him. Her ring warmed again. A paper poked her backside from under the door, and her ring warmed a third time. Annamaria grabbed the paper and read.

Annamaria,

When the sun rises, leave. Go find Grandma. I'll find you again.

~ Marianna

"Are you still there?" Anthony asked.

"Yes," she whispered.

"I promise I did not know he was heading in this direction. I would have stopped him if I had known. Please believe me. I love you."

"Okay."

They spent the next couple of hours whispering to each other. Annamaria was heartbroken she could not say goodbye to him. She drifted off to his soothing voice.

****

Annamaria woke up with a sore neck and jumped at the time her phone showed. 10:00 a.m. The sun had been up for a little over three hours. Annamaria grabbed her backpack from under her bed. She had to undo the shield spell in order to go out onto the balcony. Luckily, the sound barrier would keep Annamaria's actions unknown. She opened her balcony window and stepped out onto the edge. The surrounding air waited for instructions.

She looked back at the door. If Anthony was still sitting there, and no one else was on the second floor, she could say a quick goodbye. She didn't believe he would stop her. Maybe he would even join Marianna and catch up with her later. But if Will was also on the second floor, he could grab Annamaria before she had time to summon a fireball. Desire overpowered logic. Annamaria left her backpack on the balcony and tiptoed to the door.

She opened the door at the speed of a snail and stuck her head out the tiniest bit. Without time to react, Annamaria was yanked by her hair, dragged down the hall, and thrown into Will's room. Will slammed her against the wall. She summoned fire, but Will squeezed her wrists until the fire died.

"Oh no you don't. You are going to spend the day with me."

Annamaria kicked and screamed. Even though her

resistance would do nothing, she couldn't stand there pliant. Will cackled, his eyes bore into Annamaria's. His pupils dilated, and the familiar light feeling opened her mind to hypnosis. "Be quiet and stay still."

He lowered his head toward her neck, his fangs elongating. Annamaria's magic flowed and jolted against her bones and muscles, but she could not move or make a sound. She continued to struggle, but it was like pushing on the lid of a locked box. Right before Will's fangs contacted the skin on her neck, Annamaria's muscles twitched, and she threw her hand in front of her neck. Will's fangs sank into her hand, and she let out a bloodcurdling scream as her flesh tore. His lips clasped over the wound, the feeling of her blood suctioning out of her body a strange sensation. A new, cold substance entered her bloodstream. Annamaria's knees grew weak.

Will's door sprang open, a blur tackled Will, and his fangs ripped a gash across Annamaria's hand. Anthony pinned Will to the floor. Will kicked Anthony off him and lunged at Annamaria, but Anthony had given her time to draw a line of fire between them. Marianna ran into the room just as Annamaria finished the line. Will roared. Anthony took a step back from the fire, his chest heaving. Marianna kept her hands at her sides and motioned for Annamaria to go.

"Annamaria, can we talk?" Anthony's gaze rotated between the fire and Annamaria.

She glared. "No, I'm done talking." Her face softened. "I'm sorry." She met Anthony's, then Marianna's eyes.

Annamaria turned, ran behind the curtains, opened the door to Will's balcony, and stepped out onto the ledge. She called on the air and lowered herself to the ground. She levitated her backpack off her balcony, put it on, and ran to the gate. Calling on the air again, she rose herself up over the gate and down onto the road leading down the mountain. As soon as her feet hit the ground, she ran.

****

Anthony, Kylie, Tyler, and Marianna sat on the living room couches while Will stormed back and forth across the floor. The smell of smoke wafted through the house. They were successful in putting the fire out, but Will's room was black and crispy.

"Why the hell did you interfere?" Will asked Anthony.

"Because you always lose control." Anthony spoke through gritted teeth. "You weren't going to convince her by abusing her. Like I've been saying from the beginning, she needs to feel like a true, free member of this household."

"And look where that thinking got us." Will threw his hands in the air. "She nearly burned both of us to ash and is now running through the woods!"

"Will, just let her go." Everyone stared at Marianna. Though she had a forceful personality in her and Will's personal relationship, she had never commanded him in front of the coven.

Will got in Marianna's face. "I'm doing this for you. You have been so depressed as a vampire, we all can see it. I know you miss your magic. If she is bound to us, you can wield magic through her."

Marianna looked away from Will. How could he think she would be okay with enslaving her own sister? He had been with her every step of her journey to find her family. She looked back into his eyes, searching.

"You know how much I love you. And you've shown how much you love me with all you did to help me find my family." Her gaze held his as she gently placed her hands on his face, her eyes pleading for him to listen. "But this is not what I want. I want a sisterly relationship with Annamaria, and I want her to make the choices I never got to make."

Will stood stiffly under Marianna's soft touch, the rest of the room fell silent. His gaze stayed locked on Marianna's, but the guy she fell in love with was no longer there. "I'm doing this with or without you, Marianna."

Marianna let her hands fall from his face and stood up. "Then when the sun sets, I'm gone."

She walked out of the living room. Will caught up and slammed her against the wall. Marianna shoved against his chest, but her efforts were futile, her two years were nothing compared to Will's seventy.

"You're not going anywhere." He dragged Marianna downstairs into the basement and chained her up in one of the rooms.

The shackles had been hexed by a witch to keep the strength of a vampire or werewolf contained. Both were silent as the chains clicked the end of their relationship. Marianna listened to his footsteps return to the living room.

"At sundown we are going to go get the little brat and drag her back by her hair," Will said.

Silence.

"Okay," Kylie said. Forced out, not agreeable.

Silence.

"Tyler?" Silence. "Anthony?" Silence. "We leave

at sundown." Will's footsteps pounded across the ceiling.

Marianna closed her eyes and slumped against the wall. They all must have agreed. Not because they wanted to. Will used his power as coven leader to force it. Just like he was going to force Annamaria to be bound to him.

Kylie's voice filtered downstairs. "Anthony, what are we going to do?"

Anthony groaned. "It's 1694 all over again. I couldn't save Elizabeth then, and now I'm going to lose Annamaria in the same way."

Kylie shushed him. "You had no control then, and you have no control now. This is not your fault."

More footsteps, walking back and forth.

"You don't understand! I promised her no one in this house would hurt her. I promised her *I* would never hurt her. And now I have to break both promises tonight."

"Let's just hope she gets far enough away before the sun sets," said Tyler.

Yes, please, please let Annamaria get far enough away during daylight.

****

Annamaria had just barely finished the switchback that put the mansion out of eyesight when she had to slow down. All of her athletic ability was attributed to dance. She was not a runner. Plus, her hand was killing her. She had a good-sized gash across her palm. She could also feel the cold venom moving through her veins. Annamaria gasped and stopped moving. What if vampire venom was like snake venom?

Annamaria stepped off the paved road and found a

large rock to sit on. She breathed in through her nose and out through her mouth, trying her hardest to breathe slowly and in control. Even with stopping to rest, her blood was still racing, and the icy feeling of the venom continued to spread through her body. Everywhere the cold touched left her numb, and her eyelids drooped. Annamaria held on to the rock for support, forced her eyes wide as they begged to close, but she couldn't fight it. Losing consciousness, she fell backward from the rock onto the ground, shielded from the view of the road.

Annamaria woke up to wet on her face. Something slobbery and rough brushed the bottom of her cheek to her temple. She opened her eyes to a mass of black fur. Annamaria exhaled, and her shoulders relaxed.

"Luna girl." Her voice was raspy, her throat dry.

Luna whined and tugged on Annamaria's shirt. Annamaria sat up, and her head spun. She leaned against the rock until the dizziness passed. Luna lay in Annamaria's lap while Annamaria waited for her body to regain its strength. She scratched Luna's head while Luna panted with her tongue lolled out.

"I wish you could tell me what's going on with Marianna. I hope she's okay."

Luna looked at Annamaria and let out a little huff. The feeling returned to Annamaria's limbs, and her brain became functional again. Luna jumped up and tugged on Annamaria's shirt again. Annamaria stood up and started walking back to the road, but Luna howled and yanked Annamaria a few steps into the forest.

"Luna, I need to go that way." Annamaria pointed in the town's direction. The sun was farther west than was comfortable. Luna, however, continued to pull on

Annamaria, whining, howling, and growling.

Luna stopped for a minute, ears turning back toward the forest. A strange noise came from the trees. It sounded like a cry, but it wasn't human. The cry tore at Annamaria's heart, and without thinking, she took off into the forest. Luna followed at Annamaria's heels, no longer tugging on her clothes.

A trail of stepping stones materialized in front of Annamaria's feet as she walked. She looked behind her, and the road was nowhere to be seen. The magical trail was not behind her either. The stones disappeared with each step, but they were still in front of her, leading her on. Annamaria stopped. *This is weird.* She turned in the direction she came from when the sound called out again. As if someone else controlled her, Annamaria continued deeper into the forest, Luna at her heels.

Climbing over a fallen tree, Annamaria's gaze landed on the source of the sound. A baby black bear caught in a trap. Annamaria rushed toward it. As she approached, the bear stopped crying. Looking at her, the cub nudged its head at its trapped paw. "*Recludo.*" The trap sprang free. The bear limped toward her and jumped into her lap, nuzzling her with its head.

She giggled. "You're welcome, little fella. Let me look at your paw."

Annamaria's mouth fell open as the bear raised its hurt paw toward her. She took the paw in her hands, careful to avoid painful pressure. "*Salutem.*" It healed halfway. "*Salutem.*" It healed completely.

Annamaria was certain the bear just smiled. It jumped on Annamaria and nuzzled her. She hugged it but stopped when reality hit her. The mother was sure to be nearby, and mama bears were ferocious and protective. "Okay, go along now. Find your mom." She put the bear down. The bear shook its head no, or was that a trick of the light? The cub jumped onto her foot, wrapping its paws around her legs.

Good grief, what was Annamaria going to do if the mom showed up? Annamaria pried the bear from her leg. "Look, you are super cute, and I'm happy to have helped you, but if your mom sees us, she's going to eat me." The baby bear continued to climb Annamaria. "Luna." Annamaria looked around for the wolf. Luna lay in the brush, a few feet away, watching the interaction with a calm expression. "Luna, can you make it leave?" Luna also shook her head no. A low rumble sounded around them. Annamaria's blood ran cold. A full-grown bear lumbered out of some brush toward Annamaria and the baby.

Annamaria froze. Hold still, and the bear will leave her alone, right? Wait, no. Appear as big as possible. No. Fetal position and protect her neck. Ah, who was she kidding? She had already been caught red-handed with this bear's baby. No amount of survival training would get her out of this. Annamaria's magic hummed. No way. She could not hurt an innocent creature.

The baby ran toward the adult, humming, and swatted its mother's face. The mother nuzzled her baby and continued to walk toward Annamaria. Annamaria met the mother's eyes, and for an inexplicable reason, Annamaria sensed she was not in danger. The mother put its head under Annamaria's hand, and she petted the coarse fur. Then, the mother picked up her baby with her mouth, and placed it in Annamaria's arms.

Annamaria's eyebrows rose. "You want me to take your baby?"

The mother exhaled and dove her head down. She nuzzled her baby one more time, turned around, and walked back into the trees. Annamaria's jaw dropped. A playful swipe on her face returned her attention to the cub.

Annamaria held the baby bear up to her face. "So you're with me now?" The baby made an assenting noise. Annamaria sat it down next to her feet. "Well, you're going to have to keep up because we need to arrive in town before nightfall."

Annamaria looked around, trying to figure out where to go. The sun was closer to the western mountains than when she woke up. The town was west of the house, so if Annamaria kept the sun on her left side, she should run into the road. Annamaria began walking, and the bear tumbled along around her feet while Luna walked calmly on Annamaria's other side.

How did I hear his cry from so far away? "So why are you supposed to be with me?" It made another noise Annamaria could not comprehend a meaning from. The image of Gwen sitting on Trinity's shoulder entered Annamaria's mind. Trinity talked to Gwen, and Gwen talked back. Annamaria glanced at Luna. She and Marianna shared a similar bond. Was this bear Annamaria's familiar?

"Are you my familiar?" The bear looked at Annamaria before changing direction and heading east up the mountain. "That's the wrong way. It's not safe." The bear ignored her and kept climbing. It moved very fast for a baby, and Annamaria tripped over rocks and large branches. Luna also followed the bear, ignoring Annamaria's objections.

Annamaria stumbled upon a perfect circle of thin

trees and found the bear inside. The sounds of the forest disappeared. A soft whisper drifted from the circle and surrounded Annamaria. She somehow knew not to be afraid and stepped into the circle with her bear. A light filled the circle. Annamaria and the bear rose a few feet into the air. Light particles, similar to the first time Annamaria shot magic out of her hands, burst out of her chest, and the same light burst from the bear. The particles intermingled in midair above them before they split and reentered Annamaria's body and the bear's.

Annamaria and the bear descended back to the ground, and the light faded. "What just happened?"

We are connected.

The bear did not speak. No sound filtered into her ears. The words appeared in her heart, but she knew the bear spoke to her.

"Can anyone else hear you?"

No.

Annamaria grinned. She loved this little black fur ball already. She increased her pace and checked the sun, which bordered the western horizon—too close for Annamaria's comfort. How long had all of this taken? "We have to hurry. We have to get into town before the sun sets, or the vampires are going to get us."

The bear followed Annamaria. Luna, however, looked at them and headed back in the house's direction.

Luna says goodbye and good luck.

"Thanks, Luna!" Luna howled back. Annamaria turned back to the bear. "So are you a boy or a girl?"

Boy.

"What's your name?"

You name me.

"Hm, Pooh Bear?"

No.

Annamaria giggled. "I'm sorry. Bad joke. Do you like Nico?"

Yes.

"Perfect. Nico, let me catch you up on everything." Annamaria recounted her life's story to her new companion. When she finished, she was back on the road. The sky tinted pink, orange, and red. Annamaria's heart stopped.

"Can you run fast? Because we need to zoom down the road."

Yes. I am faster than normal.

Annamaria and Nico took off down the road, sprinting as fast as they could, their gazes trained on the setting sun.

****

Marianna heaved against the chains with all her strength. She tried running at vampire speed but couldn't gain enough momentum before she ran out of chain and it yanked her back. She summoned a ball of light and held it against the chain, but the light would never be as hot as fire. No matter what she did, she could not break the chains.

"Anthony!" she screamed upward at the ceiling. "Kylie! Tyler! I know you can hear me! I know you love her! Please, fight it!"

Marianna had spent the past two years respecting Will's authoritative power. Choosing to disobey him was as easy as turning a corner. For the others, it would be like a mortal trying to fight hypnotism. Anthony would have an easier time than Kylie and Tyler. He was centuries older than everyone else, and Will wasn't his sire. However, Anthony had lived with Will the longest, accepting Will as his coven leader.

Marianna slumped against the chains. She hoped Annamaria got herself a suitable distance away before the sun set. There was one problem. How much venom was in Annamaria's system? The right amount and Annamaria would sleep for hours, especially since it was Annamaria's first time being bitten. Marianna remembered her first time experiencing venom traveling through her bloodstream...

Marianna walked down the hall in Diego's house to her bedroom. She jumped and gasped at the sudden appearance of Luca blocking her path. He smirked.

"I'm sorry. I didn't mean to startle you."

Marianna returned his smile with a small one of her own. Though her eyes were still wide, her heart raced. "That's okay. Excuse me." She tried to walk around him.

His hand grabbed her wrist and spun her back toward him. His other hand snapped around her waist, drawing her flush against him. Luca dipped his head toward Marianna's chest and grinned at the sound of her dashing heart. He nuzzled her against the wall. Marianna's lips trembled.

"Please, let me go."

"Sh." Luca locked eyes with Marianna, and his pupils dilated. "Hold still, be quiet." Marianna's head spun, but she kept her coherence, wiggling against his powerful hold, and continuing to whisper, "Please." He dilated his pupils again, and Marianna's limbs weakened. "Hold still, be quiet." This time, Marianna's body froze, as silent tears leaked down her cheeks.

Luca licked the tears off of Marianna's cheeks and

grazed his mouth down to her neck. His vicelike grip on her wrist loosened, and he pinned his hand to the small of her back, holding her like a lover. Luca kissed her neck. Her skin erupted into tingles, then her neck numbed. She didn't feel his fangs sinking into her skin. Marianna's vision blurred as her blood suctioned out of the holes in her neck, and a strange feeling spread through her bloodstream as his venom entered her body. The more blood left her body, the more venom spread. Marianna's equilibrium turned over, her knees buckled, and Luca caught her. He carried her like a child into her bedroom, where he laid her on her bed...

Marianna shook herself out of the awful memory at the sound of footsteps and the door being unlocked. Will walked into the room. Marianna stared up at the man who she thought she had loved, who she thought had loved her. How could she have fallen for a man so similar to Luca? Both needing their women to fear and submit. Marianna wasn't going to submit anymore.

"The sun is almost down. We're going to collect your sister. I'm giving you a second chance. Have you reconsidered?"

Marianna bit her tongue instead of spitting in his face. A plan was forming in her head, and she couldn't help Annamaria if she was in these chains.

Chapter 19 To Protect and Serve

Annamaria and Nico entered town just as the sun sank below the horizon. "Can I put you in my backpack? It will make getting into someone's house easier." Nico stood on his hind legs and raised his front paws. She put him in and zipped up the flap except for a hole in the top for his head.

Annamaria ran to the first house, pounded on the door, and rang the bell. All the lights were off, but Annamaria hoped someone was inside just the same. After a minute of no answer, Annamaria ran to the next house. Same situation, no lights, no answer. At the third house, Annamaria shifted from one foot to the next, flapping her hands at her sides as she looked around. Why was no one home?

Did she just hear running? "*Recludo*." Annamaria turned the knob and found herself cascaded in light.

"Police! Put your hands up and turn around slowly."

Nico dropped to the bottom of Annamaria's backpack. Annamaria let go of the door, put her hands up, and turned around. She squinted as the bright light hit her face. A dark figure walked toward her. Please be the real police. Please be the real police.

"Care to tell us what you are doing?" a gruff voice asked from behind the flashlight's beam.

"I'm just arriving. I'm new." Annamaria squinted

over the light.

"Really?" a second voice asked. "The owners didn't mention a renter moving in."

Annamaria shrugged. "They must have forgotten."

"And who are the owners?"

Annamaria looked down at her feet. "I forgot."

"A simple phone call can get this cleared up. Let's go down to the station." He stepped toward Annamaria and touched her arm.

Annamaria screamed and jumped backward into the house. "No. I have to be inside a house."

"Miss, you don't have any keys in your hand. The owners did not inform us of renters. There are no vehicles on this street. From our point of view, this is a strange circumstance. Please, come willingly to the station."

Annamaria tried to shut the door with the plan to magically lock it, but the officer stopped her with his foot. He grabbed Annamaria's arm and dragged her onto the porch. Annamaria screamed and wriggled. Her magic hummed, but she kept the energy inside. She couldn't harm them. They were innocent humans just doing their job.

The officer with the flashlight groaned. "We don't have time for this, Dave. We have enough probable cause, and now she's resisting. Just cuff her and let's go."

The officer holding her arm adjusted her in front of him, took her backpack off, guided her hands behind her, and placed handcuffs around her wrists.

"You are under arrest for breaking and entering," he said. His partner shifted the flashlight from her face to her backpack and unzipped it.

"Don't!"

"What the hell?"

Nico jumped out of the backpack and ran into the woods.

I'll be back.

Stunned silence followed as Annamaria and the two officers watched Nico disappear into the trees. The officer who cuffed her regained control and led Annamaria to his car. Annamaria walked under the guide of his hand on her arm. Her voice was lost.

They placed her in the back seat of their car. The click of the door brought her voice back. "No, it's not safe. We need to get inside the house." The officers ignored her and started sending in information to dispatch. Annamaria continued to yell they needed to get inside. In between hysterics, she overheard them order a tox-screen and send out animal control to make sure the baby bear and his mom didn't come into town.

Annamaria's legs were like gelatin when they pulled her out of the car and led her into the station. She turned her head back and forth. Was that a figure in the shadows? The handcuffs didn't lock her magic, but they made it impossible to aim well. Please, let the vampires be hesitant to make a scene in the town so close to their home.

As they entered the station, a third officer ran toward them. He took Annamaria by the shoulder and bent down to her level. He studied her face with his mouth open. "What's your name, sweetheart?" He was the officer from the Fourth of July.

"Annamaria Lyons," she whispered.

He glared above Annamaria's head. "Uncuff her. Now."

"Yes, Captain."

Annamaria's hands were freed, and she was guided into an investigation room.

"Would you like anything to eat or drink?" the captain asked after helping Annamaria into a chair.

Annamaria shook her head. She didn't think she could handle putting anything in her stomach. The captain sat down across from her, and an officer Annamaria recognized as the one watching her from the restaurant, sat down next to him.

"Annamaria, I'm Captain John Russells, and this is Officer Craig Stevens. Can you tell us what happened to you?"

Annamaria stared at the table. There was no way she could tell them the truth. "I was taken, and I got away." She didn't lie. Will did take her to his house, and she did get away.

"Do you know who took you?" Captain Russells asked.

"No."

"What about your aunt? Is she nearby also?"

"I don't know where she is."

"Was she taken with you?"

"We were separated. I haven't seen her since May."

"You were taken in Wyoming. Do you know where you are now?"

"Pennsylvania."

"Do you know how you got here?"

Annamaria looked up and breathed. "A car. We drove for three days."

"But you don't know who took you?"

Again, Annamaria shook her head.

"You mean to tell me you have been in the presence of your kidnapper for the past four months, and you don't know their name?" Captain Russells failed to look impersonal. Annamaria bowed her head. Captain Russells sighed. "Can you at least describe them to me?"

"It's not safe," Annamaria whispered.

"Sweetheart, I assure you, you are safe here. No one can harm you anymore." Annamaria shook her head, blinking back the tears threatening to spill over. "Can you tell me where you escaped from? How did you get here?"

"It's not safe." Annamaria's voice rose slightly. "They can hear us."

She appeared crazy, but her heart pounded faster with each passing minute. She needed to figure out a way to tell the police how serious the situation was without telling them too much.

"They?" asked Captain Russells. "How many?"

"I thought only one, but the others, they lied. They tricked me." A few tears trickled down her cheeks.

Officer Stevens leaned forward. "Sir, perhaps she needs some rest, and she can answer questions later."

Captain Russells sliced his hand in front of Officer Stevens. "No. She's finally talking. Annamaria, can you tell me how many?"

Annamaria took a deep breath. "Four." She was not about to throw Marianna under the bus. Kylie, Tyler, and Anthony had known. Their friendship didn't matter anymore. They should have been honest.

"Did they hurt you?"

Annamaria extended her hand, showing the bite sustained by Will. The two police officers looked at the scab shaped like teeth. For having sustained the injury less than twelve hours ago, it was almost healed. Perhaps magic in her blood healed her without needing an incantation.

"They bit you?" Captain Russells' eyes roved over Annamaria's hand. "Those don't even look human."

A loud bang like a car crash reverberated through the walls. Annamaria jumped out of her chair and raised her hands, placing her feet in a fighter's stance.

Annamaria spun in a circle, surveying the walls and ceiling. "I'm sorry. I'll stop talking. Please, don't hurt them!"

"Sir, let's not push her," Officer Stevens said.

"You're right." Captain Russells sighed and ran his hand down his face. "We should call the FBI and Harrison PD, anyway."

"I'll call them," Officer Stevens said.

"Thanks, Craig. Annamaria, come with me. It's not luxurious, but we have a cot you can rest on."

Annamaria jumped back from the captain, her breath coming faster and sharper. "No. It's not safe. We need to get inside a house. All of us!"

Stevens and the captain exchanged a look, then the captain placed a gentle but firm hand on Annamaria's arm and guided her into a new room with a couple of cots, pillows, and blankets.

"Rest in here." He squeezed her shoulder. "I'll let you know when we have information from the FBI." He took out a key. "I'm sorry, but I'm going to have to lock this door for your safety until you are calm."

Annamaria sank onto the nearest cot, shaking and hyperventilating. She was tempted to put a lock spell on the door, but what if the police noticed? There was a small window on the far wall, and Annamaria was sure shadows passed by it. She wanted to rub her *sisters* ring, but she was terrified to risk Will showing up with Marianna.

The key scraped in the lock again. Annamaria shrank into the back corner and positioned her hands, ready. She lowered her hands when Officer Stevens' head poked around the door.

"Annamaria? Are you doing okay?"

Annamaria straightened up and walked toward him with careful steps. "Yes, sorry. I'm just very jumpy."

"I understand." Stevens walked in and closed the door. His eyes darkened as he looked Annamaria up and down. "I know why you need to get inside a house."

Annamaria's mouth fell open. "You do?"

"Yes, and I'm going to help you." He beckoned Annamaria to follow him. They walked down the hall to the back of the station. "My car is parked out this way." Stevens gestured to the back exit. Annamaria followed him outside, glancing from side to side, not seeing anything. She got in the passenger seat, and he started driving the direction Annamaria had come from.

"Where are we going?" Annamaria's gaze raked the surroundings.

"My house," Stevens said.

"They haven't been invited in?"

He shook his head. "Absolutely not."

Annamaria sighed, and her shoulders relaxed. "How do you know about them?"

"They approached me several years ago. I sweep things under the rug when tourists go missing, and they leave the residents alone." Stevens kept his gaze on the road.

Annamaria's stomach lurched. Stevens shrugged. "It's the best way to protect and serve the community. Anyway, I didn't even think of connecting your disappearance to them. I'm sorry."

Annamaria stared at the road. "What did you do about the three missing persons from the summer?"

"Their bodies were eventually found in the mountains, and their families were told they perished in a hiking accident." There was something in Stevens' voice. Embarrassment? Regret?

Annamaria clenched her teeth and swallowed bile. They arrived at a dark house. Stevens must not have a family, or they were already asleep. Annamaria didn't even know what time it was. She had turned off her cell phone to prevent them from tracking her. She followed Stevens toward the house, surveying the darkness, her hands ready. He fumbled in his pocket.

"Damn it. I left my house keys at the station. Looks like we'll have to go around back."

Annamaria followed him around the side. She shook so much her feet stumbled a few times. Stevens' backyard opened up into the woods. He stopped, grabbed Annamaria's arm so hard it hurt, and threw her into the shadows of his neighbor's house. A pair of arms wrapped around Annamaria's torso, pinning her arms to her sides.

"Thanks, Craig." Goosebumps erupted on her skin as Will's voice grated in her ear. She screamed in fury.

"I'm sorry." Stevens looked to the side. "Like I said, this is how I have to protect and serve." He turned away, then looked back. "And besides, it's not like you're fully human. You're out of my jurisdiction." He bolted to his car and drove away at top speed.

Will towed Annamaria into the woods, but he could not get a good hold on her wrists. She called on the air, flew out of his grasp, and landed in a tree.

"I can climb," he said in a singsong voice.

Annamaria thrust him down with water. Something large landed on her back, flattening her to the ground. She got up, facing Tyler. She blasted him with water as well. Will was up and heading toward her again. She threw a fireball at him. This was life and death. He jumped out of the way and backed up again, redirecting his angle.

Duck!

Annamaria did so just as Kylie's body sailed over her. She buried Kylie in earth and threw some more fire at Will, who continued to dodge it. Will screamed, but Annamaria was sure she had not hit him. He shook his leg. "Get off, you stupid thing." Nico's baby teeth gripped Will's ankle. Will kicked hard, and Nico flew several feet, landing in a bush.

"*Incarcero!*"

Annamaria threw the golden cage at Will. Annamaria could not see if her aim was true because she was forced down on her knees, her arms yanked behind her, and the dreadful pinch of her magic being kinked shuddered throughout her body. She had never been able to overcome all of them.

Annamaria screamed again and gagged as a hand wrapped around her throat. Her face was forced up to meet Will's irate eyes. Her cage was unsuccessful, as usual. Off to the side, Anthony scooped up Nico. Will squeezed, and she gagged.

"Will," said Kylie's voice on Annamaria's left

side. "Don't kill her."

"I won't, unless she makes me."

He raised Annamaria up and slammed her back into a tree. "Keep her arms tight." Kylie and Tyler kept their hold and wrapped her arms backward around the tree, looking anywhere but at her.

"Listen here, girlie. You can come back up to the house. Or I can kill you, right here, right now."

"Will!" Kylie said. Will ignored her.

"Kill me," Annamaria sputtered.

Kylie, Tyler, and Anthony took in a collective sharp breath. However, Annamaria was sure Will was bluffing. He had spent too much time trying to force Annamaria under his thumb to lose her just like that.

Before Will could respond, several lights shone on their party.

"POLICE! Everybody, hands up."

Before anyone could respond, one by one, the lights dropped. Marianna appeared on the scene, dragging four bodies, and dropped them at Annamaria's feet.

"They aren't dead, yet. But they will be if you don't come." Marianna's voice was emotionless, her eyes trained above Annamaria's head.

Her own sister had turned against her. Annamaria's heart broke right there. There was no way Annamaria could allow the deaths of four innocent people on her conscience. She closed her eyes and bowed her head. Will let go of her throat, and Tyler and Kylie let go of her arms. Annamaria collapsed to the ground, coughing and sobbing.

A pair of arms she knew too well picked her up and carried her. Annamaria kept her eyes closed. She did not want to look at him right now. She was lowered, and the cushion of the back seat molded to her weight, providing relief for her tired muscles. She looked away from him.

A rough grab on her hair yanked her head awkwardly toward her left shoulder. A piercing pain erupted on her exposed neck. She screamed and wiggled against who she was sure was Will, but he held her tight. Venom entered her bloodstream, and her body weakened right away. Her arms dropped as they became numb, followed by the rest of her body. Annamaria was sure she was dying when she lost consciousness.

****

Annamaria took a deep breath and opened her eyes. It was almost too dark to see. Her body hurt. A hard surface pressed into her buttocks. This couldn't be her room. She looked around. Judging by the chains clasped around her wrists and all over the walls, she was in the dungeon in the basement. "*Recludo*." Nothing. "*Recludo!*" Worse than nothing. Annamaria couldn't even feel her magic. Had Tyler and Kylie done what Anthony feared? Had they damaged her to the point she couldn't do magic? She was useless to them without magic. What would they do to her then?

A masculine chuckle sounded from the dark. She looked around, her gaze settled on a man standing in a corner. He stepped closer, but Annamaria did not recognize him. He was of average height, had messy blond hair, and his skin had a fleshy hue. He lacked the perfect posture vampires possessed.

"That was a cute show you put on in the woods."

Annamaria glared at him. "Who are you?"

He leered. "Oh yes, introductions. I'm sorry, how rude of me. I'm Leo."

"What do you want, Leo?"

His smile widened at her tone. "Short, sweet, and to the point. I like it. I am here to offer you two options. I will unlock these chains right now and escort you to Valentina." Annamaria gasped and scooted into the wall. "Or you can stay here, and I will bind you to Will and his coven."

Annamaria ground her teeth. "You can go to hell."

Leo cackled. "I'm already there. I'll give you some time to think." He walked out of the door, shutting and locking it.

Annamaria stared at the locked door. Valentina was involved? She had assumed Will was just being controlling and power hungry. Had Will been waiting to betray her and Marianna this whole time? And what of Marianna? Why had she encouraged Annamaria to make a run for it, only to be the one to make Annamaria come back? Now she had this impossible choice. She didn't know which was the worse option. Annamaria threw her head back and screamed.

Sometime later, the door opened, and Tyler and Kylie entered. Annamaria glared at them and scooted as far away as she could, biting her tongue to prevent painful groans escaping her lips.

Kylie's eyes roved over the chains. "We are sor—"

"What did you do to me?" Her voice sharp.

Kylie looked down. "We didn't want to, but we had to. Will's the coven leader, and there is a bond—"

Annamaria waved Kylie off. "No, I'm talking about my hands. My magic isn't working. What did you do?"

"It's the chains." Tyler gestured to Annamaria's wrists. "They are hexed to withhold a vampire's or werewolf's strength and prevent a witch from using magic."

Annamaria's face crumpled as she looked at her hands.

"Why didn't you help me?" Annamaria glared at them.

"We had to obey Will." Kylie looked up through her eyelashes, her eyes broken.

Annamaria scoffed. "You absolutely had to? You had zero ability to choose on your own? Because if the rest of you had helped me, Will would have been outnumbered instead of me."

Kylie chewed on her nail. "Well, I guess we could have, but it takes a lot of strength—"

"I'm going to be blunt with you. Vampires are selfish creatures. Will wants to control your magic. Kylie and I still want you for a dance partner. Marianna wants her sister close, and Anthony wants all of you. All of those desires led us to follow Will last night." Tyler shrugged.

Annamaria tucked her knees into her chest and buried her head in her knees. She could not bear to hear Anthony's or Marianna's names right now. Out of all the betrayal over the past thirty-six hours, what they had done was the most painful. She had also grown to view Kylie and Tyler as her best friends, especially Kylie. Had they not sworn they loved her for her? Tyler just admitted the truth, and it hurt. Annamaria was so stupid for trusting them.

"We are so sorry," whispered Kylie. "We wanted you to know."

The door clicked shut. She was alone again.

Much later, Anthony visited her. He looked terrible. He fell to his knees. Annamaria sat there, unmoving, looking at the wall.

"Annamaria." His voice choked.

She put her hand up. "Don't. I've already heard Kylie's and Tyler's pitiful excuses. I don't want to hear yours." The two of them sat in silence for several minutes while Annamaria hid her face in her knees, and Anthony was bent over, his shoulders shaking.

"Why did you take me?" Annamaria asked.

"What?"

"Why were you the one who picked me up off the ground and carried me to the car?" Tears spilled as she turned to force herself to look into his eyes when he answered.

"Because I wanted you handled gently." Anthony's eyes were sincere.

Annamaria shook her head and rolled her eyes. "Why didn't you help me instead? You threw Will off of me here in the house. Why couldn't you help me out there?"

"Will commanded it, and I caved. I didn't fight it." Anthony dropped his head.

"Because you want me back here."

"Not like this." Anthony gestured to the chains.

"But this is where we are now. What are your plans? What do you want out of this?"

Anthony followed Annamaria's words with his brow creased, then his mouth fell open, and his eyes widened. He clasped her hands. "Annamaria, I will never make you be with me. I will never ask anything of you if you can't truly choose."

Annamaria huffed and yanked her hands away. Yeah right. "What did you do with Nico?"

"Who's Nico?"

"Nico! My baby bear. I saw you take him."

"He's safe. Um, have you decided what you are going to do?" Anthony stared into Annamaria's eyes.

"What do you mean, what am I going to do? I can't do anything. I'm shackled with no way of escaping."

"I mean, with the choices Leo is offering."

Annamaria straightened her back and lifted her chin. "I will not decide. I'm sure he already has his orders, so it doesn't matter what I say."

It was silent for a minute, then Anthony spoke again. "Annamaria, I need to ask you a terrible favor." Annamaria looked at him. What could she do while chained to these walls? Anthony looked down. "If they choose the bond spell, will you... Please... don't fight the spell?"

"Are you serious?" Annamaria's magic hummed. Whoa. Anger was the answer?

Anthony looked up, his gaze pleading. "I'm sorry, but I don't want to lose you. If you fight the spell, you'll die. I can't bear that."

"You lost me when you didn't help me in the woods. You lost me when you put me in Will's car."

Anthony bent over again, dry sobs exhaling out of him. Annamaria's heart broke at the sound, but she kept her face masklike. Anthony stood up.

"Please. Please don't die," he whispered.

Annamaria stayed looking away until the door clicked shut. The click sounded like her death sentence. Annamaria wrapped her arms around her legs again and sobbed.

****

Marianna eavesdropped on Will and Leo from her bedroom.

"Are you sure your coven can handle this? Marianna hasn't left her room, and the other three have already crept down to the basement to beg Annamaria's forgiveness," Leo said to Will.

"Yes," said Will. "I have explained the benefits to them. They are just a little disgruntled because Anthony convinced them if we were nice to her, we wouldn't have to bind her. When she ran away, they all understood the necessity of binding."

There was a long silence.

"There's another problem. I thought Marianna had broken her by threatening the humans, but it appears to only be temporary. She gave me plenty of attitude, along with the others who have visited her."

"So?"

Leo sighed. "So the spell won't work in her current state. She'll fight it, and she'll die." Will snorted. "You may not care, but Valentina does. If you can't take this seriously, then I'll knock her out and take her with me tonight."

Marianna left her room and headed down the hall to Will's room. She needed to save the conversation before Will caused her to lose her sister forever. "That won't be necessary." Marianna smiled sweetly at Leo. "What do we need to do to ensure the spell works?"

"Her spirit needs to be utterly and completely broken." Leo shook his hand at Marianna. "She needs to be convinced the only way her life could be pain free and pleasant is by being bound to Will and the rest of you."

Marianna's heart sank. She hoped her grief didn't show on her face. "And how do we do that?"

Leo smirked. "Oh, I have some ideas. Would you two care to join me?"

"Absolutely." Will jumped off his bed.

"No thanks." If Annamaria was ever going to trust her again, Marianna couldn't be involved in this part. "One request." The two men turned around. "I want to be the main bonding agent."

"No, it's my coven."

Leo was also shaking his head. "Valentina is still pissed at you for taking out Scott and Priya. You need to prove yourself before she gives you something as important as your sister."

Marianna took a step forward. "Let this be my test. As her sister, I lessen the risk of the coven being killed in a rescue attempt."

Will and Leo looked at each other.

"All right," Leo said.

Will huffed. "Fine."

****

Annamaria didn't know how much time passed since Anthony left. She had fallen asleep for part of it, but she was awake now, and hungry. The door opened, and Will and Leo walked in together. Annamaria glared up at the two of them. They both chuckled.

"Have you decided yet?" Leo asked.

Annamaria lifted her chin. "My answer remains the same."

"I thought so." Leo showed his teeth. "Will, why don't you have a little snack?"

Will leaped onto Annamaria in a blur and sunk his teeth into her neck. Annamaria screamed at the pain.

There was no venom this time to numb and paralyze her. When Will slid his fangs out of her neck, Annamaria slumped down, holding her wound and fighting to control her sobs.

"Let's try again," said Leo. "Which option would you like to choose?"

Annamaria spat at his feet. Leo looked at Will and gestured toward Annamaria. Will attacked again, choosing a new spot on Annamaria's neck. This time, the venom entered her veins. She didn't lose consciousness, but her head swam, preventing her from holding it up.

Leo asked again which choice she would like. She couldn't answer, even if she wanted to, and braced herself for Will's fangs. Instead, her body filled with indescribable pain, like she was being burned, stabbed, and electrocuted all at the same time. She screamed, twisted her hair, and rocked back and forth, trying to endure the pain. After a minute, the pain ceased. Annamaria opened her eyes and could make out Leo standing above her with his hands aimed at her.

"We'll leave you for now." He and Will left the room, locking the door behind them.

For the next several days, Will and Leo visited Annamaria to torture her into deciding. Each day, Will drank more blood from her, promising her this would all go away if she would accept the bonding spell. Annamaria's body handled Will's bites better each time, and she could feel a small resistance building up in her bloodstream. The pain curse Leo inflicted on Annamaria's body lasted longer each day as well, though he gave no opinion on what Annamaria's choice should be.

On the fourth day, Annamaria broke. "All right, I'll do it! I'll do the bond spell. Please, don't touch me anymore."

Will grinned. "Good choice."

Leo didn't say anything but swept from the room muttering something about preparations. The minute they left, Annamaria regretted giving in. She could not stand the pain anymore, and her body had no more strength from losing so much blood each day. The bond spell was the lesser of two evils. She did not want to go to Valentina. With the bond spell, Annamaria was almost in charge of her destiny. If she didn't want to accept it, she could accept death. If she chickened out and accepted the spell, when Trinity came, she would kill Will and set Annamaria free.

Chapter 20 Binding

Courtney Mills watched the Reunited series for the hundredth time. "Will you stop it?" Cody asked. "I can't handle listening to those songs anymore. There are no clues, no matter how many times you watch them."

"Just because *you* see nothing doesn't mean nothing's there," said Courtney. Cody growled.

Alyssa slapped the kitchen table. "Shut up, Cody. You're not the only one who is hurting."

"Kids!" barked their dad.

Everyone fell silent. This had been the worst summer of Cody's life. Trinity's disappearance sent his dad back into the depression from when his mom died, and Anna's disappearance ate at Cody and his sisters. Cody's dad had shared Trinity's note with them, but his dad and the police chief believed the message was forced since the house had been destroyed.

The most frustrating thing was they couldn't even tell the police the truth. The Mills family were certain vampires had taken Anna, but they had no idea what happened to Trinity. The police didn't know vampires existed, let alone know how to deal with such creatures. Their family was equipped to deal with vampires, which did them no good when they couldn't find Anna.

"I got something," said Courtney.

"What?" Cody jumped over the counter to get to

his sister.

"Marianna." She smiled.

"You mean Anna?" Alyssa asked.

"No. Marianna. Anna's older sister," Courtney said.

"Marianna died with Anna's parents," Hal said.

"Dad, I don't think she did." Courtney shook her head. "I think she's alive, and I think Anna is with her."

"What makes you think that?" Hal asked.

"The story." Courtney gestured to the computer screen. "It's about long-lost sisters finding each other."

"Yeah, but the other dancer doesn't look like she's related to Anna. They aren't even the same race." Cody crossed his arms.

Courtney palmed her forehead. "That doesn't mean she isn't there, dufus. I doubt the entire coven is in these videos."

Cody's blood raced, and he lunged at his older sister, but Hal stopped him around the chest. "Get control of your temper, son."

After practicing his breathing exercises, Cody remembered something. "Oh my gosh, Dad, I'm so stupid."

"What else is new?"

Hal glared at Courtney. She bowed her head.

"Talk, son."

"I think Marianna was here before they disappeared. That last week, Anna ate lunch at home every day, and she wouldn't tell me why, just said it was 'family stuff.' And on the night of the dance concert, there was this other redhead sitting with Trinity. I asked Anna who she was. She told me she was her cousin, but what if she was her sister?"

Everyone's mouths were open. "And why did it take you four months to tell us this?" asked Alyssa.

"I'm sorry. I wasn't focused on Anna's 'cousin.' I was focused on Anna and where she could be." Not to mention moping about his stupid decision to break up with her.

"It doesn't matter now." Hal put his hands up. "I'm glad you told us now. If that was Marianna, I wonder what happened to her. She must be with Anna if Courtney's interpretation of the videos is correct."

"So both of them are captives?" Alyssa asked.

"Well, the story implies a happy ending." Courtney shrugged. "But maybe it's a happy ending from the vampires' point of view."

"That still doesn't tell us where she is," Cody mumbled.

"Well, at least we figured something out."

Hal patted his middle child's shoulder. "You did good, Courtney. I need to call Libby and give her this information."

Cody sat down on the couch and rubbed his wet eyes. Why couldn't Anna have just told him who had her when she texted him? Why did she say she left willingly? Was she forced to say that? Why wouldn't she tell him where she was when she emailed him? Did she even want to escape? She looked pretty happy in those dance videos. Cody flopped his head onto the back of the couch and groaned. He wasn't being fair to her. He had no idea what she was going through, and it's not like she knew what Cody knew. Those vampires must have told her some pretty twisted lies.

No, Anna was not to blame, Cody was. Ever since prom, Cody had sensed something, but instead of being patient with her, he broke up with her. What he would give to relive that week. If they were still together when she had been taken, she might have told him where she was and who had her.

Cody hit the arm of the couch. If his dad and Trinity had been honest in the first place, there would be no secrets between Anna and Cody. There would have been no breakup. Cody and Anna would have celebrated after the dance concert together, and Anna would still be here. Cody's phone rang. He looked at the screen and jumped.

"Dad, it's the number Anna texted me from!"

"Answer and put them on speaker," Hal said, still on his own phone. "Libby, I'm going to put you on speaker as well so you can listen."

Cody swiped the green phone icon with a shaking finger and clicked the speaker. "Hello?"

Soft, heartbreaking sobs came out of the speaker.

"Hello? Anna? Is that you?"

"Cody?" Anna's voice was choked with sobs.

Hal, Alyssa, and Courtney all ran to the couch to listen closer.

"Anna, where are you?" asked Cody.

"Cody, I tried to get away, but they caught me."

"Who? Who caught you? Where are you?"

"I'm sorry, I can't tell. It's not safe. I tried to be strong, to hold on as long as I could. But I can't anymore, it's too late. I just wanted to hear your voice one more time and tell you goodbye before I get…before things change."

"Anna, please listen to me! I know you're a witch. I know vampires have you. I can help." Cody yanked on his hair.

"You do?" Anna whispered. Good, she was finally listening.

"Yes! Now please tell me where you are."

BANG!

Anna's screams heightened to hysteric proportions.

"Hey! Give me that," said a gruff voice. The call ended.

Cody looked up at his dad, his heart racing, his voice caught in his throat. Alyssa and Courtney both had tears streaming down their faces, sniffling with each breath.

"Libby, what do you make of that?" Even Hal's voice cracked.

"Things have taken a very grave turn," Libby said.

"How can things be worse than they already are?" asked Cody.

Hal gave Cody a look. "What do you mean?" he asked Libby.

"I think they are going to change her, or they are going to put her under the bond spell."

"What's the bond spell?" the Mills asked in unison.

"It's a spell which bonds a witch to a coven of vampires. The witch must do their bidding for the rest of their life. It's irreversible unless the coven leader is killed." Libby's voice shook.

"Why would they keep her alive for this long and put her on the internet, just to change her or bind her?" Hal asked.

"Well, the time doesn't make sense for changing her," said Libby. "So I think they are probably binding her. She wasn't raised a witch, so she needed to learn how to use her magic. That's probably what has been going on this whole time."

"So what does this mean for finding her?" Hal asked.

"If they are changing her, there's no hope." Libby's voice broke.

Cody threw himself onto his knees and howled. Alyssa and Courtney joined him, throwing themselves over his shoulders, sobbing with him.

"If they are binding her, we can still find her and kill the coven." Libby hung up the phone.

"How does Trinity fit into all of this?" Alyssa asked. "I can't see her willingly handing Anna over to a coven of vampires, not when she has spent the past sixteen years keeping Anna hidden."

Hal nodded. "I agree. Trinity's whereabouts are a bigger mystery than Anna's."

"And what about Marianna?" Courtney asked.

"We'll rescue her with Anna," Hal said.

****

Will ripped Sandy's cell phone out of Annamaria's hands and threw it against the wall, shattering on impact. "Enjoy your goodbye to your little human boyfriend?" Will asked. Annamaria didn't answer. "What will Anthony think?" He unchained her and threw her over his shoulder. *Ignis!* No fire appeared in her palm. The constant blood draining and torture had left her too weak.

Up on the main floor, Will stopped at Sandy's door as she exited her room. "Sandy, I'm afraid to say your contract has been terminated. Effective immediately." He dropped her broken phone into her hands.

Sandy straightened herself and lifted her chin. "I was about to resign, anyway."

Will carried Annamaria into the guest bedroom

next to Sandy's room. He ripped off her shirt and shorts. Annamaria stumbled away from him in her bra and underwear. "No! I already said I'd do it. Please don't touch me."

"Come here. I'm just changing your clothes."

He grabbed her and stretched a knee-length summer dress from her closet upstairs over her body. In her new attire, Will carried Annamaria down the hall into the ballroom. She hung over his shoulder like a sack of potatoes. She had no more energy to fight. Will positioned her on her feet and stood behind her, her back leaning against his chest.

Annamaria's eyes took in her surroundings. Marianna stood next to her in a floor-length silver evening gown, avoiding Annamaria's eyes. Diagonally in between the two sisters was Leo. Off to the side were Anthony, Kylie, and Tyler. They too were dressed in formal attire, staring at their feet. Apparently loss of freedom was a black-tie event. The casual dress Will put on her told Annamaria where her station in this house would be once the spell was over.

"Annamaria, Leo will perform the bond spell." Marianna gestured at Leo, her eyes focused above Annamaria's head. He smirked at Annamaria, and Annamaria looked back with blank eyes.

Leo took a breath, his smile widening. "So how this works is any vampire who would like Annamaria to be bound to them needs to have their venom in her body when I perform the spell. There is one vampire who is the main bonding agent, which will be Marianna."

Annamaria's drooping head snapped up. She assumed Will would be the one she was bound to. This changed everything. How could Annamaria ask Trinity to kill Marianna in order to free her? She couldn't accept the spell now, but could she really die? As much as she didn't want to accept the spell, she also didn't want to die. Maybe she should accept the invitation to go to Valentina. She could have more time to figure out an escape plan.

"Marianna, you will bite Annamaria first, and more of your venom needs to be in her body than the others." Marianna nodded. "The rest of you bite Annamaria next, but you don't need a lot of venom. Only one or two drops will do."

The others dipped their chins once.

"Marianna, you may begin."

"Wait," Annamaria croaked. Leo looked at her. "I'll go with you. You can take me to Valentina." Anthony, Kylie, and Tyler all gasped. Marianna cocked her head and blinked. Will growled in her ears.

Leo opened his mouth, but no sound escaped.

"No! Leo, you promised me. I did my part. I got them in the same place. You guys owe me." Will's voice echoed in the deadly silent ballroom.

Marianna took a quick breath in, leaving her mouth open as she looked between Leo and Will, her eyes narrowing until they were slits.

Leo surveyed everyone in the room, his gaze landing on Annamaria. "Sorry sweetheart, that ship has sailed." Annamaria closed her eyes, and a lone tear slipped down her cheek. "Will and Marianna, switch. Will is going to be the main bonding agent."

"What?" Marianna said.

Will sighed. "As it should be."

Will spun Annamaria around and bit into her neck.

Annamaria's knees buckled. She was so weak, the first stream of venom took all her remaining strength. Will took her dead weight and held her like a baby. "Marianna? Are you still a part of this coven?" A gentle hand took her wrist and bit into it.

"The rest of you may come forward now," Leo said.

Annamaria's surroundings became fuzzy, darkness framing the edges of her vision. Footsteps echoed, and another hand took her left arm. "Sorry," Kylie said, followed by a small pinch in her arm. One tiny drop entered her bloodstream.

"Sorry," said Tyler, accompanied by a tiny pinch as well.

"Please forgive me." Anthony's bite was the smallest of all but tore at Annamaria's heart the most.

Leo started chanting, and Annamaria's head began spinning. Her thoughts were like a whirlpool, and with each spin, she sank deeper into herself. Her willpower and determination were buried with each passing second. *Wait, I don't want this, but if I fight, I'll die. I'm not ready to die. I don't want to lose myself either. What do I do?*

Annamaria's thoughts and her eyesight became clearer. Was this how the spell worked? This part wasn't so bad. Maybe staying alive was the right choice. Her gaze focused. She flew across the grounds in someone's arms. The gate was open, and they zoomed through as it closed behind them, and they stopped.

"The shield spell." Anthony's lips grazed her ear. "Could you make it big enough to go around the entire house?"

Annamaria groaned. "I can try, but I can't stand."

Anthony's arms tightened around her. "I'll hold you. Here's a healing potion. Use the strength you gain fully on your magic."

He steadied Annamaria, held the tip of a bottle to her lips, and she drank. The potion spread like caffeine at light speed, and she held her hands up to the gate. "*Clypeus*!" The shield took the shape of the gate, and Annamaria spread her arms wide, willing her magic to follow the wall and dome over the top. The spell finished just in time as Marianna and Will slammed into the shield.

Anthony threw himself and Annamaria into the back of a waiting vehicle, which started driving as soon as they were inside. Annamaria looked up front and relaxed to see Daniel driving and Sandy in the passenger seat. Sandy turned around. "Did you make it out okay?"

"I think so," stuttered Annamaria. Nico popped his head up from Sandy's lap and jumped into the back seat into Annamaria's arms. "Nico!" Annamaria hugged and kissed him.

Sandy grinned. "He missed you." Annamaria placed Nico on her chest and fell asleep with her head against the window.

Annamaria woke up as the car slowed down. She opened her eyes, and they were pulling into a Daylight parking lot. Daniel pulled up to the main entrance, idling the car.

"Wait here while I check us in." Anthony jumped out of the car and zoomed into the building.

Daniel turned around and surveyed Annamaria.

"Thank you so much," she said.

"Listen, I need to get my mom to a safe place. This is where we part ways. Anthony's car is already here, and you'll be traveling with him. No matter what he says, make sure he takes you to the Mills' ranch."

Annamaria cocked her head. "The Mills? As in Mr. Henry Mills, Alyssa, Courtney, and Cody?"

"Yes." Daniel nodded his head.

"Why?"

"Just trust me." Daniel's eyes were pleading.

Annamaria held Daniel's gaze. Cody had begged her to trust him every time they talked, and she didn't listen until the last second. "Okay." She and Sandy hugged goodbye.

"We'll see each other again." Sandy smiled and cupped Annamaria's face, a lone tear sliding down her cheek.

Annamaria smiled back. "I hope so."

Anthony escorted her and Nico into their hotel room. Annamaria stared at her feet, her hair shielding her face, and Anthony had a protective arm around her while they hastened down the hall. Inside the room, Nico jumped on one bed, curled up, and fell asleep. Annamaria next to Nico, Anthony sat across from her on the opposite bed. They stared at each other in silence for a few minutes.

"Can I order you breakfast?" Anthony asked.

Annamaria nodded, her eyes glazed. "Okay, thanks. Where are we?"

"Indiana."

"Daniel drove this far in one night?"

"It's easy to speed at night because the roads are so empty. Plus, werewolves also like going fast." Anthony chuckled. Annamaria stared at the floor. "Are you okay?"

Annamaria looked up. "No."

"Do you want to talk? Or…" Anthony extended his hand toward her, then dropped it.

Annamaria sighed. "I'm just going to lie here until breakfast." She laid down and turned her back to Anthony.

Once Annamaria ate a decent breakfast, she felt well enough to talk, but she wasn't about to jump into Anthony's arms.

"So what happened? How did you get me out of there?"

"The night we brought you back, I started texting Daniel. We drove here and met, leaving my car and making a reservation. Then we drove back and prepared Sandy and your bear. That's why I visited you so much later, after you woke up. That's also why I asked you to not fight the spell. I didn't want you to die before I could get you out of there." Anthony's shoulders slumped.

"I understand now, and I forgive you for asking that of me." Annamaria's voice was stiff.

"Then you almost ruined everything by asking Leo to take you to Valentina." Anthony rubbed his forehead and raked his fingers through his hair.

Annamaria scoffed. "I didn't want to be bound to Marianna. I couldn't accept her death as a means for my freedom."

Anthony nodded, relaxing. "It was so hard for me to bite you. But I couldn't give Will a reason to be suspicious. The spell started, and your eyes were twitching like you were having a seizure, but the rest of your body just hung there. Then your face went blank, and I was terrified you had died." Anthony shuddered.

"I couldn't make up my mind at first. Then I chose to accept it. I thought Trinity could kill Will. So what happened next?"

Anthony dropped his gaze. "I sliced Leo's neck, grabbed you, jumped out of the window, and ran. Tyler and Kylie are still so young, fresh blood would have distracted them, especially a witch's."

Annamaria put her hand to her chest. "You killed him?"

Anthony threw his hands in the air. "It was the only way to save you. You were too far gone. There was no way to stop the spell without killing the one casting the spell. Are you really upset he is gone? He would have taken you to Valentina."

Annamaria didn't answer. Of course she was happy to be free from Leo's spell, but she wished his death didn't have to be the only way. Leo was the third witch who had died at the hands of a vampire in defense of Annamaria. The higher the body count rose, the more she feared Valentina.

Annamaria spent the rest of the day going through what had been packed, just her magic book and all her clothes. When she learned Anthony left behind Elizabeth's book, her heart softened a bit. "I'm sorry. I know how special her book was to you."

Anthony shrugged. "It's just a book. *You* are alive."

The rest of the day was quiet and uncomfortable. Both Anthony and Annamaria kept sneaking glances at each other, neither saying a word. At sundown, they checked out and jumped back on the road.

****

Annamaria and Anthony spent the next couple of days driving at night and crashing in the nearest Daylight during the day. Anthony wanted to seek some of his witch contacts to get in touch with Libby, but Annamaria stood her ground until he agreed to take her back to Harrison. They were cordial to each other inside the hotel rooms, but there was no hand-holding, no cuddling, and no kissing. Nico jumped back and forth between both of them, playing, cuddling, and wrestling. Annamaria was annoyed by how much he liked Anthony. She wanted him to be just as mad at Anthony as she was.

On their final stretch of the drive, Anthony glanced over at Nico. "So what's the story with this little guy?"

"He's my familiar."

Anthony's lips parted. "I forgot about those. Elizabeth's died when we were first captured."

Annamaria grimaced. "He found me after I woke up from Will's bite. Or rather, he called to me, and I found him."

Anthony snapped his fingers. "That's why your scent was all over the forest."

Annamaria nodded. "Yeah, that's also why I barely got into town at sunset. Is that why the police had time to arrest me before you guys arrived?"

"Yeah. We were running all over the forest trying to figure out where you were. You were already in the police station by the time we crossed the city limits."

"And then you guys crashed a car."

Anthony looked embarrassed. "It was actually to tell Craig to hurry and figure something out, not to tell you to be quiet. But it worked either way."

They both fell silent as they remembered what

happened next. Annamaria still hadn't forgiven Anthony for siding with Will. If he, Kylie, and Tyler had tried harder, they could have overcome Will's mandate, and Will would have been outnumbered. Now because of their weakness, Annamaria had to flee for her life, *and* she was separated from her sister.

Right on the border of South Dakota and Wyoming, Anthony slammed on the brakes, and the car spun, but luckily stayed upright. Standing in the middle of the road were Will and Marianna.

"How did they find us?"

Anthony shook his head, his eyes narrowed. Annamaria and Anthony got out of the car, and Anthony zoomed over to Annamaria, placing himself in front of her.

Will smirked. "Mortals are so predictable. I had a feeling you would want to return to a familiar place." Annamaria didn't respond. She prepared herself for the fight of her life. "I'm tired of giving you chances! This ends tonight."

The four of them were plunged into darkness. Annamaria's *sisters* ring warmed and guided her forward. Could Annamaria trust her sister now? The ring warmed again and tugged. Annamaria took a deep breath and walked forward. She stepped into a circle of light where Marianna was. Annamaria opened her mouth to ask what was going on, but Marianna put her hand over Annamaria's mouth and thrust a piece of paper into her hands. Annamaria looked down.

Don't talk! He can still hear even though he can't see. I'm so sorry about everything! I'll explain later. Please play along and pretend to fight me. I'm going to herd you into the woods to safety. Anthony will take care of Will.

Annamaria looked up from the paper. Marianna's eyes were pleading, begging Annamaria to believe her. Could she believe her? Annamaria pondered the incident in the forest and the ballroom just a few nights ago. Both times Marianna's posture had been rigid, and she refused to look at Annamaria. Now she was back to her normal self. Annamaria gave her sister another chance and bobbed her head.

"Marianna, you're the only one who can see right now, ya know!" Will said.

"Sorry, honey. I just needed to get the upper hand."

Marianna removed the illusion of complete darkness and threw Annamaria off the road toward the trees. Annamaria caught herself in the air and rose higher while Marianna ran underneath her. Marianna redirected, jumped, and yanked on Annamaria's foot, crashing both of them to the ground. Marianna overpowered and ended up on top. She wrapped her fingers around Annamaria's throat, the pressure painless. "Get into the woods." Annamaria drowned her sister in a bubble of water, knocking her off, and ran into the trees.

Once in the shelter of the trees, Annamaria stopped and spied on Will and Anthony. They were locked in a skilled martial arts duel.

"We were supposed to be best friends!" Will roared, kicking Anthony's legs from underneath him.

"I thought so, too." Anthony growled, jumped up, and punched Will in the face.

"Then why are you fighting against me?" Will jumped over Anthony to avoid a second punch.

"Because you have gone insane!" Anthony grunted

as he ducked to avoid Will's flying fist.

Both Annamaria and Marianna were wincing as Anthony and Will beat on each other.

"What do we do now?" Annamaria whispered. Marianna grabbed her hand and dragged her farther into the trees. After a few minutes, Annamaria refused to take another step without answers. "Marianna, please stop. Tell me what is going on. Why do you keep changing your mind?"

Marianna turned around and faced Annamaria. "I never changed my mind. I tried to leave the same day you did, but Will overpowered me and chained me up, and I couldn't convince the others to disobey him. Kylie and Tyler were changed by him, so their loyalty bond is the strongest. Anthony could have, but we would only be evenly matched. We can only beat Will if he is outnumbered. So I pretended to reconsider to make sure he didn't kill you. I helped Anthony plan our escape, but I couldn't let my betrayal be known at the house because I needed to get Will away from Kylie and Tyler. They fled after drinking Leo."

"Why couldn't you tell me all that at the house?" Annamaria folded her arms.

Marianna surveyed the trees. "Leo was watching both of us too closely."

Annamaria let out a breath and nodded. "What about the light thing just now? How did you make me see with you?"

Marianna beamed. "I've been practicing. I guess the spell has more layers than I understood."

A strange gagging sound reached their ears. Marianna's head snapped toward it, Annamaria's response just a bit slower. They met one another's gaze, their eyes widening in unison before taking off running. Will had Anthony in a headlock, twisting Anthony's neck like he was going to rip his head off. Anthony's eyes bulged, his hands gripped Will's wrists in a futile attempt to free himself. Both sisters rushed forward, but Marianna was flung into the brush by a powerful gust of wind. Marianna jumped to her feet and reached for Annamaria but stopped as Annamaria zoomed past, reaching Will and Anthony.

Annamaria's blood boiled at the sight. Her magic raced through her veins, burning hot and heating her skin in the cool night air. Her hand tingled as the heat rushed out of her. She called on the air and threw Will into a tree. The wind blew so fast and strong it held Will up against the trunk. Will clawed at the invisible force holding him to the tree, his eyes widening when his struggling failed to free him.

Marianna rushed to Anthony and helped him up. They both turned to Annamaria, freezing at the scene in front of them. As the wind howled around them, Annamaria's mind spun like she was going under the bond spell again. Her chest tightened at how close she had been to losing herself. How close she had been to losing Anthony. Just a second later and Will would have ended Anthony's long life. Annamaria gasped at the image of Anthony sprawled on the forest floor unmoving, silent, lifeless. She kept the wind going with one hand and summoned a nearby tree branch with her other. Marianna lunged forward, but Anthony caught her around the waist. He shook his head and spoke lowly, his eyes pained.

Annamaria broke the branch to a sharp point and drove the wood into Will's heart. A short scream erupted from his throat before his body became limp, his eyes unseeing. Annamaria set the branch on fire, the flames spreading over Will's immobile form. In a few minutes, he was a pile of ash.

Another scream tore through the night. Annamaria turned around. Marianna's hands were over her mouth, her eyes wide, staring at the ash that had been Will. Anthony's knees buckled, and he collapsed to the ground. With his head bowed, he sobbed. "Goodbye friend, goodbye."

Annamaria looked down at her shaking hands. She had just killed someone. Both Anthony and Marianna continued to make pained, tearless noises. Unable to look at them, Annamaria ran deeper into the woods. When she couldn't run anymore, she slid down a tree trunk and panted as a few tears trickled down her cheeks. A few minutes later, Nico bounded through the trees and jumped into her lap. Annamaria wrapped her arms around him and cried.

He was a bad guy.

"I know, but my sister loved him," Annamaria whispered. "Anthony did too."

"Annamaria, are you okay?" Anthony stepped into the tiny clearing.

"Anthony." Annamaria stood up and looked at her feet. "I'm so sorry. I know he was your friend."

Anthony took Annamaria's face in his hands and wiped her tears. "You had to."

Annamaria hugged him, crying into his chest. Anthony hugged her back, his body shaking as well. Annamaria's cries turned to sniffles. Her breathing slowed, and Anthony's breathing matched hers. They returned to the place where Will's ashes and Marianna were. Marianna rushed at Annamaria and drew her into a tight embrace.

"I'm so sorry, Marianna. I know you loved him. I just… He had Anthony… I don't know what hap—"

"Do not apologize. I stopped loving him when he threatened you with the bond spell. I stopped loving him when he chained me up. I stopped loving him when he tortured you. Then to learn he has been working for Valentina this whole time."

Annamaria shook her head. "I should have used *incarcero.* I just freaked when I saw Anthony."

"You did what you had to do. He would not have stopped. Killing him was the only way." Marianna's hands framed Annamaria's face.

"But I killed someone." Annamaria sniffed.

Marianna rolled her eyes with a sympathetic smile. "And I haven't? Or Anthony? We aren't judging you."

"But I'm judging me."

Marianna hugged her again. "Don't. I love you. And I'm so glad you are alive and not bonded."

Sunrise was too close to make it all the way to Harrison, so they drove to Sundance and got a hotel for the day. Will's car had been totaled in the fight, and Marianna's car was back at the mansion. "Let's get it when we have a better idea of what's ahead," Anthony suggested. Annamaria and Marianna agreed.

Marianna and Anthony were silent in their individual grief. Annamaria locked herself in the bathroom for the entire day, unable to face either of them. Her stomach squirmed. She had killed someone. It didn't matter what Marianna said. She was a killer.

As soon as the sun set, they were back in the car, zooming down the freeway. Annamaria drove for this last leg of the journey. She drove faster than was wise, using magic to help her stay steady, make sharp turns, and safely pass other cars. In record time, she arrived in Harrison at eleven at night.

Chapter 21 Alpha

Annamaria parked Anthony's car right in front of the house. All the lights were on inside. She got out of the car, left the door open, and started running to the front door, leaving Marianna and Anthony inside.

Marianna turned toward Anthony as the fresh air filled the car. "What exactly did Daniel say about these people?" She spoke at a low pitch.

Anthony hissed. "Nothing. Annamaria was who he talked to." Anthony and Marianna opened up their doors. "Annamaria, wait! I think they're—"

"ANNA!" The front door opened, and Cody bounded out onto the porch. He met Annamaria at the top of the steps, picked her up, and spun her around. He grabbed her face and kissed her on her mouth. "Oh my gosh, you're alive!"

Annamaria laughed. "I am."

Marianna observed the boy who had broken her sister's heart. She had seen him from a distance once, and the smell was not as strong then. Cody's body stiffened. He lifted Annamaria into his house, across the threshold, and threw her behind him. He was fast. Faster than a human, but not as fast as a vampire. He glared at Anthony and Marianna.

"Did they follow you?" Cody gestured toward Anthony and Marianna.

"Huh?" Annamaria poked her head around Cody.

"We all came together."

"They're vampires." A deep growl rumbled in his chest.

Marianna flinched. This was why she feared meeting her grandma.

Annamaria arched a brow. "Yeah, I know."

"What are they doing here?" Cody growled and crouched.

Marianna and Anthony glanced at each other and tensed. They would be outnumbered in a heartbeat. They needed to be careful. Annamaria ripped herself away from Cody and stomped back down the stairs.

"He helped me escape. She is my sister. Why are you being so rude?" Annamaria stood in front of Marianna and Anthony, her arms folded.

"Please come back inside." Cody took a tentative step over the threshold.

"No."

Cody growled and leaped off the porch. As soon as the moonlight hit his frame, his skin rippled, and in the blink of an eye, a large gray wolf stood where Cody used to be. Annamaria screamed. Marianna grabbed Annamaria's shoulders and pulled her closer. Anthony zoomed in front of the girls, and the air rippled as the shield spell wrapped around the three of them.

The wolf growled again and jumped on the small group. The shield did its job, creating a strange vision of a wolf suspended in midair, attacking an invisible box. The wolf growled as he unsuccessfully bit and scratched at the shield. Annamaria squeezed Marianna's hand and pulled her into Anthony's embrace. Marianna shook with Annamaria. Anthony's body was tense as he held them.

"What's going on out here?"

An older version of Cody stepped across the threshold. His gaze froze on Annamaria. "Anna, you're okay!" He rushed outside and slammed into the invisible shield. He stepped back and surveyed the situation. He grabbed Cody's tail and yanked him down. "Back on the porch. Get control of yourself." Cody whined. "Now." Cody scampered onto the porch and shielded himself from the moonlight, becoming human again. The man and Annamaria looked at each other. Her eyes were wide and teary. "Anna, it's okay. We won't hurt you, Marianna, or your friend."

****

Mr. Mills put chairs out on the front porch so he didn't have to invite Anthony and Marianna into his house. Alyssa and Courtney shuffled outside, and they, along with Cody, stared open-mouthed at Marianna. Mr. Mills possessed more decorum than his children.

"Welcome, Marianna. I'm so happy you are…alive. And?"

"Anthony."

Mr. Mills nodded. "Anthony. Thank you for getting these two here safely."

Both Marianna and Anthony gave tight-lipped smiles. Annamaria sat in between them, facing the Mills. She tried and failed to control her shaking. She should have put the pieces together when Daniel told her to come here, but even if she had, there was no way she could have prepared herself to witness one of them shifting in midair to attack them.

Cody sat across from Annamaria. His body vibrating every few seconds. He wrung his hands and ground his teeth.

Mr. Mills sat down last. "Anna, welcome home. I'm so glad you are here and safe. If you are up to it, can you tell us what's been going on?"

Annamaria recounted the past several months of magic lessons, hiding, and complications with Will. She left out her relationship with Anthony.

"Do you know where Trinity is or what she is doing?" Mr. Mills asked.

Annamaria shook her head. "No, I don't. I'm sorry, Mr. Mills."

"Where is the other one?" Alyssa asked. "Is he going to show up too?"

"No, he's dead. I killed him." Annamaria looked down.

"Good girl." Cody beamed, his body calm. Anthony clenched his jaw, and Marianna growled. Cody's body swelled, but he deflated and bowed his head when Mr. Mills placed a firm hand on his son's shoulder.

"What happened on your end?" Annamaria asked the group.

Mr. Mills leaned forward. "Well, I could tell something was going on that week. I could smell Marianna's scent around your house, but Trinity wouldn't tell me anything. Then she sent me a message about you two taking off early. I always knew Trinity would take you to your grandma's after graduation. Her letter sounded like she stopped waiting, which I obviously respected. A couple of days later, I got a call from the police. The Jenkins had alerted the police to your house being broken into. The place was destroyed. I thought the message was forced and something bad had happened to you two. I remembered the vampire smell and figured that's what happened."

"Meanwhile, my dad finally told me we are all werewolves," Cody said. All traces of danger were gone. His eyes shone with excitement. "He barely told me in enough time. You know our first transformation is the first full moon after our eighteenth birthday?"

Annamaria shook her head. Though it made sense thinking back on what Daniel said when he had recounted his own story.

"Anyway—" Mr. Mills gave Cody a look. "—we have been in contact with different wolf packs all over the country to help look for you. Sniffing out vampire covens. But you weren't with any of them. We went on the news because we were desperate and hoped a human had miraculously seen you. Of course, I did not know that would make your situation worse. I'm sorry."

"I have also been working with your grandma all summer. We analyzed the online videos, trying to find a clue as to your whereabouts, and we analyzed the texts and email but couldn't get a correct ping. And of course, your phone call scared the hell out of us, and we thought we lost you for good. But a few hours later, Daniel called and told us you were on your way and to wait for a few days."

"How do you know Daniel?" Annamaria asked.

"He's been tracking down as many packs as he can to find his father." Courtney blushed and bit back a smile.

"Is his father in your pack?"

Mr. Mills shook his head. "Poor guy, I hope he finds him soon."

"So why didn't you tell me all of this in the texts or the email?" Annamaria asked Cody.

"My dad said not to. He said we didn't know if others were reading it, and we needed to protect the pack. Why didn't you say more than you did?" Cody pointed a finger at Annamaria.

"Because I thought you were human. I was trying to protect you." Annamaria threw herself back in her seat, folding her arms.

"Fair point," Cody mumbled.

Mr. Mills yawned. "Well, I think we all need to go to bed. Courtney, why don't you sleep in Lyssa's room, and Anna can sleep in yours?"

"Okay." Courtney jumped up, smiling.

"Um, Mr. Mills? Marianna and Anthony can't be outside when the sun comes up."

"Oh, right." Mr. Mills sighed as he ran his fingers through his hair. "I guess I can invite them into the guesthouse."

"I'll sleep there, too. I need to stay with my sister." Annamaria linked her arm through Marianna's.

Anthony rubbed her fingers. "It's okay. I'll be with her. We'll be fine." Marianna inclined her head.

"Are you sure?" Annamaria looked at her sister.

"Yes." Marianna smiled.

The small group walked with Mr. Mills behind the main house. He unlocked and opened the front door. "Marianna, you may come in. Anthony, you may come in."

"Thanks."

"Thank you."

Mr. Mills left, and Cody made his way up onto the porch. He had walked much slower, breathing in and out in a controlled fashion. He relaxed on the porch but didn't follow Annamaria inside.

Annamaria closed the curtains and shuffled up to Anthony. "I'm sorry."

"For what?"

"This." She gestured to the guesthouse. "They aren't being very nice, and I'm embarrassed for them."

Anthony played with a strand of her hair. "It's in their nature. I feel the same way. I'm just better at hiding it."

"Really, Annamaria, it's fine," said Marianna. "You haven't seen them in months. You deserve some alone time with them."

Annamaria tapped her lips. "I'm going to put a shield spell on the house so no one can hurt you while I'm sleeping." Many of Cody's relatives lived all over the property, and she didn't want an accident happening.

"Okay." Anthony chuckled, but his laughter didn't meet his eyes.

Marianna and Annamaria hugged each other goodnight. Cody's growls reached their ears. "Stay here." Annamaria ran outside. Luna, with her ears flat, was trying to get past Cody.

"Stay back," Cody said. "This is a natural wolf, and I don't know what it's doing."

Annamaria placed her hand on Cody's shoulder. "That's Luna, Marianna's familiar. She's just trying to get to her companion." Annamaria held her hand out to Luna. "Come here, girl. Mommy's inside."

Cody stepped to the side, and Luna bounded past Annamaria into the open door.

"Luna girl, you found me! You're such a smart girl. Yes, you are."

Luna responded with a happy whine.

"Your vampire sister has a familiar?" Cody looked intrigued.

"She was a witch before she was turned. She still has some power. She's a hybrid."

Cody nodded. Annamaria headed back inside the guesthouse. "I'll be out in a minute."

She surveyed Marianna rubbing Luna's belly and Anthony staring into space. "You'll be all right?" Marianna nodded, smiling.

"What texts and email were they talking about?" Anthony asked.

Annamaria grimaced. "When Sandy's phone fell out of her pocket outside, I texted him and asked him to stop going on the news. That was before we, you know."

"And the email?"

"It was a goodbye. I emailed him after my solo dance number. I told him I was safe, and he should have fun at college."

"And what about now?"

Annamaria sighed. "I honestly can't think about that right now."

Anthony bowed his head and looked away. Annamaria almost told him to not worry, but she stopped herself. She didn't want to have this conversation in front of Marianna or in the Mills' guesthouse. What if he persuaded her to forgive him and take him back? She needed more time to think. Marianna patted Anthony's shoulder and smiled at Annamaria. Annamaria waved at both of them as she left the guesthouse, casting the shield spell when she was outside.

As she and Cody walked back to the main house,

he continued to breathe in and out in large gusts, walking in a stiff motion.

"Are you all right?" Annamaria looked at him with concern.

"I need to concentrate," he said through gritted teeth, keeping his gaze forward.

As soon as they were in the main house, Cody's shoulders slumped. "I'm sorry. I'm still new to shifting. So I can't always control whether I shift under the moonlight."

Annamaria hugged him. The feeling wasn't the same. His arms were too large, heavy, and tight. Mr. Mills walked up to them. "I just got off the phone with your grandma. She wants you and Marianna to travel to her as soon as possible. I told her you could head out tomorrow night."

"Wait, she only gets to be here for a day?" Cody asked.

"Anna needs to meet her grandma and continue training," Mr. Mills said.

"I'm sure we can visit each other often." Annamaria smiled.

Cody put his arm around her and drew her into him, squeezing her too tight.

Up in Courtney's room, Courtney gave Annamaria some of her pajamas. She gave Annamaria a big hug. "I'm so happy you're safe." Annamaria curved her lips upward. Courtney surveyed her. "You're not the same."

Annamaria straightened. "Yes I am. My magic is just unlocked."

Courtney put a hand on Annamaria's shoulder. "I'm not judging you. You've been through a lot. You survived something the rest of us will never understand.

Of course you're different. I can tell you're strong but also vulnerable."

Annamaria forced out a laugh. "What are you, a psychic?" Courtney giggled. "Cody is different also."

Courtney sighed. "Yeah, he's a jerk."

"I didn't mean it like that."

"Oh yes you did." Courtney smiled. "It's okay because it's true. It's the Alpha in him." Annamaria's eyes widened, and Courtney giggled again. "Our dad is the Alpha of the pack. Cody will be the next Alpha one day."

"Lyssa won't?"

Courtney rolled her eyes. "No, werewolves apparently are still sexist in the twenty-first century."

"That is not true." Alyssa walked into Courtney's room. "It's just the way the genetics work. And I truly don't care. I wouldn't want to be Alpha, anyway."

"So has Cody been like this since his first transformation?" Annamaria asked. Both girls nodded, rolling their eyes. Annamaria pursed her lips and breathed out of her nose.

"Hey." Alyssa squeezed Annamaria's shoulder. "Courtney and I don't care what you think of him now. We will always love you, no matter what. Don't feel any pressure to fall back into his arms, all right?"

Annamaria exhaled. "Thanks. I just really need to get to my grandma's."

"Of course you do," said Courtney. "And that male vampire, regardless of how he smells, is really cute."

"I don't know what you're talking about." Annamaria blushed.

Both Alyssa and Courtney smirked. "Come on, Anna, it's us. Now be truthful. Are you with him?"

Alyssa asked.

"Not anymore." Annamaria let out a shaky breath.

"But the feelings are still there?" Courtney asked.

"I don't know." Annamaria played with the ends of her hair, where Anthony's fingers had been minutes ago.

"Well, it certainly looked like you like each other." Courtney wiggled her eyebrows.

Annamaria blushed some more. The last time she talked about her feelings with Alyssa and Courtney, Cody had been the topic. She cringed at talking about another guy with these two. She also didn't know what those feelings were. She was still hurt by everything, but it's not like she could turn off her feelings like a light switch. Ever since they escaped the mansion, she had been going back and forth between being mad at him and wanting to work things out.

Alyssa rolled her eyes. "Enough with the third degree, Court." She touched Annamaria's arm. "Like I said before, we don't care who you like."

****

Annamaria hadn't been asleep very long when she was awoken by the sound of the door opening. "Anna?" Cody's voice whispered through the dark.

"Hmmm?"

"Can we talk?"

"Sure." Annamaria sat up and turned on the lamp next to Courtney's bed.

"In my room?" Cody jerked his head out into the hall.

Annamaria surveyed him. He wasn't puffed up anymore. He looked and sounded more like her Cody from high school.

"Okay." She smiled.

She got out of bed and let Cody take her hand, leading her down the hall. Nico lumbered after them at first, but Annamaria sent him back to Courtney's room to keep sleeping. In Cody's room, they sat cross-legged on his mattress, facing each other. Cody extended his hand toward her, but then let his arm fall. Annamaria put her hand on top of his and smiled.

"I need to apologize for everything. You were going through a lot that week, and instead of trusting you, I let my own feelings get in the way. I shouldn't have broken up with you. If I hadn't, you would have been at my house the night your house was attacked. I'm so sorry." Cody hung his head.

Annamaria put her hand on his face. "Don't blame yourself. Trinity still would have sent me away. And if you were involved in that fight, you could have gotten hurt or killed. They almost took me because I couldn't defend myself."

"I could have taken them."

"Really?" Annamaria raised an eyebrow. "Before you even shifted?"

"No." Cody sighed. "I'm just being…"

"Arrogant?"

Cody chuckled. "Yeah, sorry. I feel like Jekyll and Hyde or something. One minute I'm my normal self, and the next I'm all angry."

Annamaria rubbed his arm. "Courtney said it's the Alpha in you. What did she mean?"

"My dad said it's so I can take command." Cody played with Annamaria's hand. "He said I have to work to control my anger so I can make wise decisions."

Annamaria squeezed his hand. "That sounds like a

lot to put on your shoulders."

"Tell me about it." Cody raked his fingers through his hair. "But what about you? How is your magic?"

Annamaria giggled. "Well, you got to see some in your front yard tonight."

Cody blushed and rubbed his forehead. "I'm really sorry about that."

"It's okay. Would you like to see more?"

"Yes." Cody eyes were wide and lit up.

Annamaria levitated a few things around Cody's room. She showed him each of the other three elements. She took his pocketknife from the bedside table, cut her hand, and healed herself. Cody's eyes shown at the levitation and the elements, and he gasped when she cut and healed herself. She ended by summoning some food from the fridge, and they enjoyed a 4:00 a.m. snack.

"Your turn," Annamaria said while they ate.

"My turn for what?" Cody put five strawberries in his mouth at once.

"To show me your superpowers in your human form. Daniel showed me his tricks. I want to see you do them."

Cody grinned. He jumped off the bed. "Hang on." He winked and bent his knees, gripped the bedframe with his hands, and lifted with little effort, though his muscles still bulged. Annamaria clasped her hands over her mouth to keep herself from squealing and waking the rest of the house. When Cody placed the bed back down, he raised his hand, and Annamaria grinned as his fingernails turned into claws. She looked from Cody's clawed hand to his face, and her smile grew wider to see his irises turn yellow. His teeth extended into wolf canines. Cody looked just as deadly as a vampire.

Cody returned to normal and sat back down on the bed. "Like you saw earlier tonight, I can go full wolf under the light of the moon, but the rest of the time, that's what I can do." Cody shrugged.

"Well, you look deadly." Annamaria smiled. Cody chuckled and laid back on his bed, tucking Annamaria into him. She lay her head on his shoulder. "Is it normal to wait until your eighteenth birthday to learn you are a werewolf?"

Cody shook his head. "Dad ordered the pack to keep our abilities a secret temporarily while you and Trinity lived here. Just until Trinity unlocked your powers to keep you safe."

Annamaria frowned. "Why? Are you dangerous?"

"No, my dad said we had to keep you as far away from any part of the magical community as possible until the right time."

"Did he say why or what the right time is?"

"I asked him, but he changed the subject."

Annamaria sighed. Trinity's secrets made even less sense now that she knew the Mills were werewolves.

"I'm sorry." Cody grimaced.

He stroked her hair. Annamaria judged Cody too harshly earlier in the night. They both had so much thrown on their shoulders at the same time. Perhaps they could help each other through what lay ahead.

Cody stopped playing with Annamaria's hair. "Anna, what are those?"

"What?" Annamaria was almost asleep.

"Those marks on your neck. What are they?" He guided Annamaria and himself back into a sitting position and got a better look in the light. Cody gasped.

"Are those bites?"

Annamaria ducked her head down, and Cody's gaze raked over her exposed skin. His eyes widened as he found several scars on her neck and arms and the gash in her hand. Cody's body shook.

"I really want to kill them right now," he said through gritted teeth.

"Don't." Annamaria grabbed his hand. "Most of them are from Will, and he's already dead."

"Most?" Cody's brows rose.

"Marianna and the others had to for the bonding ceremony, but they were already planning on stopping the ceremony before it was complete." Annamaria gave an unconvincing shrug.

His jaw clenched, Cody's body shook, and his irises rotated from their normal blue to yellow. Annamaria laid his head on her lap and ran her fingers through his hair. "Shh, it's okay. I'm fine. My magic helped me heal. I'm alive. I'm here." Cody's shaking slowed, and his irises changed back to blue and remained.

****

Annamaria's eyes opened to the sun streaming into Cody's window. She gasped and jumped out of his bed. Cody stretched and yawned.

"What's the matter?"

"It's morning. I need to get back into Courtney's room before anyone knows I was here."

"No one is going to care." Cody rolled over and closed his eyes again.

"I do."

Annamaria opened Cody's door, looked down the hall, and tiptoed back to Courtney's room. Cody rolled out of bed and followed her. He slipped into Courtney's room as Annamaria closed the door.

"This is not what I meant." Annamaria laughed.

Cody laughed and drew Annamaria close like they were back in high school. He lowered his head, and Annamaria accepted his kiss. His lips were nice and familiar.

"I missed you so much." Cody's voice was husky.

Annamaria smiled. "I missed you too."

Cody groaned. "I can't believe you have to leave tonight. I just got you back."

"We'll keep in touch. You'll visit me, and I'll visit you." Annamaria looked away, her stomach clenching.

Chapter 22 It's Annamaria Now

"Chief Davis and I have come up with a statement for you to sign about what happened," said Mr. Mills at breakfast. "We'll send the document to the FBI. We will not allow any media cameras on this property. Your grandma gave me an incantation for you to use which will make the FBI accept your written statement without needing to interview you."

"What does the statement say?" Annamaria asked.

"You were taken by a man. You never saw his face or heard his name. When his house caught on fire, you escaped." Mr. Mills took a sip of his coffee.

Annamaria put her fork down. "What about Trinity? I have no way of contacting her."

"Your grandma said the spell will also erase Trinity from their minds. It will be like you have always lived with Libby." Mr. Mills avoided Annamaria's gaze and scowled.

Annamaria matched Mr. Mills' glare. "So it will be like Trinity never existed? Does my grandma care at all?"

Mr. Mills' face softened. He placed his hand on top of Annamaria's. "Of course she does. I do too. But wherever she is, it involves magic, so the FBI can't help."

Annamaria didn't like it but couldn't think of a better idea. She picked up her fork again. "And once I sign this, I can go about showing my face, as normal?"

"Yes."

Annamaria beamed. "Okay, I'll sign it, and I'll cast the spell."

The signing of the statement was quick. Chief Davis didn't look surprised, watching Annamaria perform magic over the document. He also handed Annamaria her old phone, which had been in evidence until that morning. Annamaria took it but wasn't sure whether she would use it. Trinity would use the new number to contact her. Not to mention, only humans who were no longer her friends had her old number. Annamaria decided she would keep both phones, just in case.

After saying goodbye to Chief Davis, Annamaria strode to the guesthouse to take down the shield spell and see Anthony and Marianna. She passed a few of Cody's cousins on the way there, who waved, some giving her quick hugs. Wow. All these people were werewolves, and they all lived together, in a pack.

Annamaria entered the guesthouse, smiling. "Good morning."

"Morning," Anthony mumbled.

"How was your night?" Marianna's lips pursed, the corners tugged upward.

"It was fine." Annamaria cocked her head as Marianna failed to fight a smile.

"Just fine?" Marianna grinned and wiggled her eyebrows.

"What are you trying to imply?" Annamaria asked.

Marianna's smile fell. "We overheard Cody talking to someone early this morning. He implied you two might get back together."

Annamaria's heart pounded, aware of Anthony in her peripheral. "What exactly did he say?"

Marianna's eyes widened at Anthony, and her mouth dropped open as if she had just remembered he was in the room. "He said, well, he said you two slept together last night."

Annamaria looked at Anthony. "That is not what happened at all. We were talking in his room, and we fell asleep."

"He also said you guys kissed this morning." Marianna played with her hands.

Annamaria looked up at the ceiling and closed her eyes, her face flaming. "Yes, he kissed me, and I didn't stop him. But it wasn't... It didn't feel... Anthony, I'm really sorry."

"Are you getting back together with him?" Anthony's face was unreadable.

"I don't know...not right now. I have to go to my grandma's." Annamaria bit her lip. She really needed to figure out her feelings. Anthony looked above her head. "Anthony, please, talk to me."

"I'm hurt." He met her gaze, his eyes matching his words.

"We aren't even together right now." Annamaria pinched her pointer finger.

"I know, but I hoped we could eventually work things out, but..." Anthony looked away.

Annamaria's blood boiled. "Let me get this straight. You lie to me about the bonding spell, help capture me in the woods, and then bite me? But I kiss an ex-boyfriend one time and fall asleep in his bed—something I've been doing with you all summer, and you want to give up?"

"She's got a point there." Marianna gave Anthony a protective-older-sister look.

Anthony exhaled. "I don't know. I just need some time to figure things out."

Annamaria's stomach twisted. She was a hypocrite. She spent the past several days refusing to talk to Anthony about their relationship, and now she had hurt him and refused to afford him the same time and space. Annamaria relaxed her stance. "I'm sorry. Take all the time you need."

Anthony nodded. "There is something else we overheard you need to know—"

A knock on the door cut him off. Annamaria opened it.

"Hey, Anna, Stephanie is here. She wants to see you," Alyssa said.

Annamaria's face lit up. She turned back to Anthony. "Can we finish this later?"

He nodded, his lips in a thin line.

Marianna, however, grabbed Annamaria's arm. "There is one more thing you should know."

"Can it please wait? Stephanie is the one who started all my problems at school. If she wants to see me, I want to see her." Annamaria pulled her arm out of Marianna's grasp.

Marianna made a face but didn't stop Annamaria. Once around the front, Annamaria ran toward Stephanie, who was sitting on the front porch. Stephanie jumped up, and they met at the bottom of the stairs and squeezed each other in a tight hug. Stephanie started sobbing.

"You're alive! And I was so horrible to you. I can't stop thinking about how we left things."

"Shhh." Annamaria teared up as she squeezed her best friend. "There was no way to know what was coming. I forgive you."

And she did. Seeing her best friend again wiped away all the negative feelings from before. When they finished hugging, they walked up onto the porch where Cody was. He got up and went inside. "I'll let you two catch up."

"Is Jamie going to come too?" Annamaria asked.

Stephanie shook her head. "She's in Utah for school."

"Which school?" Jamie received acceptance letters to every school she applied to, so her choices were vast.

"Utah State, with Isaac."

Annamaria snickered. "Of course. Well, I'm glad to see you at least."

"Me too. Um... So why are you here at Cody's house?" Stephanie gave Annamaria a strange look.

"Where else would I go?"

Stephanie shrugged. "I don't know, your house?"

"And relive what happened to me four months ago?"

Stephanie hit her head. "I'm sorry... Do you want to talk about it?"

Annamaria waved her hand. "No, I want to hear about you. What have you been up to?"

"Well, we did a tribute to you at graduation. I spent the summer helping my parents with the store. And I'm currently working at Amy's Daycare while I do classes online."

Annamaria smiled. "That's great. Is the daycare job with your studies?"

"Yeah, I'm doing Early Childhood Education."

Stephanie nodded.

"You'll be good at that. Are there any boys in your life?" Annamaria crossed her fingers.

"Did Cody not tell you?" Stephanie narrowed her eyes.

Annamaria matched Stephanie's face. "Tell me what?"

"Cody and I are dating," Stephanie rushed out in one breath, keeping her gaze level with Annamaria's.

Annamaria was silent for a full minute. "Why? How? When?" She blinked with each word.

"Well, I've always liked him, and we spent a lot of time together when you disappeared for, you know, consolation. And we just sort of happened."

"When did you officially get together?" Annamaria was rigid in her chair, her nails digging into her knees.

"Graduation." Stephanie remained upright and confident.

A month? Annamaria had been gone for only a month, and Cody replaced her with her best friend. Heat rose into Annamaria's face. "So you used my kidnapping, and for all you knew, death, to swoop in on my boyfriend?"

"It was terrible timing, I know. But he had broken up with you before you disappeared." Annamaria scoffed. Stephanie shuddered. "I swear, Anna, I was not glad you were gone."

"Could have fooled me." Annamaria glared. Stephanie did not respond. Annamaria stood up, and Stephanie followed. This visit was over. "Well, I slept in his bed last night, so have fun working that out with him."

Annamaria turned around and stomped inside,

shutting the door on Stephanie, whose mouth hung open and eyes watered. A lump rose in her throat. That was unfair and hurtful, but she was furious. She stormed into the kitchen, where Cody was drinking a soda.

"How was your visit?"

"Oh, I don't know. How is your dating life?" Annamaria leaned against the table, looking him up and down.

Cody had the grace to look remorseful. "I was going to tell you." He set his soda can down.

"When? Before or after you invited me into your room in the middle of the night?"

Cody put his hands up. "I didn't plan that. It just happened."

"And that makes it okay?" Annamaria's voice rose. "She's my best friend. And I was barely gone a month when you moved on!"

Cody's torso swelled. "We were broken up!"

"A breakup, which you admitted last night you regret doing." Annamaria slapped the countertop.

Cody huffed. "What about your vampire friend, huh? Something's going on between you two, I can tell. I'm not the only guilty party here."

Annamaria closed her eyes and took a deep breath. Her relationship with Anthony was nowhere near the same thing. Until last night, Annamaria assumed Cody was human, so she couldn't be with him. Cody learned Annamaria was a witch and he was a werewolf the night she left. Anthony was a stranger to Cody. Stephanie had been Annamaria's best friend. The two scenarios were not comparable.

"Anthony and I broke up several days ago. You are

still with Stephanie." She pointed at Cody.

"So you can't be mad at me for dating her." Cody threw his hands up.

Way to miss the point.

Annamaria rubbed her temples. "I'm not mad you're dating her. I'm mad you didn't tell me. You snuck me into your room, cuddled with me, let me fall asleep in your bed, and kissed me! How could you do that to me and her?"

"Wow, Cody, are you really that stupid?" Courtney walked into the kitchen and grabbed a water bottle out of the fridge. Cody threw his soda can at his sister, who ducked. The can split against the fridge, spraying sticky soda everywhere. Mr. Mills strode into the room. Waves of power thickening the air. Cody and Courtney hunched their shoulders.

"All of you separate and go calm down, now."

Cody ran out the back door, past the guesthouse, which he flipped off, then out into the fields. Courtney gave Annamaria a hug. "Sorry, girl. Love you." She sauntered upstairs. Annamaria huffed back to the porch and threw herself into a chair. Mr. Mills followed her and sat down next to her.

"I know this doesn't excuse what just happened with my son, but the first few years of shifting are very difficult for a werewolf, plus he has Alpha hormones."

"Yeah, they told me." Annamaria stared forward.

Mr. Mills looked out toward the road. Annamaria studied her nails.

"Trinity was the love of my life." Annamaria looked up at this change of topic. "She refused to marry me because she didn't want to be stuck here in this tiny town. She wanted to travel. I have a younger brother I could have passed the ranch and pack to, but I wanted both. Trinity made me choose. I chose the ranch, and Trinity walked away. I can't regret it because I love my late wife and my kids. But when Trinity showed up with you, I thought we had our second chance. She refused once again. She wanted to focus on you. I was ready to try again this summer after you and Cody graduated, and the chance slipped through my fingers for a third time. I hope that wasn't my last chance with her. I hope wherever she is, she comes back."

"I'm so sorry, Mr. Mills." Annamaria wiped a tear. "I wish I knew where she was, but she wouldn't tell me anything when we were in contact, and now she's gone MIA. But I think if Valentina's followers had Trinity, they would use her as bait for me and Marianna."

Mr. Mills inclined his head. "You are probably right. Both Trinity and I were prideful and hardheaded at different times during our courtship, which cost us a life together. I don't know if you're meant to be with my son, or that boy in my guesthouse, or someone else entirely. But whoever they are, don't let pride get in the way."

Annamaria gave him a half smile. "Thanks, Mr. Mills. Do you know why Trinity didn't tell me about you guys when she unlocked my powers? Or let me tell Cody about myself? Things could have turned out different if she had."

Mr. Mills rubbed his chin. "I can only guess. I believe it is because Marianna is a vampire. Trinity wanted to protect her. And I'm ashamed to say she was right to do so. If any of us came across Marianna without being prepared, we could have hurt her."

"You didn't hurt her last night."

"That's because we were partially prepared. We knew you were coming, and you would smell like them. But as you can see by Cody's initial reaction, coming face to face with one is unpredictable." Mr. Mills stood up. "If you need a vehicle to get to your grandma's, I can provide one."

"Thank you, I'll let you know."

Annamaria sat on the porch for a while longer, silent tears falling. When she had no more tears left, she wiped her eyes and headed back to the guesthouse. When she entered, Marianna rushed over, giving her a big hug.

"Could you guys hear?" Annamaria sniffed.

"Only the yelling." Anthony walked forward.

"Was that the other thing you two wanted to tell me?"

Marianna nodded. "Yeah, whoever he was talking with asked about Stephanie and if you knew. He said no, but he would figure things out."

Annamaria snorted and shook her head. "Grandma wants us to come to her tonight." Marianna's eyes widened, but she didn't argue. "Anthony, what is your plan?"

"I will drive you and Marianna to your grandma's." His face and voice were passive.

"Thank you. And once we are there?"

"I don't know yet."

"Fair enough. Can I go fill your car up with gas? That way we can just go once the sun is down?" Anthony tossed Annamaria his keys.

****

The door clicked, and Marianna rounded on Anthony. "What the heck?"

"What?" he asked.

"You! Annamaria! What are you doing? Do you want her back or not?"

Anthony rubbed his face. "Yes… No… I don't know. When it was just our little group hidden in the mountains, things were great. My past is dead, and Annamaria's past was supposed to be human. But now we are here, and he's a werewolf, and you two have to go to your grandma, the vampire hating queen. I just don't know what's going to happen."

"Cody just got caught red-handed dating Annamaria's ex-best friend." Marianna's eyes danced. "Not to mention, he has to stay here with his pack while Annamaria and I go on to our grandma's. You get to come with us. You'll be right there to comfort her and help her through whatever is to come. As for my grandma, I have those same fears too. But Annamaria told me she'll protect me, and we'll leave if we have to. I trust her. Do you trust her?"

Anthony sighed. "Yes, I trust her."

"So you'll try to win her back then?" Marianna stared him down.

Anthony glared at Marianna. "What are you playing at? You seemed giddy enough when you thought they would get back together. Now you want me to try and get her back. Whose side are you on?"

Marianna snapped her fingers. "Annamaria's. I want her to be happy and to not get her heart broken again. If she was happy about last night, I was going to support her. But I do think you are the better choice for her." Anthony raised his eyebrows. "Cody is just as new to this world as Annamaria is. She needs someone experienced like you who can be her rock."

Anthony pursed his lips.

Marianna grabbed his shoulders. "Anthony, come on. You make each other happy."

Anthony gently removed her hands. "Let's just get out of here, and I'll figure things out on the road, okay?"

"All right." She at least agreed with him on wanting to get away from this wolf pack as soon as possible.

****

At the gas station, someone yelled Annamaria's name. She looked up to see Tally, her former teammate, running toward her. Annamaria gave her a big hug.

"I heard you returned. How are you?" Tally asked.

"I'll be fine. How are you?"

"Good. I'm the new dance coach." Tally bounced up and down.

"Wow, congratulations." Annamaria gave her a genuine smile.

"Thanks. Well, it's nice to see you. Welcome back." Tally headed back to her car.

Annamaria waved bye. When Annamaria returned to the Mills' property, Cody was back on the front porch. Annamaria sat next to him. He took her hand, but Annamaria pulled away.

"Sorry. Habit."

Annamaria remained silent.

"Anna, you're right. I should have told you before everything happened last night."

"I wouldn't have done anything with you if I had known. And it's Annamaria now."

Cody nodded his head. "I know. That's partly why I kept her a secret because I still want you. I'll break up with her. I'll come with you to your grandma's."

Annamaria shook her head, fighting back tears. "No. You belong here, and I need to figure out where I belong." Annamaria stood up to return Anthony's keys. Cody grabbed her hand.

"Please. It's just one fight, one stupid fight. Do you really want to throw away our childhood, our teenage years, us, because of one fight?"

"It's not just one fight." Annamaria struggled to speak as the tears were spilling over. "We've both changed. We are both new people. You're going to be the Alpha. I don't know who I am."

"But you at least know your feelings, right? I mean, the way you reacted to Stephanie, you gotta still feel something for me." Cody took her other hand. "We just need a second chance."

Annamaria shook her head. "I have to go to my grandma's."

"When you are done there, will you come back?" Cody was also crying now.

"Goodbye, Cody." Annamaria walked away to the guesthouse to prepare to leave.

Marianna and Luna were sitting in the back of Anthony's car. Nico was curled up on the passenger seat, and Anthony was in the driver's seat. Annamaria wrote instructions on how to get to Libby's community as the location was unknown to GPS. Mr. Mills hugged her goodbye and wished her good luck. Alyssa and Courtney hugged her together. Cody was nowhere to be seen.

"We still love you," Courtney said.

"Yes," said Alyssa. "Like we said last night, your relationship with Cody doesn't affect our friendship."

Annamaria squeezed them tighter. "I'm going to miss you two."

"We'll come visit," they said.

"Text one of us when you get there," said Mr. Mills. Annamaria nodded and got in the car, putting Nico on her lap.

Anthony accelerated the car away from the house. Annamaria looked back. Marianna placed a comforting hand on her shoulder. Annamaria placed her hand on top of her sister's and squeezed it. Everyone in Harrison knew who they were or who they were going to be. Annamaria didn't know who she was going to be, but she no longer believed she belonged in Harrison.

She glanced at Anthony as the ranch shrank in the distance. He returned the glance. Their gazes locked on each other. Annamaria placed her hand on his knee. The first time she made the first move.

"I know we have a lot to figure out, but please don't drop me off and run away."

Anthony dropped his hand from the steering wheel to squeeze Annamaria's. "I won't. I promise."

"Awww," Marianna said. "I'm totally rooting for you two, but please, Anthony, watch the road."

They all laughed, and Annamaria settled into her seat, fingers curling into Nico's fur as she took in the scenery.

A word about the author...

Chelsey M. Ortega is a teacher by day and writer by night. History is her first love, and any story involving magic and romance, her second love. She especially loves witches and is still awaiting her acceptance letter to a well-known school. Chelsey received her Bachelor's in History Teaching from Brigham Young University. In addition to writing, Chelsey teaches high school US History and ESL. She lives in Utah with her husband, three children, and two cats. Follow Chelsey at www.chelseymortega.com.

Thank you for purchasing
this publication of The Wild Rose Press, Inc.

For questions or more information
contact us at
info@thewildrosepress.com.

The Wild Rose Press, Inc.
www.thewildrosepress.com